Lilith's Dream

Also by Whitley Strieber

WHITLEY STRIEBER

Lilith's Dream

A Tale of the Vampire Life

ATRIA BOOKS

New York London Toronto Sydney Singapore

ATRIA BOOKS
1230 Avenue of the Americas
New York, NY 10020

ISBN: 0-7434-5152-X

First Atria Books hardcover printing October 2002

10 9 8 7 6 5 4 3 2 1

ATRIA BOOKS is a trademark of Simon & Schuster, Inc.

For information regarding special discounts for bulk purchases, please contact Simon & Schuster Special Sales at 1-800-456-6798 or business@simonandschuster.com

Printed in the U.S.A.

This book is dedicated to the memory of JS,
with deepest thanks.

I would like to acknowledge the support of
Mitchell Ivers, my editor;
my wife and lifelong muse, Anne Strieber;
and my agent Sandra Martin.

Judge not the Lord by feeble sense,
But trust him for his grace;
Behind a frowning providence
He hides a smiling face.

"Light Shining Out of Darkness"
—William Cowper

Lilith's Dream

CHAPTER ONE

A Different Dust

It was silver and very high, the thing that Lilith was watching. She wondered what it might be. Really, she couldn't remember ever seeing anything quite like it. Of course, she hadn't been here in some time, not out here.

She focused on the gleam in the sky. It implied things, things that disturbed her almost as much as the reason she had come out to the surface.

Last night, she had slept as she always slept, for a few deep, echoing hours. She had awakened at the far edge of a heartbreaking dream—one she'd had far too many times—and known immediately that she had been left alone too long.

She directed her attention to the lilies that crowded the entrance to her cave, listening to the whisper of the lives that transpired among them—the drone of the bee, the shuffle of the beetles, the snickering movement of the little shrews that hunted the beetles.

Her lilies were a great comfort. They made the unending journey of her life much easier to bear.

The passing of the silver object brought behind it a low and subtle sound. She listened to it gradually fade, like the roaring of a distant waterfall. Memory flashed: water dropping over a cliff, pearls of fire in the blue light of another sun.

A thrall lay upon the air, as if far away some great violence had trembled down to its end. She raised her long hands, held them out in the comfortable light. Then she clapped her hands together, the sound echoing flatly off the walls of the small canyon that surrounded her cave. A pair of jackals that had been sleeping beneath an acacia bush raised their heads and regarded her with their wary jackal eyes. Her stomach asked again for food.

A sadness came upon her and she began to sing, no particular words, just a humming that seemed to fit her mood. The male jackal became excited, and began to pace back and forth, panting. Then he rushed the female and rutted her. The bees began to whir and the beetles to stride, and their rodentine oppressors dashed about, squealing and copulating. A confused shrew mother, deep in her burrow, frantically ate the runt of her litter.

When Lilith stopped, the beetles curled their legs beneath them and the shrews tucked their noses into their breasts. The jackals went back beneath the shrub where they shaded themselves, and the droning of the bees grew low. A memory came to her, of walking narrow streets when the shadows were long and the grinders were lying at rest in their mud houses. Her life revolved around these curious memories—indeed, they felt more alive than the vespers of the days. This life was the dream; the flashes of memory, the shimmering dreams—they were her real life.

She got up and went inside, rushing so fast that the air sped past her face and made her linens shudder around her body. Then the words burst out of her as if they had been waiting in a cage to be released. She cried out, her voice so high with fright that it surprised her: "I'm starving!"

She threw herself down, grabbed a cloth to her face, and sucked in air that was ever so faintly scented from the little bit of blood she had spilled during her last meal. She tossed from side to side on the bed, admitting at last that she was not only starving, she was in agony. She had been so long without pain that she had not at first understood what it was. But yes, this congealing fire in her stomach—this was pain. It swept along her legs and up her spine, radiating out from a belly that felt as dry as ash. Runnels of sweat came from her pores, and a thick, sour sensation, as if a rat was cavorting in her stomach, made her gag.

Hunger was a danger. Hunger came upon you by inches, then exploded unexpectedly. Beyond it lay the worst of all the oblivions her kind could suffer: she would become too weak to eat, but remain unable to die. Her body would sink to a dry and helpless stillness, her muscles becoming as ropy as smoked meat, her eyes shriveling until they rattled in their sockets like stones in the pocket of a child.

The whisper of her heart became noticeable, rising to a whir of uneasy noise.

"Where are you?" Her voice had a flat echo to it. "Hello?"

The only reply was the rushing of the desert wind high above, communicating down the intricate tunnels that ventilated her cave.

She crossed the chamber, nervously aware that she felt a little weaker, a little more earthbound, than she had felt even when she awoke. It was nothing more than a certain increase of definition where her feet pressed against the soles of her sandals, but it was a signal that she was dealing with one of the rarest things that she knew—limited time.

In one sense, she had always thought of her time in this life as being limited. In her dream, millennia passed in moments. Her captivity in this life had been not yet an hour . . . according to the grammar of dream. The mystery of this was the mystery of her hope. Lilith did not think she had been born here. She thought she had been sent here. She had been here since the Mammoth trembled the air with his booming call.

She'd had children, but her memory of their creation was a secret she kept even from herself. They had come about in a stone building beside the Blood Sea, but not by her giving birth. She had told her children that she'd left their father, had explained them to themselves in that way. She had always felt that there was something missing in them, something in their eyes. It was why men said that she had given birth to demons.

A tickling sensation caused her to touch her chin. It was drool, thick, pouring from her mouth. She snatched her fingers away from the grotesque warning, then drew cotton cloth across it to dry herself. Soon she would have too little energy left and would be unable to move.

She strode upstairs and threw open her chests, looking for her cloak. It had been a long time since she'd taken a journey, a very long time, and she certainly did not want to do it now. As the human population had grown, she had come to find their filthy, jangling, squalling hordes impossible to endure.

One of them alone might smell sweet and taste delicious, but wallowing through the huge nests of cities that they made—it was too much to bear. They used rough animals for food and transportation and lit smoky fires at night to mark the way, and some of them came to cut the purse or cut the throat, and they hung one the other or whipped them or bound them upon stakes and burned them, and the smell of that would leave a nasty grease on the afternoon air. They rotted and died and were left in heaps, and rats and cats ran about making their lives in the filth.

She did not want ever again to go to dreadful Alexandria or Rome, or sit in a wagon or a litter carried by sweating men, or lie in terror upon the deck of a groaning ship. But she had to forage. To do that, she needed to go to a city. It could not be done among the few who lived in the desert, not if she expected to conceal her cull.

She groaned, the sound coming out so unexpectedly that she was startled. It had come from deep, deep within, down where her body sensed that it was dying. Why had they forsaken her, who had tended her for so long? Where was Re-Atun, who had been bringing her food for a thousand years?

She lifted a dress from the cedar chest. It floated on the air, settling slowly to the floor. She searched deeper. Now here was a cape made of the skin of a bear. It was quite old, though, and not as supple as it had been when it was still full of the animal's grease. Too long, also, it trailed the ground. In the cold times, the bears had been quite large.

Finally she chose a dress of fine linen and her traveling cloak of human leather, made from a species that she had extinguished. Though gentle, the heavy-jawed creatures had been dangerously strong, and their blood was bitter on the tongue. She'd preferred the tall, thin-skinned ones, who were not only sweet-blooded but intelligent enough to be a good beginning for her work.

She went to her table of oils and began to disguise herself as a human being, drawing eyebrows on her smooth forehead, then applying kohl and gilding the lids in the manner of the pharaohs. The Egyptians were a docile people who respected their rulers, and she would appear to them to be a great lady, and they would drop their eyes and let her pass. She would find a dark corner, make quick work of one of them to regain her strength, then go on and locate her own kind.

The cloak settled around her shoulders as if the former owner of the skin had been bred to cover her, such was the expertise of the tailor who had made it.

She went out into the mouth of her cave, pausing there for a moment to listen. She knew every detail of the silence of this place. It had been many, many years since any human intruder had appeared here, and there was no sign of one now. She proceeded down through her lilies, then paused again.

She took a single step. It felt almost ceremonial. From this point, she would be in the world of beings she had created, both human and Keeper. She felt a profound love for all of them, a complicated love, of both mother and predator.

Moving quickly now, she ascended from the humid draw that marked her home. The going along these hills was harder than she recalled. On the expedition to Rome, they had carried her in a litter. More recently, she had been taken to Cairo in a carriage with horses. This contraption had carried her into the great city by night, where she had observed creatures called Englishmen, who had arisen in the north and were of interest to some people. They were not a new breed, and thus could not be claimed by Drawghera, who had wanted to add them to his keepings and take them from those of Gilles. Drawghera had claimed that they were related to the tribes he kept in Carpathia, but it was not true.

She had been in Cairo for just a few days, and had never gone out of the palace in which she had been made resident. She remembered, and not with pleasure, how the place had rung with a din of iron wheels, the clatter of horses and the braying of mules. Its air had been a fetor of smoke and manure. Re-Atun had wanted her to live here, near him, and had brought her a gift of two luscious males to tempt her to stay. From one she had learned the language of the Englishmen, which contained only a few echoes of her own tongue, Prime, upon which all human languages rested. When the creature's time came, it had given its life unwillingly, this one. The other had dallied with her for days, and from it she had learned the language of the Arabs, which had in it Egyptian, and much subtle Prime.

She had not been in Cairo long enough to meet the pharaoh, but she wondered what he could have been thinking to allow this mad nest of starvation, sickness, and animals to grow up along the banks of the Nile. The Englishmen had claimed that there was no pharaoh. Nothing would have surprised her, in that place, but she thought their assertion an improbable one.

She reached the top of the hill she had been climbing. Here was the plateau where, last time, the carriage and horses had been waiting. But there was only the wind now, blowing steadily in the late afternoon. To the west, the sun was enormous in the sky. A few leagues off stood Mons Porphyrites. She decided that she would go and buy transportation from the Romans who had a stoneworks there.

Not much farther away was the Rohamnu, where she herself had caused *beken* to be quarried, with which she had built many things. She would have the Romans carry her there, and from thence she would go to the Punt trade road that led into Antinoe. There would be caravans on the road, and seeing her fine dress, they would carry her willingly. She remembered the builder of Antinoe, a Roman covered with sores and full of sickness called Hadrian. He had built the town in memory of a boy he had loved, Antinous, who had been consumed by Eumenes.

As she moved in her steady stride, all of these things passed through her mind. The chronology was vague, but the memories were crystal sharp. Hadrian might have lived yesterday, or still be alive, or dead for eons. But she could see his face, the shattered eyes of the most powerful man in the world.

She came out upon a spreading view, and stopped there in respect for the great world. The westward sun was as red as the blood of an infant. To the east, the moon rose, a silver sickle in a purple sky. Beneath it the land dwindled down into shadows of many colors, grays and golds slipping along the edges of cliffs, and the blood red of porphyry off in the direction of the Roman quarry.

The two jackals had come with her from home, and stood now a short distance away, their eyes blazing in the golden last of the sunlight. They were inhabited, she knew, by the impulse of her journey. The Egyptians would say that they were Wepwawet, the Opener of Ways, and her companion Anubis. They knew the use of the jackal, but were ignorant of the science with which she had made of the creature a tool for travelers of her own kind. She made a low sound, a complex word in Prime. The jackals trotted a distance, but not in the direction she would have thought right.

Nonetheless, she followed after them, confident that the two animals would do their work correctly. Along the way, they caught another animal and ate it while it squalled and struggled. At the moment of last light, she felt the sun go as if it was withdrawing from her heart. She gazed along the eastern horizon, resting her eyes upon the thin net of stars that the Greeks called the Pleiades, the sailing ones.

They always made her feel so sad, those stars, especially one of them, the blue spark of her true home. She felt, sometimes, as if she had just stepped away for a moment, but had ended up here for ten thousand years. She had been a bride, had gone to sleep beneath a plum-blossom tree and ended up here.

Or had she? It seemed to be part of the basis of memory, the plum-blossom tree, but she could not be sure. Perhaps it was only the desperate dream of a creature without beginning or end, whose greatest need was to have some sort of a foundation in time.

She turned her head away from the sky and went on, following the scent of the jackals' fur. But where were they leading her? It seemed wrong. In fact, she was sure that it was wrong. The Romans were in the opposite direction.

Perhaps they had another, quicker way to the Punt road. That must be it, a quick trip through a crack in the mountains, then down to the road. Maybe they were even going toward the smoke of a resting caravan.

Darkness rose. Now, high above, hung the glowing outer arm of the galaxy, the border of the known world. Her eyes focused, then focused again, until the firmament revealed its wonders to her. The reefs of stars became a jeweled host as she began to perceive each individual strand of light. As the rays entered her eyes, each sent its own message to her heart.

She could not keep from singing, and she raised her voice in the long, rich tones of her kind, a shimmering regiment of notes like the deep songs of the whale and the wind. The jackals laughed and yapped, and when she stopped, she heard them rutting again.

Her songs were not songs of joy, though. When she saw the night, she remembered fields bowing in night's wind, and being tired after a day of threshing, and the warm scent of bread.

But she did not eat bread. She couldn't eat bread.

Motionless, she waited for the jackals to return to their task of guiding her. Her stillness was as precise as her movement. Indeed, she was so still that a cruising owl used her as a perch, hooted twice, then swept back into the sky, its wings trembling the silent air. She thought nothing of this, who had slept upon the desert reaches in the company of lions and, in her youth, swum the waters off the point now called Aden, singing until the whales rose from the dark ocean. Aden . . . she had called it Adam, after the lost love of her dreams, and in the first days had stood there listening to the sea, and called out in her loneliness, "Lest I forget you, O my love, Adam."

But even his face and even his voice, if ever he had been, had been swept away by the running river of time. There remained only the longing.

She walked steadily and precisely, as silently as the jackals, a shadow in the shadows of the night. But for her skin glowing pale beneath the hood and her eyes gleaming with a tiger's shine, she revealed nothing of herself to the world around her.

Long before she came upon the camp, she knew that it was there. Ten leagues away, she spread her nostrils and drew in the scent of blood and cooked meat and dates, and the scintillating odor of human skin. She lived as much by scent as sight, and it was one of her favorite smells. They liked to be kissed, which was a matter of indifference to her. But she would kiss them to smell them. She knew the different ways each part of the human body smelled, and enjoyed it all.

Romans bathed and slicked themselves with oil. So these were not Romans. She lengthened her stride. The jackals scampered ahead of her, then stationed themselves on a tall outcropping, their forms dark against the sky glow. She moved directly toward them, knowing that the encampment of the humans would be in their sight.

She caught the sweet, milky scent of young children, and the odor of men with sweat in their hair. Also, now, the musk of the women, of whom there were three young and two old. She went closer, rising to the point on which the jackals stood.

As she approached, they melted away. She looked down into the top of a canyon. There were three pinpricks of light lost down there in the darkness—cook fires.

Then she noticed something odd. On the far horizon, just where the afterglow of the set sun marked the edge of the earth, there were lights moving back and forth. She listened. Below, she heard expected sounds— soft adult voices and the sharper cries of children, the rattle of flames and the hiss of cookpans—human sounds no different from any others. But the horizon offered a different noise. What was it, though? It was extremely faint, perhaps thirty or forty leagues away. Not growling, not a living creature. What, then? She could not place that noise. Almost, the rumbling of wagon wheels. Almost, the running of a waterfall. Almost, but not quite, either of those things.

She could make a nice meal down in the campsite, but her instinct was not to take even the smallest chance. Far better to do it in a back alley, to some social cull, than to cut out a paterfamilias or a valuable slave and cause the others to rush from the shelter, barking and waving torches.

What would they do if a noble came walking out of the dark of the night? They would think her a goddess, no doubt of it. That would be well. She would prevail upon their transport, and they would relate to their grandchildren the story of the deity they had conducted to town.

When she started down the mountainside, the male jackal yapped three times. She stopped. Why, in a setting that offered absolutely no threat, would it sound warning?

She drew in scent. Nothing but the peace of the cook fire and the fragrance of the bodies. She listened. The voices were as calm as the night.

She continued. Again, Anubis sounded warning. Again, she stopped, and again detected nothing. The moon rose above the mountains behind her. A chill had come into the air, the ancient cold of the desert night. The warning seemed to penetrate very deeply, raising some deep inner string to uneasy vibration. There was really no question connected with it, not if she allowed herself to see clearly. The warning was a fundamental one. It was her world telling her that she was about to do something that she had not done ever, not in all her years here. She was about to go into the places of men without guide or guard. She would enter now the land of the tall grass, the jackals seemed to say, where danger concealed itself in innocence.

As she went down the mountain, the campfires grew and became more defined. Soon she was close enough to see the creatures moving about. They were all heavily clothed, and so prosperous enough to afford ample cloth. Could they be Sumerian merchants, then? They had far more linen to weave than Egyptian peasants, and wore long robes to announce their wealth. She might take a Sumerian merchant, who had far to go before he could raise an alarm. Or maybe they were travelers from Nubia to the south.

The women were covered all over, even their faces. Now, this stopped her. It was strange. But no, when she'd gone to examine the Englishmen in Cairo, the women had gone about in the streets like that. Yes, they must be Egyptians living in this new fashion. The Egyptians were thriving, to have this much cloth. Even the children wore blue leggings and white shirts imprinted with letters and designs.

She came to the edge of their firelight. One was playing on an instrument and singing. They watched their fire with sleepy eyes.

She walked into the camp. For a moment, they did nothing. Then the one with the musical instrument stopped playing it. The children became quiet. She stood before their fire and said, in Egyptian, "Carry me to Thebes."

One looked to the other. A smooth boy went against its father's hip. She repeated her demand. It was obvious, though, that they did not understand her. She tried the next logical choice, which was Arabic. "Please convey me to your city. God is good."

"We are wanderers, by the mercy of God."

"Then to the Romans. Take me to the Romans."

They glanced at one another, muttering. Finally, the oldest one spoke, a creature with a white twist of beard and a dirty cloth turban. "Do you mean those ruins in the Abu Ma'mmal? Are you a tourist?"

Some of the words passed her by. "I am a traveler," she said. She drew back her hood. The men all gasped. Their eyes opened wide. Behind their veils, the women did the same. The children went into defensive postures, clinging to the adults. Two of the men began backing on their haunches, slipping away from the firelight.

A sour whiff of fear told her that she had only seconds to deal with this unexpected situation. She opened her hands, palms out. "I am in need of your help."

A woman whispered, "It's a djin. A djin of the night."

The elder man raised his own hand in a gesture of dismissal toward the woman who had spoken. "God willing, would you take some tea?"

Lilith came closer to them. "It would be my pleasure, sir."

It had been a long time since she had done this, but she found herself enjoying the company of her creatures more than she had expected. Really, now that she thought of it, she'd been tucked away in her cave much too long. Here, beside an open fire, beneath the blazing of the moon, surrounded by the jackals and the sailing night birds, this was good.

The old one came close to her, his eyes down, his poor hands trembling so much that he almost spilled the tea. She watched the veins of his neck throb. They were a little caked inside, and would offer a hesitant draw. With this one, she'd go straight to the main artery and with a single heave of her belly dry him to dust.

Laughing easily, she took the tea. "Thank you."

"May God be with you."

As she sipped her tea, the tension among them continued to rise. The children and women had repaired to their tent, and could be heard speaking softly together. A little boy was whispering, "It is a rich djin, look at the gold!" A female replied, "It is an American."

That was a word she did not know. She made a note to discover its meaning.

Taking tea with her were four males. From their eyes, she could see that they found her beauty very great. Her spell was coming down upon them as swiftly as the dew that falls before dawn.

She noticed, however, that they were moving themselves about, maneuvering so that her way was blocked except directly behind her, which would take her into their tent. Within, there was rustling. An ambush? She said, "How may I get to Thebes?"

The old man nodded toward the west. "The road is there. You can get the bus to Cairo. There's tours to Thebes." There was another unknown word for her list, *bus.* "A few kilometers."

There was no road off in that direction, she knew quite well. If she walked west, she would go many leagues before she reached the Nile, a journey that would kill a human. Perhaps they were trying to trick her to go off into the desert, with the intention of following her and attacking her.

If they did, she would take them all. She'd bloat like a tick, but she wouldn't need to eat again for quite a time. Her tongue was stiffening with eagerness when she heard a distant and very surprising noise: a clanking sound, followed in a moment by clattering that quickly became continuous.

"My cousin comes," the elder said. "He will take you in his car as far as El Maadi. There you can take an East Delta bus into Cairo. Is your hotel there?"

She had understood some of it. His "cousin" would be a blood relative. But the rest—whatever did he mean? How was it that there were so many new words in the language of Arabic, in just—what—oh, it couldn't have been more than a hundred years or so.

Of a sudden, the clanking sound became louder. There was a rhythm to it, and it seemed to be moving faster than was natural.

All the animals that had been lingering about her in the shadows hustled away. To the west, she saw a glow. She had no idea even how to ask a question about it, so she remained silent. In what seemed like just a moment, it became enormous and burst over the edge of a nearby hill. The light was accompanied by a terrific roar and an odor of some sort of bizarre fire.

Forgetting all of her careful poise, Lilith jumped up, cried out, and scrambled into the tent. She tripped over a child and went sprawling, her cloak settling around her as the great light swept across the thin fabric walls.

Then it went out. A moment later the noise faded, and with it, but more slowly, the odor.

"God be with you," a male cried cheerfully. "You have a lost American! What beautiful good fortune for us, my brothers!"

"She speaks Arabic," one of the young men murmured.

"Well, all the better, may God be pleased! My dear lady, come forth, would it please you."

She stepped from the tent. There was a carriage visible in the light of the fire. It had obviously come far, for it was covered with dust. It was also the source of the odor of fire. There was not the faintest scent of a horse, or sound of one, or sight of one.

Very well. It was a puzzle that would be solved.

"Look, I can take you for twenty pounds. Do you have a cell? Is there somebody to call? What hotel are you in?"

None of the questions were sensible. In fact, only the inflection told her that they *were* questions. "All is well," she said. "May I go now into the carriage?"

"She talks like an old movie," the cousin said. "What kind of Arabic is that?"

"It's her way. But look at that costume. She must be a rich one."

The cousin gave her a long, frank stare. "You are pale," he said, after his appraisal was over.

"I have not been much in the sun, in these past years."

"Hey, Abi, I have to get that line back up tonight, or the boss'll be on my ass. The fatties don't get their air conditioners at the monastery until I do."

"How many fatties?"

"A bunch. Big busload. First-class extra and a bit."

"Tips if we go to be pictured?"

The cousin nodded. "Borrow that camel from Duli. You'll get nice money. But be late. They'll not be up with the sun." He laughed then, through gaps in his teeth. Then he looked to Lilith. "Lady, we go now."

How interesting this would be, to go in a carriage without a horse. Did he pull it himself? Roman boys played at war, making their slaves pull their baby chariots about in the peristyles of their houses. But a human being was not strong enough to pull a heavy conveyance like this carriage. It had two rows of seats within, and four doors, and seemed at once dirty and beautiful. It also had wide, small wheels that would make it quite impossible in the sand, even for somebody much stronger than a human being.

She got into the thing, seating herself behind a circular rail, placing her hands firmly around it. She detested the bouncing of carriages, and there was always the threat of the ditch.

"The American fears the Arab's driving, my cousin. She thinks you a fool."

She heard this. How dare they consider her a drover. "I'll not drive," she said.

There was a silence from without. The men grouped together. As low as they whispered, she could hear them with ease.

"I tell you, it's a djin."

"There are no djin, no more than your foolish god who never—"

"No, no, Allah be praised, go with God. Look at her! Look, she looks like some kind of a—what is it? Marble. A woman made of marble. It's horrifying."

"I see money. Twenty pounds for ten klicks, and no haggling! I'm going."

"Cousin, I would not go out into the night with that thing."

But he went.

CHAPTER TWO

Tears before Sunrise

Leonore Patterson looked down at the steak that the waiter set on the coffee table before her. She cut into it and watched the blood come out in runnels, then spread in intricate rivers across the bright white china plate. She touched one of them, then brought the tips of her fingers to her lips. Memory.

She threw herself back on the couch, touched her temples, massaged them, then pushed hard, feeling the flutter of her own veins. She pressed until it hurt, blocking some of the deeper pain, the torment as if a brutal leather garrote were being tightened around her neck.

"You want something?" His tone was carefully pleasant. He did not care what she wanted or didn't. She was a job.

"I'm fine," she replied, wishing that she could keep the ugly snap out of her voice. Indifference would be less revealing. She was far from "fine," but it was also none of his damned business. She lit a cigarette, took a long, miserable drag.

"Should we do that?"

"Tell me when I smoke," she'd said, "remind me." She wished to hell she hadn't. "I'm stopping tomorrow. Remind me then."

"You're stopping tomorrow. Shall I have the suite stripped?"

Leo met his eyes. "Of cigarettes?"

He nodded. George had been her chief of staff for three years. He'd come to her from ten years of freelancing New York for Bowie and Jagger and people. Before that, incredibly, he had been on security for Jackie. He was, in other words, exactly right.

But not tonight. Tonight he was exactly wrong, because tonight she had to ditch her very pretty and very efficient George. She'd been taught to plan every inch of every move, to respect the danger of the hunt, and she could not allow George or any of the other servants to know that she would be leaving the suite in the small hours of the morning.

Suddenly her spine felt hot. She sat up, rigid. In the secret, internal war that she was fighting with her own body, another stage had been reached. She tore viciously into the steak, causing George to step back from the table, causing Malcom to ask her, "May I pour you some wine? We have a Giscours that would be lovely with that meat."

Damn them and their wine.

"No, thanks," she said, forcing her voice into an artificially cheerful lilt. She put down her utensils and pulled her feet up on the couch, then fired the remote at the big-screen TV across the room. She began surfing.

George and Malcom watched her without watching her, unobtrusively alert. She knew that there was absolutely no human feeling involved in their attentiveness. George watched an icon. Malcom had asked his question of an icon. Neither of them saw the desperate woman who sat before them, who at thirty-three looked nineteen. When she'd become ageless, she had gained the confidence she needed to become a performer.

Years of grief and fear had followed her blooding by Miriam Blaylock. Miri had been killed by a monster called Paul Ward, a crazy "vampire hunter" with a genius-level ability as a detective and no mercy at all.

Something about the blooding had changed her voice. She'd been a good singer one day, a brilliant one the next. Her voice was a dream, a curling hypnotic smoke, all because of the vampire blood that now ran in her veins. Or maybe it was knowledge that made her sound as she did, the alluring resonance of somebody who kills.

She had started at the Viper Club in L.A., and just gone on from there. "Somebody Love Me" was number one on the charts, looking certain to be her tenth gold record in a row.

Nobody understood just what that song meant to her. It sounded as if her heart was in it because it was. In her whole life, the only person who had even come close to loving her was Miri, and she'd loved her like a person would love a cat.

Her gleaming, ever-perfect beauty only made it worse. Such beauty doesn't draw people to you. On the contrary, it isolates you, frightening men and making women sad. It's a disfigurement.

"Are you ready for us to go?" George asked.

He sounded as deferential as some imperial flunky, afraid that his question might seem impertinent to her highness. But why? Her highness was just a kid from Bronxville, for God's sake, the daughter of a guy who bought media for Gray Advertising and a woman whose chief purpose in life was to attend charitable meetings. She had been a face that came down into the world and left again, and Leo knew the sounds of the house: the dripping of the kitchen faucet, the rattling of the trees against the eaves, the whisper of wind in the chimney. But not touch, not smiles. She'd been part of the furniture.

In school, she was the kind of person who was always and never there. She wasn't pretty enough to be of interest to boys, she wasn't aggressive enough to count in the rough society of girls, and she wasn't rich, so she didn't matter in spite of herself, as the rich kids did. She used to pretend to be an alien, or somebody from a foreign country. Sometimes she would speak with a thick French accent and claim to know little English. Nobody cared. If she called, she dated . . . sometimes. If she did not call, nobody called. She had been a stranger in her own life, not even important enough to be hurt.

Leonore Emma Patterson considered herself to be, if anything, even more isolated now. The merchandising was all anybody cared about or knew. Ultimately, the words that David Bowie had murmured to her on the stage at Madison Square Garden, during the Children of the East benefit—"We're all alone, you know, forever"—ultimately, those rather melodramatic words were not melodrama at all. They were just the truth.

There was also no hope. None. At the level of fame she had now reached, you could only meet people who had motives, or stars as screwed up and crazy as you were. She was just this awful freak, this ugly, perverted *freak,* and she hated herself, she wanted to walk out of her own body, to leave it behind right here on this couch forever.

What had happened to her was so outlandish, so impossible that when she was not being torn apart inside by her habit, it was as if it didn't exist, as if everything was normal, as if the tinsel world in which she lived was real. She was a woman with a womb and a heart and she loved kids and the idea of being pregnant, and she would go out in disguise, just to sit near people with children. She went to kids' movies, she went to parks, she walked the block when school was letting out, listening to the bright voices while, inside herself, she wept with shame and was twisted by poisonous memories.

If she did some really good hash and then some chrys and then dropped X, she could make it through another twenty-four hours without killing somebody.

"Am I still on pro?"

George said crisply, "You have four months to go."

"Shit." She'd been in court too damn many times, and she had to be real careful or some judge was gonna put this lady where she so very definitely belonged, which was deep in the deepest cell in the nastiest supermax this side of Texas. Down there, she would die the slow, agonizing death she so richly deserved.

She went to the window, gazed out at Fifth Avenue. "Martini," she said. A moment later, Malcom was shaking. She counted all ninety-nine (he never varied, he was perfect), then took the drink. Sipping, she shifted her gaze toward Sutton Place. There were twelve hotel suites in Manhattan from which you could see the roof of one particular house. She wandered from one of these suites to the next, living a few months in one, a few months in another. She had to be able to see the house, had to look upon it, had to remember and hate. . . and love.

She wanted to get high and drunk both, anything but feel what she was feeling right now. Compared to this addiction, alcoholism was baby stuff and drug problems were child's play. No, no, this was what you could safely call the big time.

She threw back the rest of the drink and went into her bedroom, closing the door behind her. A moment later, she called George on the inter-com. "I'm gonna crash. No calls, no visitors, until you hear from me."

"No club?"

She clutched the bedspread like a life preserver, or a rope to put around her neck. Yeah, there was an "unofficial" club date tonight. She'd made it before the hunger came upon her. She'd wanted to do it, been looking forward to the hour of release from the burden of self that singing on a stage would give her.

As a result, the half of New York that mattered was waiting for her to show up at Club Six on Anne Street. But, guess what, the very thought of doing what she'd been dying to do now made her almost spit up her guts. "No club," she whispered, and put the handset down.

She lay back in the silk sheets. City silence: the relentless sneer of the air-conditioning, the subdued boom and chatter of traffic. The top of the window revealed long clouds moving southward. Moaning wind said that this October night would soon turn cold. The full moon appeared, racing in the ripped sky. This vision from childhood winters brought a sting to her eyes. Sentimental girl, lost in the woods, looking for any welcoming cabin she might find . . . and a man, O a man, in whose eyes she was only her.

Drivel. Sentimental pap. She was all teary about a childhood that had been worse than her present hell. At least now she had the limos and the worshipers. She turned her mind to Miri, whom she had truly loved and who had taken from her more than she had to give. At first, it had seemed so sweet. She'd had a few happy months with Miri, until Paul fucking Ward blew her to pieces. Now Leo was alone, and try as she might, she'd never found another person like herself, let alone another real vampire like Miri, to cherish her and tell her that it was all a part of nature, that she, too, belonged to the cold laws that ran the world.

The moon was swallowed by clouds, and the corners of the Sherry-Netherland tower wailed. In her legs, her chest, above all deep in her stomach, there were burning points of need. All of the little points would grow, she knew, until they formed a web of fire. And then, so very slowly, she would begin to weaken.

On stage, she was Madonna with Enya's eyes and the voice of a girl who had just this moment discovered love . . . and it was all one hell of a lie. She squirmed, ran her hands down her legs. She decided that it felt like her marrow was boiling. Sitting up in the bed, she threw her shirt off and stroked her breasts until her nipples were erect.

She went into the back of the closet and took off her baggy Leo! T-shirt and her shorts, and pulled on the black turtleneck and pants that she would wear tonight. After lacing the black sneakers, she pulled back the baseboard where she kept her cache, and withdrew the fleam she kept there. This ancient blooding tool had been given to her by Sarah Roberts, Miriam's companion, who had also been offed by P. W. The fleam had been used by the doctors of two centuries ago to bleed patients. This one had an ivory handle gone yellow with age, a silver shaft, and a spotless hooking blade that came to a needle-sharp point. Leo nursed her fleam. She sharpened it by the hour as it was meant to be sharpened, with a chamois, until the mere weight of the instrument was sufficient to make it sink into flesh.

She slipped it into its case, and slid the case into the pocket concealed in her pants. Then she went into the bathroom and sat down at the makeup table. Fifteen years in the entertainment industry had taught her just about everything there was to know about makeup. A shadow here, a line there, fresh contacts and a black wig, and suddenly Leo Patterson wasn't Leo Patterson anymore. She was still tall and beautiful, but the trademark lips were more narrow, and the elegant eyebrows had a different, wider shape. The eyes, which had been blue, were now a dull brown. Onstage, she needed a miracle worker to light them, blue though they were, because they were so dead and sad.

Now, instead of saying to themselves, That's Leo, people who detected some familiarity would think, Don't I know that woman?

The next step was to evade George. First, she double-checked her bedroom door. He would come in occasionally when he thought she was deeply asleep, and kneel beside her bed and put his head on her pillow. It was kind of nice, actually, but it must not happen tonight. At least it beat having him sneaking around smelling her shoes or something. Or maybe he did that, too, who was to know?

She opened the door that the waiter used to reach the bedroom without appearing in the living rooms, and went quickly along the narrow corridor to the kitchen. There was a faint odor of cigarette smoke, a radio playing Taiwanese rock ballads. In the pantry, Mr. Leong, the night chef, sat at a small table reading a Chinese newspaper and smoking. He was there to cater to any whim she might have during the night, for egg rolls or a ham sandwich or oatmeal, or a complete banquet.

She watched him, carefully noting how alert he appeared. His eyes were moving quickly back and forth. He was reading intently, which was the next best thing to his being asleep. She stepped out into the kitchen. Now she was in his potential full view. There was no margin for error, nothing she could do if he saw her except go back into her bedroom and hope he didn't mention it to anybody.

No matter how careful she was, there could come a time when the police would be asking each of these men where she had been on this night, and each of them would have to be so certain that she was here that they could pass a polygraph. Not even unconscious doubt must be there.

When the cook took a drag on his cigarette, she could hear the crinkling of the tobacco as it burned. Then there came the sigh of the smoke being expelled through his nostrils. He picked his nose, then made some comment in Chinese, speaking angrily to the newspaper. He licked his finger, shook the paper, and turned to the next page.

As he did this, she took two quick steps into the center of the kitchen. She was no more than ten feet away from him. From the brightly lit pantry, she would be visible at first as a dark form. The next second, he would realize who it must be, no matter how she looked.

She had oiled the door that led out into the back hallway with care. It made no sound as she opened it. She stepped through, pulled it shut. A deep breath, let it out. Safe—for now. Listen, as she had been taught. The ears can hear what the eyes cannot see. Faintly, deep in the building, there was a chugging sound. She recoiled. It was somebody heavy climbing the stairs. A security guard was moving between floors. There was a silent pause, then a clang. He'd gone into one of the floors, but which one? She had no way to know. She'd have to take the risk of running into him as he came out. She heard Miri's stern words, *Do not tempt the unknown.* But what could she do, dammit? She wasn't any good at this, and she never would be. If only she'd had more time to learn. If just once, they had taken her hunting with them. But she'd had to make it all up, using guesswork and imagination.

Hard light shone off gleaming tan walls and a black, highly polished linoleum floor. She began moving down the service stairs, stepping quickly and silently beneath the stark fluorescent lights. Her feet hardly whispered on the steps as she descended. Still, though, she knew that there was sound. There was always sound.

She had gone perhaps ten stories when she heard another clank, quite nearby—just below, in fact. She stopped, stopped breathing. Looking straight down, she could see the top of a steel fire door opening. An instant later, she smelled perfume, cheap and dense. A woman appeared in the stairwell. She had bleached blond hair tied back tight and a trench of a part. A cigarette hung from her lips.

A whore, leaving by the back way. The Sherry wouldn't allow working girls to cross its public spaces. Instead, they would be using the same freight elevators and stairs as the rest of the service staff.

The girl was crying, her sobs almost machinelike. Had she been pushed out of some room, spat on, robbed, brutalized?

The sobbing faded like some indifferent memory, and Leo started down again. She passed floor after floor, watching as the stenciled numbers unwound to "MAIN" and then "BMT" and then "SUB-1." Here, the Sherry-Netherland stopped, perhaps sixty feet underground.

There was no way to know what would happen when she pushed the door open. Maybe she'd be in a police guard room, or some sort of employee cafeteria. *Planning is everything. Care and forethought.* Then teach me how, dear Miri. How do you plan for monsterhood?

All right, shut up! Just do the damn thing and get it over with. She opened the door. First thing, she looked for security cameras. Cameras were death.

No cameras, at least none that she could see. Even so, she drew her ski mask down over her face before she stepped out into the room.

Dim light, black pipes, roaring. Boilers and things, furnaces. She knew furnaces, understood fire, understood heat. Later tonight, she would draw a furnace to eighteen hundred degrees, so much heat that it would vaporize bone.

Then she found what she was looking for, something that was present in all of these buildings—an exit from the subbasement to the outside. It had to be there by law, an emergency escape. It consisted of a black iron spiral of stairs that led up to a steel door . . . which was elaborately alarmed. If you went through, you set bells ringing in the guard room on the next level up.

She'd confronted many of these doors over the past fifteen years. They all relied on the same mechanism to trip the alarm—a hard push against the crossbar. She took our her flat toolbox and inserted a thin but very strong blade into the lip of the latch, pressing against the angle of the tongue until it came free. Being careful not to move the crossbar, she drew the door open and stepped quickly out.

A reek of garbage, the nearby sound of a horn honking in an underground parking lot, closer silence. She took off her ski mask and stuffed it into an inner pocket in her car coat. Then she climbed the steel stairs to the surface and stepped out into the street. A moment later, she was just another quick figure, as isolated as the rest who hurried up and down the sidewalk.

Wind gusted, steam sped from a Con Ed ditch, a bus came clamoring down Fifth Avenue. She moved east. She would go to First Avenue, start at Fifty-ninth and work her way down under the concealing shadow of the Queensboro Bridge and into the upper fifties. She'd find somebody, she always did, wherever she went, here or on Third Avenue with the working girls, or down on Greenwich Street, or just about anywhere.

The bridge thundered, the Fifty-ninth Street tram bobbled in the sky on its way to Roosevelt Island. A Lexus full of bridge-and-tunnel boys passed her slowly. No good, too many of them. Then there came a figure huddling north into the wind, wearing a sports jacket pulled closed by a fist. As he approached, she evaluated him. His eyes painted her quickly, flickering with short, flylike movements. He was softly made, no athlete. Good. He appeared healthy enough. A second check mark on his death warrant. Look at the hands—no ring trench. Three marks and you're in.

"Got the time?"

"Uh, it's—" He made a show of looking at his watch.

"Eleven-forty. I have a watch, too."

His eyes met hers, flickered away. So he wanted a kink. He was out looking for something odd. Fine, she'd done it all five times over. Guys looking for anonymous sex weren't generally interested in the missionary position. He offered her a weak smile.

"Look, honey, you want a date or not?"

"What're you—uh—"

"It's a date. Whatever you want."

"Uh, I, you know, it's just ordinary."

"C'mere." She put her arms on his shoulders, smiled up at him. "Now nobody can hear us but us." She met his eyes. "Honey, you look like you lost your mommy."

"Maybe that's what happened. I did. You know, what about the, sort of, that I'm—I have a big job. A lot of people work for me. I spend my life giving orders and my wife, she's not—she can't . . . she just can't."

She took his hand. "You just forget it, okay. Okay? 'Cause I know what we're gonna do."

"You do?"

"Baby, don't you worry. You found the right girl. It's lucky. I'm looking for it. I love it. So just—here, come on, don't you pull away, now, honey." She took him by the wrist, led him until he resisted.

"Where is it? Is it a hotel?" His voice was higher, edgy.

"It's a private house. Just you and me."

"Is this expensive, because—"

"Don't worry about it."

He was silent but resistant, still very wary. She held him firmly, moving quickly toward the old house, the place where she had found her miracle and lost her humanity. She didn't actually enter it often, not unless she had to.

She drew out the old brass key.

"Here?" he asked, raising his eyes to the dark facade.

"Come on." She laughed, drawing him up the steps. "It's gonna be just us, total privacy, nobody can hear, nobody can see. You ever get that before? You can do anything."

"Look, lady, it's not that I don't trust you, but I've never contemplated anything quite like this."

Interesting use of language. Was this an educated man, a professional, the kind of guy whose disappearance would get a lot of notice? She opened the door, turned on the hall lights. "Okay, okay," she said to him when he hesitated on the stoop. Just come in the damn house, mister. For chrissakes.

When he entered, she immediately pushed the door closed. He could not know that there was now no way for him to get out, not through that or any door or any window, not without her keys and her knowledge of these intricate locks. No matter who he was or what he was, a dead man now stood before her.

He smiled, revealing neatly kept teeth. "Well, wow," he said. "Wow."

"It's very old."

"That ceiling, it's lovely."

She turned on the lights in the ceiling.

"Tiffany," he said, "Is it the real thing?"

"The real thing," she said. She ushered him into the living room, turned on the lights there.

It was so marvelous, this room where her life had begun and ended. There, on that Louis Quatorze chair, she had sat while Miriam and Sarah played on the cello and the pianoforte. Here was the center of her heart and her love.

"This is—I don't know, you're just a little girl and this place—is this your folks' house? I don't know. I don't know what I'm doing here. I visualized, I guess, I thought some older woman—you know, a working girl— that would just, you know, a kind of quick thing in a hotel room or something. Just quick, fifty bucks and good-bye." He smiled again. His cheeks were flushed, his lips trying to smile, his eyes blinking continuously.

She reached out, grabbed his crotch. He was tumescent, and immediately became hard. "Look," she said, "you just do as I tell you, and it's gonna be like nothing you ever thought you'd get. It's gonna be the best experience of your life. The best, you got that? I mean, I'll tell you the truth, mister. I won't lie. You're getting this, this ultimate fantasy, here. Do you understand that? Do I look twenty?"

"You look—"

"Kneel *down!*"

He shuffled to one knee, sort of squatted. "How old are you? I mean, this could be very illegal, here. Illegal for me, you know."

She raised his chin, looked down into his eyes—and slapped him hard enough to snap his head to one side. He yelped, and she said, "It's as illegal as hell, mister. I'm your dream, mister. Your fantasy, am I right?"

"Fantasy—"

"To be like you are, a scumbag—say you're a scumbag."

". . . scumbag . . ."

She slapped the other cheek. "I don't hear you!"

"Scumbag! I'm a scumbag!" He took her hands. She drew them away. On his own, he went down to the floor. He embraced her feet.

In that moment, she felt a vast loneliness within her, something akin to sorrow and beyond sorrow, beyond the tears and the pain in her bones. "Strip," she ordered. She laughed, a girlish tinkle.

He got up and took off his sports jacket. "If there's a—you know—do you have a special room?"

"You'll do as you're told right here." She folded her arms. "This is where."

He went down to his skivvies, then stopped. She drew them off. She'd seen so many naked men in her life, dozens and dozens of them, it seemed, more when she was a sort of half-star, less later, far less now. Now, in fact, the only naked men she saw were guys like this, who were dying.

She reached out, took his dick in her hand. It shot up to full stiffness. His eyes got kind of glassy. He looked as if he was turning into a fish. Pulling him by the dick, she led him to the main staircase, then upstairs.

Although he was apparently to play the slave, she hated him with the dull, hopeless hatred of a captive who understands that no escape is possible. What flowed in his veins was more important to her right now than heroin to a strung-out junkie.

He said, "Hey," and she gripped the hot, dreary thing harder and pulled at him more roughly. Come on, come on, don't talk anymore, just let's get it done.

She didn't take him into the master bedroom. She hadn't been in there in years. Instead, she went to the smaller of the four bedrooms on this floor, the one toward the back where she had lain in anguish while the new blood had been pumped into her veins, in the most loving, dearest, and cruelest act that perhaps could be done on the earth.

"Oh, man," he said, "this is nice. Are we really the only people here?"

"Just you and me."

"Because—"

Now he would say his dismal, boring fantasy, face flushing, eyes all moist, trying to make whatever sordid, disgusting thing he wanted to do seem somehow reasonable and viable. But it would not be reasonable, it would be infantile and grotesque, maybe extremely grotesque. But she would do it, some of it, if only to disgust herself more and hate herself more.

"What's the game, honey? We can't do it if you don't say it."

He remained silent.

She sat down on the bed, drew him down beside her. Then she saw that his face had changed, that he was not a sweating, nervous fool any more, that there was something acute in his eyes, and something inside him that seemed to be in motion, as if he contained another, darker version of himself that had been waiting for this moment to reveal itself.

His hands, which had seemed as soft and loathsome as the rest of this bloated maggot, came around her throat, and proved to be not at all maggoty. No, the pudgy fingers concealed iron.

She felt her throat closing, heard her breath start to hiss. Outside, the wind hissed against the window. He rose up and plunged down on her, crushing her beneath his weight. He stank of cigarettes and stale, unwashed skin. His erection pushed against her thigh.

"Fuckin' cunt," he snarled.

"What are you doing?"

"You stupid piece of filth!" His fingers pushed at her windpipe.

"You're killing me!"

"So. The fuck. What?"

She writhed. He was strong, dammit, real strong. "You're a—"

He smiled, thrust against her. "You're number twenty-one, filth! You goddamn fuckin' piece a shit, in this nice house, how dare you. How dare you!"

As his fingers jabbed deeper and her windpipe threatened to collapse, her mind registered the truth: she had picked up a serial killer. He was strong, too. He was very strong. He was humping her, not entering her but thrusting against her as he killed her.

She could let him. She could do that. But then where would she be? Sarah had taught her carefully: We do not die. No matter how shattered the body, it lives on. Twilight world. Half life.

His eyes bulged with rage, and his breath went fast. She tossed her head and writhed. He was strangling her quite seriously now, and it was time to put a stop to that. His weight, however—and to her great surprise—prevented her from moving but one of his hands away.

Incredibly, she actually *was* in trouble. Then his mouth came down on hers and covered it, and suddenly his sour, smoked breath was gushing into her, penetrating her with the spittle and phlegm of his soul.

She lay still, and in his eagerness he shifted just a bit. This gave her the chance to use her hidden strength, and she exploded out from under him. He flew up and back and landed with a thud that shook the house.

The vampire blood made you strong. It made you much stronger than anybody thought you would be.

Snarling with surprise, shaking his head in confusion, he leaped at her. Her hands shot up as quick as the flicker of a falcon's wing and took his wrists in a grip that he would not be able to break.

His eyes bulged with the effort. He growled and shook and struggled until purple veins throbbed in his delicious neck. She watched, waiting until he bent down, preparing to throw himself back away from her. Then her knee came up and connected with his face. Howling, his teeth bared, he flew back ten feet into the wall, which his head hit with a sound like an egg cracking. As he sank down, she took handcuffs out from under the bed and snapped them around his wrists.

She marched the astonished, spent man straight down to the basement and hooked the cuffs to an eye in the wall. It wouldn't be long, now. She wasn't cruel, she didn't like them to suffer . . . although with this one, she was tempted to prolong his agony just a little bit. How pleasant it would be if all of her victims were as worthy of death as this one. She took the fleam out of its case. He stared at it.

She went over to the furnace and pulled the firing lever. Then she started the high-pressure gas, which made a cruel hiss. She fired the thing, then adjusted the gas while her victim shook and kicked and snarled like a wild animal. She went upstairs and got his clothes, which lay in a pile in the music room.

Entering it, she stopped. She stood surveying the intricate parquet floor, the Fragonard murals on the walls, of a garden musicale that Miriam had actually attended, at Le Petit Trianon in 1769. She sat at the piano and played a few bars of Chopin, some prelude, she didn't recall which one.

She realized that she was making him wait, contemplate the fleam lying in its case, and listen to the furnace that would soon consume him. Still, it was essentially just another person going to die because she had to eat.

She held the clothes to her face and inhaled. God, but he was foul. She forced herself to suck the air in again, to smell the greasy, rotted essence of him, to smother herself in it. Maybe she did it because it revolted her, and maybe she liked that. She wanted more, to inhale more, to feel more, to suffer more. Maybe she should have let him rape her longer. Now, was *that* a sick thought.

She took the clothes down to the basement. He watched her with the empty eyes of a shark. "Look," he said, "I got overexcited. It's my fantasy, that's all. I never hurt anybody. Oh, I couldn't do that. It's my fantasy, is all."

She opened the furnace, tossed in a shoe. It evaporated in a white flash.

"How am I gonna get down the street, you bitch?"

"It's okay. It's all okay." She tossed in the other shoe.

"Oh, no. Oh, God, please, please."

She got the rest of the clothes.

"Don't do that!"

She threw them in, wallet, belt and all.

"Listen, please, this is crazy."

She took the fleam from its case.

"Shit! What is that thing? Oh, Christ, put it down! Oh, Christ, Christ.

Hey. Help! HEY! HEY! HELP!" He shook and he kicked and he twisted against the steel that held him pinned to the wall.

"It would've been nice to make love," she said as she slapped his neck with two fingers to bring up the vein, holding his head still via a fistful of hair.

"We can make love! Oh, I'm good, I'm beautiful. Please, lady. Oh, shit, why did I ever do this?"

She laid the fleam against his neck, flicked it into the vein, drew it out.

She caught the spray of blood in her mouth, even as he jerked his head to the side and shrieked, his eyes screwed shut. It was always like this. She stopped the stream with a fingertip. Male or female, young or old, they all reacted, at this point, exactly the same way. "Calm down," she said. He lurched away and started spraying again. Again, she blocked the flow. "Don't move," she said. "Stop. Just stop."

He snarled at her.

"If you don't let me control this, you'll die."

He became still.

She drew closer. She watched his teeth, his glaring eyes. With her free hand, she stroked him down below, and actually got a bit of a rise. Now, that was impressive. Brave man, for a serial rapist or whatever he was. She exhaled to the point of almost collapsing her lungs, then withdrew her finger in favor of her mouth.

With all her might, she sucked. He realized what was happening and gave out a high, frantic yell and lurched away from her. She was on him, though, like a leech stuck to a hippo.

The blood came in slowly at first, annoyingly so, but then some inner resistance collapsed and it flowed, then gushed, sluicing down her throat like water down a rapids. It shocked her from her toes to the top of her head, a bolt of electric life. The sensation was so magical—his living, squirming essence transferred into her thirsting organs and bone-dry bones—that she groaned with pleasure as she sucked. Waves of vibrant new life swept up and down her, from her toes to the top of her head, great, white waves sighing ecstasy as they broke on the shores of her starvation.

The fire entering her bones turned to sweet vibration, the itching that had been driving her mad ended as moist softness suffused her skin.

Beginning down deep below her navel, where lay her body's center of gravity, there spread outward in every direction a sense of well-being so profound that it was like an actual glow.

She withdrew her mouth from the neck, and looked upon a body transformed. What had been plump was now as shriveled as dry fruit. His pudgy biceps were like ropes of beef jerky stretched along his bones. The bones themselves were black and dry. His eyeballs glittered in his head like moist prunes. The mouth, drawn wide by the sudden desiccation of the jaw muscles, revealed a tongue that pointed straight out, a screaming finger. Pooling on the floor were feces and urine. She cursed mildly. She'd forgotten to put down paper. Miriam used to recommend standing them in a catbox.

She found paper, and got a shock. It was a Sunday *Times* from fifteen years ago—the last *Times* ever brought into this house. Leo had gotten it herself. She even remembered that Sunday, going down to the corner of Fifty-fifth and Third to the newsstand and thinking, I'll be reading the paper in a hundred years, if there is a paper then, or a thousand . . . and feeling as if she was rich beyond calculation or dream.

She got the mess cleaned up and thrust the paper into the fire. Then she unhooked the body. It dropped into an angular heap. She opened the furnace door again, opened it wide. The corpse was still somewhat pliant, so she straightened it out, arranged the hands down the sides, and slid it in like a log.

She closed the door quickly on the hissing and spitting of the grease, and trotted upstairs.

A body meant homicide detectives. A missing person meant that the case would be filed and forgotten in seventy-two hours. Never, ever leave a trace.

She went to the second floor, careful not to turn on lights, and stood for a moment in the pregnant silence of the back hall. Then she entered her old room, sat on the narrow bed of her girlhood. She took off her shoes, then stripped naked.

Lying back on the bed, touching herself with idle fingers, she giggled a little. Something of him, a slight dampness, still clung to her down there. Usually, she was pensive at this point—feeling absolutely marvelous, but also a little sad. A life, after all, had been destroyed, a human being's hopes and dreams shattered. People had been left in grief, never to know what had happened to their loved one.

This time, however, she felt much better. She'd actually done some good, killing a man who was at the least a rapist, and most likely a murderer.

She walked into the bathroom, turned on the water. She was careful. From experience, she knew that it would be exceptionally hot when the furnace was running. Miriam would have taken a soak, then wanted an hour of careful massage. Leo wasn't like that. What pleasure she got from life, she got onstage. The rest was hell, especially this, even when the victim deserved it.

She took a quick shower, using the now dry crust of soap she'd left behind when she was last here. She raised her face into the water, letting the hard, hot stream blush her a little. Then she made the streams into needles and held her breasts so that they pummeled the sensitive crowns and nipples until she squirmed.

She got out of the shower, went to the makeup mirror, and turned the makeup lights on. To make it as brutal as possible, she'd put in two-hundred-watt bulbs. She swabbed away the steam with a towel and beheld the face that looked back at her. Carefully, clinically, she examined the area around the eyes, the corners of the mouth, the tender skin between the brows that could so easily constrict into a frown. What looked back at her was a sensual, vulnerable girl of perhaps eighteen.

That was enough, done. She wasn't interested in enjoying the miracle, only in doing what she had to do. The idea of getting old and dying no longer horrified her. On the contrary, what horrified her was the reality that she could never do so. Either she must live endlessly or die endlessly. "We linger, Leo," Sarah had said. "If they kill you or lock you away, you'll be rendered helpless, but you won't die. So don't take any chances."

She returned to the Sherry, walking through a windswept night. The East River was in tidal flow and covered with quick, angry waves. A barge went past, its tug hooting as it struggled against the current. Sometimes she wished that her magical blood could also speed up time. She'd like to go somewhere far into the future where maybe there would be a cure for her, a way to roll back the clock to the time when she had been human.

The Sherry stood above the silent corner of Fifth and Fifty-eighth. A cab drifted past, a prowl car slid around the corner. Malcom and George would have made their discreet exits by now. Mr. Leong would be asleep in his chair.

Still, she entered the Sherry by the employees' door, slipping in with her key. At this hour, there was little chance of encountering a waiter in the halls. She didn't dare to use the elevator, though. That was pressing luck too far. Instead, she went back up the stairs. The way she felt now, the climb was effortless. Her hearing, also, was a hundred times more acute than it had been before the food, as were her eyes and ears and smell.

She listened ahead, but no security man was afoot in the building. She returned to her suite, closing the door behind her. All quiet, all well. She went into her room, lay facedown on the bed, and cried and cried and cried.

CHAPTER THREE

The Endless Soldier

The radio turned on at six, awakening Paul Ward with the news. As he came to consciousness, he turned to the miracle beside him— the woman who had stayed. She sighed softly, welcoming his invasion of her side. "Uh-oh," she said when she felt him slide over her. Then he was looking down on a flickering morning smile, eyes half opened or half closed. As he settled into her, he kissed her lips.

The familiar wonder of the sensation enveloped him, rising from his loins. She sighed a little, laughed a little—and the voice of Leo Patterson blared through the house.

He felt himself faltering, then stopped. "Oh, God," he whispered in her ear.

"Oh, Paul . . . Paul."

He ended up on his back, glaring up at the ceiling, listening as "Grrl, Grrl, Grrl" sneered to its bitter end, to be replaced by the blunt irony and rage of "Evil Doll."

"Why does he do this?" he muttered, rising out of bed. He dragged on his underpants and stormed down to his son's room. Paul was a huge man, a poor fit for the narrow halls of this ancient dwelling. Dutch farmers had built it in 1653, and Dutch farmers had been compact. He stopped outside his son's room.

"Ian!" No response. He hammered on the door, then tried the knob. It was locked. "Turn that thing down!"

"Evil Doll" rolled into "Catch Me If You Can," and Paul considered breaking the door down. It wouldn't be hard at all for him to smash the big oak door—just a little push.

"Open up!" It was a highly specialized skill to love a teenager, even as hard-won a child as Ian. "Catch Me If You Can" screamed and warbled and roared.

Why her, of all the damn singers in the world?

If what he was beginning to fear about Ian was true, it wouldn't be a matter of wanting to throttle a kid who blasted his peace all to hell at six in the morning, it would be a matter of carrying out the most agonizingly painful duty in his life.

"Ian! Ian, please!"

The music went away. Paul waited into the silence for the voice of the boy-child he had adored, or the cry of the baby he had held beneath his robe on cold mornings. The silence extended.

Paul returned to his own room. Becky was sitting up, and tried to soothe him with a come-hither smile. She was not by nature gentle; she was as tough a cop as you would ever find, every bit as tough as Leo Patterson pretended to be in her music. But there were many layers to Becky's personality, and right now his ruthless professional killer of a sexy lady was pink and soft. "I think he heard us," she said.

"I was being quiet."

"He's got your hearing, Paul, you know that."

Paul went into the john, turned on the hot water until it steamed up from the sink, then covered his cheeks with the luxurious Italian shaving cream that he favored. Shaving mechanically, he tried to push back his concerns about Ian. The boy was just a teenager. Leo Patterson was all over the television, in all the magazines. She was the girl that every red-blooded seventeen-year-old in America—or the world, for that matter—dreamed about.

He dressed and headed down to make his eggs. Before descending the stairs, he paused and listened at Ian's door. He heard breathing—very soft, very close.

"Ian?"

No response.

Paul turned the handle. Locked. "Ian, come on."

Still nothing. He turned it harder, rattled the door. No response, but he was still right there, literally leaning against the other side of the door. Paul felt the familiar urge to just explode into every direction at once that his teenager was so damn good at evoking in him. But losing your temper with Ian didn't help anything.

"Come on, guy, let's get past it." Nothing. "Hey, we're on the same side."

The breathing faded, to be replaced by the small sounds of Ian getting ready for school.

Being ignored did it. Paul kicked the door. From down the hall, Becky said, "Oh, for God's sake," as Paul slammed his foot into the door a second time, so hard that it split down the middle and the free half flew into the bedroom.

Ian screamed, and the sound of it—the warbling, boyish surprise of it—set a fire in Paul, and it was all he could do not to tangle with him.

"Goddammit, Ian," he yelled. "Goddammit!"

Ian slid back against the wall, knocking down his bedside table and radio. His lamp shattered. And then something happened that had never happened before. Instead of cowering, his face covered with tears, instead of Paul getting hold of himself and there developing a trade of damp apologies, Ian laughed. He did not make any sound, but only bared his teeth and shut his eyes and shook in silent laughter.

"Don't you touch him, Paul Ward!"

Everything slowed down. Ian's laugh became a fixed, brittle grin of fear. Becky's hand drifted up, impacted Paul's cocked arm with all the effect of a landing butterfly. Then his arm began to move, and he could not stop it, he could not because the rage was running him and he—the reasonably civilized man who normally inhabited this big, rough body—was on hold, neutralized, put aside.

The hand—open now, at least, no longer a fist—impacted. It hit not the boy but the table, which hopped and shattered into an explosion of kindling. Paul stumbled, staggered, and then was leaning against the wall breathing hard, feeling his heart go *slamslam slamslam* and thinking, *The kid's gonna kill me yet.*

"You asshole," Ian shrieked, scrambling to his feet and leaping back across his bed, trying to put something more substantial between himself and his onrushing dad. "I hate you, I hate you!"

"You don't hate your father."

"He's a jerk, look, he wrecked my stuff, he's a total out-of-control jerk, Mom! Why don't you see that and get us out of here!"

"Ian—"

"You shut up!"

"Don't you tell your father to shut up!"

"Shut up and get out, old man! Go on, get out!"

"You listen to me. You open your door when I knock."

"You did not knock, you just kicked the damn thing down, Dad."

"Why did you turn that goddamn *bitch* on like that at six o fucking clock in the morning?"

"Come on, Paul, for God's sake, it's obvious why"

Paul stopped. He'd overreacted, way overreacted. Ian, blushing bright red now, hung his head. "Son," Paul said, "look—it's . . . nature. Oh, Christ . . ."

"Dad, just shut up."

"Why do you listen to that woman?"

"Shut up and go downstairs and eat your damn eggs."

"Lemme help you, here." He tried to pick the pieces of the table back up.

"I'll go to Wal-Mart and get another one, Dad."

"Listen, son—uh—"

"Dad, forget it."

"Ian—"

"Come on, Paul, you're hungry, and you're mean when you're hungry."

Ian said in an undertone, "He must always be hungry."

Paul's anger flared again, but this time he managed to grab it and stuff it back into the cave where it lived. He told himself, He couldn't make you so mad if you didn't love him. But it sure as hell did not feel like that right now.

He went downstairs as Ian and his mother set about cleaning up the boy's room. He could hear Ian sobbing now, no longer able to put up a show and, in front of his mom, feeling no need to do so. To Ian, Becky was the mother of his heart and blood. He had no idea that he was adopted, and he sure as hell didn't know who his real mother was, let alone what.

Paul started the coffee in the French press, enough for the three of them. He hardly thought about his breakfast, making it mechanically. A few minutes later Becky came in, wearing a bathrobe and slippers, and took over from him. Drawing his own robe close around his neck, he went out the back door, stopping for a moment in the larger, colder air of morning. It was absolutely dark and absolutely still, with not even a hint of dawn in the east. The morning star—Jupiter, he thought—hung just above the tops of the pines that crowded the woods. To the north, the Endless Mountains tumbled off to the black horizon. He breathed in the pure, knife-cold air and regretted that he had to be in this wonderful moment while feeling so damn sad.

As he hurried along the path that led out to the road, he passed the old tree where his father's remnant had been found. His dad had been devoured by the East Mill Vampire, long before the existence of the creatures was known. The vampire had operated in the area for generations, ranging as far east as Danbury and Bridgeport, taking its occasional victims from isolated farms, and from the slums of places like Poughkeepsie and Newburgh.

It was disturbing to destroy vampires, because they were intelligent creatures with lives every bit as complex as ours—more so, some thought—but he had found unequivocal satisfaction in the death of the East Mill Vampire. He'd shot it until its head was reduced to chunks, then his team—very efficient by the time they arrived in this comparative backwater—had burned the remains to grease and ash. The site of the thing's destruction was a hike from here, one that Paul took often. You went across two hills, then through the van Aalten orchard, and finally through a pumpkin patch that belonged, now, to some city people. Beyond the pumpkin patch was Aalten Kill, a speeding little stream of perfect water that was the residence of brook trout far too wise to fall victim to fishermen—including a very frustrated Paul Ward, who'd been working the Aalten's eddies and pools since he was nine. In a tumble of stones above the brook was the blackened place where the East Mill Vampire had been rendered down. It had died slowly, as they always did, its headless body twisting in the flames like a great decapitated reptile. It had left a tiny, ancient house and a small garden of lilies.

He reached the road and got his papers, the *New York Times* and the *Kingston Freeman*. Returning to the predictably silent kitchen, he ate his eggs without a word from his wife. He pushed away the ritual desire for a cigar that followed every meal. No more cigars, no more steaks, no more Mexican food. He felt great, but the medicos told a different story: his heart was struggling, and he had to take care.

As he started down to his basement office, Becky asked, "Aren't you going to talk to him?"

"Apologize?"

"You were wrong. Badly wrong."

"No."

He arrived at the bottom of the stairs and stepped out into the familiar cellar of his childhood. Here, he had made spook houses. Here, he and his dad had built their train set and played "Trains in the Dark," with all the tiny streetlights glowing and the tiny passenger windows lit as their train raced through the little town with its garage and its church and its people who had been painted with single-hair brushes, detailed down to the color of their eyes.

The third week after Dad had disappeared, Paul had huddled right over there behind the fat, black furnace and begged the good lord to take him, too. He had been greeted with what he had come to see as mankind's defining truth, the silence of God.

Becky came down, as he'd known she would.

"Paul, look, Ian's becoming an adult. You have to make room for him."

"Ian is seventeen, and he needs to open his door when his father knocks."

Paul went through another, very different door, that led into a very different sort of a room. He flipped on the lights, which filled the room with a soft blue glow.

"Paul, you need to talk this out with him. Come on, now, this is—you talk about childish."

"Oops. Nope. Wrong approach. Ian needs to come to me. He needs to apologize to me."

"Sometimes I have a hard time believing that dinosaurs are actually extinct."

He was going to control the anger. He was going to get her to see what was needed here.

He waited. He wanted her to show that she at least understood that he *had* a side, that it wasn't all Ian here and no Paul. But she did not come in. In fact, she pulled his own door closed in his face. He heard her feet on the stairs.

He shut his eyes and took the slow breaths that would ease his aching chest. Far away, as if filtering down from some mad heaven, he heard, *"Love me please love me, love me please love me . . ."*

Who was playing the damn CD this time, her or him?

Christ almighty, of all the singers in the world, why did he have to go for that one? Goddammit, dammit, dammit!

He would have pounded the wall, but his hand still hurt from shattering the table. Instead, he decided that his instinct to come down here had been the right one. Throw yourself into work. He'd been a damn fool up there, it was true. But he shouldn't have to gobble crow the way Becky wanted. Kids heal, for God's sake.

Prescription for an upset and regretful old dinosaur: lose thyself in thy work.

He lumbered over to his slot of a desk and pressed a button, which turned on a group of three computer screens. He tapped his keyboard a few times, then stopped, waiting for the New York Overnights. These were crime reports that were on their way into the National Crime Database. He glanced at two murders, one in Brooklyn and the other in Manhattan. A drug dealer had come to his inevitable end in Bay Ridge. On the Upper West Side a man of seventy had killed his cancer-ridden wife. He had given police a tape she had made begging him to do it. Poor damn people.

A kidnapping in Buffalo merited a little attention, but not much. Leo Patterson was not in Buffalo. According to Joe Leong, Leo had left her suite wearing a black turtleneck and slacks at 2:17 A.M. She had returned at 3:22. It wasn't enough to get him any support, not in the absence of hard evidence.

There were no missing persons reports from Midtown North. Midtown South, however, had three: a girl of seventeen with a history of runaways, an elderly man with Alzheimer's, and a Catholic priest.

This third case Paul went into more carefully. A Father of the Holy Rosary called Joachim Prester had walked out of his rectory on Eleventh Street and never returned. But the case was three days old. They'd waited quite a while before they reported him. Then he saw why: Father Prester was a binge alcoholic and had last been seen wandering the South Street Seaport. Probably lost with the tides by now, a victim of the unforgiving waters that surged around Manhattan.

So, once again, there was nothing solid to pin on Leo. Once again, he would put in a request to allow him to detain her and obtain a blood sample for analysis. Once again, he would be denied.

Leo was not a vampire, she was a human being who'd been "blooded," that is to say, had vampire blood infused into her veins by a real vampire. A creature that called itself Miriam Blaylock had done it to her, then died in a hail of bullets a few weeks later. After that, Leo had disappeared into the world, another trashy bit of flotsam on the nightclub and cruise ship circuit, singing tired old ballads for tired old people. She'd appeared to sink without a trace.

But then, to his growing amazement and horror, Paul had watched her resurfacing. When he actually saw her again, a couple of years after Miriam's death, she looked eighteen but sounded—well, she sounded like an ancient child, wise and knowing and infinitely wounded. Her voice broke your heart, just shattered you.

And then her albums began appearing on charts. And then people started talking about her. Her concerts became large, then huge. Her fame exploded like some kind of out-of-control tumor.

A year ago, the first Leo Patterson poster had appeared in Ian's room.

Long before that, Paul had begun fighting the CIA bureaucracy to get some of his old team reactivated and assigned to her surveillance. CIA didn't like him, and they feared that his work, if it was ever revealed, would lead to all kinds of unwanted repercussions. He'd killed hundreds of highly intelligent beings, who'd had names and a language and writing. It would be easy to see this as a gross violation of the prohibition against assassination that the agency had been working under at the time. Worse, they were genetically similar to man, so much so that their blood could damn well run in our veins. So CIA kept him under deep, deep cover, and wished that all of his work and his tremendous accomplishment of freeing mankind from a great curse would just disappear.

In the end, he'd been given one guy. They'd had Joe Leong doing close-range intercepts in China—setting devices that were designed to pick up conversations in private apartments and offices. Joe was good at tunnels and basements. He was good in the dark.

Thumbs dug into Paul's neck. He leaned back into Becky's eyes. "You're acting weak," she said, "and that makes me mad, because I know you're strong."

"I'm down here working."

"You're down here obsessing. Paul, you go up and be with him."

"Leo fed."

The hands disappeared. He could feel a change in Becky as she stood behind him. The careful professional replaced the worried mother. "You have evidence?"

"Joe followed her to Sutton Place. She went in with a victim, came out alone. During this time, the furnace was fired."

"That's all?"

"That's all."

"Any missing persons report fit? Did Joe get a look at the guy?"

"Mid forties, stocky, not real pretty. Short brown hair, carried a briefcase. Came out of a bar on Third Avenue. Went into the roach motel with America's Sweetie, did not return."

Becky dropped down into her own chair. "You want to go in and see Jack Binion?"

He thought about that. The chief of detectives was fairly cooperative, but real careful around a Central Intelligence Agency official with a secret brief. Had he known just how much of an outsider within the company Paul actually was, he wouldn't have given him any time at all.

But he didn't know that, so fifteen minutes in the man's office might be productive.

Paul picked up the phone, dialed.

"Chief Binion's office."

"This is Paul Ward. I'd like to meet with the chief today. Tell him it'll take about fifteen minutes, and I can do it anytime from ten on."

There was a short silence. "You want me to tell him, like, right now?"

"Yeah."

"Call him at home and wake him up?"

Paul muttered that he'd call back, and hung up the phone. "I get up too early," he said.

"And you go to bed too late. When you do sleep, you look like somebody waiting to be executed. You have nightmares that you never remember, like last night."

"I had nightmares?"

"You cried."

"Christ, that again."

"And you woke up mean, just like you always do when you cry in the night."

"None of this is news. Anyway, I'm working."

"Look, you're also down here hiding from Ian, which he knows perfectly well."

"I have an urgent case, for chrissakes!"

"Paul, the Leo evidence you've just presented to me is absolutely worthless, as you know. And even if it isn't, whatever you're doing now can wait half an hour."

"A man died last night."

"Maybe, but a father's relationship with his son is dying right now. Why not go up and sit with him while he eats? Talk to him, be with him."

He was silent.

"Dammit, Paul, then don't talk. Just *be*. There's something important happening here. Right now, today, you two either build a wall or you don't, and dammit, I say you don't."

He met her eyes, found he could not bear that, and looked away. Why had he ever, ever picked that little baby up out of its exquisite antique cradle? But how could he not? You couldn't just leave a baby, and especially not your own damn son. Ian was pure vampire on his mother's side, about a third on Paul's. That made him more than half vampire. And it made his future a huge unknown. He had never fed, never wanted to feed, had no idea that vampires were anything real. As far as Ian was concerned, Becky was Mom and Paul was Dad, and that was that.

The question was, would puberty bring with it an urge to feed? It was already bringing an affinity for vampire blood, Paul felt sure. That was the origin of the Leo fixation. So would he also, one day—

Paul pushed the thought out of his mind with a fury that almost made him groan aloud. The rage that had invaded him told him the hardest truth there was about himself: he loved this son of his more than his own damn life, but if he turned vampire, then he would have to kill him.

How far will she go to protect Ian, if it comes to that? he wondered. Becky was an extremely effective operative, quick and ruthless and as sharp as a knife. She might not be Ian's natural mother, but she was more loyal to him than she was to her own soul.

"More coffee," she said, a false lilt in her voice. "Shall I bring it down?"

"No, no, I'll go up." There was no other choice. In a family this close to exploding into blood and death, he had to do everything he could to keep things going.

"Well, good," she said. "That's good. Come on."

He followed her up the stairs, trying not to think about gallows. He was an adult. He could handle this.

Ian was in the kitchen, his blond hair glowing in a shaft of morning light. As a little boy he had been so beautiful that he unsettled people. Men and women alike found themselves wanting to hold him and touch him, to the point that it frightened some of them, made them uneasy. But that was Ian's nature, to draw, from deep within all whom he encountered, things that they did not even know were there.

"Hey, Ian."

"Hey, Dad."

The boy's knife slithered in his breakfast steak, his fork worked the eggs with busy clinks. The sound that came when he guzzled his milk revolted Paul beyond words. Then he glanced up, and his eyes were the blue of morning. "Sorry about the music."

His heart said, All is forgiven, O my son! His voice said, "No big deal."

"You'd think they would've made thicker walls back in the old days."

Translation: I heard you fucking Mom and it embarrassed me so bad I'm still congealed inside. Paul's heart opened to his boy. "Yeah," he said. "But look at it this way, Ian. Your olds are tight. Better than a lot of kids, where the olds hate each other. You want the olds to be tight."

"For sure, Dad. Melissa Smith's parents go final today. We're celebrating."

"Oh? And why is that?"

"Why?" He swept the air with a closed fist, innocently showing off his smooth, gracefully muscled arm. "No more bruises for Missy."

"Her dad hit her?"

"Slapped, mostly."

He tried to call up a picture of Dick Smith, but could recall only a pallid executive with beat-up old glasses. "That Mr. Peepers guy?"

"Get him drunk and he's deadly. Especially to girls. He left Dickie pretty much alone, except when he tried to get him off Missy. Then he'd come after him with a belt."

What was it he was hearing in Ian's voice? Was it curiosity or compassion? Ian had never been hit. In fact, he lived in a home where a raised voice was a rarity, and punishments consisted of expressions of disappointment.

For Becky and Paul, ultra-violence was work. Their private lives had to be as peaceful as a Trappist oratory.

"So," Ian said, "you no like Leo?"

"No like Leo."

"She's redefining the feminine, Dad. She's politically, like, important. She's going beyond feminism into grrl power. I mean, she's this incredibly sweet, vulnerable girl who's totally tough at the same time. Athene, goddess of wisdom and war, Lilith, mother of demons. Leo's reempowering the myth of the feminine. Good-bye, Tinkerbelle."

"It's just that . . . it was kinda loud."

"My loudness is mine, not hers. Let it sink into your soul, man, let it—" He laughed, suddenly, a brief, embarrassed chuckle. Ian was remembering why he'd turned it up so loud. He shut his mouth so hard his teeth clicked, as if he'd felt pain in the laugh and was trying to bite it off.

"I'm sorry we disturbed you," Paul murmured.

Ian smiled a little. What son cannot see past the masks of his father? It struck Paul unexpectedly this time, the depth and power of his love for his boy. He'd been astonished to hear a baby crying, in the moments after the battle with Miri. Then he'd found the crib behind a curtain in the bedroom of the lavish San Francisco apartment they'd tracked her to. Paul had known instantly that this was his son, and why Miri had seduced him: to get this child.

Paul had lifted the wriggling life from its bed and had instantly and completely loved the baby he knew he should kill. He had tightened his hands around the tiny chest until the kid squirmed, until he could feel the heart fluttering like a captured moth. He had remained like that, his own sweat dripping down onto the squalling thing, his fingers trembling, his jaw clenching.

The baby had seemed so vulnerable, so tiny, at once more deeply a part of Paul Ward than anyone else could ever be—and more alien and more dangerous.

"I'll take him," Becky had said, and swept him up in her arms. Paul had raised his head and seen in his sweating, tough fighting companion something so deeply true, and so unexpectedly soft and just very damn appealing, that it had made him cover his weapon with the blood-spattered edge of his jacket and say, "Marry me." To which she had replied, "Yeah, right."

Thus are born romances, and father and motherhoods, and the journeys of children. Tentatively, he reached across to Ian, who did not react. He immediately withdrew. "Look," he said, "I'm gonna drive down to the city. You want I should drop you at school?"

"I drive?" Ian asked.

"Go for it."

They headed out. "Seriously," Ian said, "she's making a statement. That's why kids like her. This is the postfeminist era. You and Mom— you don't see that. It's not enough for women to get the boardroom.

There's a level of psychological and cultural empowerment that they have not yet captured. Leo is about a whole new way of looking at what women are."

Given what he knew about Leo, it was all Paul could do not to spit his contempt. Women were soft and good, not dangerous.

But Becky—his sweet, soft Becky—was one of the most dangerous human beings he'd ever known, dammit!

When Paul said nothing, Ian spoke again: "Women will never become all they can be until we respect their danger. I love Momma, but sweet is not what women need to be right now."

Paul smiled to himself. What would you think, little boy, if you'd seen your mommy as I have seen her, filthy in a black cave, face to face with a monster that can throw a goddamn knife faster than a bullet, pounding away with a pistol as big as your head?

But he said—could say—not one damn word. The dark power of women has a good side and a bad side, though, and this innocent boy was being attracted to the bad side.

When they arrived at the school, Paul contented himself with a pat on the shoulder for his son.

"Bye, guy," he said, "love you." And, God, he felt that. He felt that so deep, and it hurt so much.

"Love you, Dad."

Then he was gone, disappearing into the morass of losers that populated his high school. Paul knew that they should have sent him to prep school. But the idea of letting him go out in the world on his own like that—it was just impossible. When Ian was so much as late coming home from a dance, Paul paced, worrying that he was out there in the hills somewhere, sniffing around some lonely cabin.

Paul headed for the parkway, powering the vehicle expertly through the hairpins of East Mill Road. On the trip down to the city, he listened blankly to the late repeat of *Morning Edition* and remembered not a word.

He pulled into One Police Plaza at exactly four minutes to ten and took the elevator up to the fifth floor. The duty officer was so beautiful that Paul practically had to glue the image of Becky onto his brain to avoid becoming terminally distracted. She had big green eyes and, beneath her starch-scented uniform blouse, two very shapely reasons that a blouse was different from a shirt.

Would Leo the grrrl approve of the way I think? he wondered.

"Mr. Ward, please come in. Coffee?"

"Yeah, black and mean as you can make it."

She went out, and Binion said, "You're gonna have to cut it before you can eat it. She doesn't like suits, and you gave her license." He gestured toward a chair, then dropped into his own. "You said fifteen minutes, no more."

"I'm looking at a possible murder."

"All right. That's my kind of business."

He wanted to add, Committed by a vampire, but that was, of course, impossible. Then he wanted to say, Committed by Leo Patterson. But that was, if anything, even more impossible.

"I want to see all the raw MP sheets for yesterday."

The eyebrows flickered. The coffee came. The chief busied himself with his mug. "I'm trying to figure out which parts of the ethics code I wouldn't be violating, and I can't seem to find any. Except the prohibition against killing rats on Sunday. We're okay there."

"Then just for Midtown North. Stuff that might not be in the computer."

"That you know isn't in the computer, because you already looked. Stuff the detectives didn't bother to post. The bullshit calls from drunks and paranoids, that kind of shit—am I right?"

"Exactly right."

"Leave no tone unsturned, right, CIA? Thing is, if you guys are so careful, then why do we always lose?"

"We don't lose. We never lose."

"Oh, yeah, I musta got my doublethink backward." He pushed a button. His orderly reappeared. "Sergeant, could you get MN to fax over all the shit outa the detectives' trash cans. Gum wrappers, everything. Gum."

She withdrew.

"You know, Paul, if I had some inkling of what you were doing, I could help you more. Offer insight. Resources."

"Need to know, I'm sorry."

"Look, let me put this another way. If you're going to get any more help from this department, I'm going to need some kind of supporting authorization. I don't mean to be a bureaucrat—"

"You are a bureaucrat. Covering your ass."

"Covering my ass."

The sergeant brought in a couple of faxed sheets. "Quiet night," Binion said, reading them. He handed them to Paul. The first was a list made by somebody taking phone calls. It was cryptic, but he could guess what things like "Drnk asshl" meant.

He stuffed the fax in his pocket. Maybe the trip had been a bust. And yet, the man that Leo had murdered last night had been real. He had been alive, and now he wasn't. Unless . . . could she have been meeting another creature like herself? God forbid. His firm belief was that she was the only one. He and his team and the others around the world were good. They were damn good. She was the only one.

So this Mr. Whoever had not been missed—at least, not yet. Maybe somebody would report him in a few days, but Paul did not have a few days. If there was any evidence of this man's death left in Leo Patterson's house, it would soon be gone.

"I think I'm running out my time," Paul said.

Something approaching a smile of relief flickered in Binion's face. Paul decided that he probably couldn't even imagine how much this man wanted him out of his office.

He took off, thinking that he would have to proceed with his investigation on the ground, in the time-honored way of the policeman. There was a reason they used to be called flatfoots.

Paul thought he might approach the house. As soon as she'd started getting rich, Leo had bought it from the trust that Miri had set up to hold her property. Miri had needed to be able to disappear for a century or so, and return to find that her taxes had continued to be paid. She had created a trust in Liechtenstein that did all the bookkeeping and made sure everything was running properly.

Leo had known about the trust, and had somehow gotten it to sell her the property. How had she ever convinced them that they had the right to do this? No matter, it was now owned by Leo Patterson, big as life, the deed properly filed downtown.

Paul had not entered the house since the debacle he had experienced there, those dizzying, maddening days of love, after Miri had seduced him. She'd known the secret of his blood before he knew she was a vampire. Realizing that her fellow Keepers, as they called themselves, were being decimated, she'd used him to make her pregnant. He had just enough vampire blood to do it, something he'd found out too late.

In the end, after she was sure she was pregnant, she'd turned on him. He'd been completely blindsided. They'd had him trussed up in the damn basement, with the furnace door open, for God's sake. Whereupon Becky had dropped down through a skylight, an angel from on high. Good woman power had saved him from bad woman power, the angel with the gun besting the angel with the hungry, sucking jaws.

Even though it was forested with alarms and various electronic trip-wires, there was a way into that house. He had known about it for years, but never used it before. No, he'd stayed away, far away. Only a fool would expose himself to a place that had been owned by a creature as hard to kill, and as intelligent, as a vampire.

Paul wanted to believe that they were all gone. Wanted to. But if he really did believe that, then why hadn't he taken the early retirement CIA had offered him six years ago?

Because he believed nothing.

He left One Police Plaza and got in his car. The morning sun shafted down through cathedrals of golden cloud; Manhattan sparked and roared. He negotiated Park Row to the Bowery, using his quick little Saab to outmaneuver trucks and cabs, whose drivers raged at him as he cut them off.

Passing University Hospital, he thought of Dr. Sarah Roberts, that lost soul, and her twenty-year struggle to make sense of Miriam Blaylock's blood. She'd been seduced, in the end, blooded before Leo was blooded. She lay now in some coffin somewhere, trapped in the strange, half-conscious nightmare of a creature that cannot die. He couldn't despise her, she had been an excellent scientist. Really, she had discovered Blaylock. In a sense, she had discovered vampires. Too bad Miriam had found the soft, lonely place in her soul, and gone there, and exploited her weakness to make her a slave.

By the time he flashed past Fiftieth Street, he realized that he was going seventy, whipping in and out of traffic so fast that people could only stand and stare. He hit the brakes. His reflexes made such maneuvers easy for him. He could have done the same thing at a hundred, just as efficiently. But you didn't do high-speed driving in Manhattan, not if you didn't want to attract some pretty upset traffic cops. He dropped back to forty and let the car slide into a right onto Fifty-sixth Street.

He pulled into a garage on First Avenue. Up here, the brownies might or might not understand that his plate number said he was a federal officer. He got out of the car, gave the attendant his keys, and crossed the avenue. He passed then into the magical world of Sutton Place, which had once been a fabulous enclave of homes with gardens stretching down to what was then called the North River. The gardens were still there, but they had been rendered into walled stumps of their former grandeur when the East Side Highway was built.

Among the fables of Manhattan is that of the tunnels. The abandoned Second Avenue Subway and other, more ancient tunnels—the first New York Central tunnel, the Crosstown Walkway, among others—snake beneath the streets. There are deeper, more hidden passages, too, the access tunnels for Con Ed's steam lines, the sewers, and the access tunnels to the great water lines that shoot down from the upstate reservoirs at a depth of two hundred feet.

There are also other tunnels down there, tunnels that have not been mapped on any map, and in those tunnels lay the undead vampires of New York. It had been a methodical carnage. It had also reduced the annual missing persons count by five thousand. That's how many lives had been saved in this one city alone, five thousand a year.

His team hadn't even known of these tunnels. They'd thought that New York had few vampires. But Miriam Blaylock had escaped from her house into a tunnel, and that had led them to the rest of the infestation.

He and Becky had not dared to follow her, not into that dark unknown. Later, though, the team had conquered it completely.

It was a branch of Miriam's escape tunnel that Paul would now use to enter her house. It would be tricky, though. His eyes were sharp enough to notice the twists and turns, but not as sharp as a vampire's. Even though he was going only a couple hundred feet, getting lost was a distinct possibility. If that happened, he'd probably end up starving to death before he found his way out.

He walked down Fifty-sixth Street to its end, then vaulted the wall that concealed Miriam's garden from the world. He dropped down into it, looked immediately up toward the leaded glass windows of the music room. This was taking a mad chance, he knew that. But he also knew that no progress would be made without such chances.

He took five quick steps to the back of the garden, then touched the pavement around a birdbath. Doing it just right caused a crack to open in the green of the lawn. There were a few hewn steps, and the rattle of busy water. It was low tide, so a faint glow could be seen from below where the tunnel opened onto the East River. For a few hours each day, the mouth was above water. He'd seen it from a boat. It was identical to the other drains beneath the esplanade that supported FDR Drive. There would be no reason whatever to suspect that it led to the hidden warrens of a vicious species of predator.

He descended to a small landing at the bottom of ten steps, then pulled a lever which closed the entrance above him. Like everything made by them, age and long disuse had not reduced its efficiency. The trap above closed without a murmur or a creak.

All he had was a penlight. But he had expected to get some information from the police. He had not expected that this situation would arise. For that reason, also, he was not armed. He stepped carefully, his head down, one hand guarding his forehead. Paul was easily as big as the striding horrors who had once used this tunnel.

The long downslope led to the water, the upslope to the house. Paul went to the stone steps that rose into the cellar, climbed them, and confronted an ancient door with a cunning lock. He knew the secrets of these locks, with their gravity-driven systems that would defeat any normal means of opening them.

He leaned against the door. His eyes closed, his jaw hanging with his concentration, he made a series of movements, alternately pressing the door and then releasing it. As he did so, he could hear the tumblers click-ing. He'd learned this technique from his French colleague and dear friend, Colonel Jean Bocage. Bocage had learned it from the vampires. They did not travel with keys; knowledge of the locks and the tunnels meant that their whole secret world was always open to them.

The door swung softly back, and the cool air of the house surrounded him. There was a scent, very subtle, not pleasant. What was it? He inhaled again, realized that he was smelling age—old cloth, old furniture, things so ancient that they were part of a kind of twilight. It was the scent of memory, this sweet, sad odor, and it filled the house.

Careful in his method, he looked along the baseboards, then the crown moldings, then up and down the walls. He was seeking the glitter of the camera's eye, the dot of the laser's source, any sign of alarm equip-ment. There was nothing, though, not this deep in the house.

He remembered this room—there was the door into the little infir-mary where Sarah Roberts had been his doctor and Leo Patterson his nurse. They had subtly tormented him with desire, these glorious women, their dresses whispering as they moved, the sun from the high, barred windows playing in their hair.

Down the lower stairs and around a corner was another sort of a room altogether, and it was there that Paul went first. Above, the clinic had retained its pristine, starched appearance. Obviously, somebody was keeping the place up. Here, though, things were different. An iron bed-stead sat against one wall, on it a rusty set of springs. The chosen had been bound to this bedframe, Paul knew, left to await their end while scream-ing themselves hoarse. Was it used still? He could hardly imagine some-body as soft and sweet-looking as Leo putting other human beings through that, but look at her onstage. Onstage she was blue steel.

Paul put his hand against the black door of the furnace. This was not the same as the furnace in his own basement, a great can of iron. This was a very different design, ostensibly built to fire a high-pressure boiler. But its interior was no compact firebox.

He drew the bar that closed it back, listening to the high grinding of iron upon iron. The door swung silently and easily open onto an absolute blackness. He shone his penlight in—and saw there dozens of gas jets and what looked like some sort of forced air device. Firebrick lined the interior, which, he was surprised and disappointed to see, contained not even ash. The thing was so clean, it was as if it had been built yesterday. Had it not still been warm, he could have made himself believe that it hadn't been used in years, if ever.

He drew back and slammed the door. The clang echoed off through the house, was instantly absorbed. He looked up the stairs that led into the basement proper. At first, he trotted. Maybe she'd kept some sort of a souvenir—a damned ear or a finger or something.

He stopped on the wider stairway that led up to the pantry. She hadn't kept a crumb of evidence; he knew it without looking. Further exploration would gain him nothing, and expose him to the very significant risk of being discovered. After all, this was Leo's place. She might be living at the Sherry just now—she migrated restlessly from hotel to hotel—but she could come and go from here whenever she pleased. The front door could fly open at any moment.

He mounted the stairs, went through the hospital-clean pantry and into the breakfast room. These rooms had never been used, of course. They were here because Miriam could never have built a house without a kitchen and dining areas.

He went into the wonderful front hall, an ivory-colored oval with a grand, sweeping staircase behind it that led up to the festival areas, the ballroom and the large banquet room. On this floor, the closed double doors before him led to Miriam's favorite music room, as lovely a private space as existed in New York.

He drew the doors back.

Oh. Oh, God. It was absolutely, exactly as it had been so many years ago. In this room, Paul had fallen in love, deeply, madly, with what turned out to be a murderous, cunning monstrosity . . . that had swept his heart away and then crushed it dry between her vampire fingers. The ancient pianoforte still stood overlooking the back garden, and before him, the great window of mullioned, leaded glass saw the side garden, and farther off, the prancing East River waters. There was no hint that the FDR Drive even existed.

He walked into the room. His eye was attracted by a particularly fabulous chair, as wonderful a piece of furniture as had ever been crafted. Miriam had said that it pre-dated Egypt, this marvel of the cabinet-maker's art. Paul had sat in it, had felt the way its grace added to its function. It was as if it had been tailored not only to fit the body, but to ennoble it. Where it had been made, she had never said.

His eye was drawn, then, to a face. He found himself looking up into something he had entirely forgotten was there: the portrait of Miriam that had been painted by Vermeer. He gasped as a blade of longing sliced his heart. He had forgotten, quite forgotten, the beauty, the majesty of the creature.

And he had also forgotten just how much he loved her. It shook him, it made him groan a little. She had the finest face he had ever laid eyes upon, her nose thin and sculpted, her lips at once laughing and set gravely, her eyes infinitely gentle, heartbreakingly gentle . . . and as hard as diamonds.

He sank down into the chair, not because he wanted to but because his legs failed him. He bent forward, his face convulsing, then rigid. He wanted her, just to see her once again crossing to the pianoforte, to hear her playing with those long, angelic fingers of hers, to see the tilt of her chin and the glow of the sun upon her brow.

For a long time he remained there, fighting to control himself and failing. The painting was a trap that had closed him up in the prison of his own denied love. He remembered the touch of her fingers upon his thigh, he remembered her voice as she said from the Bible on one of those dear nights, "I am the rose of Sharon, and the lily of the valley. . . ."

Across the echoes of the years, he sat before this sacred painting in this sacred place, and knew that his heart was ruined for love, had always been ruined for love.

The thing was, had he really killed her? He had shot her, but he had not shot her head, had not been able to. He listed her as dead, and there had never been a sign of her, but the real reason that he kept his investigation going was not Leo Patterson, it was the knowledge that he had not done his duty with this vampire.

Becky said he had. Becky said she was dead. But could he really trust himself, this man who loved too easily, to have properly killed the love of his life?

Becky knew, in the patient way of a woman who must conduct her own love affair in the shadow of another, greater one, that he still loved Miriam Blaylock. Paul saw how she had crafted their life together by details and particulars, creating little islands of closeness, waiting for his sex to swing round with the slow seasons, taking advantage when she could, making something for herself that way, and for the boy.

He sank forward, overwhelmed by the explosive emotions of desire and loss that were sweeping him, and knelt there, his graying head bowed, his hands clenched as if in abject prayer.

The silence of the house was profound. More time, it seemed, rested here than it did in other places, spreading across the glowing furniture like a fragile, infinite snow.

Then he heard something, as subtle a sound as had ever penetrated his consciousness, like the distant tap of his own heart, or the slow of his breath in the deep night. It was a long, expiring sigh, as if a sheet had been dragged across a polished floor, or somebody who had been sleeping for a very long time had sighed in the first gray of morning.

Slowly, he got to his feet. He looked up into the ceiling of billowing clouds and angels rising. No matter how hard he tried, he could not entirely rid himself of the notion that there was, somewhere in the nature of the relationship between vampire and human, some deep peace or goodness that transcended the violence and the horror. But surely that was just sentimentality, an echo of lost and foolish love.

He went quickly across the quieting carpets and the slick marble floor of the foyer, and down and back the way he had come, disappearing as swiftly as a shadow, leaving the house to its silence, its lost mistress, and its dreams.

CHAPTER FOUR

The Blood Eagle

L ilith awoke in the man's arms, feeling the delicious tickle of his hand running up and down her thigh. At once she was glad, she was grateful . . . and she was lonely. His attentions had drawn her to enter what she thought of as her life's dream, which had been unfolding as long as she could remember, of an afternoon in a place of perfect joy.

In this part of the dream she is leaving. To do this, she steps beneath a plum tree covered with blossoms, into its fragrant, bee-humming bower. As she leaves, a man lays his fingers on her cheek and touches her tears. He says, "Only an hour." His strong, sweet voice, when she hears it in her dream, makes her glow with the vanishing light of longing.

She'd heard it just now, "Only an hour." It had become for her the watchword of the eons, this enormous hour.

"You are my passionflower," the man breathed into her ear in his own poetry, his slippery, jaunty Arabic.

Instantly, there came a silent riposte, *You are my dinner.* She gazed at him, thinking that they did not have such complex faces in the long-ago. "Ibrahim," she breathed, "love me." And he did, oh, he *really* did. His eyes bulged, and his lips hung slack as he pumped away at her. But he also tried to pleasure her, speeding up, slowing down, watching to gauge it in her eyes. And he did see it, because it was there. He was giving her pleasure, enough pleasure to make her feel a most unaccustomed feeling, which was regret.

She had come to feel a certain tenderness toward him. He sang, he told her stories of his youth among the camels, he bragged to her about his little possessions, his auto, his timepiece, the black "business suit" he kept in a bag. "I am a businessman. In Cairo, I am respected. I must wear such a suit."

She felt him swell within her, saw his eyes flicker as he experienced the little death of coitus. Then he sank down upon her, and she enjoyed his weight. Her pleasure in him was not physical. It was, and this was a surprising truth, a pleasure of the heart.

He rolled off, breathing hard. "Oh," he said, "oh, my. Was it so good for you?" It could not feel for him as it would with a human woman, but he said nothing, so neither did she. She turned to him and kissed the edge of his beard.

In recent years, she had taken less of an interest in the prey species. At home when she fed, she had come to prefer that they bring it to her wrapped in linen and so trussed that it could not even struggle. She would see only the neck, taste only blood drawn from carefully cleaned skin.

She did not want to experience Ibrahim in such a detached and sterile manner. She wanted to take him in the old way, with loving gentleness, even a sweet touch of regret. That was the way to eat, with respect.

But even so, look at his dark and shining eyes. He was so pleased with her, so grateful. Perhaps, as hungry as she was, she could delay a little more. If she began to lose too much strength, she could always just reach over and do him. It only took a moment.

She lay her fingers along his carotid. "Boomboom," she said, "boom-boom."

"What do you feel?"

"Your blood."

He threw himself on his back and began to laugh silently, his beard bobbing, his face twisted with pleasure that was also pain. "I am not a good Muslim," he said. "I am not a good Egyptian."

"You keep saying that. What would a good Muslim do?"

"Not fornicate. And a good Egyptian would not consort with a djin and bring misfortune on himself and all his family."

"You think me a demon?"

He scoffed. "I know it." Then, suddenly, he rose. She went up, too. They sat face to face, naked, in the smoky light of the one old lamp that lit the caravan. "Your skin is not like ours," he said. He reached out and touched her hand. She looked down at his fingers, then up to his face. In it, she saw a dangerous wonder.

"If I am a djin—"

"I did not know that such things could be."

"—you should run for help."

"But your . . . eyes . . . I am enchanted."

She did not think that his enchantment was centered on her eyes. "It's dangerous, is it not, to love a djin?"

"It is not something I thought was possible, because there are no djin. But your body is so cold, and you have the name of a great djin."

"Lilith . . ."

"The first wife of Adam. She divorced him and spawned a race of demons."

"Adam . . ." How that name resonated! She had always loved it, had kept it deep in her heart. Adam, a name from her dreams. She repeated it, "Adam . . ."

"But I am only Ibrahim. Can you ever say 'Ibrahim' with such love?"

She lay back in their ragged sheets, indolent in the lazy light. "I wonder sometimes if ever I knew an Adam. It's a name that's just on the tip of my tongue."

"If you are Lilith the demoness, then perhaps the memory has gotten like that because it is so old. Nobody knows what it would be like to be that old."

She knew how she appeared to them. Cocking an eyebrow, she asked, "Do you imagine that I am old?"

" 'Love is from before the light began, When light is over, love shall be . . .' "

"That's lovely."

"A foolish Arab wrote it. 'To lighten my darkness, I look for the red crescent of her lips, And if that comes not, I look for the blue crescent of the sword of death.' "

She found this suddenly quite interesting. "You would die for me?"

He nodded, his face mock-solemn.

It made her laugh, and at first he laughed, too, but then became silent. Late into the night, she lay beside him and felt him watching her. She pretended to sleep, and in her false sleep she falsely sighed his name.

Each morning, a boy-child brought dates and milky tea. At noon, Ibrahim went to a tent with the other men, and in the evening servants even more bedraggled than he was came and set up a table beneath some trees, and she and he would sit together. He would eat and watch her, his eyes shining with desire. He observed that she never ate, but asked no explanation.

Now, as she lay beside him for what must be the fourth night, she thought perhaps the time had come to eat. Gravity was controlling her more and more. She was sluggish.

She went up on one arm. There he lay, his face slightly sweated, his form motionless but for the slight rising and falling of the chest. She ran a finger through the curly, graying hair. He stirred a little. His eyes seemed unfocused, as if he was at large in his inner life.

What might he be looking for within himself—the images of his wives, perhaps? Not likely. When he wept, as he sometimes did, he claimed that he was missing them. "But I have been captured by you, my demoness. I cannot leave."

She gazed at the flame of the lantern. He had trimmed its wick in the afternoon, and it was very steady tonight. It was run, he had said, by the same oil that ran the unhorsed wagon.

His genital organ glowed faintly pink. It was fully engorged with blood. Without speaking, she mounted him and put him in her. Let him have a last run.

The muscles in the edges of his face tightened, making it seem to extend, gleaming, into the lantern light. He had said that he did not like her to do this. It wasn't seemly, he said, for the woman to go boldly on the man. So perhaps, this time, he would want to do violence to her afterward. There was a part of her that enjoyed the illusion of helplessness at the hands of a human being. In her inner world, she would imagine being captured by them, and bound so that she could not move. The idea of being carried by them, of suffering pain from their hands with no ability to prevent it, of being ravished by the hurrying little thrusts of the males—these thoughts would amuse her—as indeed, they amused her now.

Tears came into his eyes. But then he expended himself, and sank back. She dismounted him. He made an expression with his face, drawing his lips back across his teeth. Then he sucked in air, hissing like an uneasy snake. "I must pray," he said.

She laid a hand on his breast. "Not now."

"Yes, now. The hour is late. If the others see that I do not pray—"

"You don't believe any of it."

"But I cannot take the risk of being thought impious. You cannot imagine what they would do, and I don't want to. Already, they have seen that I pray only once in the day. And they see that a djin is here with me. If I do not pray, they will kill us both, I sense it."

"Who is your god? Amon-ra?"

His eyes, subtly clouded, looked upon her with curiosity. But he said nothing.

All of this prayer of his, she wondered, where had it come from? They still had their precious "beliefs," the humans, that were not grounded in fact. Did they not notice the silence of their gods? Well, Ibrahim did. He prayed only for show. She wanted to be impressed with her Ibrahim, but no, not now. Now, things must change. She put aside sentiment.

"Should I pray?" she asked. "Will they think ill of us if I do not?"

"They will think ill of us if you come out of the caravan but to draw and wash and get supplies. If a woman prays or does not pray, what does it matter?"

She found some dates that he had, and fed him one. As he took it between his lips, his eyes closed. "I am seeing you like the star of heaven," he said. He sat up on the side of the bed. "But, you know, where are you from? You came out of the desert. Can it be that demons are real? Is that why you have taken me from my family?"

She laid her lips on his neck. He muttered something—a prayer, she supposed, to his silent god. When her tongue penetrated the skin, he made a small, internal sound of surprise. She felt intake of breath, then the beginnings of speech in his throat.

She clenched the powerful muscle that encased her stomach, doing it so tightly that a bit of digestive fluid issued from her nose and ran busily down her jaw, hot and swift. Then the muscle unwound, opening her gut with hydraulic smoothness, the suction swooping his blood from his veins. The poetess Ashtar had called it "that movement beneath all others."

He made a long, babbling utterance of mixed confusion and fear, high with question, higher with complaint. Then his tongue began sputtering in his mouth, and his heels drummed the sodden bed. A fly rushed about her lips, frantically seeking the blood that bubbled out.

Ah, nice. An edible little man.

There came tapping. The sudden arrival of other humans didn't concern her, no matter that the moment was inopportune. She laid her hand on Ibrahim's wrist, detected no pulse. Very well, his struggles would raise no alarm. She got up, threw on her great cloak, and opened the door a bit.

The boys had arrived with dinner, lamb in rice. "My master is not disposed," she murmured through the crack in the door. "God is great."

"God is great," the leader of the boys replied. But they lingered. No matter that he was unwell, they still must be paid for the food they had made. To reward each other for services and such, the humans nowadays passed around bits of paper and nondescript metal.

She had no clear idea of the way this all worked. How much should she give them? She went to his leather packet, an ugly little thing made of some sort of extruded material that had been subjected to heat. There were Egyptian pounds in it, numbered in Arabic numerals. Inventive creatures, the Arabs. She took a few out and handed them through the door.

"May God grant you many blessings," the head boy expostulated.

She pulled the door shut and went to tend to the remnant. Ibrahim was dark brown, his skin stretched so tightly on the bones that it shone. He had a lovely clean back. Never one to waste, she took her flaying knife from the pouch where she kept it in her cloak and skinned off the good part, detaching it from the fascia with expert strokes. She rolled it and put it into the inside pocket of the cloak. This would make something nice, perhaps slippers.

She saw some damp in the abdomen, flipped the remnant over, and sucked into it, penetrating the cavity with her tongue, running it about and draining the last.

Now the remnant was crisp. It smelled of rawhide, a dense, musky odor. She began at the feet, crushing the remains and reducing them to powder between her fingers, letting the material flow onto a cloth. In a few minutes, all that remained of Ibrahim was a pile of material not dissimilar to the granules of his everlasting damnable coffee. Wrapping herself against the cold of the desert night, she went out into the oasis, looking for a disused fire.

There were quite a number of the poor in this place. Many of the people here were without even a tent, and she knew that eyes were watching her from beneath the piles of cloth that lay here and there near the guttering fires. Ibrahim said that they thought her a djin. Well, they were not so far wrong, were they?

She went to one of the fires, where there was a coffeepot steaming near some coals, and dusted them with the powder. Ibrahim sparked merrily into the sky, his red-hot crumbs twirling up in the smoke. So there he went, with his pink organ and golden brown skin, and his poetry. His hair gave the smoke a displeasing pungency. She moved quickly back to their hut.

Inside, she prepared for her journey, drawing her heart closed to the misfortunes she might observe along the road, or what she might find at the end of her quest. It was disturbing that her people had abandoned her. The reason had to be discovered and understood. She very definitely sensed a threat.

She'd come to understand that, just across the mountains from here, lay Cairo, which, she now knew, had displaced Thebes.

Moving about under the eyes of the human creatures was eerie. She walked out into the desert a short distance. She felt quite good now, with Ibrahim's life spreading through her body. She'd been as dry as sand inside.

A glance at the stars told her exactly where she was on the planet—just forty royal miles south and east of Giza. In that direction, the sky glowed as if with perpetual sunset. She could not imagine that the glow could be a human nest, but apparently it was Cairo. If this was true, then it had grown to be the greatest city of the earth, and meant that Egypt had retained the ancient importance she had given it in the world of men. Giza was on the far side of the Nile. In the past, only little Tanis had been on this side of the river, in the desert below Heliopolis.

She considered how to get into Cairo. Forty miles would be a long, but not an impossible, walk. However, Ibrahim's chemical wagon could get her there in a matter of minutes. He had said so himself, by traveling the black wax road eastward.

She approached the thing, drew her cloak around her linen gown, and peered at it. If a human being could control this wagon, she could do it too, and far better. She had observed the various movements Ibrahim had made while directing it about. If she made the same movements, she would succeed. She returned to their caravan and removed the key from his trousers, which lay upon the floor.

As she crossed the dusty clearing, she heard a child's voice whisper, "The djin is getting in his car."

It still made her uneasy, this cunning machine. Nevertheless, she worried the lock, inexpertly rattling it. Shadows began moving about in the oasis, and she heard somebody calling for Ibrahim. A shuddering, uneasy thrill passed through her.

Then the door came open. She entered the thing in the driving position, found the keyhole, and inserted the key. Out in the darkness, a voice shouted, "Ibrahim, Ibrahim." She waited a moment for the key to work, but no sound issued from the wagon. There had been a hand motion involved, which she emulated, turning the key. At once, the mechanism began to chatter. Bobbing lanterns appeared in the darkness. "Stop," shouted a male.

Now what? Use the feet, pressing the pedals in sequence. Move the hand on the lever. However, when she duplicated these actions, the machine went backward, and at significant speed. She sat in the proper position, but the backward motion did not cease. Wondering at it, she watched the lights of the oasis disappear into the dust cloud spread by the rushing wheels.

The gradient changed. She was backing into the mountains. Soon, the oasis would be many miles away. It occurred to her that the device would not stop if it came to a cliff. It had no mind, and she could not see to direct it. She turned the key again, and in a moment, was rewarded with the stopping of all motion and sound.

Now, where had she come to? A mile, perhaps, due south of the oasis. She had not known that the thing would go backward. What had happened was in some way related to the pressure she had put on the pedals, and the manipulation of the lever. She should have realized that the movements of the lever were not arbitrary. It was hard to remember that machines only did as they were commanded. They were not unruly, like horses and mules.

She sat for a moment. How was it that the humans had created such an object as this? It might be the only one, of course, the work of some peculiar genius. Certainly not Ibrahim. He would have bought it from the genius with some of his paper bits. However, what genius would sell such a wonderful thing to an idiot? Surely Great Cairo would offer more desirable buyers than her little rodent of the desert.

Again, she set the fire within the thing. It consisted, this fire, of a series of explosions, she could hear that. The odor of its burning was not pleasant. Ibrahim had given over Egyptian pounds for the liquid to run the wagon, to a man who had carried it in tin jars slung upon the backs of camels.

This time, the thing went forward, clanking and jerking first, then sounding and moving more smoothly as it gathered speed. She learned to make it go a certain speed by keeping the pedal pressure steady. He'd had lights that lit it at night, but they impeded her vision ahead, so she left them off.

The others at the oasis must already be aware that something was amiss with Ibrahim. She would not return to the oasis. Instead, she would go north and west, toward Cairo.

He had used that waxen road before, and now she sought it again. For quite some time, she did not see it. But then the wagon shot up a berm and out into the air. With a great, rattling crash and a growl from within, it landed on the black material. It would have gone all the way across, except Lilith brought it to a halt using the pedals, which was quite easy to do. Actually, the thing was easier than a horse. Horses had always been something of a curse for her kind. They were apt to become uneasy, to bolt unexpectedly, and otherwise draw attention to the fact that they were frightened.

She descended from the wagon, bent down, and ran her hand along the black wax. It was quite warm to the touch, and filled with pebbles. An interesting substance. She bent closer, sniffed it. Pungent, smelling faintly of the same liquid that burned in the lamps and the wagon. This was all alchemized from petroleum, she thought. They had sprayed a thick petroleum on stones, and made from this a path that would not be much affected by rain. A thinner petroleum, perhaps a boil-off of some sort, had been condensed into fuel. There were pools of this ichor south of Thebes, a day's journey into the desert. That was where they must have gone.

At that moment, and without warning, a great noise arose. Huge lights bored into her face. She realized that something was going to strike her in seconds. Reflex caused her to leap into the air. As she went flailing down into the dust of the berm, an immense machine went past her. She glimpsed curtains in windows, and sleeping humans within, in rows of seats. Then the thing was gone, bleating off down the path like a ram in heat.

She looked after it. How could something so large move with such speed? It had shocked her so much that she was trembling like an innocent child—which was absurd. She forced herself to stop. Very well. Now she returned to the wagon of Ibrahim, got in it, and began proceeding again toward Cairo. She did not care to move at such high speed, because it felt as if the breath would be pulled from her lungs. She kept it at what felt like the speed of a fast camel or a good team of horses. She did not use the lights, because she could see easily with all this moonlight.

Nevertheless, light filled the compartment. Then a horrible bleating broke out behind her. She glanced around to see a massive silver jaw not three feet from the rear of her wagon. This thing sailed back and forth in the road, bleating and snarling. Shocked by its size and its aggression, she turned the wheel on hers and it went away to the far side of the road. A truly gigantic machine passed her, making her wagon rock and shudder. The driver cried out, "Son of a diseased whore!" and made a gesture with his fingers. She felt anger tighten the skin of her cheeks, felt her skin grow colder than the desert night. Had the arrogant little creature that was riding the giant come within her grasp, she would have sucked it as dry as sand and thrown the husk into the face of the night.

The wind left by the giant slowly died away. The thing could have crushed her. It would have brought terrible wounding, followed by lingering years of agony. They would have buried her in the ground, where she would have remained conscious, waiting.

Perhaps it was that Ibrahim had the smallest wagon. The enormous ones were normal. This was why their drivers were so aggressive. They were not used to seeing such a small one. She would cause it to go more quickly, and would use the lights to give the night-blind human beings warning of her presence. She wondered if the wagons grew like plants.

She traveled on for a time, and for this time the road remained absolutely dark. It was eighth month, and the seven stars of the Pleiades lay low on the horizon.

Then the wagon mounted a long rise, and there appeared before her one of the most magnificent sights she had ever beheld. No matter how dark the cave of memory, such a vision as this would never be forgotten. Stretching from the southern to the northern horizons was an ocean of lights, as if the stars had grown so fat that they had come down to rest themselves upon the earth. She stopped the wagon. For some little time, she stared through the glass screen. Then she stepped out and stood with the wind in her face, her hood down her back, absorbing the wonder.

Re-Atun had never told her of this formation. When she had come to Cairo before, she had seen nothing like this. But what was it? Who would make such a thing? Who could? It was this strange decorative creation, or artwork, that had been making the sky glow, not the human place that was invisible beneath its brilliance. The wax path led straight down and across a plain, into the dancing forest of the lights.

When she began to draw closer, things seemed to be not as they had at first appeared. The glimmering mass—it wasn't an artwork at all, but something much stranger. When she began to see specific buildings, houses on the roadside, she realized that the jewel-like points of light were coming from sparks that had been captured in glass. Had man learned to take crumbs from the sun, then, in preference to the torch, the candle, and the lantern?

The closer she got to Cairo, the more her wagon was surrounded by others. She soon discovered that they came in all shapes and sizes. Quite a few were as small as Ibrahim's. Some were even larger than the ones she'd seen in the hills. In addition, buildings were springing up on both sides of the path, and people were moving about in numbers.

Seeing the wealth of food around, she thought perhaps she would eat again, a small one or maybe two, to fill her completely after her long hunger. She wished that Re-Atun was here to help her, and began to feel a distinct anger that he was not. It was his duty, to serve the mother of them all. Why was he ignoring his duty?

The wagon had come into a densely populated area. The place was richly scented with human smells, the odor of skin laced with whiffs of sweat and urine, and the deeper odor of offal that rose from grates along the edges of the path.

The place was rushing, complicated, and, above all, bright. Colorful strips of light flashed, globes glowed—it was all very different from the lamplit world of man. The Keepers preferred shadows, so they would certainly not be seen in this glaring, onrushing maelstrom of light-flooded activity.

The place positively teemed with people. In fact, the scent of all this flesh was putting an edge on her appetite, a strong edge. Ibrahim now seemed like not nearly enough.

Ibrahim . . .

How strange she felt right now. But she did remember his smiles, and the gratitude in his eyes when she had given him pleasure.

Wiping her cheeks of the moisture there, she decided to stop the wagon and get one of the creatures and eat again. She'd take a small one, just a tidbit. When she'd gone abroad in Thebes, taking a babe had caused some wailing from the woman, nothing more than that. Human children died so often, they made little of their deaths.

When she stopped her wagon, all the others behind her began bleating and flashing. She opened the door, rose to her feet, and drew her cloak tight. Then she lifted her hood, putting her face in shadow. Best to take some precautions. Sometimes the woman would complain more than others. She'd need to blend into the crowd, then.

She swept through the tangled mass of wagons, into a side path upon which many men and a few women walked. It was not seemly for one of her station to look behind her, but she began to get the sense that the people she was passing were turning to watch her. A snapping glance revealed people with narrowed eyes. Beggars stopped their pleas in midsentence, merchants stepped back into their doorways, slipping away among their sheaves of scarves and hanging masses of rugs.

She turned down a crooked path between enormous buildings, great boxes that smelled as if they were literally packed with humans. The commotion of the big path died away behind her, and she decided that she would not return to Ibrahim's wagon, not face that tangled, glaring chaos of humanity.

Then, suddenly, she was in a tiny square filled with peace. The sight of a fountain in the center of the square for an instant split her heart with a shaft of memory so sweet and so ancient that she actually cried out. She stopped, momentarily stunned. What was this recollection? And this agony—an agony of love, where was it from?

There was singing, soft, echoing in the silence. Two little girls were sitting beside the dry fountain, girls in patched gowns, with little scarves covering their hair. Her heart in turmoil, her mind full of the confusions of this new city and the powerful and unexpected emotion she had just experienced, she went almost automatically forward. One of the girls looked up at her, and she saw the child's eyes and was horrified— mankind had changed! Look, the child was awake, full of spirit. Still, by instinct, she did what her body demanded, and lifted it to her mouth and locked onto its warm, sweet neck. She took it with a powerful gulp. The remnant crackled to bone and disappeared into its clothes. A child's thin gristle was not strong enough to hold the skeleton together, and the bones, tight-sheathed by the skin, came tumbling out of the bit of cloth the thing had worn, and scattered about Lilith's feet.

The other one spoke, a quick question that Lilith did not quite understand. It had wonderful, smooth skin. It was so beautiful, she thought she had never seen such an exquisite face. She took it and held it to her lips, and the perfume of its skin filled her nostrils. She hunted for the tiny artery with her tongue. But then—then—

She drew her head back. The child turned to her, and laid upon her lips a kiss as soft as the wing of a dove. The fountain—she saw it alive, pure water bubbling, in it the blue fish of home and childhood.

Childhood! O, she had played by such a fountain. And somebody had said—had said—"I will wait for you. . . ."

She put the exquisite child down. It looked up at her with sparkling, vastly intelligent eyes. Secretly in the eons, the human soul had rowed far upriver from its animal origins, much farther than she had thought. This was no blank creature of the past, this was a conscious being.

Her gut wrenched, the taste of the blood she'd just eaten threatened to sicken her. She mourned within herself for dear Ibrahim and for the girl whose life she had just consumed.

An extremely bright light flashed, and a woman's voice was raised in frantic babble. As the words changed to shrieks, Lilith began to move off. She went down a crack of an alley, looking for Keeper sign. A city like Cairo would be honeycombed with secret Keeper passages.

She found one, just an irregular two bricks in a wall. Pressing them with the heel of her hand, she opened a narrow door to an equally narrow passage and went in.

The silence here was tremendous, the darkness absolute. She reached out and rubbed the wall, bringing up the soft glow of the paint they used to make the little light that they needed in places like this. Ahead, a passage went curving off. She hurried along it, soon finding the exit. She'd hoped that this led to greater tunnels, but apparently she'd hit on nothing but a short escape route. Very well, she exited.

She could not be far from where she had started, but hopefully far enough. She was before a large building, perhaps a palace, distinguished by tall spires. She could do with a palace, with its abundance of pure water and its bathing-maids. Her heart hammering, she made for the entrance.

As she was crossing the square that lay before it, she heard a bird of a kind she had not seen in many, many years, a great eagle, dark of wing, which had once ranged the Valley of the Nile. These birds had taken the children of men, and rent them with their beaks, while the parents ran along below wailing in the rain of blood. She looked up, expecting to see one of the creatures fall on some loose tot, but instead a small wagon filled with men came whizzing into the open space. The wagon's lights were flashing blue and red, and it was uttering this scream from its stiff silver mouth. Was there a bird in the wagon, or had they somehow taken its cry? And why?

She watched curiously as the wagon sped past her, stopped in a cloud of dust, then wheeled around. She moved toward the palace, from which a guardian began crying a warning in Arabic. He was atop a high tower. "God is most great," he cried, "I testify that there is no god except God. I testify that Mohammed is the messenger of God. . . ." And she thought, Him again. She had decided that Mohammed must be the pharaoh of this time. Perhaps he was even within this palace. She would go to him.

At that moment, there came a *cr-a-a-k* that echoed through the open space before the palace, causing ordinary birds to rise from their roosts and swirl about in a terrified flock. The sound had emanated from a man in brown clothing. He was pointing a small stick at her and calling out, "Come here, in the name of God. We are the police wanting you."

She did not understand the word *police*. In any case, she did not come at human command. She ignored the cry. It came again, and then another crack of sound. The birds continued swirling about in the darkness. The man in the tower finished his melodious call and withdrew. Lilith mounted the wide steps that led into the palace. Another voice shouted, "It's desecrating the mosque," and there were more cracks.

Then she was flying. She was flying quite far and high, it seemed. But no, she was falling. She put a hand out and steadied herself, but fell heavily upon the steps she'd just been climbing.

There was an odd sensation in her. For some time, she lay trying to understand why she was not walking, and what this sensation actually was. Finally, she realized that she had been knocked to the ground by something that had struck her in the back, and the sensation was pain.

There was the sound of running behind her. Pain or no pain, she went to her feet. Three men, all dressed in identical brown, were pounding across the wide plaza, coming toward her. She watched them with mild interest. The blow she had felt and the fall she had taken were still a matter for wonder. Had they struck her? If so, how, from such a distance? Their arms were not long, and she saw no bows in their hands, nor quivers at their backs. So how?

Then flame spat from the end of one of the sticks that they carried, instantly followed by a wind beside her head. So they were slings, and she had been hit by one of the stones. The little devils were trying to hurt her, and from the pain in her back, they had.

She took a deep breath, heard bubbling coming from within. They had pierced her with a projectile slung from the devices, the fire-spitting slings. But why? She had done these creatures no harm.

From out of a side alley there came women, all laid over with shrouds, all running along, wailing and crying out, "There she goes, stop her, stop the monster."

Again the slings made their explosive sound. Lilith felt a stone pass her face so close that it left behind it a hot wind. She rushed along the steps but did not enter the palace. Better, when being chased, to leave as many paths open as possible. She would rather dare the night than enter an easily searched warren of rooms.

But she was being *chased*. How incredible. How fearful. Gangs of humans could chop you up, burn you. It had occasionally happened to Keepers, as she was well aware. She needed sign, she needed to find the house of Re-Atun.

She looked for more sign, but saw nothing. There was darkness ahead, however, so she went that way. Here was a fruit-seller's stall. She recognized some of the fruits, but not all. There were red and yellow and green fruits, golden fruits, fruits with textured skins, and fruits gleaming like ceramics. It seemed to her that this must be the best-stocked fruit-seller's stall in the world. How odd a coincidence, to happen upon what must be a famous place. She passed into the stall, where sat a man in a turban doing the "smoking" that had so pleased Ibrahim, and sipping hot liquid from a glass. He glanced up at her and asked, "Where are you going?"

She didn't answer. A moment later, in fact, she heard the cries of the wagon of the angry men, and then also a cry from the fruit-seller, who went outside and began to shout, "The thief is here, the thief is here."

She was slowed by the complexity of the surroundings. Moving blindly, not knowing which door led where or which alley would aid her escape and which thwart it, she nevertheless continued ahead. The wound in her back continued to give her pain. She could feel the stone lodged in her skeleton, making every movement a torment.

Then, very suddenly, there was a feature she recognized immediately, that she could never forget and that had been there since she had first walked in this place, when Egypt was a land of green grass and trees. The sight of the Nile almost shattered her composure. She sobbed, a sound that amazed her so much that it momentarily pushed aside her pain.

Her own kind had always lived along the Nile, in houses that communicated to the tunnels that led to Giza, and the halls of conclave and record that lay deep beneath the pyramids. It had been thus in the days of Thebes, and it would be thus now. She looked up and down the long, curving quay, and soon found signs of her own kind. Yes, they were here. Of course they were. In this greatest of human places, the Keepers would be in secret control of everything. That was the way the world worked, as she had intended it to work.

In the distance, she could hear the little wagons as they rushed about, trying to find her. Cairo, however, was a maze that made Babylon look simple, even when one could not find Keeper tunnels. She had crossed into alleys that could only be negotiated on foot. Even so, she looked up and down the open space, searching for more of the little men with the stone or dart throwers. If those things were to strike her head, it would be very dangerous.

Pain. Danger. How amazing. She moved quickly along, going to a place in the quay where the bricks of its wall were laid in a subtly different pattern. Standing there, she faced the buildings across the road, looking at their bases. And yes, she saw another variation in pattern there, a balustrade that had a row of carvings of fruits on it, one of which, looked at in a certain way, could be seen as an arrow.

At last, she had come to the house of Re-Atun. Now he would answer her questions and give her shelter. Now, she would be safe. She trotted across the street, moved in the direction indicated. Re-Atun would gaze at her with such fondness that it would make her anger melt.

She went down the steps, one two, into the fetor of the lower alleyway. At this level, it was designed to be unappealing, to appear abandoned. She felt along the seventh seam of the wall's masonry, then made the intricate series of movements that served as a key.

There was silence. Nothing. She stepped back. She had not opened this door before, but all doors opened to all, so this one—

It swung in toward darkness absolute. She stepped in, quickly pushing it closed behind her. Speaking in her elegant, perfectly articulated Prime, she called on him to come forth.

This time, the silence was confusing. Could it be that she had, by some bizarre coincidence, come here while he was out foraging? She felt along the low ceiling to the light, then rubbed her palm quickly back and forth until the sensitive phosphors painted there glowed.

A face, leering. Gray objects dangling below it, oozing with some sort of life form. And—were those wings? No, they were not wings. The chest had been split open and lifted, exposing the lungs and heart, which were seething with maggots. The lower body was laid open as well, the long, curling gut tied into a hangman's noose. The body itself was riveted to a thick metal wall, where once, she suspected, there had been an elegant door leading into the subterranean palace of Re-Atun. She stepped back, too horrified at first to utter a sound. In her immense life, this was among the most repulsive things she had ever seen. But what, exactly, was it? She peered closer, looking directly into the rotted face, trying to understand.

NO! She reeled, turning away in loathing from the slowly struggling body, away from the awful, seething whisper that had started up in the lips, that she knew were words, *"Kill me . . . kill me . . ."*

He was still conscious enough to know to whom he spoke, because his Prime was formal with respect.

Her immediate impulse was to run, but she dared not. What had happened here? Oh, he had been split—and she knew the torment. It was called the blood eagle, the opening of the chest of a living creature, an ancient way of torturing one who could not die. Some ancient flags—that of the Russian czars, for example—displayed the blood eagle as a warning to the Keepers.

She could kill him, though, using her ancient and intimate knowledge of their kind.

"Who did this?"

The lips remained frozen. They would speak no more. But the eyes, the eyes seemed to look right through her. She turned around. On the distance, she heard the banshee wailing of many more of the little wagons, and the cries of hurrying humans.

To destroy a Keeper, you needed fire and time, and she had neither. Where she was standing right now, this very spot, was a death trap. She leaned close to him, into the stink and rotted vileness of his black flesh, bearing the mites that rushed onto her skin. She opened the flower of her lips, and a dying goddess kissed a living corpse. Then she stepped back. The whole flesh of him, the whole bone, seemed to twist on the spikes that held it to the wall. "Re-Atun, beloved of my womb," she whispered, but then stopped. She could say no more.

He knew, and she knew, that this would be his last chance at mercy, maybe forever. She looked about, wishing that she could open the skull, could reach in—but the wailing ground down just outside, and the voices became sharper, more crisp. They had her, and they knew they had her. Of course they did: she had gone straight into their trap.

CHAPTER FIVE

The Monster of Cairo

S weet Girl Pie" came on, and Ian turned the radio up as far as it would go. He jammed the gas pedal to the floor of his dad's way-cool '65 Mustang. Dad just loved this dumb old car. It was like all of Dad's stuff, still perfect no matter how old. He could spend any amount on what he loved—keeping this baby as perfect as she was the day she rolled out of the showroom, or maintaining his terrifying antique float plane—or buying his new plane, for that matter. Hell, he could spend anything on what he loved, but Ian was still at East Mill goddamn High School.

"I'm alive, Dad, I'm SOMEBODY!" He yelled it out, blasting the words louder than the music. "I AM SOMEBODY!" It was a cry to the silence of the night and the twisting road down which the 'Stang was now screaming at 80 mph.

With an expertise that would have shocked even his father, who knew the truth about his extraordinary physical excellence and superb reflexes, Ian spun the gleaming old car in three complete circles in front of East Mill High, then headed into the parking lot, where Mr. Sleicher was frantically waving his flashlight. "Ward," he said, "holy moly, you just about got yourself killed."

Ian pulled into the space Mr. Sleicher was indicating. "I'm sorry, Mr. Sleicher," he said, "you know these old 'Stangs don't have a front end. Fortunately, I managed not to lose control." He smiled politely at the history teacher known as Mr. Sleeper for his habit of falling asleep during his own lectures.

"Well, Ian, you . . . pulled it out. You oughta—you know there's a good stock car run over in Danbury. Don't tell your olds I said this, but you'd probably be able to qualify, you can drive like that. They take 'em at eighteen, you know."

Ian thought, Exactly what I need. Ian Ward, stock car racer. He was tempted to ask, "Mr. Sleeper, just offhand, what was the Treaty of Paris?" But Mr. Sleeper taught his history by reading from his teacher's manual and going for the class discussion suggestions at the end.

Ian had known since he was nine that he was a sort of freak in regard to intelligence. He kept it carefully hidden, but his parents knew. Hell, they were always praising him for it. So what were they thinking to stick him in this rathole when all the kids he'd grown up with had gone off to prep school? Tommy Royal was at Taft, the Singer sisters were at Andover, his best friend of his life Kev Potter-Jones was at Exeter . . . and he was here, so Daddy could keep his widdle-bitty boy close to home. Dad was a Choate alum. By all rights, Ian should be a legacy there. Mom—had she gone to high school? Or school at all? Sometimes he thought she'd been grown hydroponically by the Company, picked, and plugged into that spyhole of theirs in the basement.

Ian had wanted to see the inside of their little cell since he was old enough to think, but it was no go. Classified. He had no idea what his parents did except that they worked for the CIA. Dad was rich somehow, because they always flew first class and family vacations could be, frankly, fairly amazing. Plus you didn't go out and buy a quarter-of-a-million-dollar sport plane if you weren't pretty well off. In school, Ian was, like, the rich kid.

He trotted across the parking lot toward the gym. Kerry Logan's dismal band, Bad Boy, was defecating noise into the night. He arrived at the cash table and plunked down his five bucks. Sherry Gleeson stamped his hand. "Why am I here?" he asked her.

"I don't know. Why are you here?"

"Looking for survivors."

He was female-challenged, always had been. Officially he was good looking, but in reality there was too much of the little boy in his face. He'd tried growing a beard, but had gotten only some blond junk that looked like it had been pulled out of some waitress's beehive and pasted on. He was thinking about getting a swastika tattooed on his earlobe.

"Hey, fool," Terence van Aalten said. His parents were apple farmers. His family had been apple farmers since before the Headless Horseman galloped up from Sleepy Hollow, which was about thirty miles south of here.

"Hey, Aapples."

Glorious Gloria Gunderson looked through Ian so completely that he had the creepy sensation of being invisible. He leaned close to her ear. "Lick my bag."

Her eyes went wide. East Mill scandal! East Mill scandal!

"Now, don't look so shocked, I'll give you a buck." He fluttered his eyes at her. "I'm *sooo* sweet."

"You're just gonna get yourself beat up again, Different," she said. "Do you want that?"

"I love punishment."

Kerry Logan leaned into the mike and said, "Dis ova *oeeennnee . . .*" He leaned out. He leaned in again, *"Oeeeeee . . ."* Child Barley was somewhere backstage shooting the gain on the mike every time the Bad Boy from the Eagle Scouts tried to sing. So *baaaaaaaaaaad!*

Ian thought he might go back there and give Child Barley some assistance. Also, the Child could sometimes produce the odd little pill. Ian didn't indulge, not the son of intelligence officers, not if you respected their security clearances. But the possession of a tab of X would adjust the attitudes of any number of the flouncing beauties out on the dance floor. A tab of X would ensure a conversation in the depths of his car. The console was an amazing problem, of course, but there was always her house.

Irie Dearborn smelled like some kind of wonderful raw fruit, a trembling aroma of purest feminine sweetness. He leaned over to where she was sitting and said, "Your perfume smells like a dog in heat."

She said, "I'm cut," and held out her hand. She'd sliced it on a busted plastic glass that was lying on the floor before her pretty little feet. He lifted its white softness to his lips and kissed, but really so that he could smell her smell more closely. Ian knew that it was extremely odd to love smells the way he did, but he did.

She yanked it away. "Thank you."

He whispered in her ear, "You'll get melanoma in a week, from the touch of my lips."

"What's that?"

"Cancer."

Dream: He lives in Chelsea down near the docks, in one of those huge old derelicts where they throw raves. He runs the very most phat rave in the whole community, and he is, he is SOMEBODY. (Oh, yeah, like he would have the nerve to do that. Mr. Goodboy. But his mom and dad, their jobs depended on things not happening, like, he is tossed for raving.)

To go to the sound booth, he had to get up onstage, and when he did, some asshole threw a screaming fit and did a fake faint. In seconds, a dozen other guys were doing it. "Bite me," he yelled as he pushed his way through the curtains and into the dark wings.

Thinking that the outburst was because of his ridiculous band, Kerry hopped and jerked his hips. Ian picked up a power cable connection and plugged and unplugged it a couple of times, listening to Kerry's guitar live and die, live and die. "Hey, man," came his voice from the Outer Beyond. "I know that's you, asshole."

Saying "asshole" onstage, Kerry—is there a merit badge for that?

The Child was indeed in the sound booth, enveloped in so much smoke that he was actually hard to see. Ian went in. "Hey."

"Fuckaroo," the Child said, handing over a surprisingly tiny joint.

Ian dropped the blinds and locked the door, then waved the joint away.

The Child, who was probably the coolest freshman to hit East Mill in history, convulsed with laughter. "God, listen to him. Is he singing with his bunghole?" He shot the gain up and down, up and down. "He's gonna beat my ass up again."

"Lucky you." Ian sat in one of the folding chairs that were scattered around the room. The Child closed his eyes. "I'm really back here looking for X."

The Child laughed silently. "As am I, as am I."

"You don't have any?"

"So you can't get any from—who's that guy in—uh—that junior? My beloved competition?"

"Robinson. Robinson's been, like, tied to his bed by his parents. They suspect him of being a drug dealer, or some such nonsense."

"That girl did herself."

"What girl?"

"Robinson, Brittania, of bag nose fame."

"Britt Robinson is a bag nose? Where's she get that kind of money?"

"Ask the cocaine angel in the sky. She's with him now." He rolled his eyes. "She went, like, *eckeckeck*"—he convulsed furiously—"in the Gilford Road McDonald's. In the la-a-a-dies."

Britt Robinson had been in Lit. 6 with him last semester, and she'd just offed? This had happened? "You're shittin' me."

He shook his head. "Life goes on."

Not hers, though. He did not want any X, all of a sudden. Kerry sang, and the Child played the gain. "I'm gonna *ooooooeeeee* . . . ."

"I'm—Jesus."

"You suckin' face wit her?"

"No—no, it's just a shock. Do people know?"

He shrugged. "Sure. But she was, like, a bag nose. Nobody cares."

Ian left the dance, walking out into the starry night. Why was there even a dance going on? What about honoring the dead? They all knew her, she'd been around just yesterday. Now she was just another kid dead, goombye. It was like war. In war, somebody dies, you don't cancel the dance. "*Oooooeeeee* . . ." from inside the gym.

Ian wanted his dad's big arms around him, like when he was a kid. No, he didn't, dammit, he *did not!* He got in the 'Stang and drove off, jamming the gas to the floor, listening to the tires scream, feeling the lousy front end wallow. Driving fast and too fast, he swept through East Mill, went out Gilford Road past Jergen's Ice Cream Stand and past Amon Antique Village, past the glaring Taco Bell, and pulled into the McDonald's.

A couple of people were inside, there were the usual busted-down kids behind the counter, the neon was humming. That was it, life goes on.

Somebody died, hey! Hey!

He drove on, past the abandoned radio station and the Exxon station, leaving the last lights and then turning north into the hills, pushing the car hard on the cruel roads, driving on. He did not want to stop, not ever, just to drive, to somehow catch up with her soul. He slammed a cassette into the deck, fast-forwarded to "Hey I Matter."

"Hey I matter, please look at me, Hey I matter. I matter, I got a name, hey I matter." And then the mean drums, and then her voice again, "I matter, I got a name, hey I matter . . ."

One thing, Leo, you're wrong about. We don't matter, we're fodder, or not even that. Just names slipping into memory and then gone, lost names. "WE FUCKING MATTER!"

He'd yelled so loud his throat hurt. Up the road he saw a deer, swerved, listened to the tires squeal, felt the front end contemplate his death, then decide he had a couple more minutes after all.

He drove on, pushing the car maybe hard enough to kill them both, deep into the night.

Becky Ward read the e-mail again. It wasn't that she couldn't believe what she was seeing, but that she wasn't sure what to believe. The agency's search engine had found a link to a story in the on-line edition of a Tunisian newspaper about the apparent murder of a child in Cairo that fit their alert criteria.

Under the headline, "The Monster of Cairo," the story described how a tall woman in a black cloak had rushed into a street where some children were playing, and immediately killed one of them, "leaving the remains dry and hard, and as light as paper."

They hadn't done Cairo, the Egyptians and the French had. She recalled that Jean Bocage had found the Egyptian sterilization team to be extremely efficient. Given that they had to work against what was probably the world's most long-standing infestation, and that Colonel Bocage handed out praise with the generosity of an anorexic miser, that was quite an affirmation.

She went to the Tunisian paper's website. The story was brief, and mentioned no names. She next tried some of the keywords in the

Egyptian press. Nothing came up, so she printed the story for Paul and left it at that. He was upstairs in the den. She'd heard him pacing back and forth, back and forth.

His den was as his father had left it, but exactly. Even the magazines that his father had been reading the day of his disappearance were still in the stand beside his old leather chair.

In her heart, Becky knew that the huge grief of his loss dominated his life more than any love ever could, except perhaps for the love that his damned blood made him feel for Miriam Blaylock. Paul had not married her, he had taken her in from the storm. That was the truth of it—she'd been adopted. She tried not to blame Paul for bringing all this emotional baggage to their marriage. By rights, she ought to really hate what she had here, the obsessed man and the boy who was not hers. But they were needful and sparkling with charisma, both of them. She couldn't help but feel as she did, the fierce loyalty, the equally fierce love.

Back and forth he went, back and forth. She should tell him about the Monster of Cairo. She locked the communications center, set its alarms. Ian had gotten used to his curiosity about this room, and it had been a long time since he'd come down here to challenge the system. Still, the way he'd been lately, so sullen and bitter and withdrawn—she didn't know what he might do next.

Last night, he'd come in at three, his eyes broadcasting to his mother that he was both high and drunk. But he'd been as stable as a rock, his voice careful, sharp, and entirely unslurred. Just like his father. Paul could get fantastically drunk. He could put down a fifth of Scotch and still draw his gun from under his arm aimed and ready to fire in two seconds flat.

"Paul," she said, walking into the den, "I have something here." She handed him the printout.

He read it at least three times before he so much as moved. Then he said, "I'm going down to Langley."

Their mission survived for one reason only: out of sight in a big bureaucracy was pretty much out of mind. "That's a mistake."

"Oh, okay. We have vampires on the loose, and that's a mistake? Thank you."

"Won't Bocage be right on top of it? I mean, the French were on station there. Plus, that Egyptian—their team—it was supposed to be top drawer."

He took another long, careful look at the story. "The French program is still active, that's true enough. I don't know if the Egyptians got decommissioned or what happened to them."

"In either case, it's not our problem."

"So what's your suggestion? Just sit?"

"You've been on my case lately, Paul."

"I haven't been on your case."

"And I'm beginning not to like it."

"I'm not on anybody's case, okay? I just see this thing coming back to life, and I think we're going to need help, and nobody cares. That's the problem." He tossed the printout onto his desk. "I want to get some more assets assigned to Patterson."

"That won't happen."

"Well, that's blunt, at least. Why won't it happen, considering that there are holes in coverage the size of the damned Grand Canyon? I know she left the suite under cover three nights ago. I know she took somebody to her house, and I know why. I need people on her day and night, from now until as long as it takes."

"Paul, if you go to Langley—" She stopped. She didn't want to say it. It would only make him worse.

"What?"

She turned away from him. "You know what."

She felt him staring at her back, and the fierceness she felt thrilled her, even when they were on the knife edge of a blowup. Maybe she would never stop being excited by this man, and maybe she would never feel entirely comfortable with herself for putting him first when he did not reciprocate.

"I got myself fired and reinstated. Once you win one of those hearings, the morons leave you alone. I need more bodies on Patterson, and I need them now, and I *will* get them."

"Paul, you're going to broadcast a very clear message down there, and that message will be that you're fishing without a hook in an empty pond."

"The furnace was hot, and the man is gone! For chrissakes."

"That's the evidence you're taking to Langley?"

"Yes."

"You'll not only get no additional assets, what you have now will be taken from you."

He smiled at her, the explosive intensity of it lighting up the room. His son did that, too, when he smiled.

She just suddenly kissed him and let herself melt into his clumsy response. He was a clumsy dancer, too, and she adored that about him as well. "If I wanted my face sanded, I'd go to a carpenter," she said, laughing.

He felt his beard. "I shaved."

She ran her fingers along his blue cheek. "Two days ago."

"That long? Are you sure?"

"I was there."

He looked down at her, and for a moment she was gazing into the eyes of a giant child. It always startled her to see the face he had shown to his father, and the shadow of his own son that flickered there. In a way, she was not a wife and mother but the keeper of two strange, incredibly appealing beings. When she'd told Dr. Rhodes—Allie, her shrink for three years—"My husband isn't quite human," Allie had taken it as metaphor.

"We're in trouble, big-time," he said.

"Not if you stay away from Langley, we're not."

"We have two vampires still operating in two vastly different parts of the world, and that is what I define as big-time." He paced to the window. "The guns," he said softly. "I want to bring out the guns."

"Oh, come on. What if Ian should see them? Or—my God, you talk about Langley. If Langley finds out we kept those guns, they're liable to take the legal route."

"We had to keep them! Jesus Christ!"

"I know we had to keep them. I helped you keep them. Remember whose name's on the returned property manifest? Not yours."

"If there are two, what if there are twenty or fifty or five hundred?"

"You know that isn't true."

"I've got a meeting with Briggsie."

"That's a fascinatingly bad idea. You not only bust the chain of command, you show up in the office of the person who likes you the least."

"He has authority. I need somebody who can say yes."

"I think you need to start with Cici."

"Cecelia's a drone."

"Cecelia is fair, and she's also your direct superior. Go into her office with good evidence, and she'll listen. You don't respect the chain of command, Paul, you start out from behind. That kind of approach is why we're hanging on by our teeth when we ought to be like Bocage, with a whole operation still in place, waiting, watching."

"Oh, so it's my fault. Of course. And to think all these years I thought it was the fault of deadwood administrators."

"Paul, I don't want you to go down there and blow it. We could lose what little is left of this operation."

"So what? You think it's over anyway."

"Of course it isn't over! I wake up night after night in a sick sweat because it isn't over. And I know—oh, God, Paul, what's happening to Ian? What's he becoming? Paul, is Ian—is that why you're so—so frightening lately, Paul? Is Ian . . . "

"What's Ian got to do with this?"

"Ian has everything to do with it! He has to do with us. And I'm scared for him. I don't know what's happening to him." She paused. "What will happen. Might." There it was, on the table.

"Nobody knows what Ian's going to become. Watchful waiting, that's the prescription."

Paul had been about to say more, but his jaw snapped shut, and his head whipped around. Becky turned. Ian was standing in the doorway. Paul's face went rigid. She went to their son, asking herself the same questions that she'd seen in Paul's frightened eyes: How long has he been there? What has he heard?

"Ian," she said, "good morning."

"It's afternoon," Paul growled.

"Watchful waiting, Dad? For what?"

"It's shop talk. We can't discuss it, and you know we can't."

"Yeah, you can, Dad, because that's a lie. It's about me." He came into the room, came close to his father. "What are you watching for?"

"Ian, for chrissakes."

"What's wrong with me?"

"Ian—"

"Shut up, Mom."

"Don't you tell your mother to shut up."

"Then you tell me what you're watching for, Dad. What's wrong with me?" He flushed; his eyes widened. Becky had never seen a look like that in his face. *"What's wrong with me?"*

Anger was radiating from him like nuclear heat. How long had he known that there was some issue about him that they did not discuss with him? How much did he know?

"Nothing's wrong with you," Paul replied, and the love in his eyes shocked Becky, shocked her and made her heart hurt for both of them.

"Oh? Then maybe I've got it backward. Because if nothing's wrong with me, then I have to ask, what's wrong with you?"

"Ian—"

"Mom, *something is wrong!* Because this family has changed. It isn't like it used to be. Dad, you and I, we used to—" His voice broke. He was silent for a moment, as the man inside struggled to control the boy. "Dad, do you hate me, deep down? Is that it? Or is it that you're scared of me?"

Paul sighed exactly as a man did who'd just had his aorta sliced through by a well-thrown knife.

"He doesn't hate you."

"If I do something right, he's a damn tomb. But if, God forbid, I do something he slightly does not like, then he's coming at my head with a jackhammer. Am I right, Dad?"

Paul remained silent.

"You say it, say you don't despise me or fear me or hate me or whatever in hell it is. Say it, Dad!"

Paul's cheeks drew inward; his eyes dropped. From her interrogation training, Becky knew that he felt threatened by the demand, and there was a danger he would blow up right back. "Paul," she said, warning in her tone—she hoped.

"You do not do drugs. You do not get drunk. You do not disappear in *my goddamn car* until three o'clock in the fucking morning!"

"Oh, God. God, I can't believe this. I just cannot *believe* this." He looked at Becky, his young eyes glistening, the tears that were swimming there making her want to cradle him, to cradle them both, to somehow make this family heal by the sheer power of her will.

"Read the fucking obituaries," Ian spat. "I guess I spent a little too much time driving off my grief—as trivial as that probably is to you—in *your goddamn car*. So please let me apologize."

He ran upstairs. Listening to his thundering feet, Becky could not help but follow him. The husband she left behind was hurting, too, she knew that; but Ian was the son, and so the husband had to wait.

She found him throwing clothes into a backpack, and in that moment wanted the days to come back when her kisses were magic on his wounds. She took a shoulder, trying to turn him to her, was shaken off. She tried again.

"Mom, will you please just back off!"

"Honey—"

Ian pointed to the door. "That man—that man—he ruined my life."

"Ian!"

"Mom, I got straight A's from the first grade on, I speak four languages, and he's forced me to stay in this stupid, god-forgotten hellhole of a school—and he can only say those dumb, meaningless things to me when I hold out my hand to him and ask him for the truth." He strode to the door. "Thank you, Father! Because you've made it easy for me! You've made it so damn easy!"

"Where will you go?" she asked him. She was defeated, she knew it. The tension between Ian and Paul—the awful, grinding, destroying tension—had been too much. Things had always been headed toward this end; she'd known it for years. And now a secret part of her mind, a part that she did not often face, opened itself to her, and a voice whispered, *Let him go. At least he'll be safe from Paul.*

She went to him and held him. He let her, but did not encourage her. She laid her hand against his magnificent blond head. "I remember when I got your curls cut the first time," she said.

"Momma . . ."

"I cried."

They were silent then, the woman and the child, and Becky from Jersey, who'd done it early and gotten most everything wrong, knew again, and from deep within, that one thing about her was true: she was a mother, and this was her son.

Paul trusted Becky to handle Ian. He could not handle Ian. He couldn't even face him. The older the boy got, the more uneasy he became that letting him live had been the cruel gesture of a man too proud to believe that a child of his could become a monster. Well, his mother had been one of the most horrible of all the vampires, a brilliant, bloodthirsty sophisticate with a spectacularly lethal ability to blend into the human world.

What had he expected—that the laws of damn nature wouldn't apply to his kid? Yeah, that's right. And he had reason—Ian wasn't full-blooded, Ian wasn't raised to the vampire life, he had never fed on human blood. To make sure he'd never be even slightly tempted, he'd been told nothing about vampires.

But now he was reaching puberty, and this obsession with Leo Patterson was terrifying Paul. "I love you with my soul," he said into the murmuring of the voices upstairs. "Oh, my son."

He went out and got into his 'Stang, noticing immediately that Ian had used about four gallons of gas last night. This old lady drank about a gallon per sixteen miles, so he'd taken a fair journey, more than the few miles to the high school and back. He had indeed been driving the hills, just as he'd said.

But what did that mean? Had somebody gone missing in the hills last night?

No. God, no. He had not fed, not yet, and probably never would. For God's sake, x-ray him, and you did not see that strange barrel of an organ that passed in the vampires for a stomach, or the enormous heart. Only Ian's brain was the same as theirs, with a third more folds in it than human.

He gunned the engine, started for the airport, with an effort pushing his worries about Ian out of his mind. He opened his cell phone and called ahead for the en route weather, found out that it was going to be just peachy. At least something was falling together right. Hell, maybe it was a portent of things to come. Maybe it meant that Langley was going to be helpful.

He had his meeting at twelve-twenty. It was now nine-twenty. He'd be in the air about two hours in his turbo Mooney M20M. This was a beautiful little airplane, capable of doing 230 knots. He flew from the Storm King airport, a patch of concrete and old Cessnas where you had to worry seriously about deer on the runway. But he loved it. He also owned a Piper Super Cub seaplane restoration that he and Ian used to take fishing way the hell up north, dropping down onto lakes in Canada so isolated that five-pound wild trout weren't out of the question.

As he stopped at the hangar, his cell rang. "Go on."

"Honey, he needs you. He needs his dad."

"Christ. Tell him I'll be back by five."

"He is up there packing, and he is leaving. He's leaving, Paul!"

"You can handle that. He's seventeen, you can make him stay."

"You can make him stay by just treating him like a human being for three minutes. Now, you forget that damn meeting. You get back here, and you help him. This has gone far enough, and it's over. It's over, Paul!"

What was over? Was she over? Were they over? "Listen, I have to do this, and you know I have to. I have to do this!"

"Paul, it's gonna be a failure. Face it, you'll never get another chance with the agency. Ever since you won your board, they've hated you. Hated you! They are going to early retire you, and if you make too much disturbing noise, they might just haul off and kill you."

"The agency doesn't kill it's own. For God's sake, you know that. This isn't the damn movies."

"So I gather you're not coming back."

"I'll be there by six, tops."

"Ian will probably not be here at six, Paul. And if he isn't, I have to warn you, I may not be, either."

He listened to the silence that followed this remark. She was given to melodrama, it was one of her weaknesses.

"Wish me luck," he said—asked, really.

"No."

That made him mad. That was unfair. "Okay. Then I'll wish you luck. Maybe I'll crash, and you'll get the insurance. Sound good?"

With that, he hung up. He waited for a ring, but there was no ring. He considered calling back. But he couldn't, somehow.

It wasn't pride—at least, so he told himself. He didn't know what it was—his essence, he supposed, refusing to bow . . . or his heart, telling him to let his son go.

Maybe if Ian was becoming a vampire, he needed to hide.

And maybe—God's truth—Paul wanted him to hide.

Suddenly he was crying, damn well *crying*. He had to pull the damn car over. Oh, shit, this was real asshole stuff. If Ian turned, then Paul had a job to do.

He sat there, his heart crashing, his temples pounding, feeling towering feelings of love and loyalty for his son. Tears were pouring down his cheeks.

Deep breaths finally controlled the ridiculous display, contained it, enabled him to stuff it back inside.

Okay. You are about to fly an airplane. You cannot do this if you are distraught.

He pushed it back, suppressed it, buried it alive. Then he pulled out into the road and started off again. In barely a minute, the turn to the airport raced up at him, and he had to brake to make it. "You're running," he said, realizing that his thoughts about Ian had caused him to accelerate the car to eighty. He'd done that in Manhattan yesterday. He had to watch that.

He turned into the parking lot and went over to the flightline, where his baby stood awaiting Poppa, a low, sleek BMW of an airplane, looking like a young god amid the flying Chevies and Fords that made their homes at little country airfields. Reg had gassed her up and rolled her out as ordered. Paul opened the gull-wing door and got in, enclosing himself in the black leather luxury of the cockpit.

Leather, a faint odor of aviation fuel, a general smell of newness, beautiful instruments ready to serve—this was a wonderful place to be. As if pushed by a hand from above, he bent over, his fingers closing around the stick, his body rolling forward until his forehead touched the soft nacelle that shielded the instrument panel from the sun. Behind his closed eyes, he saw Ian's face as clearly as if he was standing somewhere in the dark of his mind.

Paul took a deep, ragged breath, sat up. Instinct made him look around, fearful that his moment of weakness had been observed. But no, the field was empty, just a lot of grass and old hangars, and a couple of tired old tie-downs a few feet away.

He fired up his engine and taxied across the bumpy apron. Then he did his engine test, ran through the rest of his checklist, and taxied again, this time to the runway. The airport didn't have a tower, so he squawked Regional with his vector out and got a confirm. He was fully instrument rated, and the plane carried a transponder, so he could pretty much go where he wanted to, even into secured airspace, if he got Langley to clear him in advance.

Gone were the days of open navigation near Washington, D.C., though. He sat on the runway waiting for a response from Regional that his flight plan into tiny Potomac Airport was in the system. He didn't want the embarrassment of being given a look-see by F-15s.

"Mooney 7821, you are cleared via airway 21 to airway 22-A into Potomac Regional Airport ETA 1140. Acknowledge."

He repeated the clearance, word for word, got his okay, and let out his throttle. The engine's hum rose to a deep, satisfying roar, and he took off. The airplane loved to fly, hopping off the runway like an eager gazelle. The sun shone hard on his face, and he took out his dark glasses. Below him, the long ridges of home slipped away to the north, and with them Ian and Becky and his mom and dad, and East Mill and the debris of the East Mill Vampire. He was almost tempted to go back and circle the house a couple of times, something that had been routine in better days.

Time passed, though, and he rose high enough to be picked up on FAA radars. He couldn't depart from his flight plan now, not without setting a whole complicated chain of events into motion. He opened his cell phone to see if he'd missed any messages. He had not.

He started to dial home, then stopped himself. This would blow over. They'd be there when he got back.

He watched the sky almost constantly during the flight, wary about being put at six thousand feet with all the pleasure craft and flying jalopies. In the event, though, the air was clear, and he was soon sliding along the new runway at Potomac, then powering down and getting out.

He signed in and listed himself for departure at 3:40. He'd be home before six. The drive to Langley in a rented Taurus was uneventful, and he got into the facility without difficulty. Considering that he didn't come here often, he was surprised at how efficient everything was at the gate. There had been a time in the past when he'd worried about getting out of this place without being arrested, or even alive.

Always, when he crossed the lobby, he glanced at the Wall of Honor, knowing that his team had contributed six plaques to it. Considering that his staffing level had called for fifteen front-line personnel and forty in the support group, that was a brutal attrition rate. In fact, it was so brutal that it had gotten him noticed all the way to State.

"Paul Ward," he said to the secretary who sat outside Brigg's office. He'd replaced crusty, cunning old Justin Turk as director of special operations. Justin had been an old-guard officer, working his way up through field ops. He'd had men under his command die, and done things that he regretted. To a degree, he actually understood Paul Ward.

"Hey, Paul," the much younger Briggs said. "Glad you could make it."

"I've got evidence to present, Henry."

"Cici sends her regards. She can't sit in, unfortunately."

That was a good sign, at least. Paul's private name for Cici was Miz No.

Briggs sat down. The office had been refurbished since Justin's day. The desk was the kind of thing somebody who expected to be upwardly mobile would buy—a little too big for its present surroundings. But it broadcast one thing loud and clear: this particular bureaucrat was powerful enough to decorate his own digs. Another thing, less flattering, was also communicated: he wanted you to know that.

"What sort of evidence?"

"Two levels. First, there's been a murder in Cairo that the French and the Egyptians have under intensive investigation. It looks like one of ours, and I want to send an observer, but I haven't got an observer to send. Second, my target in New York is looking more and more believable. Basically, what I'm here to say is that I need more people."

"Interesting."

After that, silence fell. What was this supposed to mean? "Four agents and a comm unit would be what I'd need," he added.

"This is the business about Leo Patterson, am I right?"

"Yeah."

"The singer, Leo Patterson?"

He knew damn well who it was, and Paul had a mind to knock that supercilious tone right out of this soft little biscuit of a man. All he did was say, "I've been gathering evidence for years. She was blooded, in my opinion, by Miriam Blaylock shortly before she was killed."

"This is when a vampire feeds blood to a human being and makes them a vampire, too? Wife of Dracula effect."

"It happens, and we have the autopsy reports on Sarah Roberts to prove it."

Briggs barked out a laugh, quickly suppressed. "I'm sorry. But this is just—it's so *outré*. Your reports read like some kind of novel."

"You've seen the scientific work. It's all there. The vampire was real, may still be real, if the Cairo report is accurate."

At this point, Justin would have paused to fill his pipe, smoking rules or no smoking rules. Briggsie didn't need even that little bit of time, though. "Paul, we're going to pull all personnel off this vampire business." He smiled brightly. "You've done great!"

Paul had been down this road before, many times. He knew how to spar. "I have a dead child in Cairo, plus a string of murders in New York. And your response is, the hell with it? I'm not sure I understand."

"You and Rebecca have the option of being reassigned. If you accept, you'll both be working here at Langley."

He had heard it all before, true enough. But this time, he realized, he was hearing it for the final time.

"And don't go calling your former team on an ad hoc basis, Paul. We don't want any more of that."

"They're private citizens."

"If they carry guns illegally, if they commit acts of violence, if they use restricted radio frequencies, they are liable to end up with jail time."

"Oh, come on."

"Paul, this is over. Whatever happened in the past, we don't know, and we don't want to know. But this—if Congress gets wind of it—frankly, it's going to end up with you and Rebecca and two or three others being charged with murder."

The word hung on the air, and in Paul's mind. There was something about the way the man said it—the air of indifference, the tone that said he relished what he was doing—that made Paul so mad he couldn't talk, almost couldn't move.

"Why is it," he finally managed to say, "whenever I come here, I get gutted?"

"Paul, you'd be looking at a good assignment. East Asia Desk, doing liaison with field offices."

"Get a file clerk."

"The issue of early retirement's come up before. If you don't accept reassignment, I'm afraid it's likely to be the only option."

Paul was not used to failure. It took him a while to understand that he'd been not only stripped of the few operational assets he had left, but fired into the bargain. "The Patterson case is urgent!"

"An international superstar who lives in a fishbowl is secretly a serial killer. Paul, it's just so spectacularly implausible. It's even kind of funny. Don't you see that?" He smiled again, his face twisting as if it was in some subtle, awful way paralyzed.

"I'm afraid I don't."

"The humor is, you're obviously nuts about this woman, and you're fixated on her, and we're getting these thirty-page e-mails about her that—I'll give you this—occasionally make sense. But most often, no."

He wanted to burn the ignorant mirth out of those eyes. At least Justin Turk had considered Paul Ward a player, had taken his work seriously.

"When I think of the people I lost—"

Briggs held up a hand. "That's another issue, that particular fact. We don't like to see people dying in this service."

"But they do die."

"This organization tries to keep its people alive. You do not, however, keep your people alive. A forty-percent casualty rate—well, it's famous in management, would be the best way to put it."

"I'm not accepting reassignment, and I'm not quitting."

"Then you're quitting being paid. And you're well within early retirement parameters, if you're considering going for another hearing."

An honorable retirement at his age wasn't subject to appeal, he knew that. "People are going to die because of this."

"People die every day."

Paul's surprise had turned to anger, anger to rage. He found himself on his feet—whereupon Briggs stood up at once and began moving him toward the door. Paul went quietly, careful to control himself when Briggs drew near. His fists were a bad habit at a moment like this. There was no reason to turn a routine screwing into an assault charge.

Driving back to the airport, he found himself compulsively opening and closing his cell phone. But he would not call them. No, best not to worry it. Let it blow over.

He'd flown the plane down here, but on the way home he set the autopilot, throttled up to cruise max, and settled back to wait, keeping an eye out for traffic. He played a CD, a compendium of antique Broadway chestnuts from the twenties and thirties. "In Ole Virginia," "Till the Clouds Roll By," "Whoopee."

It was well dark when he arrived, and it took some doing to find Storm King's minimal runway lighting, which was the least the FAA would let you get away with and still call yourself an airport.

He parked the plane, opened the door, and sat listening to the night.

The cocoon of technology and communications had sheltered him from the raw night wind, but no more. Now he felt it worrying his collar, seeping down below his shirt, caressing the tender skin of his neck and chest. It was gentle now, just a little cold, but soon winter would come, and the wind would roar through the mean old hills that he loved, bringing with it snow and lightning, and it would be clear why the mountain that stood just behind this airport was called the Storm King.

He sighed, walking across the grass to his car. Becky had been absolutely right: he would have been much better off not taking this trip.

Driving home, he looked at where he was. The reality of it was stark: he was outside, out here where nobody gave a damn about some crazy guy with funny ideas about a famous singer. He'd been demoted from high-powered investigator to garden-variety nutcase.

By the time he reached the house, he was so entangled in his own miseries that he had entirely forgotten the fact that he shouldn't be surprised that it was this dark and this quiet.

"Hello?" No faint thudding of music from behind Ian's door, no "All Things Considered" playing in the kitchen while Becky put supper together.

His job, his marriage, and his relationship with his son had all burned down on the same damn day. He smashed a fist into the wall so hard the whole house shook. If he hadn't spent time punching a bag—a lot of time—that little outburst would have split his knuckles very nicely, thank you.

He went into the den, opened the bar, and poured himself a huge Scotch. He drank it, poured another, drank that. And then Becky said, "Cairo is a disaster."

Her shadow was pale in the dark doorway. "Cairo?"

"I've been on with the French all afternoon, on the secure line." She turned on the light, went over to his desk, threw herself down in his chair. She pointed at his drink. "That isn't iced tea, Jesus."

"Brief me."

"Three deaths confirmed so far. The entire Cairo police department, the Egyptian security police, their whole apparatus, and all their experienced vampire people are unable thus far to catch something that seems to have come in out of the desert about a week ago."

"Out of the desert? How could a vampire live in the desert?"

"It arrived in a car belonging to a Bedouin smuggler named Ibrahim Sarif. Who is missing. They lived together in an oasis in the Arabian Desert for a few days. The creature is described as female, as pale as paper, and wearing a head-to-foot leather cloak. Sarif's brother said it came up to their camp out of the desert and offered Ibrahim a fortune to drive it into Cairo.

"In the city, it definitely took a child and possibly another individual, but it threw that last remnant in the Nile, and they haven't been able to retrieve it."

"How close are they?"

"Not close enough. It went to a lair where they'd staked out one of the old vampires—"

"Staked it out?"

"They do things differently, Paul. Remember, this has been an oppression in Egypt for thousands of years. They really, really do not like these things. Apparently, they'd staked one of them to the door of its lair and left it in half-life, thinking that it might attract others trying to help it. Which seems to have worked. The thing went to the lair, tripping alarms all over the Egyptian security services. They sent an army."

"And there the trail ends."

"There the trail ends."

He drank more of the Scotch.

"Paul—"

"Want to hear my news? My news is that you were dead-on right about the wisdom of forcing a meeting with Langley. We are decommissioned, not to put too fine a point on it."

"Decommissioned? Now?"

"With their usual uncanny timing. It's almost enough to make you a conspiracy theorist."

She took the glass from him and drained it. "Okay, we have a vampire and no support. And no son. He went to New York to seek his fortune."

"Christ, I'm so damn sorry about this morning."

"Why didn't you call?"

"I—goddammit! When did he leave?"

"About noon. I took him to the train."

"You took him to the train? You did this?"

"You want him to throw his underwear into a backpack and hitch to the city? And get sucked up in that?"

"I want him here!"

"Oh, yeah, like that's gonna happen now. You blew that, Dad."

He tried to take the Scotch from her, but she wouldn't let it go. "Do you know where he is?"

"He's got an apartment. One of those short-term furnished deals, until he can find something more permanent."

"He's quitting school?"

"Maybe he'll get a place at Stuyvesant or one of the private schools, finish out the year that way."

"That sounds kind of reasonable." But Paul would hate it, hate not being able to watch him, to be sure each day that he was still clean, to feel his presence in the house late at night.

"It is kind of reasonable. It's more than kind of reasonable, because he is a reasonable, brilliant, and in fact a glorious young *human being*, whose life you so compassionately and intelligently saved."

He wanted to be in her arms, and she felt it, and drew him there. She held him, and he held her, for the little couple was right now being tossed here and there in dark water, and they knew it, and the shore was very far away, and they knew that, too.

CHAPTER SIX

The Voyage of the
Seven Stars

Water hissed restlessly outside the wall, and the idea of being trapped in water had always been great among Lilith's fears. The slow, infinitely painful loss of consciousness, the gradual, dying dream as you rotted or were devoured . . . for her, drowning was the worst of all nightmares.

She'd been running, it seemed, forever, but now she was here, in this ship so vast that it dwarfed every machine she had ever seen. She lay along a line of pipes, high up in the workings of the thing, listening and watching, and feeling as if it was an echo from another dimension, the slow rising and falling that told her the ship was at sea.

She'd slept here, and she ached in her bones. She had also dreamed, and it was curious, this dream. Looking back, it seemed more vivid than reality, her frightened passage into the bower of the plum-blossom tree. But what was reality—this impossible life she had lived, an existence that had lasted so long that it had become its own meaning and its own end? When she looked back across the gulf of her life, she felt that she was plying infinite water. And yet, there was the voice in her dream, calling her, telling her that it was but an hour she would be gone.

She choked, twisting and turning in her wretched hiding place. This sense of being unable ever to leave was horribly claustrophobic. Being trapped in eternal life and being trapped in a coffin were much the same thing. She wanted to be dead, but was terrified of being undead. She was cold and scared and hungry and more alone than God. Cairo had been a catastrophe, a scrambling maelstrom of desperate escapes. The shot that had made her lungs bubble and burn was almost healed, but the one that had thrown her right arm forward and sent a bolt of searing torment down all the way to her hip would need more mending.

She had learned in the past few days that the car ran faster than any horse, the gun threw darts of lead, and human beings now had rich, haunting eyes. She had also learned that the Egyptians were far more numerous than before, and far more organized. When she closed her eyes, she heard their calm, quick voices, always so much closer than she thought possible.

Not a Keeper was left alive in Cairo, not one, and she was now on this journey into the unknown, wet, filthy, dressed in rags, and more lost than she had been even on the first day she had awakened here, confused and frightened, by the banks of a pellucid sea, mourning for her lost Adam.

She would have wept, but she had done enough of that. Now, she must think. She must learn how to elude the monstrous dogs they had trained to hunt her, how to live and eat in this world turned upside down, how to find other Keepers—if there were any left anywhere—and if not, then by the holy world of her birth, what would she do?

A voice, speaking in Arabic, said, "We're redirected, you know that." Another voice said, "That's the hell. I got my wife, she doesn't know."

She no longer considered human beings simple little creatures. They had grown powerful and terrible and extraordinarily dangerous, and extraordinarily—well—*conscious*. The humans of today were vastly different even from the ones she had encountered even as recently as a hundred years ago. They were intricately formed, delicate spirits, every bit as richly endowed with self and awareness as the Keepers who had drawn them up out of the earth. And she, God curse her, had to eat them for the only food that she could digest. Now, though, their blood tasted sour and hung in her gut. The worst was the child. Before the child, she had not seen this. But the child—the little girl—her eyes. And the eyes of the one she had been unable to take—they were with her still, staring back from the half-light of pipes and cables that surrounded her. She squirmed and twisted on the pipes. She was suffocating in her own being.

They'd nearly captured her along the Nile, again in what she'd thought was pharaoh's palace, again on the roofs of a great building filled with habitations. Oh, they had come close, close and closer, sometimes even putting their hands on her. She'd run with the cats, gone down in the sewers with the black rats, climbed to heights, hidden beneath beds and tables and boxes, disguised herself in a head cloth snatched from a shop, and run, run, run.

The yowling of the dogs they had begun to use came to her ears again, and she sucked in a hard, scared breath, listened. Only the humming of the ship, the deeper throbbing . . . only her mind weaving strands of fear.

It had been night when she'd found this vessel—seen it as distant lights in stately motion across the desert. Her speed had been what had saved her. To make man easier to catch, the Keepers had bred against his natural speed, and thus could outrun him and outleap him by enough of a margin to always win against him . . . but things like cars had not entered the equation, had they, or guns?

Behind her had been the dogs, ahead an expanse of dark night desert, and then the lights. She'd run and leaped and found herself on a throbbing pavement of metal. In a moment, she'd realized that it was in motion. Looking down the cliff she had just jumped, she had seen swirling water. She had been forced then to conclude what seemed to be impossible: this immense thing was not only in motion, it was on the water. In some sense, it was a ship.

Not even in the bright fragmentary memories of home was there anything like this. Home was blond fields waving beneath a blue sun; home was a cliffside and the vast ocean, and tall, pale sails above a slim quick ship.

She felt tears going down the dirty grooves in her face, of fear and relief and so many other things. She'd never thought much of home before. This was home, this place she had come to call *"Ur-th."* Like all words in Prime, it bore many meanings. *Ur* was a foundation, place of thriving, also cave and a womb. Woman bore *ur* between her loins; a cottage was *ur,* so also a homeland and a school. But the *th* ending suggested the feeling at once of going away and of having come from far away, loneliness and a sense of loss. It was a sigh, *th*, that began with a hard edge and then whispered itself to silence.

Ur-th was a home, but also a place that was lost.

She took in a breath and said in her deepest heart, "I hate them." Or rather, wished that she could.

For eons, the Keepers had counted about 12 million human beings in the keepings. Two hundred years ago, Menes the Counter had been of the opinion that there were 300 million. Now, she thought that there must be an almost uncountable number of them in the world, the majority concentrated in great Egypt and, above all, the teeming labyrinth of Cairo.

She listened. The space she was in had been silent of man now for some time. She stirred herself and leaned over the pipes, looking up and down the bright orange catwalk twenty feet below her. There was not a shadow to be seen. She had to move about, to understand where she was. She knew the ship was sailing, she could hear the water. So maybe there was some second city in the world, perhaps a distant colony of Cairo, and maybe this thing was going there. She remembered the layout of the oceans of the world, and the great glacier that covered the northern part of the planet, making it cold and uninhabitable. So this other nest would be to the south, or along the centerline of the planet. Of course, there was much land still to the north, and Keepers in it, she knew that. But the human population was sparse there. The weather was too harsh for large concentrations of human population. They were hairless, after all. That made them cold-averse.

She slid across the pipes and dropped down. Stretching so far in each direction that she could hardly see their end were great black tanks with huge red lids. She thought that there must be whole worlds concealed in those tanks. Any one of them was large enough to contain an entire temple or palace or a great tomb.

She strode along the catwalk, her tattered cloak flying out behind her, the black and filthy ruins of her gown clinging to her lean form. She took breaths, as deep as she could. The air was fetid with the stink of petroleum. In its various forms, this chemical was everywhere among men—in their wagons, in their stoves, and now, in this vast thing. They seemed to have found many, many uses for it.

"It's the Bayonne Depot," a voice said, echoing flatly in the humming silence.

"Oh, New York. Lala, you know."

"What do I know?"

"Of the girls."

"Perhaps."

She had to crawl over the catwalk railing and drop down into the area beneath. But she could not allow herself to fall that far, not those hundreds of feet down alongside one of the great tanks, into the thick, black water she saw there. She hung with her fingers onto the grating of the catwalk itself, hoping that they somehow wouldn't come too close to this point, or wouldn't see her fingertips if they did.

They began shining torches of directed light down into the canyon below the catwalk. "It's a slow pump."

"If we have leaks here—"

"Work to do. Let's see, here, this is Position 2001.240. Input that."

They were working with a small box, tapping it with a twig. Its glowing face altered with each tap. She had not the faintest idea what they were doing. They came closer to her, again shone their torch into the depths.

"That's normal, the level there."

"Ah. God is good."

"God is good."

Now they were just above her, and the beam of the torch shone not a foot from her shoulder.

"Also."

As they moved on, she listened to their voices dwindling. She'd smelled their human smell as they passed, an odor that had once intoxicated her but that now filled her with very complex emotions, none of which had anything to do with food. She waited until she could hear them no more, then began pulling herself back up onto the catwalk. Her legs kicked air, and her shoulder and chest sent white-hot comets of pain through her whole body. Despite her massive effort at self-control, the pain made her produce a sound, the hissing of air through clenched teeth.

With a final, great effort she drew her arms tight, rising until her face was even with the top rail of the fence that protected the catwalk. She pulled herself over and stood bent and gasping, her head bowed. A hand groped for the rail, grabbed it, and hung on. The catwalk swayed, and with it the whole vast space, and the sounds of the machinery slipped into an echoing distance, a moment later to be replaced by the banging of her heart, the ripped whistle of her breath. All too slowly, she came back to the world around her, of stench and brute light and cold iron.

She'd almost fainted, that was what had happened. She took a deep breath, held it, then slowly released the air. Another, then another. Slowly and tentatively, she raised her head.

She found herself looking directly into the eyes of a young male. He smiled. Then he reached out and grabbed her wrist.

"You stink, do you know that? You smell like a filthy sewer."

She stared at him.

"Come on, or I'll toss you in the bilge. You think the captain will not put you off at Alex if he knows of you? He will, most certainly. You must be my friend. Do you want to do that, or go off at Alex?"

"I don't know."

"Where did you get that accent? You sound like an idiot. Are you? Well, all the better if you're stupid. You'll probably enjoy us all the more."

He pulled her along while she frantically cast about for ways to escape him. But what good would it do? He'd only tell the others. She could kill him, and maybe she had to. She must not become the captive of man. Above all things, that must not happen.

Perhaps she should throw him off the catwalk, make them think he'd had an accident. Unless, of course, he somehow survived his fall. The way her luck had been running, that's what would happen. He tugged at her and she cried out, shocked by the flaring pain that shot up her arm. What if she couldn't overpower him, if she was still insufficiently mended?

The catwalk ended in steel stairs that led up into another unknown area. "You go ahead," he said. She started up the stairs. When she had gotten to the top, she lifted her leg and kicked backward. Her heel connected with his forehead, and he went flying out into the air. His cry echoed in the huge space. In the distance, there was a clang. It reverberated as if a bell had been struck, and then died away into the all-present thrumming. Looking after him, she saw from the broken wreck just visible in the gloom far below that she need have no concern that he had survived.

However, they would notice that he was missing. She'd learned that disappearances now counted among the humans for a great deal. No longer did they take such things for granted. Now there would be a search. They would find him. She hoped they would conclude that he had fallen as the result of a slip. In the meantime, though, she had to find a better place to hide. The direction he had been taking her was no good, it was where the other humans stayed. Perhaps down among the works of the thing there would be more concealment.

But what if they had dogs? Then she could not hide. She could not escape from dogs. They would rend her limbs, rip them off, leaving her helpless. Then their masters would tear her chest open and make a blood eagle of her. She moved quickly along catwalks, down narrow stairways, descending into the darkest places she could find. She came then into a room filled with pipes and stinking powerfully of oil. There was no scent of man here. But also it was a miserable place, with nowhere to lie down and try to heal except among more of the accursed pipes. She went on, hurrying like a ghost up and down catwalks, along passageways, until she found a quiet, dark area. At the end of the corridor was a gray metal door with a round handle. She twisted it, then found that it was to be pulled.

Frozen air came out into the thick heat, making clouds arise around her. Beyond the door was a freezing cold cave, with the carcasses of cattle and pigs hung on hooks. So this was the place where the human food was kept. Originally, they had been gatherers of berries and fruits, but her greedy children had bred them to eat meat, so that they would become bigger and juicier, and do it faster.

She could not stay in this cold, so she went out and back down the hallway. Here she noticed a hatch, which she climbed into. A well-lighted stairway wound upward at least fifty feet. She went to the top and through another door. Absolute silence here. She found a room with a table in it and an array of silver knives and hooks and other sharp implements behind glass. Above the table was what she now recognized as an electric

light, huge, designed to cast the whole thing into brilliant illumination—
to light the table top. Against one wall were iron tanks of some sort. There
were dark green gowns hung on hooks, and strange cloth face masks.

Was it perhaps a ritual chamber, where they sacrificed themselves to
their imaginary gods?

She had no way to tell when the humans would return here, so she
could not stay. She went through a door marked "Morgue" and found
there three coffins, each resting in a table with lips around it, designed to
keep it from sliding off. She opened one, and then another, and then the
third. They had room enough for her, and they were confined enough to
be warmed by her own body warmth. She could sleep in one of them,
maybe for a long time, maybe even for the two or three days needed for
her body to heal itself.

After feeding, you required sleep, but these past few days she'd gotten
only snatches. She needed the long, helpless sleep that was the only kind
that would truly rejuvenate her. The Sleep, her people called it, the deep,
enriching excursion to the edge of death that kept them perpetually
young.

The humans would not come here except to put their dead friend in
the first of the three coffins. She went to the one at the rear of the room,
opened it, and got in. Wrapping her cloak around herself, she pulled the
lid closed, leaving a corner of leather out so that there would be some cir-
culation of air. She didn't need much. In fact, a grave made an excellent
hiding place for a sleeping Keeper.

Body warmth began to make her cozy, and for the first time in what
seemed like eternity itself, she felt safe and at least a little comfortable. Her
tongue was dry and her throat was swollen. She needed water, but the
problem would have to keep until later.

She closed her eyes. There was the long ridge she'd climbed once, she
was sure, and the tree covered with flowers like long feathers of the
palest, most delicate pink. As she went beneath it, the bright, innocent
voice of a young man said, "Only an hour," and she cried, for she had
been hearing that promise, it seemed, since before the beginning of time
itself. "Where are you?" she whispered into the dark, "Please, where are
you?"

Her eyes grew heavy, and sleep came upon her. She dreamed of a little town snuggled in a gap in the flower-tossed ridges, with stone houses and sheaths for roofs. And she was a new bride, and he was there, a shadow among the bright shadows. He said, "The ringer stands by the bell." In his voice she could hear his smile.

Then another voice spoke, rough and quick. It said, "Allah be praised, there's already a corpse in here."

Another said, "That can't be."

Light flooded her eyelids. She was disoriented. It felt as if absolutely no time had passed at all. Then she remembered that she'd been sleeping here, and dreaming, and it had been such a good dream, she hated, oh, *hated* coming back from it.

Wallowing up from the formless, timeless sleep of her kind, she first felt her healing and knew that she had slept for hours, and the hours had served her well. Then she opened her eyes into two twisted, glaring human faces.

She fought for composure, but her heart was breaking. "I am sleeping here by the will of God," she said in her archaic, painfully formal Arabic. She'd been discovered! Now, she would know the terror of destruction.

The older face disappeared. His voice said, "Bridge? This is the coffin room. We have a stowaway. No, in the coffin we were going to use for Emil. She looked dead, but her eyes opened. She's looking around. Listen to me, with God's help, send First Officer Tahrir please." Then he whispered: "With a gun. There is something that is strange."

She sat up, her eyes flickering toward some direction of escape. There was only the one door, which they were blocking. They manhandled the stinking remains of their fellow crewman into one of the coffins.

As they were completing this, another man came in. He was wearing an open jacket of dark blue and a white, rumpled shirt. In his right hand he carried a black, mean-looking gun.

The man said, "Who are you? Can you speak?"

She thought it better not to.

"Hear, then? Can you hear?" He turned to the others. "Has she said anything?"

"It's the djin that was in Cairo."

"What djin?"

"Eating people and leaping over buildings. Up two stories, five stories. It was all over the television."

"I didn't see anything about it."

"You officers, you only watch CNN. It was on Al-Jazeera every day."

"Al-Jazeera. So it's an absurdity. But this girl is—look at her. Under all that grime, she cannot be twenty. And certainly she's not the Monster of Cairo."

"Then you did see."

"Of course I saw, you fool. Do you think we live in a mosque because we're officers? I am an Egyptian just like you."

"I'm Yemeni."

"That's right, Mahmood. Yemeni." He picked up a black object and held it against his face. "Captain, yes. I am escorting a stowaway from the morgue." He glanced over at Lilith, who gave him a tiny, hopeful smile. "No, no, you will be surprised," he said into the object. He looked again at her. "You will be in amazement, Captain." He replaced the object onto a hook. "Come," he said, "come out of there now, girl. What is your name, please?" His hand was laid upon the butt of the gun.

She could reach over and take it, but she wasn't sure how to make it expel the darts. She had never held a gun, but she wanted very much to hold one and examine it, and understand the workings. Not now, though. If she did it now, she would soon have others with more guns coming in while she tried to duplicate the hand movements she'd seen them use on the things. So she said instead, "My name is Lilith."

"Oh, the djin of the night! You are not Arab, not Egyptian. Are you a Jew, then? Lilith was the demoness of the Jews, yes?"

What was he saying?

"Adam's first wife, yes? You must be rather old, Lilith. But you look rather young." He chuckled.

She could not mistake his leer, but she also could not answer him. She didn't know how.

"Not talking, eh? Well, that's understandable. But it doesn't matter. He's not turning back for a stowaway, not this far out. You'll make it to

New York, all right." He laughed. "Then they'll put you in INS lockup. That's a pretty way to see America."

Not much of this made sense. This "America" was apparently the Egyptian colony to which the ship was being sailed. But what the "INS" might be, or how a lockup worked—these things were not clear at all.

"Come on, silent beauty, let me introduce you to the man who's going to spend the rest of the trip fucking your brains out." He laughed again, higher this time—she thought, with a little madness in it. "Captain's a blondie, too."

They went into a small room that hummed. There they stood for some moments. Lilith was aware of the sensation of movement, but could not tell the direction.

"My God, have you been shitting yourself in there? You smell like the sewers of fucking Lagos."

"I thirst."

Now they passed down a corridor, and the man threw open a door into a bright room with a large wooden chest in it. On the top of the chest were piled papers and a machine with a panel on it that glowed. A man in white clothing sat behind the chest, using an instrument that was easily recognizable for what it did. He had a stylus, and was writing with it, or scribbling, rather, like a child. There was no ink pot.

"Now you have me a stowaway, Mr. T., how nice. How very nice. Have you informed the company?"

"No, sir, I brought her here first."

His head came up from his doodling. "Well." Their eyes met. She saw his pupils dilate. In a low, strained growl, he said, "And here you are . . . God . . ."

"I thought it best to inform you first, you see."

"Abdel, thank you." He arose from behind the chest, came around it. He drew back her hood, which she had raised to conceal her filthy hair. "My, my, an innocent girl. Are you from home? Or perhaps Sweden?" He turned to his friend. "Does she have any ID?"

"She calls herself Lilith."

"Ah, the famous demoness. How promising. Are you fancying your-self a demoness, Lilith? Or, look at you—are you maybe the real thing?"

She could not think how to answer him. He was a commoner, and would not know the language of the rulers. Nevertheless, she tried. "I am the Lily of the Valley," she said in pharaonic Egyptian.

"That's not Swedish," the man said with a smile. He waved his hand before him. "Get her a shower, for God's sake. And something to wear—oh, let me look at that." He came around the chest and took the hem of her cloak. Then he met the eyes of the other man. "This is very fine," he said. "Lilith, you must have a family. Am I wrong about your age? Are you a runaway? Because you know that this calfskin, it's not cheap, this."

"Why would she be dressed in a cloak? And look at the dress, Captain. Of linen."

"You're an interesting specimen, Lilith. Let's get her cleaned up, Mr. T. You can use my bathroom, Lilith."

She was directed through a mean little apartment of rooms where there was a bedstead and table and some chairs thickly covered with cloth. They came into a cell of tile and metal. She smelled water here, but could see none. "I thirst," she repeated in Arabic.

"You know, you speak Arabic like someone out of the *Thousand and One Nights*. Where did you pick up antique talk like that? Your teacher must've been an ass, Lilith."

"How could an ass teach a language?"

"Not well. Look, I'd love to hang around, but I've smelled better smells coming from under the tail of an overheated camel. Please avail yourself of the captain's incredible generosity in allowing a stinking stowaway to use his beautiful bathroom."

From this garble of words she gathered that water would be brought here. First she would drink, and then allow the servants to bathe her. So far, she had seen only males in this place, but that was of little concern. There would be serving women, of course. The men were all fed, clean, and dressed, so there had to be women somewhere about.

He went out, drawing the door closed behind him. It became dark. She waited, but did not hear him speak or leave the outside room. His breathing was steady. From the shadows under the door, she could surmise that he was standing, listening. But why? What would there be to hear? She had nothing to do except wait.

After some moments, there came a hesitant tap upon the door. It was him. Did he wish to enter? If so, why not simply do the thing? The tapping was repeated. "Are you decent?"

What a strange question. She was the essence of decency, the most decent of all the beings on the earth. This man would not even exist had it not been for her work. She had given eons of service here. Of course she was decent!

He opened the door, then stood looking at her. Then he turned and went away. Soon he returned with the other one, whose pale face was now flushed red. He had the skin of a northern tribe, this one did. He looked her up and down. "Look, hey—do you speak English?" This was the speech of the Englishmen, which she had heard in Cairo two hundred years ago. She recalled little of it. "Parlez-vous français? Sprechen sie Deutsch?" He looked her in the eyes.

She saw that he needed proper nutrients, and was lacking in body water. They had very little pure water, it seemed to her. She hadn't really tasted any since she left home. Without pure water, the human body could not thrive.

"You know, Mr. T., I think that this is an autistic. Do you know this, autism?"

"They're withdrawn. The Arabs call them blessed of God."

"You and your God."

"Hey, it's not my deal. I'm an atheist, as you know very well."

"Well, this is an autistic. She's run away from some rich family. My guess, Swedes or English or Americans. That cloak was worth—" He kissed his fingers. "Did you see the stitching in that lining? And that silk. Plus the leather. I believe it's that incredible Moroccan that's made from the split skin of unborn calves or something. That thing must have cost in the thousands of dollars U.S." He regarded her again. "So who are you, sweetheart, and how did you come to be aboard the *Seven Stars?* I'm going to squawk the company about her. There's probably some fat cat looking for her across half the world."

"A reward?"

"It's certainly possible. By the time we get to New York, the INS will have her all sorted out, would be my guess."

"Unless her fat cats want to come get her."

"That's their privilege, as long as they can connect with a moving supertanker in midocean. Now look, we'd better treat her with kid gloves. And bathe her, Abdel, if she will not bathe herself."

"I can't bathe somebody! A girl of twenty, Kurt! Come on."

"I thirst."

"And give her a Coke, if she's so damn thirsty."

The one called Abdel glared at her when Kurt left. Then he disappeared, returning again with a large phial containing dark brown liquid. He handed this to her. "Drink," he said.

She lifted it to her nose, smelled it. Coming from the bottle was a sizzling, as if it was hot. But for some cunning reason, it was instead cold.

"Drink, come on, and take off that rag if I'm going to get you showering."

Drink. But how? Where was a cup? Where was wine, beer, or water?

"Drink!"

"I thirst."

"For the love of God, you've got a Coke!" He grabbed her hand, held the phial to her lips. "Drink the Coke."

Out of the thing there came something strange indeed, candied water full of dancing bubbles. The sweetness had been married to some sort of a fruit. The water was pure enough, though. She was to take it into her mouth from the phial. She did so. A moment passed. She felt gas building within her. But she could not burp, for that was only to be done at the end of the meal. Surely this was not a meal now, among the humans.

He came behind her and drew off her cloak. So he was a servant, after all. He had spoken to her in an ungracious manner. Pharaoh would have had such an impudent servant whipped. But pharaoh was not here.

He manipulated handles, and water came spitting out of an opening. She went to it to slake her thirst, but it was unexpectedly warm, too warm to drink. She stood in it, enjoying the feeling of it upon her face, dreaming with her eyes closed of when the rain would come to her little valley, and she would watch her lilies dance, and raise her face to the weeping sky, and let the pure water soak her skin and make her as fragrant as the clouds.

"No, no, take off the damn dress! Holy God, how did you ever end up on an oil tanker? Were you dropped from Pluto?"

He handled her most roughly, trying to remove her garment. Well, then, she stepped out of it. He gasped, his eyes blinked, he turned his face away. Her beauty could shock her own children. A human being, it could stagger.

She stepped into the room of rain and lifted her face. The waters flowed strongly. He went away.

Abdel was in a state of some sort of sexual fever. He'd never known anything like it before. But seeing this filthy, crazy runaway naked had caused him to almost explode with desire. He dashed down the companionway and into his own stateroom. He was bursting. He'd never even known that such feelings were possible. He pulled off his trousers and stood in his shirttails, naked from the waist down. And there, all over his abdomen and running down his leg, was what he could not believe he was seeing. Just like that, the instant she was unclothed, he had ejaculated.

He was damned if the Lybian pigs who did the cleaning and laundry were going to see this mess. He went into the john and washed the trousers under the tap until he was sure there was nothing more than a water mark visible. Then he put on fresh pants and went up to Kurt.

"Captain, we have to do something about this woman. You know, the men say she's a demon. They say she's wanted by the Cairo police for killing people."

"Oh, come on. That's an autistic child. She couldn't swat a fly. Or if she did, she'd probably eat it."

"Have you e-mailed about her yet?"

"Sure. Athens says to keep her in confinement. They've already informed the INS and put out a description to Interpol. Her people will undoubtedly be sending us a congratulatory bottle of champagne on arrival."

"Nothing about turning around?"

Kurt looked up, his eyebrows raised. The instant he'd said it, Abdel had realized that the question had carried with it the gulf of difference between a man of the East and a man of the West. "The men call her a devil," he repeated hastily. "I think that we're going to have problems."

"I'm sure we are. But she's here, and I hardly think that we're going to go off schedule for her. So that's it. She's your responsibility, Mr. T. I don't want her stealing anything or sleeping in any more coffins." He leaned back, lit a cigarette. "That's something—a long black cloak, sleeping in a coffin. No wonder the men are concerned." He laughed. "The vampire of the *Seven Stars.*"

"They're all believers in djin. It's a bad business."

Lilith drank by laying her mouth open to the stream, and slowly took her fill of a water that had in it the thickness of various chemicals and was not a really good water. But it would do, it was slaking her thirst. The fruit-gas water had not been satisfactory.

A great deal of desert dust went down the drain at her feet, so much that the water in the bottom of the closet became slow. She would have rubbed herself with sand, but there was no sand, only a block of green clay. This clay was obviously intended for a servant to use in washing, but she used it herself, and found that drawing it along her skin was really a rather pleasant thing to do. Embossed on it were letters in the Roman alphabet: IRISH SPRING. She wondered if they were words, or the initials of an association, like SPQR, Senatus Populusque Romanus, the Senate and People of Rome. They had all sorts of associations, the Romans. Perhaps this was a Roman ship.

She began to enjoy the clay. The idea of this bath was to melt it by the heat of the water. She needed only for a serving woman to be here with her. But no, in this little closet you must bathe alone. She put it all over herself, and when she ran it in her hair, a great deal of dirt came out.

Again, she raised her face into the swarming rain. Steam rose around her as if from a bubbling pot, or from the water in the *calidarium* at Alexandria. She let the water roll off her skin until she felt well and truly clean. Then she went out into the larger part of the room, but there was still no servant there. Finally, she laid what appeared to be a part of a toga around herself and dried her skin in the manner of the Romans.

Dropping the cloth to the floor, she stepped out through the door.

The man was there, but he leaped up and rushed away when she appeared. She went into the corridor, and then saw through a glass panel the single most magnificent sight that she had beheld since she had cruised with Hadrian and his boyfriend up the Nile. It was so vast, and so vastly blue, this water. She went a short distance to a doorway, then walked out to the front of the row of windows through which she'd first seen it. From here, the ship was almost unimaginably huge. A thousand of Hadrian's most magnificent ships could have been laid out upon this deck, had it not been complicated with pipes and machines.

She raised her arms and cried out to the sea, "You child of earth and sky, O leap, leap to the sun, you waves!" The words were from the hymn to Poseidon that Hadrian's child-friend Antinous had composed one afternoon when the ribs of their ship were creaking from the slaughter of the waves.

Hadrian had been the last of the human beings she had thought of as pharaoh and treated accordingly. There had been jealousies. One of her own people had devoured Antinous, then said he had fallen into the Nile.

"My dear girl, get out of there! My God, child, what can you be thinking!" The fair-haired one came running up to her and threw a coarse jacket over her shoulders. "You poor, mad thing," he said as he drew her away from the majesty of the sea and the admiring crowd of men who had gathered on the deck below.

"Why do you call me mad?" she asked him. She was hot with anger that this impudent human being would so describe her. How dare he make comment on his betters?

They went into the large room full of machineries and glowing screens that lay behind the long row of forward-facing windows. He pushed at her, his impotent strength expending itself against her shoulder. "God, she's strong."

"As a demon," Abdel Tahrir said.

"Look, you put down any talk like that, Mr. T. I've got the little bitch on my passenger manifest now. If the men do anything to her—anything at all, Abdel, my friend—there's going to be trouble in New York." He switched into another language. "Do you understand English, missy? Look at her, Abdel, what do you think?"

"I don't think so."

"Then we'll use English. My God, how could anybody be so beautiful? Look at her, look at her!"

"It's a caution."

"A caution? They'll tear her apart. I want her up here at all times. Either in my cabin or Officer's Rec or here. And one of us—you or me— we must keep her in sight at all times. Is that understood?"

"Yes, sir. But I think that the men will not rape her. They fear her too much."

"Oh, then it's a shiv across the damned throat, eh? Kill the beast. I've already had one death aboard. If I have another, it'll be my ticket, no questions asked. You remember that." He advanced toward the other man. "Because if they take my ticket, I'll take your balls. Custom of the sea!"

Whatever the long string of gutturals had been about, they ended with Kurt bursting out laughing. He did not seem to understand how angry he had made Abdel. When an Egyptian smiles like that, he has been humiliated, and should be feared.

However, Lilith was enjoying this loud, rough northerner, and feeling a distinct sense of conflict. She thought that she would like to lie with him. Look at all that muscle, that youth and health. But also he was food, rich, satisfying food. There was in his eyes a sweetness made the more endearing because the gruffness in his voice said that he himself did not know that it was there.

Abdel yanked her arm, causing the still-tender parts within her to smart. He drew her along the corridor to a chamber. In this chamber was a bedstead, a chair that at least was not covered with those odd, plump cloths of theirs, and a basin. It also had a window that overlooked the ocean, a most wonderful window.

"I'm placing you under house arrest," he said. "Do you understand me?"

"No."

With the speed of an enraged cat, he leaped at her. "You'll be locked in here, see! You'll not come out, not even for meals. Because if the captain loses his ticket, I lose mine. And some damn—I don't know what—some damn crazy female isn't going to be the reason."

His hands were shaking, his eyes blinking rapidly, which indicated unsureness in a human being. He closed and locked the door.

She waited for some time, lying on the bed until she grew restless at the idea of being imprisoned. Just a little while ago, she would have been content to remain here forever, or anywhere she happened to be, as long as she could eat what she needed. She had been empty, incurious, and, she realized now, so afraid of the ominous presence of time that she had reduced herself almost to a state of catalepsy. She thought that she had slept for days, for months—how long, she did not know, perhaps would rather not guess.

But now all that had changed. She had successfully escaped from Cairo, had eluded the men who wanted to kill her—and they had been good hunters, oh, indeed. With such ones about, the day of her capture would certainly come, perhaps already had. The door was locked, although she could break through it. Where then?

She got up and went to the small, round window. Outside, there was nothing but great Ocean. She knew that they were beyond the Pillars of Hercules, where the ships of man had not gone in vast immemorial ages.

She paced uneasily to the door and shook it, assuming that she would shake the simple iron tumblers right off their stems. But it did not happen. There was no sound of grating metal from within, no click of a lock tongue falling free.

A flash of anger crossed through her, making her stamp and growl. She ought to tear the door off—that, she knew, she could certainly do. But then they would only find some hole deep in the ship for her, a place enclosed by iron.

She stepped back from the door. She'd seen the way they looked at her. She knew the effect that she had on the male, her own kind or human. So she went to the mirror and patted some color into her cheeks, then began smoothing her hair. Once, she would have wanted to paint her eyes, but she had seen women as they were now, and knew that the formal making up of home was no longer done here. Her careful fingers worked long on the hair, until the sun had gone low and the waves turned gold with his last grace. Then she made from the tight-woven bedclothes a *stola* of sorts, ripping strips until she had a band to raise her bosom, and a flowing skirt to conceal the curves of her hips. Her arms she left bare. She smelled her skin, which was as sweet now as the juice of the pomegranate. Her sweetness mingled with the scents of human cooking coming up from below.

As she had expected, it was not long before the men returned. It was Abdel and a bearded servant with a tray. The food was strange—two round slabs of bread with slices of cooked muscle between them. A glass contained more of the candied liquid, hissing like a baby serpent. Both men's faces had been impassive until they saw her. Then they changed, in ways that made her so happy that she tossed her hair and laughed. Abdel's eyes became hooded and his cheeks flushed as humans did when they were agitated. The servant began trembling, his spittle running in his beard.

"There is your supper," Abdel mumbled. The two of them left at once, locking the door. She went and gazed out at the last light, watching as much of the orange horizon ahead of them as she could see. This window, she thought, could be forced. But she did not think it necessary. In a mirror, Lilith could see many things, and in this mirror she saw a man coming, the northerner, and she saw herself drawing him to her breast, and singing to him . . .

And indeed Kurt Regen soon said to Abdel, "I'm leaving the bridge for the night."

As he headed toward the meeting he had imagined already a thousand different ways, Abdel's long fingers came down upon his shoulders. "Kurt, no."

"Abdel—"

"You know I don't believe any of those superstitions. They're nonsense."

"Well, yeah, that's one way of putting it." He moved on.

Abdel followed him. "Kurt! Listen. Listen to me. I will tell you, I had experiences with her—"

Kurt laughed, but he was angry. "Already? Before me?"

"No, no, not that. For God's sake. I mean that she has—she has a very strange effect. Stranger, I have to tell you—really, Kurt—than you can know. She's come onto this ship from nowhere—out of a coffin—" He laughed, a quick, false sound in which Kurt heard all the superstition of his world, heard it and quietly scorned it. Then he added, "And that clothing—I mean, did you look at it?"

"Of course I did."

"The stitching isn't just fine, it's microscopic. You'd go blind to do that—a seamstress, I mean. And the leather—that is not calfskin, Kurt. That's something . . ." He trailed off. "Not calfskin."

"So what is it?"

"It must be something exotic," Abdel said at last.

Kurt went on. "I'll ask her."

Abdel said no more, and Kurt did not turn around. He proceeded along the corridor, thinking that he had beer and whisky in his cabin, and plenty of excellent American cigarettes. He wondered what music she might care for, what food.

He stopped at her door, inserted the key. Before he entered, he tapped lightly. "Lilith?" There was no response. He opened the door to a dark room, his immediate thought being that she had somehow escaped, or jumped out of the porthole into the sea. That thought had worried him most of the day. If she really wanted to, she might open one of these ports. It would be death, of course, either sucked up in the propellers, drowned, or torn to pieces by sharks, whichever came first. But with a crazy woman, maybe it would happen that way.

As he stepped into the room, he noticed an extraordinary sweetness in the air, an odor of jasmine or some exotic southern flower like gardenias. He turned on the light—and almost cried out, she was so close to him and so still. "Oh," he said. "I thought you had gone."

She smiled slightly and raised her hand to his cheek. In his surprise, he had spoken German and thought she would not have understood. But she said, also in German, "I had not gone."

"Oh," he said, "oh." He forced himself to smile. This was not going at all as he had expected. "You speak German," he blurted, and said to himself, What a fool you are, Kurt, can't you be a little cool?

"I speak German," she replied, but like a schoolchild enunciating before her teacher.

"Are you German, then? I don't place the accent."

"You don't place the accent. I am not German."

He realized, to his great astonishment, that she did not speak German at all. She was actually constructing her replies out of his questions and statements. "From Norway, then? Sweden?"

"Not from Norway, not from Sweden."

"Will you come into my cabin and have a little entertainment with me? We can pick up satellite very nicely, and I've got some good Scotch, we can settle down and perhaps you can tell me a bit. I might be able to help you, you know. It isn't going to be pleasant with the INS."

The gravity of her eyes, the innocent seriousness of her expression— it was literally thrilling. No other word for it. Dressed up even in that sheet, the woman was making him feel feelings he had not known since he was a boy and Ingeborg Schleicher had unzipped his fly while he lay back against a tree trunk. She had reached in, and paralyzed him with pleasure when her cool fingers contacted his rigid shaft. "Does that feel like anything?" she had asked, and he had thought that his whole body was going to explode.

Lilith said, "I will come into your cabin and have the entertainment." He reached out and took the lightest, most delicate hand he had ever held. He drew her along the corridor as if he was luring a recalcitrant kitten. She laughed a little in her throat.

He got her in, got the door closed and locked. She moved into the middle of the sitting room and twirled around very prettily indeed. "I have come into your cabin and will have a little entertainment."

"How much German do you know?"

She smiled, leaned her head to one side. Oh, how beautiful, how incredibly, wonderfully beautiful she was. "I know as much German as you are entertaining me with."

"You're picking it up from talking to me! That's exactly it, isn't it?"

"I am picking up German from talking to you. This is it exactly."

She must have one of those wonderful minds of the idiot-savant that one read about, the sort of person who could calculate out numbers to the thousandth place and such. "How many languages do you speak?"

"Speak. Yes. As many as I hear."

He wanted to be the cool, imposing captain, to give her a drink and a fine cigarette and perhaps watch a little television with her beforehand. But instead he stepped forward like a schoolboy ordered to the front of the class, seized her hand, and kissed her cheek in an absurdly clumsy manner. He was like some sort of old German militarist. Almost, he had clicked his heels. Absurd, he was becoming a cliché of himself. But as he kissed the milk of her skin, the soft, almost airlike coolness of it just brushing his lips, he also inhaled a scent so wonderful that for a moment he could not move. Again, he smelled her skin—it was the odor that had permeated her room after she had bathed, the very soul of the sweetest flower in all the world. Nothing like a damn bath. What a change.

"How is it that you have perfume?" he asked her. "There is none in the ship."

"I may say in Arabic?"

"Yes, of course."

"There is no perfume in me. Perfume is the sweetness of myself when there is kindness in keeping me clean." She held out her hand, dangling it before him. "Yes," she said, "thank you, please."

He took it and smelled the scent of her. It was marvelous beyond words, this scent, it almost split him in half with desire, almost caused him to actually cry out. Then he saw, beneath the blouse she had made of the sheet, her nipples making small points behind the cloth. The nipples, the curve of her skin down into the neckline, the suggestion of her perfect breasts, seemed to combine with the scent of her to challenge his very consciousness.

"My God, you're beautiful."

"I am beautiful," she said again in German.

"And you know it?"

"I know it."

"How does it feel to be so beautiful? Do you find yourself beautiful? Because I do, I say this, I find you so awfully beautiful."

"You say awful. But you—" She smiled, oh, so wonderfully, like Botticelli's *Venus* standing in her clamshell in the Uffizi in Florence.

"Awful, it is a word we may use also to mean, very serious. I am finding you very seriously beautiful."

She went to the couch and sat down, then swiveled herself and rested her legs along it. "Come you here," she said, pointing to the cushion. He slid the coffee table aside and sat. It was impossible not to sit close. "Now," she said. Her tongue appeared behind her teeth—a curiously narrow, questing, tongue. He thought it must be a bit deformed, and perhaps that was why her accent was so odd, as odd, really, in German as in Arabic.

"May I ask you some questions?" He switched to Arabic, doing his best. "Questions. Do you know? Your surname, your place of origin?" Oh, what a fool! Why was he doing this now? Could he never escape the compulsive *Ordnung* of his nationality, his fool genetics? But it was not that, it was a lifetime of being careful, of learning one bit of technical knowledge after another, of pass-exams and politics, up the ladder rung by rung. Now a senior captain, he was obliged to ask his foolish questions of this maiden who reclined beside him.

"I am Lilith," she said. "Of Egypt."

If he did not make love to this woman, he would go mad. It was that simple, he would jump off the damned boat and let Mr. T. get his ticket at last. Let him sail the damned thing into the Statue of Liberty. He went to the bar. "Scotch? Or Baileys Irish Cream, or rum, you name it—ha ha! Yes, what's your preference?"

"Come back here."

She had risen to a sitting position. He went and stood. With a deft motion, she reached up and drew down his zipper. Before he could say or do another thing, her fingers were meeting his shaft, which was broaching like a whale. Her touch made it seem as if Ingeborg's fingers had been made of cold, wet clay. They slid around it with a motion that made him imagine them as tendrils of smoke. Then she said, "May I—I wish to gaze upon your nakedness."

It was Arabic, but so peculiar, out of some old book. Her voice was a whisper of breeze in summer trees, the sigh of a long wave upon a surrendered shore. She withdrew her hand, then rose and stood before him. Smiling slightly, she offered her moist lips to him.

Her mouth tasted of some unknown fruit, heady with spice, dense with a suggestion of . . . something raw. One of her hands had come behind his head, or he would have turned away, so surprising and so awful was this flavor. Her other arm, around his waist, seemed to lie lightly until he attempted to break off. Then, to his horror, he realized that he was not able to move away from her. He was not able to at all, because she was as strong as steel. It was not as if he was encountering even a superior animal strength, but something far stranger and more perplexing. It was like being in the grip of a machine, yes, a vise.

She'd been going to make love to him! She had no intention of—oh, but her belly contracted, her tongue jabbed, and she was eating, her body doing what her spirit denied. He poured into her, the sheer enjoyment of it making it completely impossible to stop. His heels drummed and his body convulsed. Death agony. She embraced it tens of thousands of times.

The suck ended with a wet *snap*, its vacuum breaking as she withdrew her lips from his neck. As the body slumped to the floor, she followed it, cradling it. Tears welled up in her eyes, and she raised an agonized face to the emptiness of heaven, and felt inside her the fire of knowing that she had killed somebody who was completely alive, and had deserved the right to live fully and as long as he could, and express his essence into the world.

She bent then, kneeling, covering her face with her hands. The silence that joins to death settled into the room. She had to hate man, but she could not—man had become too beautiful, a dark god of machines, a wonderful god.

But her stomach spoke, too: You have a right to live. You have a right to eat the only food that will sustain you.

"Only an hour . . ."

She remembered flowing stands of grain, and fat, sizzling cakes in the morning, and the slow fish that lived in the town's fountain, looking up out of their sweet, intelligent eyes.

No, she didn't. She couldn't. All of those dreams—they were nothing but the fantasies of a creature who did not know who or what she was except that she was different from every other creature in the world, even her own kind, and was lonely unto perishing. She'd never come from another world. She'd appeared out of the clay, the sky. Whatever cunning dark muscle in the concealed meanings of nature had formed her and her kind to need humans for food was monstrous evil.

She tossed her hair, making it flow back from her face like a falls, and went to the door and opened it, and went out into the corridor. Nobody about. So she took the remnant down to the end, and found her way out into the roaring air of the ocean night. As she threw the remnant overboard, she heard a mad howl behind her.

Here came the other one, the one called Abdel. His face was distended, his hand was brandishing a gun. She said, "What is he to you?" But it was too late. Behind him there were many more of them, all furious, all clamoring after her.

She ran along the narrow iron path, above the deck of the ship. But then there were more of them at the other end.

Well, her stomach had been a fool, had it not, and now she was well and truly trapped. She could fight them all, could survive their shots, but in the end forty or fifty human beings would overpower her.

So be it. She stood awaiting them. And they came. Hoping that they would put her away and enable her to live another day, she offered them no resistance.

She let them carry her, thinking that they would take her into the bowels of the ship and store her there. But they did not do it. Instead, they went to the side. Only when they were preparing to heave her overboard did she understand what was about to come.

But this could not be! They must not, no—she cried out, she met Abdel's eyes, she howled her terror of the sea, *"No! No—"*

She was falling, the wind roaring around her, the sea coming up, black and full of phosphorescence from the ship's wake.

She hit with a splash and a tumult of bubbles, going deep, deep into the inky water. All around her was the thrumming of the powerful vessel. She knew that she had to get away from it, to avoid whatever slashed and thrashed the water to push it along. Her legs pumped, her arms pulled, and she went deep, speeding like a fish herself, until the thrumming had receded to a mere vibration.

Her lungs began to ache. She must breathe, but if she breathed water, she knew that her dying would begin.

Kicking furiously, she rose to the surface. Her chest was burning when she finally broke into the air. She took long, trembling mouthfuls of it, filling her lungs with the living scent of the sea.

Then she was alone, and it was silent on the gentle swell of evening, and the stars were her only companions . . . and the dark water, of course, that now possessed her.

On the near distance, a huge shadow moved, its outline defined by brilliant points of light. She cried out, bellowing for them to come back, shrieking and kicking as if to somehow rise from the water and run to the ship.

But they did not come back, and she could not walk on water. The swells battered her and covered her. She came up spitting from one, only to be struck by the next. In the cold, she felt a great body brush her roughly and powerfully, and saw gleaming daggers of teeth and a cold, empty eye.

CHAPTER SEVEN

Dark Journeys

P aul lay gazing at Becky's sleeping form. The only light came from the late moon. Beyond the window, the limbs of the backyard oak rattled in a freshening wind. An owl mumbled. Far away, a night freight's horn moaned its passage through the dark valleys of the Endless Mountains. In the moonlight, Becky appeared to Paul as a gathering of miracles upon the sheets, her face filled with the peace of sleep in an accustomed bed, her wide spread arms exposing her breasts and their secrets, her open legs revealing more.

He leaned into her warmth and laid his lips on one of those full and sweetly curved breasts. A small sound of surprise came from her, followed by the soft *mmm* that signaled that she was awake, and yes. Her hand sought him, and she raised him with her cool fingertips. Then they joined together, two melding into one silver, moonlit body.

Pleasure is only the first gate passed through by lovers as familiar as they were. If they ever think about it, such lovers might say that their love-making explores a deep connection between them, sets old wires to humming, perhaps, in new ways. So when he emptied himself and whispered, "I love you," it was as if he had never whispered that before, and the little familiar kiss that replied—it was as if that was the first kiss.

He lay back. They were silent. Finally, he turned on his side, faced her. "I'm not gonna be getting to sleep."

"Me neither."

"Can we call him? Do you think it's okay?"

"At four in the morning?"

"Goddammit, I can't live like this! I can't live without my boy, Becky."

"He needs some space, Paul. No matter how hard it is for us, we have to give it to him."

"The older he gets, the more I see how vulnerable he is and how just damned unlikely his whole life is, and it's breaking my heart, honey. It's just tearing my heart in pieces." He took a breath, settled himself inside, forced his voice not to waver as he spoke. "I want him to have a good life. I want him to fall in love and have kids and see them grow up. Oh, Christ, Becky."

She held him to her, her hands barely covering his big shoulders. She was glad that his anger at Ian had faded, even if it had to be replaced by this misery.

"I'm going to New York."

That made her open her eyes and sit up. "No, you aren't."

"I swear to God, he's in trouble. I can feel it. He's gone to some damn club and done some drugs, and he's in trouble."

"Paul, hey."

He got up, started throwing on his clothes.

"Paul, it's not your concern."

"He's my child, and he's not of age. It's my concern."

"Oh, for God's sake, Paul, give him some space! Ian needs breathing room."

"Ian needs his dad."

"Paul, he needed you the day before yesterday when you went flying off to Langley. That's when he needed you."

"A kid is gonna get killed in New York. Anything could happen."

"And it probably will. And Ian will not get killed."

"How can you possibly know that?"

"Because he's Ian! For the love of God, Paul, you know what his assets are. He's smart and down-to-earth and as straight as a street. He'll survive. More than survive, he'll probably thrive. If he's at some late-night party right now, I hope he's raising hell, Paul, and having lots and lots of fun. You want to go down to see Ian, you go down later."

"Where is he?"

"We've been through that."

"He's my son!"

"Why don't you go down and fix some coffee?" she said mildly. "I have a surprise for you. I'll give it to you then."

"What in hell is it? A pussywhipping?"

"Don't be so crude," she said. "Anyway, I'm not the type."

He embraced her, and she let him, and loved it. They kissed, and he drank her eyes. "I wish I could learn how to be pissed off at you," he whispered.

"I'm glad you can't."

In one of the abrupt changes so typical of him, he suddenly got up. He went to the window, drawn, it seemed, by his own restless nature. She doubted if she knew half of what went on in the mind of her husband.

He got his robe and slippers on and padded down the creaking staircase to the kitchen.

Soon the aroma of coffee began filling the house, and the tang of bacon. He was making a predawn breakfast, God love him. Afterward, she knew, they would come back to bed and maybe doze until eight. Then another day of companionship and work would begin.

Enclosing herself in her fluffiest robe, she went down and joined him. "Oh, you sweetie," she said as he laid a plate before her with a flourish.

"So, what's the surprise?"

"The surprise is, I got us two impossible tickets for a concert."

His face didn't fall. It became careful. He was a strict Bach and Mozart man. A lot of concerts just would not work for him.

"There's a very intimate, very private concert being given for a thousand of Leo Patterson's dearest friends, and we will be there."

He poured the coffee, sat down, and said, "May I know how?"

"Your enemies at Langley fixed it up. These ducats involve a ten grand contribution to the Environment Fund, plus you have to be on the right list."

"Which we most certainly are not."

"But Mr. and Mrs. Richard Akers are, and we're going in their place."

"*The* Richard Akerses? Of General Financial?"

"The same. He's friendly, more than happy to assist the Company in its endeavors."

"Briggs okayed this?"

She had done a lot of backing and filling for her man. He was like all the old operational lions, completely incapable of handling the bureaucracy. "Briggs didn't want you out. He just wanted you careful. It's best not to go into his office and act like somebody who needs to be fitted for a straitjacket."

"I didn't! I was nice!"

"You did, and you weren't nice. Did you know that he had your plane shadowed by F-15s all the way home? You scared him that badly."

"Then he's the one who's crazy."

"I convinced him that you don't actually bite, at least not hard. I explained that I keep your teeth in a damn safety deposit box."

He started what she knew would be the usual hopelessly misguided defense of his own indefensible foolishness. She held up her hand. "Now, you listen to me. No more going to Langley and throwing weight you don't have around. Face this: you have been on an assignment that has turned up no results in years. None. It's one of the great masterpieces of nonproductivity, to the point that the general opinion down there is that you're a con man."

"Oh, come on. They have my record."

"You leave the bureaucrats to me. Is that understood?"

"I leave the throwing of weight around to you?"

"I repeat, you have about as much political weight down there as a birthday balloon full of helium. Nobody cares, Paul, except to the extent that they wish that you and all those blood-soaked boxes of operational records that go with you didn't exist."

"How much weight do you have? Given that you're with me?"

"None of your business, but that's beside the point. You are a good man with a gun, and you make Sherlock Holmes look like Goofy when it comes to detective work. But you are not—repeat, *not*—any damn good at all in the human relations department, as witness the terrified Mr. Briggs and your own bitter, infuriated son."

"Okay! Okay! Admitted."

"Again. How many times have we had this conversation?"

"Well—"

"A huge part of a marriage is when you realize that the bum is never going to change, not because he doesn't want to, but because he can't. He's a big old brontosaurus, and that's it." She leaned across the table, put her hand on his cheek. "But he's my big old brontosaurus, and I'm gonna take care of him. Keep him in his cage where he can't scare the kiddies."

He truly did not know how to react to this. He leaned back, sipping coffee and thinking just how very pleased he was that he was finally going to get close to that little vampire bitch Leo Patterson, in among her rich friends.

He made a gesture with his hand, shooting a gun.

"That better not be pointed at me."

"At Leo."

At exactly 7:00 A.M., Ian's alarm rang. He reached out and pushed the button on top. Ian liked old-fashioned things, and he'd bought this clock at a secondhand store. Today was to be his first day at his new school, Stuyvesant High. It was the best public high school in Manhattan, and he'd managed to interview his way in, convincing the admissions officer that he could keep up with the fastest track the school offered. He was eager to start, hungry for the challenge.

The family story had been that they'd had to move to Manhattan suddenly because of a job transfer. Mom had backed him up brilliantly. She was as smooth a liar as you'd find. No doubt it came from living her life in the spy world. Funny, though, Dad was no good at all with a lie. When he bluffed in poker, everybody else folded. You'd have to be in a coma to miss that much blinking and leg crossing and harrumphing.

But Dad could walk into a room and notice the slightest change. He'd do it automatically. Ian had been curious about things that his friends were studying in prep school. Classical Lit, for example—their e-mails said it was dull as death, but what was it? He'd gotten down a book of ancient Roman poetry from, like, the second-to-top shelf of Dad's study. He'd been reading it in his room when he'd heard floating up from below, "Not yet does parting summer gentle the sun's steeds . . ." Dad had noticed the book's disappearance, and was down there reciting a poem from it from memory.

Now Ian was at a school where there were courses like Classical Lit, so at least he could find out what was so dull about it. He wanted the privilege of hating what his friends hated. Except the truth was, he didn't. He loved literature and poetry and art and music—especially music. He enjoyed everything from Palestrina to Patterson, and especially her.

As he made eggs in his tiny Pullman kitchen, he felt himself getting an erection and laughed aloud. Mom had told him it was okay to be like that. A seventeen-year-old boy is normal if he gets an erection because of any crazy reason. Looking at an egg white was fine, if in some weirdly convoluted way it reminded you of a fem you were crazy about. Or the sight of an apple, or a passing nun, for chrissakes, she'd said. It's just being seventeen. Dad, on the other hand, did not talk about sex. He'd occasionally choke out a question like, "You doing okay in the down-below department?" Ian was tempted to say, "No, Dad, I'm not doing okay. My masturbation techniques are getting boring. Got any pointers?" Except he'd give Dad a stroke.

It was neat to sit down to his own self-made breakfast in his own apartment, and it would have been really fun if he hadn't been getting tears in his plate. He did not want to cry because of Dad, but it just hurt like hell that it was turning out this way. It was like ocean currents you couldn't even see were just pulling them apart.

He did not want to be alone here like this, hoping Mom would show up and visit, and just watching TV at night because he didn't know anybody and it was totally uncool to go to the movies and stuff by yourself, like you were such a bump nobody would even be seen with you.

But he didn't want East Mill ever again in his life, that dreary rundown high school full of would-be gas station attendants and burger flippers, and girls who stuck cigarettes behind their ears and thought you were ultimately cool if you did them a tab of X. Brigit Finney had gotten high on a Rolaid he'd shaved down. She'd danced for hours.

In the bathroom, he stared at his peach-fuzzy face. God give me a beard, God take away my friggin' zits! Christ, there was one on the side of his nose. Thank you. Thank you so-o-o much.

When he squeezed it, blood came out and touched his lips. He wiped it away immediately. The taste of blood was like the smell of glue, awful and good at the same time. When he was a boy, he had secretly tasted his own blood, and once with Kev Moore, he had made up a blood brothers club, and they had cut each other's fingers and held them together. The real reason for all this was so that he could suck Kev's blood off his own finger to see what it tasted like. As long as he lived, he would never do that again.

All of a sudden, he realized that he was in a hurry. Where had the time gone? Without Mom to say, "Get yer fanny packed and yer tail in gear," the time had just slipped through his fingers.

He ran down the four rumbling flights and along the narrow central corridor of the old row house where they'd found him his $1,750-a-month garret. At home, the same place would have been $300 a month.

Then, with shock and delight, he found himself facing New York in the morning. The traffic was roaring. Ninth Avenue was filled with sun. He bought a *Post* and hopped the bus, and read page 6 standing up, thinking just how extremely cool this was. He was going to do great, get excellent grades, and prove to Mom that she'd made the right decision, letting him do this. A kid living by himself and not getting into trouble or screwing up—that was his aim. Mom had said, "I trust you, Ian." Ian had replied, "I swear to you, Mom, I'm gonna do it right."

He kept this very much to himself, but he did not have it in him to break a vow. He just couldn't do it. When he swore something, it was just plain over. So he didn't make many vows, knowing the way he felt about it.

But his vow didn't prevent him from making friends at school or partying. Mom expected him to party pretty hard. It'd be way, way cool that he had his own apartment, and lots of kids would want to know him. He expected to be popular. Mom was so great.

Then he saw on page 6 that Leo was having an exclusive charity concert in a few nights. This was neat, this would be something to do—not go to it, for chrissakes, it probably cost in gold bars, but to go be a fan and cheer her on and make her feel great when she got out of her car and went in, that her people were there, and they loved her.

* * *

There had been a definite change in the rumble of the machinery that drove the bounding, filthy boat. Also, the relentless swaying of the thing seemed to be distinctly less. Lilith raised her head and looked miserably up toward the rectangle of light that was her only view out of the fish-filled hold. The hefty silver fish, their bodies cold and flaccid, came almost up to her neck. At the least sign of a crewman, she would immerse herself in them.

Alone in the sea, she had known the very worst moments of her life. At first, sea creatures had come, great slabs of darkness slicing through the water, sliding past her at a distance of inches. No matter that she sank, she had made herself absolutely still. Let them think her a log. Things had nosed her, pushed her about. No matter how much she wanted to struggle, she had remained still.

Eventually their visits had become less frequent. They had followed the ship, drawn by the offal it left in its wake, the scrapings of plates and flushings of toilets. She had wept in the lonely sea, her body trembling with the cold and the fear.

Almost from the beginning of her ordeal, she'd known that land lay somewhere to the west. The reason was that she could catch a scent of it from time to time, the faint odors of vegetation and smoke.

She had fought the current for hours. The stars told her that she was making barely a league in two hours. She did not know where this land was—perhaps an island of the ocean, or some remnant of a sunken continent.

No matter, after four days she had grown tired, and the sea was coming to seem more like a friend. She had closed her eyes, and at once a druggy sleep had come upon her. What had awakened her was the pressure of the water as it bore into her ears and crushed her eyes back into her head.

She'd opened them to darkness absolute, and known that when she breathed, it was going to be water. Drowning would not kill her, but it would choke her and weigh her down, and down in this darkness she would sink until the ocean's weight smashed her to pulp. But still she would linger on, consciousness clinging to every wrecked atom of her body—to the pain and the emptiness, until eventually she was consumed by ocean creatures or dissolved in the chemistry of the deep. But when would that be? A year, ten, a thousand . . . a million?

She had lashed out, grabbing water, her legs going like palm fronds in a screaming gale, and been about to scream when she had drawn her mouth shut and closed her hands over it, and held the air that was in her lungs.

No matter how much it hurt, she had to keep her air, because in this blackness there was no up or down, and floating was the only way she had of returning to the surface.

There had been no sense of motion. She'd felt the frantic hunger for air that would be with her forever if she drowned, the awful, cloying urgency that made her gobble for breath, and the idea that this torment might never end had so frightened her that her guts contracted, causing Kurt's still undigested blood to gush out of her in both directions.

Time began moving slower, and the pain went on and on. Every orifice had emptied its contents. Her hands twisted into fists, her legs drew up under her. Still, though, she did not breathe. There had to be enough air left in her to allow her to rise. That was what she had, and all she had. Otherwise, she was drowned.

It was at that moment that something passing strange happened, something that continued to resonate even in this present hell of fish and stench and deadly crewmen. It was so vivid that it seemed even now more like something that had happened in a dream.

She had suddenly not been in the water, she had been lying in a shady, fragrant bower. Close by, it was very quiet. She could see that the sun was bright beyond the flower-heavy branches that drooped to the ground all around her. Far off, she heard ringing—a bell, it seemed, that had been tolling all of her life. Her whole being and soul were set to longing by that bell.

She opened her eyes. She even sat up. She looked down her chest, which was covered by a bodice of the most intricate lace, as soft as a cloud. Touching it with wonder, she had a vision of a woman sewing by the warm light of a candle, sewing and singing, and outside the summer wind was singing in the trees.

Then she was back in the water, just like that. Her head raised as she torsioned her back in an agony of suffocation and sheer disappointment—and she glimpsed the moon bounding in the sky, and took in a massive, gulping breath of the best air she had ever smelled in her life, and she cried out in triumph and relief, and began to tread the surface, and her hungry eyes gazed at that moon like the eyes of a prisoner freed.

As she rose along one of the long, predawn swells that were sweeping past, she had seen another light—quite a bright light, low to the water. Swimming toward it had caused an outline to appear against the moonglow. She'd heard voices, the rattle of machines.

It was a fishing boat. She'd struggled slowly closer, begging her lucky stars that they wouldn't start their engine and plummet away. Then she had seen their nets overhanging from spars. The moment when she had reached out and closed her nearly numb fingers around one of their many ropes had been one of the holiest she had ever known.

She had drawn herself up the net, so exhausted that she could barely put one hand above the other. Sick from a stomach full of salt water, as naked as a baby, she had dropped into the hold of the ship, splashing into the seething fish and plunging down among them to hide herself. She lay, just breathing, waiting to be dragged out by the crew. But the crew did not react. Somehow, they had not seen her.

She had spent two days here, trying and largely failing to avoid being gouged by the vicious fins of the fish. But now the motion of the boat was changing. The voices of the crew were loud and excited. The sea on the other side of the hull was restless with hurrying chop. She longed to raise herself up, to look out and see what was happening. But she dared not. Her idea about man had changed entirely since she'd begun this journey. Man was much too dangerous to confront. No, she must become a creature of night and shadows, and the time to start was right now.

With her superb ears, she could hear not only the voices of the crewmen up above but the thutter of their hearts and the whisper of the blood in their veins. Over the grumble of the engines, she could hear other sounds that she thought might be coming from a nearby shore.

What she could see by looking in the only direction she could—straight up—was a rectangle of sky, glowing dully in the early hour.

She was trying to get her bearings when the few visible stars were suddenly blanked. At first, it was shockingly unclear what had happened. Then, as its trailing edge slid past, she realized that they had been passing under a massive object. There was silence from the deck above. It did not seem to have alarmed the fishermen, who continued to move about, doing their work in their black slickers. Her mind was so filled with question, though, that she went to the access ladder at the far side of the hold and risked a quick climb out of her hiding place to see more.

She lifted her head into a vision of human construction so great that it sent a cold steel spike of horror deep into her heart. At first, it seemed as if she was looking at the wing of a gigantic bird.

But no, this was not a wing, not the way it hung there between dark ridges of land. Also, the rows of lights like shimmering beads strung above it, and the brighter lights moving across it spoke eloquently of the fantastic truth: this was a gigantic bridge that spanned the neck of a broad inlet to the sea.

At that same moment, a shaft of light struck the top of the fishing boat's mast. She turned and saw, burning through a forest of what she took to be immense tree trunks, the first rays of the sun. Small waves raced before a fresh northerly breeze, and golden clouds filled the eastern sky. But instead of the sound of the wind and the calling of gulls, there arose from all sides a great, indefinable roar, as if a giant was bellowing at the dawn.

They were entering the largest bay in the world, spanned by a bridge that must be the wonder of ten planets. Surrounding this bay was a sea of light that made Cairo—great Cairo—appear dim. Overhead, blinking sky-ships pushed their way through the air.

When the boat altered its course a little, Lilith's view changed. She saw before her a statue of such splendor that it made the Colossus of Rhodes appear a dark and pitiful dwarf of a thing. This fantastic object was flooded in light so bright that it must defy the darkest night. It held aloft a torch with a golden flame, and upon its head was a diadem crown. This must be the goddess of this place, fittingly tremendous.

There came then into view a construction so unimaginable that for a long time she perceived it only as a soaring, shimmering jumble of light.

When she realized that she was looking up a majesty of cliffs that had been made into palaces with thousands upon thousands of windows, all glittering with light, she almost wept. How mighty had become the works of man! Coming to this place naked in a sodden pile of fish made her clench her jaws with frustration and anger.

Glaring defiance at the goddess and the palaces, shaking away her tears, she slid down into the shadows again and hid herself.

Leo had come back last week, just to see that absolutely all the evidence was gone. She had a fear of forgetting some small thing that would land her in prison.

She'd found nothing out of order—at least, not at first. She had come down into this cellar, looked in the furnace, and found its interior to be pale gray, just as it should be, empty even of ash. But then, standing there with the door open, she had begun to think that perhaps she hadn't had to pull back the bar just now to open it. Or had she?

She'd stood there thinking and wondering, trying to recall each tiny movement. And no, she did not think she'd had to unlock the furnace.

Since it had run, and it had to be locked to run, that meant that somebody else had been here and had opened it, then not closed it down completely. It was an easy mistake to make. The handle was not large.

Her immediate reaction had been straightforward: get out of the house. She'd left by the back and gone down the tiny alley, coming out in Sutton Place and hurrying away. She'd planned never to return.

But—and it was a large but—

Then had come another disturbing event, the disappearance of Mr. Leong.

She'd hired a private detective, only to find that his social security number belonged to a dead man. So maybe he was an illegal immigrant who had skipped. Or maybe not. Maybe he'd been something altogether different.

Paul Ward's name had come to mind. More than anybody alive, she hated Paul Ward. She knew that he was a CIA agent. Sarah had told her. She didn't know much about the CIA, but planting somebody on her staff seemed the kind of thing they would do.

So, had she been under surveillance that night? Had sneaking past her drowsy little cook been a sucker's game? She hadn't felt followed, but maybe she was wrong.

So here she was again, scared to death, trying her best to find out once and for all whether or not somebody other than her had touched this furnace. It hadn't been easy to get what she needed. Provided with limitless resources but crippled by limitless recognition, she could not do something as seemingly simple as buy a fingerprint kit in a spy store. She'd had to go to the website of the Lightning Powder Company and order the things she thought she might need, hoping that her L. Patterson credit card wouldn't cause them to get all excited. She'd had it all sent to the Mailboxes, Etc. on Sixth Street where she kept a box, then gone in and gotten it wearing her brown wig and dark glasses, and hoped that they weren't just pretending not to recognize her. She'd also gotten the *Manual of Fingerprint Development Techniques* from them.

The oily, adherent fingerprint dust was almost invisible as it went on, but when she turned on the black light that had come in the kit, the prints blazed forth.

The furnace door was covered with smears. They didn't even look like fingerprints. But then, as she kept examining them, they began to make some sense. Miri's were there, easily distinguishable because there were none of the whorls associated with human prints, just a series of vertical ridges. They were old, though, you could tell. The book said that fingerprints might last hundreds of years, so they could be from fifteen years ago or fifty.

What she was looking for were prints that had been laid on top of her own. But which ones were hers? She had printed herself before coming here, and now compared the card to what she was seeing. One after another, she found prints of her own. Again and again, they were unsmudged, obviously recent. She dusted the edges of the handle. Looked fine.

This was good, this was a relief.

And then she saw it. It wasn't a clear print on top of hers, but rather two of her own prints that had been partly smudged away. Her stomach felt as if it would crawl up her esophagus. A flush went down her, and she knew that she was red from her forehead to her chest. Her breathing became harsh. "Don't let them lock you up," Sarah had told her. "Because starvation for us is worse than the worst hell they can imagine. Eventually, you cannot move. Your body digests everything but bone and skin. But your life, Leo, it will go on, even in the skeleton."

She looked again at the smudges and knew, again, that they had been left by gloved fingers.

"Goddammit!" When she slammed the iron door, the clang echoed up through the house. She'd known it, oh, yes. She had smelled him out, the murderous bastard. He was right on top of her, just as she had suspected, breathing his vile breath down her neck. The bastard.

So, he'd be next. Fine. She'd take Paul Ward down. Son of a bitching bastard. She was a damn good hunter, the best there was. She probably should have done him a long time ago. But she'd thought, Leave him alone. Put him in the past. Miriam had loved him, and he had killed her and torn her baby from her. He was a monster. No other way to look at it.

She had better get him, or he would get her. If he'd really come in here and seen this furnace, then he suspected—or knew—something. She had to assume the worst: that he knew everything, and he would try to kill her.

What had she done to attract his attention? She thought for a moment. Another moment. She couldn't know. Maybe the night cook was indeed the answer. Little bastard.

She'd been a fool to have that extra person on staff. She hardly ever ate anything anymore, anyway. She'd compulsively gobble egg rolls or peanut butter or suddenly want a Cornish game hen or some crazy thing like that. The hunger had turned her into a damn bulemic, that was the truth of it. She'd stuff herself with human food, then vomit it all up. The hell—her body kept sending these messages—"I'm starving, I need to eat lettuce, steak, peppermint candy, yogurt." So she would eat and throw up and eat and throw up, especially at night, and that was why she had let that damn Chink spy into her life!

Okay, now, calm down. Take it easy here. You're not in jail and you're not dead, and this is for two reasons: first, he ain't certain; second, he doesn't know that you know. That's your edge, and at all costs, you have to keep your edge. So, think. Think, woman!

She grabbed her bag, dragged out a cigarette, and lit it.

She returned to the door. Yeah, it was definite—a gloved hand had obliterated some of her prints. She looked around the room. The question of how he got in was the next one to answer.

Okay, lady, how? She strode into the old infirmary and turned on the light above the operating table. They'd had the sucker on this table, once. They should have opened up his guts and then brought him back to consciousness and let him smoke that particular pipe. Bastard.

He'd come in past the alarm system, which was still secure.

Oh, fuck. Now *think*, woman!

Conceivably, Paul Ward wouldn't need to breach the alarm. No, there was another way into this place, as there was into any house owned by the Keepers. But a human being would never be able to find it—at least, not a normal human being.

Back in Paul's ancestry, though, there was a Keeper, back hundreds of years ago when they had been trying to create a new species, a genetic mix of humans and themselves. The effort had collapsed in bloody failure, breeding a race of superintelligent humans that the Keepers could never allow to continue. All of the families of mixed blood had been killed. The way Miri told it, they had believed that the destruction of Ward's father had ended that line, but it hadn't. The boy had been mistakenly left alive.

His blood was what drew him irresistibly to Miri, what made him fall so crazily in love with her, what made her able to conceive a child by him.

Dr. Sarah had typed it: He was 16 percent Keeper, Paul Ward was. He had the intelligence and power of the master species, along with a huge dose of male aggression. She'd never met a Keeper male, but Miriam had told her that the gods Apollo and Amon-Ra were mythologized Keepers, which gave her some idea of just how powerful the genes Ward carried must be.

If he could detect Keeper sign, then this house would be wide open to him. He would have come in across the garden, moved some bricks near the fountain, and descended into the entrance tunnel, or even come up from the deeper tunnels that crisscrossed the city. She crossed the basement, ducking her head beneath the pristine, white-painted brick arches that held up the house. Then she descended the three steps into the corner where the tunnel door stood. It was made of ancient iron, Keeper iron. She wouldn't go as far as a single step into the tunnels, no, never. Many Keepers had been incapacitated or destroyed in them, and what crawling, twilight horrors might remain of them now, she dared not imagine. Sarah had told her, "You must never let them touch you, *never*."

Sarah had herself been destroyed before she could explain what she'd meant. Leo had been left knowing only that the entrance to the tunnel must be kept locked at all times.

She put her bag down and took out the feather duster and the lycopodium-based powder. She dusted the door. Sure enough, there were the glove smears again, just slightly smudged where he had pushed at it.

She stared at them . . . and almost felt that she could hear him breathing off somewhere in the house. She looked outward through the infirmary, toward the dull light that filtered down from the high basement windows. How the stillness of this place oppressed her. She remembered the days of music, and thought sometimes that she wouldn't mind all that much following Miri and Sarah into the twilight. But what was it like to be like that? Did you think? Get hungry? Did you hear or see?

Maybe she'd like it—the peace, the silence. But she didn't really think so. What she thought was that it would be the most horrible, claustrophobic torture imaginable, and it terrified her beyond words.

Miri had assured her that the furnace burned away every trace of forensic evidence, that the heat it generated was almost that of an atomic fire. But Miri had lived halfway in the past. She could be dangerously overimpressed by what was now simple science, and Leo wasn't at all sure that the eighteen hundred degrees that the furnace attained was enough.

She went up the iron circular stairway that came out in the pantry. There was a bottle of 1832 Napoleon standing on the sideboard. She yanked out the cork and drank from its lip. Her Keeper blood hadn't ruined her taste for liquor and drugs, thank God. It had made her almost impervious to them, though. It took a lot, and she sucked back another big swallow, coughing away the fumes when she finished and wiping her lips.

Paul Ward: was he close by, watching her now? Could be . . . easily. She had come in by the front door, but now the idea of leaving that way made her gut churn cutting, bitter acid. No matter what she did, though, how could she ever hope to escape the man who had taken Miriam?

She went out the back door, into the concrete side yard. From here, she could see one end of the garden, with the hibernating roses along the north wall of the house.

She lingered there, if only because the spot was hidden and felt safe. She had to take a sort of journey. It was a long, strange journey into the life of a man, but it was urgently necessary if she was to be saved. She had to do what Miriam had not been able to do, nor any of the Keepers that Ward had so far confronted. She had to hunt the hunter, kill the killer. She went along the alley, to the high gate that prevented access from the street. Unlocking it with a key from her ring, she passed into Sutton Place. Now she was just another well-dressed woman on the sidewalk of the exclusive neighborhood.

She looked up and down, alert for any lingering figure. Then she went two doors down, crossed the street, and entered the Hildridge Apartments, which had doors both on Sutton Place and East Fifty-fifth Street. She went in one and out the other, looked back, and saw nothing unusual.

Her unpracticed eye failed to notice the almost motionless figure at the dead end of Fifty-fifth Street, aiming a small video camera at her. But she didn't expect a woman. In her mind, Paul was the threat. She knew nothing of the life or feelings of a wife, or what she might do to protect her man.

CHAPTER EIGHT

A Ruined World

Machines screamed, men in overalls sent nets thundering down into the hold, and a cursing crew of loaders shoveled fish. The smells of fish blood and burning fuel and sweating workmen assaulted Lilith's nostrils. She'd expelled Kurt during her ordeal, and she was absolutely famished. When humans came near her, it was all she could do not to leap out of her hiding place in the bilge and devour them in an instant.

To her great annoyance, she saw that the closest to her was a bearer of Scarcher blood, which meant a miserable meal. The Searchers had been a great disappointment.

She'd lived then along the banks of a quiet inland sea, in a land of grasses and oaks, where lions roamed and the humans traveled in packs, gathering berries and roasting wild fowl. While there, she had heard of a remarkable event among the Egyptians, and traveled to see. They had become sun worshipers, following the idea of a clever pharaoh. This sun-worshiping group was of exceptional intelligence, being composed of the best of the Egyptian herd, the lords and scribes, and the cleverest of the priests. Lilith saw that they could be the beginning of a new evolutionary thread in human life.

Posing as a human, she had become Akhenaten's wife, calling herself Nefertiti. As Nefertiti, she had contrived to gain power. Then she had secretly encouraged the return of the old Egyptian priesthood of Ra. The people of Akhenaten were expelled from the country, meaning that they became an isolated tribe, and absolutely devoted to their god . . . and their new, more accurate idea of god.

Under their leader Thutmose, they had gone into the Sinai, where she had bred and rebred them until they were truly brilliant, easily able to survive without Keeper shepherds. For two generations, they had been tested by being made to wander the desert. The survivors were the cleverest of all, and she had given them a land called Kana, populated by a ragtag of berry and rodent eaters. Sadly, though, theirs was a bitter blood, which she discovered when she ate Thutmose himself, who had been driven mad by all the adversity in the desert and come to espouse inconvenient ideas.

To this day, over all this vast gulf of years, the Searchers, now called Israelites, still remembered her by her name of Lilith, and told stories of the goddess who had given birth to demons on the shore of the Red Sea, known then as the Blood Sea.

The demons were merely the children of other Keepers. Even she did not know exactly where the Keepers had come from—where she herself had come from. Sometimes she thought they had fallen from the stars; at others, that they were part of the earth. But the Searchers were full of imagination. They filled every blank space in every story with an invention. And so she became an impertinent wife, then a night-hag wandering the world, ever on the hunt to drink the blood of children.

Ironically, she had done just that. All the Keepers had done it. Children were easy to capture, pleasant to eat, and the parents soon got over it.

For the most part, the Keepers were known to humans only in vague legends. The Searchers knew of Lilith, though, had known of her across many generations. To explain her apparent age to themselves, they theorized that she must have been the first wife of the first man. But since she now lived near the Blood Sea, she must have left him.

She had never been a wife. She loved the idea of being one, though—but not to one of these humans, and certainly not to one of her own spawn of keepers.

Now she was down here in this filth, naked and cowering, desperate for food, with only a bitter Searcher to eat. He spoke to the others in the guttural language called English. She'd been listening to this whorish polyglot ever since she got on the boat. It was far debased from the English she had learned in Cairo during the last century. Only the lowest of the low would jabber in such an argot, so at least she would not be hearing more, not in the magnificent city of palaces that stood just beyond the quay to which they had docked.

The Searcher had his back to her now. He was but three feet away. She could hear his blood racing. He was working hard. He was also, now, almost alone. Two of the other workers had climbed to the deck of the ship. He yelled, "Get 'em in, Rini."

"You get that lift going," the other man shouted back from above, and the Searcher pushed a round, black button. Cables tightened, and the fish, now gathered into a net, rose dripping out of the hold.

In that instant Lilith darted forward, grabbed the Searcher, locked onto his neck, and drained him dry. She practically gagged the blood back up, it was so foul, but she managed to control herself and toss the remnant, now nothing but a spider of narrow bones stretched with skin, into the dark bowels of the hold. She threw on the man's overall and his hat and climbed the ladder to the deck. Behind her, she heard Rini call out, "Hey, Jew-boy, whaddaya gonna get, ham and eggs?"

She crossed the deck. "Hey, Jake," somebody called. She waved vaguely, huddling under the hat. She strode down the gangplank and off into the teeming fish market, losing herself among the stalls, never stopping, looking for Keeper sign.

But the place was huge, it was completely confusing. "Hey, lady," somebody said. She passed quickly on. She'd seen how easy it was to attract attention in Cairo, and she did not want to try to cope with another strange human community. Then, abruptly, she was in sunlight. She looked up a narrow street between two rising cliffs. The humans must have carved this whole place out of a gigantic rock. What patience it must have taken—and look, the street positively swarmed with vehicles and people. But there was a distinct order here, none of the madcap of Cairo's streets. Still, though, the motors bleated at each other.

She looked up and down the street for sign, saw none. Usually, there would be some marks along the byways of a dockland. She went up the street, and soon found herself facing a wide stairway down. There was a sign on it in the Latin alphabet: "Fulton Street IND." Along with it were other words. She decided that they were incantations and spells to protect those who descended into the underworld.

She went down. There was a female in a cage, sitting quietly. She was probably being punished for some infraction, going uncovered or some such. Women had originally covered their heads because they did the picking and the harvesting, and were thus out in the sun more than the men, who hid in shady brush to hunt. Why covering of the head had become a religious law for human women was a matter for scientists to debate.

She yanked the fisherman's hat off her head and shook out her blond hair. If any approached her with a protest that she was uncovered, she'd suck them dry.

Another room, a sort of corridor, lay beyond a barrier. She peered over the barrier and saw that it was a tunnel. This was well. The Keepers would certainly have put sign in a tunnel.

She examined the barrier. It came up only to her waist, but the circular gates would not move when she pushed them. It was so low, its only purpose must be to keep out wandering animals, cattle and no doubt the odd lion. So she simply vaulted it.

Behind her, the woman in the cage began to chatter in English. She didn't listen. The poor creature was probably praying to the grand goddess in the harbor, and very justifiably wondering why such a magnificent female deity would not help a woman in need. Apparently they still did not know that their deities were only stone and mortar, the poor creatures, and this despite thousands of years of the post-solar god YHWH.

A moment later, two males dressed in similar blue clothing came hurrying toward her. One of them was from the land of Punt or perhaps Nubia. The other one, quite pale, belonged to a northern tribe. "Slow down, sister," the dark one called.

She'd listened to enough English to know that he was directing a threat toward her. But the exact context was elusive. "I am not your sister," she shouted, her voice echoing up and down the tunnel.

The men ran faster, drew closer. She came to the end of the raised platform, jumped off, and went down into the body of the tunnel itself. Two bars of iron ran away into the distance. A third one, hidden under a wooden lip, followed them.

"Come on, lady, you don't wanna do that."

"Aw, *shit!*"

She saw guns. She had not the slightest doubt that they intended to put her in the cage with the human female, no doubt for the absurd infraction of not having her head covered. She would not go in a cage. When she heard them scrambling down to the floor of what she had decided must be some sort of a mine, she ran faster.

From the distance ahead, there came a clanging noise. Soon, she saw two lights. A load of ore, and it wasn't being drawn by donkeys. It was coming fast, and there was no obvious way to get around it. The two men were gaining on her.

"Get off the line, lady!"

"Come on, lady, we ain't gonna hurtcha."

"Jesus God, she stinks. Christ, I can smell her from here!"

Stinks. That, she understood. She'd learned all about it on the *Seven Stars*.

The thing that had been in the distance was now close by. It began to bleat, signaling, she realized, that she must go to one side. She stepped up on the wooden bar that covered the third of the rails.

"Oh, Jesus, get offa there! Lady—"

She stepped back, then went into the farther side of the tunnel. The next moment, the machine with the lights went flashing past. The din was so amazingly loud that she screamed against it. The noise blanked her mind, blotted out her being. It was like death itself, this shrieking, ringing, roar.

As the thing passed, she saw in brightly lit windows a fantastic sight: human beings. Not ore, but people. There were masses of them, packed together more tightly than the fish in the hold of the boat had been, or the coach riders in Egypt. More incredibly, they were not suffering from the roar, but rather eating, staring at the same sort of paper flags she'd seen them carrying about in Cairo, or chatting amiably.

She stepped out onto the other rails, only to hear a huge blast of noise.

She looked behind her, and found herself staring right into the lights of another of the machines. She stood, transfixed, as the man driving it stared down at her.

And then she did the only thing she could—she leaped forward and threw herself against the low wall on the far side. Here, the sound was more than sound, it was a pulsating thunder, the voice of a raging storm.

Then gone. And, before her eyes, a slender, perfectly straight line. She gasped, cried out. Her fingers scrabbled along the surface. Keeper sign!

"Okay, sister, it's over."

"Come on up. Here, hon, I'll help you."

She felt hands upon her, the hands of man. But she could also lay her hand on that line, could touch it three times just right . . . and roll.

"Holy shit!"

Then, muffled, "Beats fuckin' all! What in fuck's under there?"

There came hammering, but she wasn't interested. This was a Keeper place in here, and those two creatures would not be able to enter it.

"Lady, are you okay?"

"It's the electricals in there. Somethin'."

She went on, moving slowly in the absolute darkness. She raised her hand to draw some light out of the ceiling, but when she rubbed, nothing glowed. So she had to go ahead in darkness. She drew air deep into her nose, but could smell no telltales. Behind her, quite far now, she heard the men still hammering and yelling, trying to break into the tunnel.

Her hand brushed something soft. She felt it again—a thick hanging of some kind. Why didn't they have any light in here? What was the matter with these Keepers, that they would not provide even the minimal light that their eyes needed? Feeling along the cloth, she thought that it must be a curtain. She dropped to the floor, felt for the hem, found it, and lifted it.

There came a different scent now, something hard to define—mildew, certainly. But also something else—what? She went past the hanging, and dropped it behind her. This muffled the clamor being raised by her pursuers, who were now hollering like madmen and pounding on the wall. They had realized that they could not follow her, and they did not understand. Ahead, she smelled closeness, a smell of old cloth, and again, that indefinable odor. She also heard something. Was it the sound of somebody moving?

"I greet you," she said in Prime.

No reply.

She waved her arms around . . . and struck something, which went over with a clatter. Feeling for it, she came to a familiar shape: the wax body of a candle. She took it in her hands, touching for the wick. But there was no wick. She squeezed it, then felt a harder area on it. She ran her finger along this ridge, trying to visualize what it might be. The base of the object was ragged and dry. There were places along the shaft where rats had gnawed at it. But they had not found it appetizing, apparently.

She noticed that it had curved slightly. Now, this was odd. It had a sort of animation of its own. She laid it in her palm. The slight tickling she felt told her that it was continuing to move. She picked it up, gingerly took it to her nose. There was a slight—very slight—smell of rot. She sniffed the ragged end.

She threw it and leaped up, flailing, struggling, trying to find her way in the blackness. But she could not find her way, and fell over something else, fell hard, landing on her back, hitting her head with a hard *crack* that left her momentarily stunned.

All around her, she heard rustling. She knew what it was, exactly what it was—the tiny movements of the dismembered body of the Keeper whose ripped-off finger she had been holding. Sensing her presence, it had begun to stir. She scrambled to her feet, crying out in this hellhole, screaming her pain and her agony and her monstrous fear.

What she had seen in Cairo had been so horrible that she simply hadn't made sense of it. It was possible for humans to hurt Keepers. Every few hundred years, some Keeper—usually one of the ones who disregarded warnings and lived too close to human society—was caught out and killed. But this—this was something worse than killing. This poor Keeper—man or woman, she could not tell—had been torn to pieces by someone who knew well how to torture her kind. Like the ones who had spiked Re-Atun to a door in Cairo, they had understood what you needed to do to leave a person in a hideous, lingering state of half-life.

"Oh, please, please be at rest," she moaned. "I cannot help you, my love. I cannot even help myself!" She sobbed—then stopped. She shut her mouth tight. Listened. Nothing . . . except the hopeless, whispering struggle on the floor and in her heart. But humans had been in this place, for humans and only humans could do this. Had it been the man of Punt and his northern friend? No—if they knew how to cross the barrier, they'd be chasing her now.

In Cairo, then, and also in this colony, there were killer humans. She shook her head, trying to shake out the confusion that it was bringing her. The humans were so alive now, so conscious, and yet also so cruel. You wanted to despise them, needed to fear them, but even that poor Searcher she'd just eaten—even that wretched fisherman—seemed to be worth so much more than his food value that killing him was rather awful.

Man had grown up; that was the only way to think about it. After all these generations, there had been, in just the past few decades, this amazing, explosive change in the human world.

She closed her eyes. She could have been floating, the way she felt now, as if she was in some way detaching from the world. But this was no place for dreams. She wasn't going to the home of her dreams, because there was no such place. Keepers had evolved on Earth just like the rest of her creatures. She hadn't come from some pastoral garden in the sky. And she had always eaten blood, never damned wheat cakes or whatever it was she dreamed about. Wish fulfillment, that's all it was.

"I must have light," she said aloud. She felt the walls, touching hangings, stepping over what she hoped was furniture. There had to be a form of light here, had to be. They didn't need much of it, but not even a Keeper could see in this maddening blackness. She slapped a wall and rubbed it, crying and begging, rubbed it and hammered at it—and, of a sudden, realized that she could see her hands.

The glow rose from the wall, just as it should. This painted chemical phosphorescence—it came from a lichen—was universally used by Keepers in their lairs. As the light increased, she saw why it had not worked in the front of the place: the walls were encrusted with so much lime from long abandonment that the paint was coated with it.

As the glow increased, she could hardly believe what she was seeing. Before her was a pile of body parts—torsos, legs, heads, arms, hands, fingers, strewn about, all seething with hopeless, mindless, tormented life. She gasped, gasped again, staggered back. Then she looked more—the hangings were of the finest materials, and there were lovely objects all covered with lime and rot, jades and dull, golden things, strange paintings of girls in sunlit gardens in some impossible heaven of a world.

Destroyed Keepers and their collection. It was the habit of her people to collect from earlier generations of humans and sell to later. Time made things rare among the humans. Their generations were so short and their lives so violent that treasures were quickly lost.

What kind of human beings would do something like this, though, and not also loot the place? Unless these were the things not worth taking. She raced around the miserable space, trying to think what to do to alleviate the suffering here. The only thing would be to burn them—to burn her own, dear creations, the almost-real beings she called her children—but she had not any fuel. Real, thorough killing was hard work. It took time, it took care. All she could do for them was to survive.

She scrambled to a chest, opened it. Herein were clothes. She grabbed a dress, held it against her, then another, until she'd found one that was the correct size, more or less. It was complicated and fragile, but she had to dress so that she could go among the humans. She had work to do, and there could be no delay.

Just now, in this horrible place, she faced the fact that a world catastrophe had overtaken the Keepers. Mankind had risen up against them and destroyed them with exceptional, savage cruelty, and that was why she had ceased to be attended: there was nobody left.

Shaking, her body roiling and heavy inside with the meal she'd eaten, she drew the dress over her head, struggling with the tangle of damnable petticoats and lace. Oh, she should never have just tossed that remnant back in the boat aside; what had she been thinking? They'd find it, and when they did, somebody who knew a lot about Keepers would know that there was one here, and they would hunt her down.

How did they do it? How *could* they? She had bred man to intelligence, but not that much intelligence.

She found sandals of a sort, odd things that closed with little hooks, completely encasing her foot. They weren't comfortable, and they made her feel as if her legs were the stilts of a lotus gatherer, but never mind, they were what was here. She had learned enough in Cairo to know that she would need the paper the Egyptians called "pounds." Gingerly, she probed into the clothing that hung on the torso of one of the victims. There was nothing there. Disgusted, her hands shaking so badly she could hardly control them, she went to another poor man. In his pocket was a leather case containing many greenish colored pounds, marked with various Arabic numerals.

She found something else there, a black tube, one end of which was fitted with a tiny version of the light balls used by the humans. It was not lit, though, and she could not think how that might be done. She turned it over in her hands. She could use the light it might make, if she was to learn more about the place in which she found herself. As far as she was concerned, she would be pleased never to go to the surface again except to eat. She well understood why the Keepers had retreated beneath the earth.

She turned away, stuffing the packet of pounds into the belt of the garment she was wearing. As she did so, there was a brief clatter and a flash of light. She turned. The glow from the wall revealed that the little tube was lying on the floor. It had dropped, and in doing so, had flashed. She picked it up, shook it. Again, it flickered. Again, she shook it and got the same result. What was to be made of this? Surely it wasn't necessary to shake the light out of it. No, it rattled when it was shaken, meaning that there was something loose within. What might it be? Perhaps— well, she didn't know. The fuel for the fire in the tiny globe, she supposed. Then she noticed that it had a raised bezel, and that this could be tightened.

Light came—not strong, but definitely usable. So, she had managed to prepare herself a little. She was dressed in human clothes, she had pounds, and she had portable light. Now she needed water to drink and bathe in, and a place of rest. The idea of making herself beautiful again, though, seemed very distant.

In the objective part of her mind, which was as cold and clear as a mind could be, she thought that this journey would soon be over, and it would conclude in the same way it had for those around her. Somewhere out there in those tunnels lurked her fatal end.

Becky ran the videotape again. Why would Leo have come out the alley door? Why not simply leave by the front? She'd almost missed her, had caught her only because of a flicker of movement out of the corner of her eye.

It was time for her husband to discover that they were still very much partners. "Paul, could you come in the den, please?"

There was no response; then she realized that he was on the phone in the kitchen. As she went in, he was concluding his call. "Bocage," he told her. "They've analyzed a cloak worn by the one in Cairo. It's made of you know what kind of skin."

"Oh, Jesus."

"That's not all. There was something in a pocket. More human skin, Becky. Off somebody's back."

They made purses, wallets, you name it. So he had been right, just as she'd told Briggsie that he would be.

"Are they close to it?"

"According to Bocage, the trail's gone cold."

She looked into his eyes. When she had first begun loving him, she had also begun fearing for him. They had gone shoulder to shoulder in the Paris catacombs, sterilizing them of vampires in the company of some of the bravest people in the world. Again, here in New York, Paul had found a way into the lairs, which were laid in abandoned subway tunnels and cunningly disguised pipelines.

After New York, they had believed that the vampire was extinct. Leo— if she was really blooded—was a leftover. But now, with this new case, and with the vampire disappeared—well, everything had changed.

"I've been watching Leo," she said.

He raised his eyebrows.

"I just did a stakeout at the Sutton Place address a couple of times."

"Thank you for telling me."

"I am telling you. I'm telling you now."

"Becky, it's dangerous."

She didn't even bother to shrug. "I saw her once. She had a bag. She carried it into the house."

"*It is dangerous!*"

"What was odd is that she came out through that alley that fronts on Sutton Place. Instead of the front."

"Becky, goddammit, this is rule one we're looking at. Nobody operates alone."

"I'm an expert."

"Becky, if anything happened to you, I don't know what I'd do."

"Come on, Paul, it's a dangerous business we're in. Live with it. Anyway, I got her on tape."

He sighed. "Good work," he said after he'd watched it. "The bag was full on the way in?"

"Yeah."

"It's still full here. Either it has nothing to do with the house, or it's equipment that she used in the house and took away with her."

"Any way we can enter the house?"

"The tunnel in from the garden."

Her gut tightened. That tunnel communicated with all the other tunnels.

"What's on your mind?"

"Oh, Paul, I'm just remembering."

"Yeah, it's rough. I've been remembering ever since that bastard *thing* killed my dad."

"I think we should go into that house."

There was a silence.

"Paul?"

"I've already been in the house."

"Why, Paul, we don't operate alone. Remember rule one?"

"I'm a goddamn expert," he rumbled.

They ran the videotape again. Leo came out the little door in the wall, looked up and down the street, then hurried off.

"Maybe she's making it ready," Paul said.

"The house?"

"Sure. There's a vampire on the run, and Cairo to New York is twelve hours. They've got phones, e-mail, same as everybody else. Cairo was too hot for whatever's out there, so it's coming to New York."

"Why not Beijing or Rio or Mexico City? Any one of them'd be a damn sight easier than New York."

"Leo's here, and she's rich and she's powerful."

"What's it like—the house?"

"Even that portrait of her—Miriam, I mean—it's in the living room." He looked away.

Becky knew that she could never replace Miriam in his heart. "She was a beautiful creature," she said softly, "until she kissed you."

He laughed a little. "What I want to do is wait and hang back, and keep our eye on Leo. Then, when the two of them meet up, we can do them both."

"Leo is a citizen. She gets due process."

"She's a—God, I don't know what to call her. Whatever the hell they made of her. But she's not a human being, Becky, not anymore."

"I said citizen."

"We do with her what we did with the other 'citizen.' That Roberts had been a doctor, for God's sake."

The phone rang. Both of them moved toward it with the same thought: Ian. Becky picked it up. "This is George Fox," the voice said. "Is this Mrs. Ward?"

"Hi, George."

"I need to talk to Paul."

What the hell was this about? Inspector Fox had provided lots of support during the sterilization of the city, all without knowing—or asking—exactly what a bunch of CIA officers were doing in concealed tunnels under the streets. "George Fox," she told Paul.

He pressed the speaker-phone button so she'd be able to hear the call. "George, hello," he said.

"He's in custody."

Becky's heart froze.

"Okay."

"He was apprehended in a raid on a rave in Chelsea. We have him in Central Holding. You gotta get down here, or he's gonna go to Rikers. I can't control it past booking."

What the hell was this?

"I knew it," Paul said.

"Just a second." She turned to him. "Give me that." He held the phone away, but she took it. "Okay, George, what's the situation?"

"It's a felony count of Ecstasy possession. He had a tab."

"That's a felony?"

"Class C, but it'll put him in Rikers overnight unless you get him out. And if he goes in there—well, you can't allow that."

"We'll be there in an hour." She would do the driving. He was good, but she was damn good. She hung up the phone. "He's in on an X charge. They're gonna ship him to Rikers."

"We gotta post bail. I'll call—"

"You'll call Morris Wheeler from the car. I have a feeling that somebody's gonna have to talk the night court judge into dropping charges, and a lawyer can't do that. That's a job for parents."

"You're gonna drive us down to the city in one hour? It's a two-hour drive, even with me behind the wheel."

"But you won't be behind the wheel."

She hung out her blue light and made sure her credentials were in her purse. Strictly speaking, this wasn't official business, but it was hard to tell that to the mother in her. Her boy was not going to go spend the night getting raped, for the love of all that was holy.

Rounding the first curve, Paul grabbed the handle above the passenger-side window. "We gotta get there alive," he muttered.

"Never you mind."

When they reached the parkway, she accelerated to 120, then settled in at 115. This would give her just enough anticipation time to cope with traffic ahead. Any faster, and her reflexes wouldn't make it. Hopefully, no trooper would be dumb enough to try to pull a blue light over, not when he saw the plates and knew this was a federal car.

Not five minutes later, she had a siren on her tail. She left it there for a while, hoping he'd read the plate and peel off. But she could see the rigid face under the Smokey the Bear hat. This guy was steamed. He was not going to peel off.

"Goddammit!"

Paul said nothing.

She pulled over so fast the cop practically overshot her. He came out, walked up to the window.

"This is official business," she barked.

"Driver's license and registration."

She pulled out her credentials.

"Driver's license and registration!"

"Are you nuts? This is an official vehicle, and I'm an officer of the law! Get the hell out of my face, and do it NOW!"

"Lady, you were doing a hundred and twenty."

"And if you don't move your hiney outa here, I'm gonna have to do a hundred and forty, and if I have to do that, I'm putting you up on charges, buster, and those charges will be serious."

"An Audi won't do a hundred and forty."

Oh. An asshole. Now she understood. "This one will," she said as she rolled up the window. She accelerated into traffic. He did not follow surprisingly, given that he was a complete prick.

"You scared him. Impressive."

"Yeah, yeah." Becky knew damn well that he wouldn't have come near them if she hadn't been a woman.

Fifty-two minutes later, they were in front of the municipal building in lower Manhattan. The place was a maze, but they finally found Part 176, Judge S. Gutfriend presiding. As soon as she threw the swinging glass door open, she saw the back of Morris Wheeler's head, and beside him, sitting tall, her son. She strode past the lounging cops, the miserable families, the sullen defendants—or defen*dants*, as they were called here—and put her hand on Ian's shoulder.

He turned. How young he looked—just a damn baby. Salt trenches gleamed on his cheeks, where tears had flowed and dried.

Morris shook their hands. "I was afraid we were gonna go it alone," he said. "I think you guys can figure out what to say—honor student, made a mistake, don't give him a record. Momma, you say, 'He's a good boy.' You use those words."

"The judge must hear that fifty times a night."

"You'd be surprised at how little he hears it. There are sixteen other kids on this docket, and exactly two parents have shown up. You two. And Paul, you say how proud you are of him."

"He's not proud of me," Ian muttered.

Becky squeezed Paul's hand, but she felt like wringing his damn neck. This absolutely would not be happening if Paul Ward would just let himself trust his own son. A trusted Ian would have followed his dad to Choate. He would not have been left to rot and fester and fill with hate for his own father.

Then suddenly Becky was being called. There was a little podium to stand before. "He's a good boy," she intoned into the microphone, her voice echoing oddly. She told how he was an honor student, how they'd just moved to Manhattan, and he'd gotten overexcited and made a mistake. She defended him, she thought, eloquently, before the dead eyes of Judge Gutfriend.

Then Paul took the stand. "Ian got hijacked by hype," he growled, his voice rumbling with such power through the courtroom's speakers that every single soul there fell silent. Even the judge's eyes seemed to spark a little. "He's got a midnight curfew, which he's busted for the last time. You don't wanna give this boy an adult felony record. He has the makings of a good lawyer, among other things. But you and I both know the licensing requirements. No felonies need apply. Let me take my son home and give him what he needs."

"What's that, Mr. Ward?"

"I think—to be frank, Your Honor—I think that he needs more of my time. He's been getting shortchanged."

"And so you're here."

"We're here."

The lawyer for the state read the charge but offered no argument. A mumbled couple of words and a snap of the gavel later, and the case was dismissed.

They were in the hall before Becky threw her arms around Ian.

"Does this mean I have to go back?" he asked.

She looked around for Paul. He should be here. He should help her make this decision. But he was standing at the end of the corridor like a statue. Of all the damn things, he was reading a newspaper. Becky thanked Morris for getting out of bed for them. Then she marched down the hall with Ian.

"Paul Ward—"

But he was pale. His face was frozen. He looked like he'd had a stroke. In his hands was the early edition of the *New York Daily News*. Wordlessly, he handed it to her.

Under the headline "Dried Body Apparent Accident" was the following story: "The body of fishing boat captain Jacob Siegel was found in the hold of his boat, the *Sea Bream*, after a search at the Fulton Fish Market today. Siegel's crew had reported him missing and presumed overboard when he disappeared from the boat at approximately 5:15 A.M. while it was unloading its cargo at the market.

"Mr. Siegel's body had been completely exsanguinated and was reduced almost to a skeleton in what police believe was a freak accident. 'I never saw anything like it,' said police superintendent B. J. Harlow. A coroner's report on the death is expected to be filed today."

Long before she had finished reading it, the world around Becky had slipped into silence, Ian and Paul and the corridor had slid away, and her mind had gone back again to the terrible times under these streets.

"Mom? Dad?"

She looked at him as if across a gulf of shadows. "Ian," she said, "the apartment isn't going to work."

He slumped down on the bench. But what could she do? She would never, ever leave him here to wander these streets, knowing that the vampires had returned.

CHAPTER NINE

Eaters of the Dead

The Music Room was the hottest intimate club in New York. Monty Sauder had put millions into it, banishing the awful hugeness that made so many faux café gigs so unpleasant. Who wanted to sing to an ocean of a thousand little tables, each one with its dinky little lamp? The only way you were going to sing like you were in a café was if you were. Monty had solved this problem. There were just sixty tables on his floor. The rest of the place was all balconies, so there might be a thousand people there, but you felt like you were in this really intimate space.

She stood on the bandbox stage looking out over the floor and contemplated a larger question: Why did she do this at all? She had a ridiculous amount of money, three houses she hardly ever lived in, her own plane, cars at every house just sitting there being maintained by a faceless horde of people who quietly kept everything just right—she literally had it all.

So, therefore, she was going to come out here on this stage in a few nights and bare her soul to a bunch of fat-faced rich people and reviewers whose talentless, disappointed lives and insupportable arrogance required them to dump on her. Was it really because she cared about the Environment Fund? Well, she did care, but not enough to risk all that you risked in front of an audience—smoke in your throat, nasty reviews in the *Times* or *Rolling Stone,* or even some kind of weird embarrassment, like nobody shows up. Or some asshole with a gun.

She watched Hillyard doing the lights, watched Sam Hitchens fooling with the sound. She didn't need to watch them—they'd do everything perfectly. She could afford the best.

Monty came sailing in with the presells, which mostly consisted of ten-thousand-dollar checks made out to the Environment Fund. He looked terrible, Monty did, but he always looked terrible. He smoked constantly, and his daily rest consisted of a downer at four in the morning. "Two million dollars," he said, handing her a blue packet of checks. She gave him his own check, a hundred and seventy thousand dollars. The show would ultimately net the Environment Fund $3 million. As for Leo Patterson, she would just about break even.

"How many are really coming?" she asked.

"That's an interesting question, actually." He shuffled his papers. "The issue is who's seated—" He nodded toward the floor. "And who's consigned to the dustbin of history. I seated Jewel and her truck driver and put Kitty Hart in the balcony. Ain't I bad?"

"Jewel's friend is one of the world's great bull riders, not a truck driver, and do I really want to put Kitty Carlisle Hart in the *balcony?*"

"She'd be ancient history if she wasn't so old, my dear."

"Bring me the seating chart."

He ran off, his shirttail flying behind him. Idly, she picked up the paper he'd had under his arm and left on a chair. Monty read the *Post.* Okay. Personally, she preferred the *Times.* Except for page 6, of course. The celeb gossip page of the *Post* was required reading for anybody doing the public-eye thing in New York.

She would have turned straight to it, but she dropped the paper. When she'd gathered it up, she found herself staring at something that was horribly, darkly familiar to her. For a moment her mind was blank; it was something she could not be seeing in a newspaper. But the picture could not have been more clear: it was of a man who had been consumed by a vampire—not one like her, who left a lot of the blood, but a real, natural-born vampire with an *ebius* powerful enough to suck a human being absolutely dry.

She realized simultaneously that she was no longer alone, and that this vampire—so heedless that it would leave a kill right out in the open—was in mortal danger. She crumpled the paper. Involuntarily, she moaned. Monty, George, and Monty's assistant, Fred Camp, all turned toward her. They'd been huddling together, frantically plotting how to keep the seating chart out of her hands.

"Leo?"

"I'm okay." She plastered a smile on her face. She had to get out of here immediately. She needed something, anything—a drink, a toke, a tab of Special K—to put her down. *Way* down.

"I've got some coke left over from last night," Monty suggested confidentially, seeming to sense her need.

George, who was far more perceptive, realized that something in the paper had shocked her. He picked it up. "Jesus Christ," he said. He looked at her, his eyebrows raised. Then he showed the paper to the others. "Look at this. They shouldn't print shit like this."

"Oh, our poor baby," Monty said, enclosing Leo in a long, thin arm. "This must have really shocked us." Then, sotto voce, "She's so sensitive, Georgie, I don't know how you manage her."

George said nothing. He knew well that Leo could probably have watched gladiators slicing each other up without batting an eye. So he simply stared quietly at her, his face betraying fascination and a little curiosity.

Leo fought for composure, but the walls were throbbing, the place felt like the interior of a coffin, the air was dense and foul, and she wanted only one thing: find and save that vampire.

Or no. No! God, what was she thinking? She couldn't become part of that world again. It was dead, and the vampire that had blundered into New York was doomed.

She sucked in breath, twisted her hands together, tearing at them until her knuckles sounded like snapping twigs.

She had to go into the tunnels. That's where the vampire would be, imagining itself safe in that charnel hell where Paul Ward ruled.

"If you'd rather do this another time—"

"We'll be back tomorrow," she heard George saying.

"Okay, that's good. It's fine."

If she didn't want to think about anything—and she really, really did not, not just now—well, she didn't have to. "Take me home," she said vaguely.

"To the Sherry?" George asked as they left the club.

Oh, God. This was an incredible moment. In her mind's eye, she saw the iron door to the tunnel. She could not go down there, dared not. But there was somebody needful, and she had to at least try. "My house," she said. "I'm going to spend the day at the piano."

"Beautiful," George said.

"Alone. No kibitzers."

They got in the limo and rode silently uptown. Leo closed her eyes. What if it was a man, a beautiful male of the vampire species? One of her deep night fantasies was that a male vampire, tall and powerful, showed up in her bedroom, and was so strong he made her feel like a leaf.

"Hon, do you have any food in there? Do you want me to send Bobby over from the hotel with lunch?"

"Lunch?"

She realized that the strange jittering she was feeling wasn't the car, it was her. She felt like she had a fever. George looked carefully, professionally concerned. She knew that he was thinking about what he'd do on the day off he'd just been granted.

"I want Kitty Carlisle Hart down in front. And Jewel and her boyfriend. Monty's too contemptuous. All he's ever done is throw around Daddy's money."

George remained silent.

"But it's a beautiful club, I have to agree with that."

"It's beautiful. Also good acoustically. You'll barely have to whisper."

"You know how long it's been since I sang in front of an audience?"

"Twenty-one months, including two missed informal dates. Except if you count the time at Katz's."

She'd burst into song one night at Katz's Delicatessen on Houston Street. It had quickly become a bizarre media thing, with camera crews coming in from all sides. They ruined that fun fast.

The car turned onto First Avenue and headed uptown. "Get me a *Daily News* and a *Newsday*," she said.

She held the papers tightly, not reading them, forcing herself not to think about what might be happening right now beneath the streets. Because you could bet that Paul Ward had read the paper, and he would be down there right now, an expert hunter in a territory he knew well.

Would she be able to find this vampire at all, let alone first? What if he or she didn't know anything about what Miri had done to her? Could they tell, or would he simply take her?

"Who is Miri?"

"Miri?"

"You just said a name: Miri."

She shook her head. Now she was talking to herself. That was all she needed. "Got a cigarette, George?"

"We're quitting, remember."

"Which means you haven't got one, or you're holding back?"

He held out a pack of Galoises. She took one, and he lit it. She dragged in the smoke gratefully. As far as she knew, smoking couldn't hurt her, not with Miri's blood flowing in her veins, but she was convinced that it was reducing her vocal range. Something was. But no matter, she needed this now.

"Gimme," she said.

He held the pack away from her, but she took it, and the lighter. "You quit," she said.

When the car arrived at the house, she got out and went up the steps without another word to George. She knew that she ought to be more careful, that Paul Ward and his team of murderers could be watching, but she couldn't deal with that right now. The first thing she had to do was to try to rescue that vampire. Maybe he was sick. Did they get sick? Or hurt. They could certainly be hurt—she knew that too, too well.

She unlocked the door and stepped into the house. Waving at George, she closed it behind her. God, how quiet could a house be? It was as if the very air of this place absorbed sound. There was a timelessness to it that was just awesome, as if you were floating in eternity as soon as you crossed the threshold.

It was a very wide house, seventy feet, a true mansion rather than an expanded row house. Silvers Phillipot had told her that it was worth $15 million, maybe more, and that was unfurnished. She didn't know what the furnishings might be worth. She dared not have them appraised. How could she explain chairs from ancient Egypt and Rome, or the Greek krater that stood against the far wall of the sitting room, or the Delft and the Dresden and the nameless wonders from across the length and breadth of the world? There were Titians and Canalettos on the walls, a Reubens and a Rembrandt, all portraits of the same person spanning centuries. It would be completely inexplicable to an art historian. And upstairs in the sun room, the mystery would deepen. There was an Alice Neel of the same woman sitting naked, with that same grave, infinitely noble face. How could Leo explain the fact that the great artists of the world had painted the same woman over a period of seven hundred years?

No, the house remained closed, its collections secret. But she had always wanted to make a grand entrance down the central staircase, before the assembled cream of the world. When she was just a girl here, running along behind Sarah and Miri, serving them and hoping to be blooded, she had dreamed of the dress she would wear—she thought a Hardy Amies would be fitting—and of just how she would walk, casually but grandly, as she descended into this wide foyer, with its pink marble columns and gold-inlaid marble floor.

She went through the dining room with its fabulous Tiffany glass ceiling, of doves in clouds floating on an azure sky. The table was so impossibly wonderful that she'd longed to have it identified and appraised. It was not of recent manufacture—not, that is, from the past three or four centuries. The teak actually glowed, it had been so deeply and lovingly rubbed. And yet it seemed light, almost as if it would float. She thought that it might be from some unknown culture, perhaps an ancient Indian civilization that had been entirely lost.

When you gazed into its surface, it sometimes seemed as if memories or dreams might flutter there, slipping in and out of visibility as you watched. Had she not seen a city in that reflection once, rising like a memory and then gone? Or maybe it had been just her imagination.

She climbed the back stairs into the long, narrow serving corridor that opened into the various second-floor rooms. Then she went into Miri's magnificent bedroom. This was untouched, waiting for Miri to return. As far as Leo was concerned, it would wait another thousand years, or forever. She went to the Roman cedar cupboard that stood against one of the eggshell blue walls and opened it. She slid back a drawer and put her hand into the place where a Roman senator had kept his most precious documents. From this hidden cranny she withdrew a black pistol, a weapon that Sarah had commissioned especially from the High Standard Custom Shop in Montana. She'd fired it, they all had, back when it had still seemed possible to survive. They had brought in a master gunsmith from the manufacturer especially to teach them, so that they would be the equal of their adversaries.

It had never been used. There hadn't been the chance. She hefted it, opened and inspected the ten-bullet magazine. The pistol was fully loaded. She chambered a round and turned off the safety. The trigger pull was tuned to four pounds, so she would have to be careful. She liked guns, truth to tell. Loved this one, because it was just so superbly made. They should have all had them and kept them on their persons all the time. Then they would have had a chance. Too bad Miri hadn't been able to believe in the danger, not really, not until he started firing.

Striding now, Leo went into her own room, got her shoulder holster off the top shelf of her closet, and put it on. She changed from sneakers to boots and holstered the pistol. Then she got her long, black leather coat and leather hat and put them on.

She went back downstairs, opened the tool cupboard behind the pantry, and got the flashlight.

So she was ready. Her legs felt heavy as she went down the cellar stairs and into the other part of her world, the dark part, where real life was lived. How many men and women had been sacrificed down here? Hundreds, possibly thousands, since Miri had bought the house. To her, the process had been so completely casual that it had seemed almost normal. She'd enjoyed seducing them, then terrifying them, to season the blood with a flood of adrenaline. Leo was not so skilled. Hers just died, usually in total confusion and panic.

The thing was, she liked it when they were scared. She'd been brought up under the heel of her dad, and she *liked* it when she had the power of fear over them.

She went through the infirmary where she usually did her killing, and down to the iron door that led into the tunnel. Fingerprint powder still covered it. She drew back the bolts and pulled it. It opened easily on its carefully oiled hinges. She stood staring into the blackness. How could a place be so dark? It was as if the air absorbed light. A faint wind came out, as it always did, smelling of mildew and water and the indefinable, cinnamony rot that she knew came from the remains of vampires.

How would she ever do this? The tunnels were full of switchbacks and cunning turns, including many that a human being like her would have trouble even seeing.

She stepped across the threshold and turned on her light. When she shone it into the dark, what she saw seemed straightforward enough. She'd been in here with Miri, gone through and up into the garden with her. The brick tunnel, seven feet high and wide enough for two people to stand side by side, sloped gently downward. In the distance, she could hear rushing water. There were openings along the East River, she knew, but she'd never seen them.

Paul Ward had been almost in Miri's hands when things had suddenly changed, and she'd had to escape through this tunnel. Leo and Sarah had prevented Ward from following her then, but he had tracked her like a hellhound for months, following her across the world.

Leo entered the tunnel. She started along it, then hesitated. Maybe this was a mistake. Maybe the vampire didn't know about the tunnels. But no, they all knew about tunnels. They'd dug tunnels under ancient Rome, for God's sake, and Paris and Tokyo and London. They lived in tunnels. So it would have come here by ship, which is how most of them preferred to travel, and somehow ended up on the Fulton Street Pier, probably after making its way along the Manhattan waterfront from the West Side piers where ships like the QE2 docked.

She went a few steps farther along. Suddenly she was facing the much narrower passage that led up to Miri's garden. "Never go beyond this point," Sarah Roberts had said. "You might not be able to find your way back."

Leo shone her light off into a blackness so deep that it seemed to absorb it. She had the curious idea that she was entering a kind of organ of the world—a hidden part of its circulatory system—that had died. "We are nature's balance," Miri had said. "We're the best friends you have."

Tell that to Paul Ward, sweet princess.

Moving step by step, dragging her fingers along one wall, she proceeded deeper. I know what to look for, she told herself; that's my advantage. And indeed, her fingers soon came to a subtly raised area in the masonry. Even under the light, you couldn't see it. She pressed against it. Nothing seemed to happen. She wasn't surprised. This was something she'd been told about, not something she'd ever done before. So maybe the ridge had been nothing, just a small defect in the wall.

When she shone her light at it to get a better look, however, she had to stifle a cry. There had been no sound, no sensation of something moving, as the wall had opened. She stepped in, went about five steps along the steep downward slope. Here the air was still and thick. There was no sound of the river. In fact, there was no sound of any kind except her breathing.

This tunnel was narrow, and so low she had to bend. She didn't like it. In fact, she couldn't handle it; she was just too claustrophobic, and this wasn't going to work. She turned around to go back—and confronted a brick wall. She shone her light around, frantically looking for the entrance she'd just passed through. When she saw only brick, she cried out, stifling it instantly. Then she swept her free hand along the masonry, searching for a raised area, anything that would enable her to open it.

When her fingers touched only ordinary brick and mortar, she got sick, she was so scared, bending double and retching. She pulled out the pistol and was going to fire it at the wall until she realized how stupid that would be.

She was totally and completely alone. She'd come here for the same reason that she always did things—she'd just taken the plunge.

There was only one thing left to do, and perhaps she'd known from the moment she'd come in here that this would be what happened. She started off down the tunnel.

All of her life, Lilith had bathed in clear water. Scent derived from her own lilies had filled the wide, airy rooms of her cave, and she had wanted for nothing. Now she was filthy beyond speaking, wandering in this char-nel of narrow passages, dirt, and the whispering dead.

Too bad Re-Atun had kept the sorrows of the vampires from her. The human population had been growing fast even as the species became more intelligent. She had believed that she ruled this world, but she had only reigned, a passive empress of hollow edicts. She'd been nothing but a symbol, and a lost one at that.

Why hadn't they asked for advice? Her knowledge of the past was greater than anybody's. From the time she'd left Eden, she had been—

She stopped, froze in her sidling progress. Somewhere ahead, busy lit-tle water tinkled. Eden? *Eden.*

She had not thought of that word literally in all of her time on Earth. But now suddenly it returned, bringing with it incredibly ancient memo-ries. She whispered it, *Eden,* said it aloud: Eden. It was a name—of a place, yes, the mythical garden of the Hebrew Bible. But it wasn't really that, no. Eden was home. In Prime, the word meant "granary," but it called to memory a specific place. She saw wheat fields waving in the wind, and birds sailing in the tall clouds, and she heard the cries of children. . . .

She wept, standing there alone in the tomb of her children, hearing the name of home in her mind and heart for the first time since she had—had—

What had she done?

Why was she here?

Who were these people who were here with her, the Keepers? Had been here . . .

Eden of the heart, Eden of the long nights, Eden lost . . .

A slow hand came around her ankle, the dry tips of the fingers clinging like a beetle's claws. Stifling a cry of revulsion and sorrow, she shook it off.

The long, lacy dress hissed as she hurried along. Her progress was aimless. She was looking for life, but she smelled only death in this place, only death and an occasional whiff of dirty human skin. They were down here somewhere, she knew it, and so flashed her light only as needed, to see a turning or thread past an obstacle.

She really had no idea where she was going. She was running, that was the truth of it—running in fear through a death trap, not knowing who had killed the Keepers who had lived here, knowing only that her own danger right now must be very great.

She did not want to remain in these tunnels, not given that who or whatever had been killing Keepers might still be about. She sought ways upward, but each time she approached an exit, she was confronted with a fantastic, blasting hell unlike anything she had ever seen before, a hell in which she felt she would be entirely helpless. She watched vehicles careening past, pedestrians swarming the streets, all unfolding amid the most extraordinary chaos of noise she had ever heard, far louder than Cairo.

Then she smelled something. It was a new odor, warm and smoky, very different from the sodden stink of death that pervaded the black walls of this enormous tomb. She took a deep breath of it. Yes, there was heat in it, and smoke, and also some sort of meat.

Human cooking. She took the odor in, raised her head high and sniffed again, seeking for its direction. The scent was warm, running along the top of the tunnel.

She moved in the direction of its greater strength, thinking that she would kill them, for the first time in all her years taking life for a reason other than the need to eat. In Cairo, she had seen the brightness in their eyes, and actually been unable to eat a human child. She had put it down. And she regretted Ibrahim, and even Captain Kurt.

No more. Re-Atun had been bad enough, but the horror of this place was beyond forgiveness. Now she hated man. Man was the enemy.

Surrounded by the seething ruins of her beloved people, she made a shaking vow to kill them, to kill them all.

Soon she saw ahead of her a dull light. It was flickering, of lower frequency than the globes and tubes. A fire, yes. It was firelight. She came to a narrow stair, barely wide enough for her to ascend its steep upward curve. As she negotiated it on the narrow, slippery boots, she began to hear voices, low and brutal—the voices of human beings. Now the cooking odor was strong. There was a faintly familiar aspect to the scent, an odor that clung greasily to her tongue. She approached carefully, until she was at the top of the stairway. A tight squeeze would be required, but when she moved slightly to the right and backward, she would be in a space that, from the way it sounded, was just beside the human chamber. At all costs, she did not want to appear suddenly among them. If she did, they would certainly blow her to pieces.

Light flickered against the sides of large, silent machines. The great iron boxes had circular wells on them, and doors along their fronts emblazoned with the words ROYAL ROSE. She did not know what these things were, and could not discern the meaning of the words imprinted in the Latin alphabet, but the pots hanging from the ceiling and scattered across the dusty floor made it plain that this was—or had been—a kitchen.

The cooking odor was not old, though. Whomever was doing it was just beyond the next passage, near the glow of the fire. Seeing no sign of a human in this room, she slipped around the corner. Here was a much larger space. It was furnished with many tables and chairs, all broken and atumble, and centered on a large U-shaped counter that was covered with dust and bits of glass.

Behind the ruined counter, four dark forms were huddled around a kettle that was placed on a brazier. Under the brazier there danced a merry little fire. The kettle boiled, and the humans kept dipping and sipping its contents from chipped white cups. Three males and a female, she observed. The female was a splendid specimen, arrayed in a glittering gown that revealed plums of breasts and pale shoulders. Her blond hair hung down gracefully, but without her eyes properly made up, her lovely face seemed expressionless. Two of the males were identically dressed in black jackets and white shirts. The third, by contrast, was a scruffy, scabrous mess . . . but he had the face of a boy-child. In human years, he looked not fifteen.

He had a knife, and was cutting something and dropping bits of it in the pot.

"Come on, man," one of the males said to him.

"I'm givin' you what you bought, man."

"Goddammit, Henry," the female said, "I want this to work, man. It isn't going to on a damn nickel."

"Fuck—" the third male said, removing a leather case from his breast and giving the boy some pounds from it. The boy got up and went over to a dark stack of something. He used a small lamp, and in its light Lilith saw what they had.

He cut a bit off an arm and returned to the fire. He dropped the bit into the cookpot with a faint splash. "That's good," the female whispered, "oh, that is good. . . ."

Those were the remains of her people—her children—in that pile. But what was this unholy horror? They were making a stew of them, infusing their cells into the water with heat.

And then she understood. Over the years, Keeper and man had grown close genetically, so close that a Keeper could infuse his blood into a human being's veins. The human would live in perfect youth for about two hundred years, but only at the price of drinking the blood of its own kind. Then it would die, aging the whole two hundred years in a matter of days.

Lilith had forbidden this practice if it was done to save money on slaves. Only doing it for love was permissible, but those who did it—who fell in love with the prey—were considered a little . . . well, off.

But what were these humans doing? Why did they make this foul soup?

Then it hit her—slapped her across the face, slugged her in the stomach.

To stifle the cry that leaped to her throat, she thrust her fist into her mouth.

"What was that?"

"What?"

"Somebody out there?"

"Shit, man."

What these creatures were doing was extracting the still-living essence from ripped-apart Keeper bodies, and drinking the liquor to make themselves young for a month or a year or so, until the pale whisper of Keeper blood they would absorb had gone.

Every time she thought, on this dreadful journey, that she had seen the worst, worse seemed to appear. Those bodies still bore life, suffering when they were cut, feeling with a dim and anguished awareness that they were being slowly consumed.

She stepped into the light. "Allo," she said.

The female jumped up, its gown glittering. It said, "What in fuck is *that?*"

"I thought I smelled something," one of the black-clad males muttered.

"I have a gun," the boy said, hardly even glancing at her.

"Where'd you get that dress, lady?" a male said. "You look like—"

"Shut up," the boy said. He came over to her. "Get outa my face," he said softly. "I got a business here, you wanna buy in? Fuck, you smell like a pig." He went back to the others, strolling, his hips waving, arrogance oozing out of him. He said, "'S jus' some old tunnel rat. They come up inna here alla time."

"Well, you oughta get a apartment."

"I ain't takin' this stuff up. Jesus!"

"This stuff," the girl said, her voice lilting with new youth. "This stuff, oh, ah, heeeyy! Oh, I sound *fabulous.*"

Lilith stepped closer. The three well-dressed ones came to their feet. In a few minutes, they had shed years. It was the most unholy and revolting thing she had seen in all of her time on Earth.

She reached down and picked up the boy, who at once began struggling, his voice echoing in the filthy room. With a single, quick movement, she sucked him completely dry. Her action made no noise, but the speed with which his tissues dried out created a sound like the ripping of paper. The remnant sank down in the now-floppy clothing. She crushed it beneath her feet and went for the others.

They ran, their voices pealing out incoherent, shrieked babble. Never mind, they would not escape her. She raced forward, following them up a staircase and along a corridor, then up another, narrower stair.

At the top a door opened into a room lined with containers upon which were painted images of various human foods. She was running fast now, just dimly aware of passing through another room, lighted, very hot, in which there were bubbling cauldrons and men in tall white hats. But they were not cooking the flesh of Keepers. This was all ordinary human food, she could smell it.

She grabbed the female by the neck, staggered, and was carried forward by momentum through a door that swung back on itself by some uncanny means.

Human beings were everywhere. Dozens of them sat around low tables arranged with foods. Her three victims raced out into this crowd, tumbling tables and shouting. Surprise froze her. What was this place? She could not stand against so many. They were bound to kill her, and in just moments.

She turned to go back the way she had come, but the creatures in white were coming out of the swinging door carrying axes. Now she felt a shudder of fear. Was she to be trapped here? Was she to end up in one of their shameful, hidden pots?

With a snarl of rage, she dashed on, using her strength to knock down any human who came near her. She rushed through another door, then along a dim hallway that opened into another wide, glittering room. This was a palace, certainly, and all these creatures must be rulers. No wonder they wanted youth. All rulers wanted youth.

In the mirrored walls she could see herself, and was surprised that she appeared radically different from the human females. The clothing she wore was covered with lace, and draped about her like some sort of robe. By contrast, their clothing was svelte and close to the body. She recalled that the dresses of the Englishwomen in Cairo two hundred years ago had looked as hers did. Apparently the humans had changed the way their clothing looked. She must not forget that.

Voices were rising, there were screams, there were howled words. One of the men in the blue clothing appeared. She darted into a door and found herself on a stone staircase. She ran up it, heard voices below. "Stop," one of them cried.

She went through another door. This hallway was very quiet. She ran along it, trying doors. On each, there were Arabic numerals—457, 459, 461—and then 463 started to come open. She threw herself inside, pushing the creature within backward so hard that it slammed against the far wall. It slumped, rendered senseless.

She was in a room, not large, dominated by a flat couch. There was a window, behind which humans sat speaking. Strangely, they did not react to her presence, but merely continued talking as if she was not noticeable to them. "What's more, we see only double-digit growth on the horizon," one of the creatures said to her.

"Excuse me," she replied in her awkward English. At least this one didn't run away. She dashed through the only other door, and was delighted to find a water room like the one on the *Seven Stars*. She stopped, listened. Without, there was only the jabbering of the man in the window. She went to the creature she had stunned. It was a female, wearing the correct clothing. She lifted it and stripped it. The clothing was in three layers and many parts, not simple and elegant like her own linen and silk, not complicated with lace and tassels like this awful thing she was wearing.

She dropped it off, went to the window, and peered in. Still, the creatures did not see her. "Allo," she said to them. They continued their droning. She touched the window. It was of a heavy glass. Also, they seemed much smaller than human beings ought to be. Finally, she took a cloth from the couch and covered it. This was some sort of spell-driven thing. Magic had run mad among the humans. Everything was magic, from the wagons that rolled by themselves, to the ship the size of a pyramid, to this strange enchanted glass.

She had learned on the ship the trick of the drawing of water, and in a moment had a wondrous lot of it coming down upon her. She opened her mouth into it, let it pour in. It tasted less of chemicals than the ship's water, and she enjoyed its coolness and sweetness. She watched the waste curling down the drain.

After a time, she came out, taking down from the wall a length of what felt like cotton and wrapping herself with it. Phials of unguents and fragrant oils lay about, but when she attempted to anoint her breasts from one of them, it left a slick material that got bubbles in it if she swept her hands through it. Finally, she went in the water again, and was slowly covered with bubbles. More of the filth that caked her came off, much more. She got the phial and poured it over her, wiping herself with her hands until her whole body was anointed with the golden ichor that became white bubbles when alchemized into the water.

Now her skin was rosy, and she smelled again like a maiden. She took the cloth to her and held it against her breasts, and gazed upon her own face in the mirror that covered an entire wall of the chamber.

Off in the distance, she heard the surging roar of man's works. Behind her, the people in the strange window jabbered continuously. The human creature remained stunned on the floor.

Looking at herself, Lilith saw that she was comely indeed, with her soft lips and bright eyes. The years, she thought, will not bow the mother of the world.

But loneliness might. She went into the other room, sat upon one of the thickly built chairs, bent her head upon her hand, and remained there in silence, alone in the vastness of a world that was hers no longer. As she sat, the weight of her feeding made her want to sleep. She lay back on the chair, listening to the drone of the hypnotized people in the window. A careful look at the woman she had knocked out revealed that she would not come to for some hours.

Lilith thought to kill her. But no, not now, she couldn't eat again so soon, and the blood would go dead. She'd sleep a while and make room, then tuck the creature in. It was thin, it wouldn't provide much blood.

Blood. She was an eater of blood. She didn't really remember why. Or, really, even where she had come from . . . except for this word *Eden,* that meant land of grain.

She closed her eyes. Off in the distance of her mind, she saw stone cottages clustering under broad trees, and heard the grinding of the grain.

Once, she had been an eater of grain . . . she had been so young. . . .

"We need one innocent enough to do it well," he had said, the one they called the boy master.

Chapter Ten

Fast Walker

The only sound in the neat little apartment was the ticking of the wind-up alarm clock. Paul moved through the room, impressed with how his son had set the place up. Look at this neatly made bed, clean kitchen—he'd surely started out in good order. Maybe Paul shouldn't have done what he'd done. But he had to have the boy back, there was just no other choice. Poor Ian had been so damn humiliated, and who could blame him? He knew that the drugs had been planted on him. But why, and by whom—those were things he would never know.

He unrolled the old map he had brought with him and tacked it to the wall. The pencil lines were a little faded, but still precise. It had been made many years ago by Charles Frater, one of his earliest team members. Given that Charlie had died creating this map, it should have been drafted in blood. As they had gone through the tunnel system, Charlie had worked out the details of every lair and run that he could find, assisted by what everybody considered Paul's uncanny ability to see the vampires' marks and signs.

When Charlie was killed, the Company had not offered a replacement. The Company never replaced anybody on Paul Ward's team. Justin Turk, Briggsie's predecessor, had put it pretty clearly: "We don't kill people, Paul. Putting somebody on your project is a death sentence."

"Goddammit!" They were damn well back, and he didn't have shit to throw at them. Him and the woman he loved, and a few old guns. *"Goddammit!"*

If she got killed, he would feel like he'd killed her, and that would never change.

He looked at the East Side tunnels. One communicated with the ruins of the unfinished Second Avenue Subway. The other angled west, then went up Sixth Avenue. That one they had named "Condo Row" because of all the lairs that lay along it. Thirty-four of them, as Paul remembered. The New York vampires had reacted pretty much the same way—when threatened, they had rushed to protect their possessions. There had been all sorts of things down there—Renoirs and gold coins and clothing and rare books, jewelry and watches, you name it.

Condo Row, which paralleled and snaked beneath the Sixth Avenue IND, had numerous entrances into the subbasements of midtown hotels and restaurants. Paul had once come up and found himself in the coat room at "21." Other passages ended in seemingly inappropriate places, until you understood that they'd been created during the Prohibition era to open into the newly created basement speakeasys. The vampires had found it convenient to steal people out of places where they weren't supposed to be. One branch had even gone into the pantry of Billy Rose's Horseshoe Club, now a disused ruin in the basement of the Royalton Hotel. During its lifetime, no fewer than fourteen missing persons had either last been seen at the Horseshoe Club or had attended the club around the time they disappeared.

Who would ever have imagined that such a danger could lurk behind a cloakroom door, or around the corner from the famous horseshoe bar?

The other main tunnel, nicknamed the Sutton Place Express, led up along the East River. It communicated to ten or twelve escape hatches that opened into the river. Vampires were strong swimmers; they could stay underwater for an amazingly long time without becoming incapacitated. They would come up to the street out of their tunnels, take a victim, and fade back into the system, taking the remains with them. The bones would be crushed to splinters and tossed in the river.

The Miriam Blaylock house, radically different from the dirty lairs where most of the vampires lived, also communicated with the East Side tunnels. This was why they'd come to be called the Sutton Place

Express by his team. It was into the East Side system that Blaylock had escaped on the day she'd almost succeeded in killing him in that house of hers.

Paul sat down with his gun. The big, highly specialized pistol was a dull, gleaming blue. It carried a twenty-bullet magazine, and the bullets were fat, mean magnums, capable of blowing a human—or vampire—head into four or five pieces upon impact. Three shots would tear a vampire to bits. The French had an even better weapon, but this would have to do. Paul dropped it into his underarm holster.

"Charlie was a hell of a draftsman."

Paul turned. Becky was supposed to be in East Mill with their son. "Where's Ian?"

"In his room with the door locked, feeling sorry for himself. He wasn't doing X, by the way."

"Momma believes."

"He says the tab was dropped on him during the raid, and Momma does believe."

"You know something, Momma? I believe him, too."

She looked at him sharply. An instant later, realization dawned. "You bastard," she said quietly.

"I had to!"

"You—" She stopped herself. Her eyes flashed with rage. But then she, also, saw the necessity.

"You did it before you knew about the new vampire."

"I did it because I didn't want him in the same damn city with Leo. The blood attracts, you know that."

"Paul, you crushed him. You just plain crushed him." She strode to the window. "Jesus, you are a piece of work."

"It wasn't even a real tab. When they tested it, he'd've been let go, even if he got sucked up in the system."

"You had no damn right to do this! You and your damn cop friends. Jesus Christ, you just cut the kid's heart out!"

"He's up at home instead of down here with these damn vampires, and I don't happen to think I cut his heart out at all. I think I saved his life."

She hated it, he could see it in her face. But she was also grateful. He could see that, too.

He pressed his advantage. "What would we have done? 'Hey, Ian, there's a big old vampire here in New York, and if you see it, you're gonna fall in love, and ain't that just dandy? Bullshit, Becky. Bullshit! I did the right thing."

Her silence was blue with rage. But she swallowed it. What other choice did she have? "Okay."

"So now I'm gonna go in there"—he indicated the tunnels—"and I'm gonna repeat the sterilization protocol." He hauled out his gun, slapped it against his palm.

"You're not going in there alone."

"I am."

"That vampire is going to be desperate and well aware of the danger."

He shrugged. "I'm gonna be just as well aware."

"Paul, you stay out of there."

He loved her. But he would not do that. "Unless I destroy that animal, people are going to start disappearing again. Maybe it'll be somebody's kid—a kid like Ian, out to have a good time. He takes a shortcut down a side street, and Mom and Dad spend the rest of their lives waiting. Or a father—some night watchman from the Dominican Republic, got three kids and a wife in Bushwick, he evaporates into thin air."

"Like your dad."

"And his wife and his kids are sent to hell, and they didn't do a damn thing to deserve it!"

"Just like you and your mom were. Paul, I love you, and I respect your motives immensely. With all my soul. But you are NOT going down there, because you cannot go up against a vampire alone and win, and you know that, and I know that, and I am not going to lose you."

"I have a sworn duty."

"What about your duty to me? Your *sworn* duty? Or to your son—the duty to that wild blood you two have lurking in your damn veins?"

He gazed at her, his brilliant eyes telling her that he thought he would checkmate the monster that was down there. "The way I figure it, the thing's gonna spend a day or so exploring. It's going to find all the vampire remains down there and get real worried. It'll hole up in some dark corner."

"This thing came from God only knows where, when we thought they were all gone. Extinct. But here it is, one hell of a survivor, you ask me. It doesn't seem like the holing-up kind."

"It came from Cairo."

"You know that for certain?"

"A trail goes cold there, picks up here ten days later. Bocage has it pegged as a female, about five-eight, blond, blue-eyed. Also weak on street smarts. It lived somewhere in the desert, all right."

"Feeding on what?"

"There are people in the desert. Bedouins."

"Too noticeable."

"It's a wanderer. That's why we've never caught it. It stayed ahead of us."

"Paul, have you ever considered that it's surviving because it's better than the others? It knows we're here. This public kill is bait on a hook."

"That had occurred to me."

"No vampire would do a kill like that and not hide the remnant, not unless it was stupid, and they don't come that way, or it was inexperienced, and this thing is probably thousands of years old, or it had another purpose altogether. And Paul, I'll tell you right now what that purpose is, because I know. That purpose is you."

"Becky, I'm going down there, and you aren't. That's the beginning and end of it. I'm doing a recce from Sutton Place to Fulton Street, then working my way up Condo Row all the way to the end. If I don't have an encounter, good. I'll find another way. If I do catch up with it, even better. We can send the damn skin to Briggs."

"That'd be a masterstroke of diplomacy."

He closed his jacket. He was going. He was doing it right now.

She backed toward the door, staying in front of him. You never gave up your ground, not if you wanted to win a confrontation with Paul Ward. "I'm going to cover your back," she said carefully, putting as much force into her voice as there was.

He tried to get around her.

She stayed in front of him. Just. "We never defeated one of them if it was ready for us. Not one."

"Miriam Blaylock was ready for us."

"She died to save her baby."

"By getting herself killed? I doubt it."

"By surrendering to his father! She knew what you'd do."

A long silence.

"And you brought home a wonderful son! Please, Paul, we need you. Especially your son. You're the only person in the world remotely like him. He's going to have to learn to control one hell of a powerful and very alien personality. I can already see it growing in him, Paul. He's struggling with some amazing demons, and if you aren't there to help him make it, he isn't going to make it."

Now he would push her aside. He would be gentle, but there would be no point in resisting. The hard eyes glittered. "If we both go down there, he could lose us both."

"You admit it. You're risking death. What if you die, and the vampire doesn't?"

"You're next."

"Back to back, we have the best chance. One by one, we are defeated in detail. If we're going to survive, we have to do this together. If it can get you, it can sure as hell get me. You know that as well as I do."

"There is no other way!"

"We're going in together."

"And Ian?"

"Maybe he gets us both back, and maybe just one. But we win down there, if we go in together, and you know that's the truth."

"I know I can do this vampire."

"And I agree! With me rearguarding you."

Long sigh. Cold, steady look. Admission that she was right, expressed as a slight softening in the corners of the eyes.

The best place to enter the tunnels would be the Blaylock garden, but that wasn't a real good idea. They had to do it from an unexpected point, somewhere that the vampire wasn't likely to be waiting for them.

"I'm planning to go in through the subbasement of the Royalton."

"I know the location. We got a family of five down in there."

"Five," he said in a hollow voice.

They took a cab up to the hotel, entered the lobby. The Royalton was high Manhattan glitz aboveground, but its basement was a very different matter. Billy Rose had built the Horseshoe Bar in the 1930s. The place had served everybody from Eleanor Roosevelt to Frank Sinatra's Rat Pack. It had been closed down in the 1950s.

They had found it by accident, going up one of the tightly wound staircases the vampires used to access their grab stations. Instead of emerging into some basement that used to be a speakeasy, they had ended up in this wonderful, ruined room.

"Should we involve the manager?"

"Why?"

"He's gonna get told that we went through. What if he calls the cops?"

In a few moments, they were sitting in the office of Gene Forrest, general manager of the hotel. Forrest was both carefully and casually dressed. He looked exactly like he belonged at the ultra-cool Royalton. Paul showed him an artificial credential.

"Office of Environmental Analysis? I'm not familiar."

"We're planning a rodent sweep."

"We don't have rodents."

"There's a space under your subbasement that does."

"There's that old bar down there. But it's sealed."

Paul nodded. "If it isn't, we'll seal it. Just want to let you know we're going to be doing a little testing down there."

"We had some guests go down there the other night. Drunk. One of them was in costume."

Becky could feel Paul's tension rise. It didn't sound like it meant anything, but maybe it did.

"Do your guests often go down there?"

"God, no. They had to get keys. How they did it, we don't know. We're still investigating."

"You got their names?"

"They were dinner guests, unfortunately."

"They made a reservation?"

"The Smiths."

"What exactly happened?"

"They were first noticed when they burst out into the kitchen, screaming."

"From below?"

"Four of them. Nobody had seen them go down, so the staff were quite surprised. One of the women was dressed like Sarah Bernhardt or somebody. A turn-of-the-century ball gown."

"Did you see them?"

"Actually, yes. I stayed on that evening. We had an important table. Catherine Deneuve, with four guests. Lovely, lovely woman. I wanted it all to be absolutely wonderful. But then this group—I hadn't noticed them when they were at their table—suddenly they burst into the dining room. They actually turned over tables. It was fantastic. A disaster."

"You called the police?"

"Immediately. We had an officer here in about three minutes. Plus our own security people. But they were already gone."

"All four of them were gone?"

He nodded.

Paul sighed. "We'd like to do our survey, anyway. We'll be down there for about an hour."

The manager had become so tense, he seemed almost coiled, his face compressed. "You're not that." He gestured toward the fake ID card.

Paul remained silent.

"Is there some kind of drug operation going on down there? I've always hated that place. We keep it locked. We don't know how they got in."

"We're not cops. The hotel isn't going to be raided."

"It was horrible. They were horrible."

"Yes, I'm sure they were."

They went down through the hotel's glittering, shadowy dining room and its pristine kitchens, then down through the pantries and the storage basement. The manager showed them a steel door, securely locked. He took out a key and opened it.

"Can we take that?"

"Of course." He handed them the key. "But lock it behind you. We never leave it open. Ever."

"You've had trouble?"

"I don't like it down there. I'm going to have this door sealed. Absolutely. I'm walling it up."

"That's a good idea, mister. A very good idea."

They went through into the darkness of a cave.

"Why are we here?" Becky asked. "The vampire's probably gone."

"We'll see."

Paul opened his briefcase, which contained an array of compact but powerful devices. They strapped new light-amplifying equipment on their faces. This system bled out tiny quantities of infrared light to compensate in areas where the darkness was complete. They put on their overshoes, specially designed with wide, hollow rubber soles to minimize sound. Neither of them spoke. They didn't need to. All the old training and familiarity had returned the moment they got into this place.

Becky shone her light around the large, low space. There were chairs jumbled against one wall, a broad floor, and a small stage. The famous bar dominated the room.

Paul said, "What the shit?" He vaulted the bar with the ease of a powerful athlete, landing behind it without a sound. He was looking down at a body. There were things running on the dead skin. The one visible eye was heavily involved with insects.

Becky saw gray hair, wrinkles. "It's an old man." But he was wearing the T-shirt and sneakers of a kid.

"We don't know what it is, Becky."

She gasped when she saw, in the zinc ice chests under the bar, legs and arms stacked as neatly as cordwood. "Oh, God, Paul."

There was a can of Sterno and a little griddle. A spilled saucepan lay on its side nearby. Bits of gray material were scattered around it on the floor. They looked organic, but the insects weren't bothering them.

Paul squatted. He remained there for a long moment. Then he stood up. "He was eating the remains of the vampires we killed here."

"Jesus. And somebody broke his neck."

"The vampire."

"What would happen if you ate them? Would you become young?"

"Sure, for a while. Be my guess."

"That explains the clothes. He was living as a boy. The corpse returned to its real age after he died."

Paul went to the far back of the room, into the club's old kitchen. He felt along a wall in the liquor safe. She saw his hand move slightly, watched the darkness thicken as the concealed door he was looking for slid open. She gave him some light. The blackness in the tunnel beyond seemed to absorb the beam, to suck the life right out of it.

She had the urge to take out her cell phone and call Ian. They might be in here for hours, maybe all night. He would be frantic.

"Paul, I want to know something. I want to know why you came here to this specific place."

He slowly turned. In the powerful beam of her flashlight, his face was shockingly changed, the skin powder-white, the blue eyes like glass. The lips were set hard and straight. He lifted his hand, waved it past his eyes.

She moved the light. "Sorry."

He stared down into the dark of the tunnel.

"Paul, what I want to know is, why are we here? How did you know to come here in the first place?"

He came toward her, three steps. There was in the movement a quickness that made her see what he normally hid, and hid well—the thing about him that was so very different—the sense of an alien presence that lingered about him like smoke; the animal that peered from behind those slow eyes of his. "I just know," he said. "It's the way I am."

"You deduced it. Hit it right on the button."

"We've got a lot of work to do, and no time."

"Can I call Ian first? I've still got a little signal here. But down below—"

"We're not going down there."

"So it's out?"

"It's out."

It was loose in the city.

* * *

Leo was crying, and she couldn't stop crying because the flashlight was getting dimmer and dimmer and she couldn't find her way and she had been a damned fool to come down here in the first place. What had she been thinking, that she could guide some vampire up to the surface and take care of him and maybe there would be love? Is that what she'd been thinking? Because now that seemed like a very stupid thing to be concerned about, especially when she was going to be onstage in a few hours. If.

The truth was, she hadn't been thinking at all, she'd been acting on impulse, doing just what she wanted to do in that particular moment. That was why she'd let Miri blood her, because it had been a sensational experience, the combination of being totally surrendered to Miri, feeling the boiling cold of Miri's life force going through her veins and making her heart race so fast it seemed about to explode, and feeling like she was going to become eternal and powerful and just as incredibly glamorous and wonderful as Miri.

This was the same kind of decision—impulsive, crazy, and wrong. The thing that she could never understand about herself was why she would suddenly do something like this. She didn't lead her life this way. Absolutely not. She led her life like a marine drill sergeant with a chess pro override. You don't become a superstar any other way. It's never a damn accident. So why was she here? What was driving her?

"Help! Help me!"

Her cries echoed away into the distance. She'd been blundering along this messy tunnel for a long time now, dodging pipes and sagging wires and rusty machinery. There were rats literally everywhere, a whole city of rats that must be going up at night and feeding on garbage, then coming down here during the day. They were big, fearless, inquisitive rats. They weren't particularly aggressive or anything, but their casually interested stares left no doubt about what would happen to her when her light went out.

"Help! Help me!"

The echo called back to her, of that voice of mixed youthfulness and age that had made her so famous. What damn difference did it make now? All that fame and money and her eternal youth were just generally worthless here.

Her flashlight finally did what it had wanted to from the beginning—it went out. She shook it. Nothing. She burst into tears. Standing in the middle of this dark and treacherous place, hugging herself, cold and completely helpless, she cried like people must cry on the night before execution. She cried for a long time, bitterly and angrily, until there was nothing left but snuffling and choking.

When she stopped, she heard a sound at her feet. It was close, a sort of frantic sputtering noise. But what was it?

A pain shot up her right leg. Instinct caused her to slap at it, and her hand encountered rough fur.

It was rats, rats all around her and now nipping at her, trying to draw blood so that they could get more.

Her hands shaking so much she could hardly control them, she got the gun out. Holding as far from her as she could, she fired it.

The roar was mind boggling, it made her scream, it made her ears ring, but what she saw in the flash made her whole heart and soul howl with sheer, blinding terror, because it was a seething, tumbling, circus of rats.

She fired. Again. Again. Again. And in each flash she saw them, she saw them turning tail and running. Fired. Fired. And then it was clear. No more rats.

Kicking, shrieking at the darkness, she moved slowly along. She waved her hands in front of her, fighting the persistent sensation that they were going to drop down on her from above.

"Help! Help me, please!"

Another sharp, twisting pain in the fat of her calf. She swung around, fired again—and they were back, a stormy gray ocean of them swarming toward her in the flash. Again she fired. Again. They kept coming. Again, again, again, *click click clickclickclick.*

She hurled the empty gun at them and tried to run, shuffling along, scuttling, waving her hands in front of her. She gagged, retching up the acid that was making her stomach twist itself into burning knots.

She fell, crashing to the floor with a dry, scraping thud. They seethed over her, covering her in an instant.

What would happen? Would she die, or would she become part of them, of their stomach and their shit—what would happen?

She clawed her way to her feet, dragging them off her like leeches in the Congo, bellowing like a wounded heifer, begging God for deliverance.

Then she remembered something. She thrust her hand into her pocket, and there it was, the lighter she'd taken from George back in the limo. Crying, screaming in her throat, she pulled the little Bic out and raised it high and lit it, grotesquely mocking Lady Liberty out there in the free air of the harbor.

The rats didn't like that, not really. But they sniffed into the pool of light. They would get used to it.

Bending low, she thrust the flame at them, screaming as she did so like a Valkyrie . . . a very scared Valkyrie.

Then she felt something, a new sensation. It was deep under her feet, a throbbing that came and went. She moved a bit more, going toward a pile of debris that choked the tunnel ahead. As she was walking, she felt the throbbing again. It had a rhythm to it, and she thought she knew what that rhythm was: she was hearing a subway.

Everybody knew about the old Second Avenue Line, which had been abandoned and left unfinished back in the 1970s or '80s. Somewhere back then, anyway. Was that what she was in, and therefore she was hearing the Lex, somewhere nearby? She moved a little farther ahead. Seeing that she was active again, seeing the fire, the rats had backed off once more. But not far. They were everywhere, looking at her like pedestrians watching a burning building.

Again she heard the sound, and this time it was a little louder. It was definitely the subway, that was clear now. She moved more quickly, clutching the lighter, afraid that it, too, would soon go out. Every few steps, the sound was a little more distinct. She knew a lot about the subway. She hadn't always been a little rich girl. Life for Leo Patterson had started out in Bronxville, but by the time she was fourteen, her whole existence was centered on Metro North and the subway, her umbilical cord to Manhattan. She'd dress up in her stardust gown and go from club to club with the other bridge-and-tunnel girls, trying to suck, fuck, or bribe her way into someplace worth going. And failing. Always. You had a mark on you that only Manhattan could see, you who crossed the bridges and slid through the tunnels.

The lighter was getting hot. She turned the flame down. Another train passed, going pretty fast. She must be somewhere near one of the crosstown lines. She looked for some kind of a door or something, some way of getting into the living part of the subway.

She thought that the line was actually above her. Raising the light, she looked up. And there, she saw something that might matter. Along the roof of the tunnel were dark rectangles, possibly openings of some kind. They were dripping, with long stalactites hanging from them. Her guttering flame couldn't reveal much about where they went, if anywhere, but at least they weren't here on this floor amid the confederacy of the rats. She went to the concrete wall and looked upward. She was tall enough by half a hand to grasp the edge of the sill above.

She turned off the lighter and put it in her pocket. Immediately, rustling began. As she reached up and grasped the edge, they reached her, and when they did, they began to scream. They did not squeak like the rats one might find behind a country woodpile. They screamed with the harshness of their lives and their hunger, and perhaps some nameless change that had come to them from whatever nibbling they did on the remains of vampires.

As she pulled herself up, her naked arms wallowing in thick greasy debris that immediately made her itch, they leaped at her like raging dogs, snapping and grabbing at her jeans, her boots, her exposed skin. Revolted, choking back her own cries, she kicked them off as she drew herself into the space above.

She fell, and hard—it felt like a good three feet, hitting a concrete floor. Behind her, the gun fell into the mass of rats far below. So, no gun now and no way to get another. Empty anyway, empty and now gone.

Wallowing in the filth that had cushioned her, she struggled to her feet. Her head cracked the ceiling so hard that there was a flash in her eyes. But at least there were no rats here. Rubbing her head, she was gathering herself together when something flew at her out of the blackness. Pain shot up her neck, and she grabbed into the black, finding fur, a thick, squirming body, a wildly whipping tail. She dragged the rat off her and dug her fingers into its neck until the screaming was reduced to a low crackle, then to silence, and the squirming gradually became disorganized, then ended.

She listened. Nothing, not around her. They didn't infest this place, they couldn't get up here. This one must have come up clinging to her jeans. She threw it down and got out the lighter. Holding it high, she lit it again.

She was in a sort of room . . . and all around her were wonders. Gilded frames glowed in the half-light, knights marched across a rotting tapestry, golden objects lay in a pile against the far wall. Amazed, her hands shaking, she put down her lighter and lifted one of them from the heap.

She recognized it at once, and what she saw stabbed her heart through with the dear torture of fond memory. She was holding a monstrance, used in Catholic benedictions to display the communion wafer, called by Catholics the host, and believed to contain the actual spirit of Christ.

Leo had not laid eyes on a monstrance since she was twelve years old. She had been a member of the choir at St. Agnes School, Bronxville, and the sudden, totally unexpected appearance of this object in this impossible place shocked away a lot of years and a thick crust of life.

She held the heavy object, gazing into the dark crystal porthole where once the white wafer had been placed by reverent priestly hands. She saw there her childhood face, its heart shape so perfectly beautiful that she groaned aloud.

"It's gold," she said to the darkness. She had come upon a horde of stolen treasure. And what treasure. The paintings were ruined, just rotting canvas and a few pitiful, flaking patches of paint. But they were magnificent examples of the Hudson River School, revealing the ghosts of grand Catskill vistas and distant, sunny days. It was the world in its truth and perfect beauty, and she saw with total clarity that the hand that had painted it was guided by something that could only be described as sacred—deeply sacred—and she regretted deeply that these miraculous creations had been left here to their ruin.

There were craters in the walls, each one filled by a dark lead meteorite, and she knew what those craters were. Bullets, huge ones, had blasted this place. They accounted for the ripped sockets in the paintings and the unrecognizable colored glass fragments on the floor, and the pearls and rubies and emeralds rolling in the dust, and the oddly twisted frock coat and splayed cellophane collar that she knew contained a broken body, gray with dust and torn full of gaping holes, but undecayed.

Then she saw something gleaming there that she thought was a diamond, and instinctively reached out, drawn to the glitter as men have been to shiny objects since we swept the forest tops of the past in screaming packs. And when she did, she reached toward the living eye of a vampire who had lain here these long years, too broken to mend himself, but still possessed of a deathless consciousness.

Don't ever touch them, Sarah Roberts had warned her, and when the arm moved and cold, bone-hard fingers closed around her wrist, she knew why, for she was trapped as certainly as she would have been by a blue steel handcuff. And then she saw the teeth appearing behind the crackling, shattering lips, as the black, dry-cured ropes of muscles twisted the parched skin in a smile that managed to communicate hate and cruelty and wicked, sneering irony. How could you do this, it seemed to say, you wretched little animal?

Instinct took over, and she hammered at it and shrieked and threw herself back. The body came to pieces, the whole arm coming with the hand that had grabbed her, ripping off the shoulder with a dry, crunching sound, and the dull *pop* of the bone leaving its socket.

When she dragged it off herself, the fingers began clattering like a scorpion's pincers as the hand expended itself helplessly in the muck that covered the floor.

She leaped up, clawing at the ceiling as a drowning submariner might claw at the iron that confined him. She stumbled forward, falling toward and then through a rotted Gobelins tapestry. She staggered, fell again, hit a wall, and slid along it. She turned, feeling something soft, then pressed deep into some kind of material.

Light appeared, *light!* The lighter was gone, but it didn't matter now, because there was light behind this wall of cloth. She pushed her way through and suddenly was in a place so altogether different from where she had been that she wallowed in confusion, tumbling to the floor in a heap of cloth. Swimming, struggling, she tore the material away from her face and dragged herself to her feet—and found herself standing in the lower-level men's department at Bloomingdale's, which she had entered by crashing through a rack of overcoats that had been recessed into a wall.

The monstrance still clutched tightly in her hands, she looked from face to face—an elderly customer whose tongue was slowly passing behind his lips, a woman who barked out a sound somewhere between laughter and terror, a salesman whose face filled with question so innocently pure that it melted the years in an instant, and turned him into an astonished little boy.

A tall man, black, who had been trying on the jacket of a very fine suit, had the presence of mind to say, "Well, damn." Then his teenage daughter, fumbling in her purse, asked in a sweet, neatly composed voice, "May I have your autograph?"

CHAPTER ELEVEN

The Music Room

Lilith clicked a button on the thick wand again, surfing as fast as the controls would allow. It still seemed slow, as the screen changed from image to image. When she had calmed down enough to explore her new surroundings, she had understood that the SONY wasn't a window, but rather that it contained thousands upon thousands of pictures painted in such extraordinary detail that they seemed real. They were being run rapidly together to create the illusion, in a slow-registering human eye, of movement. If she unfocused, she would also see them that way. However, a little attention revealed the truth: she was really looking at streams of discreet images.

It was hard to imagine the number of people that must be involved in creating them, but the motive was clear enough. The pictures were used to inform. Although there was writing involved in human life as well, this seemed the more important means of communication. Using the clock that she'd found on the wrist of the woman who had occupied this chamber, she had counted 750 of the pictures in half a circuit of the sweep hand across its face. She did not measure time in such detail, any more than she could imagine anybody making so many pictures. And they flowed onto the screen from many different directions. How there could be so many in the SONY and yet it not be filled was quite a mystery.

One or two of the picture sequences were in other languages, but most were in English. She'd heard nothing else spoken here, so she had used the SONY to improve her smattering. She had followed conversational exercises with Humphrey Bogart and Lauren Bacall, Robert Mitchum and John Wayne. These were distinguished from other material in the SONY by the fact that they involved long dialogues about the persons and items pictured, and so could be used by the student to learn the language. She would stop at the images in gray tones, as they afforded the best likelihood of getting useful conversation.

From looking at the pictures, she had concluded that mankind's world had become vast indeed. Cairo wasn't the center of anything. This mighty place was the center. Or another one, full of white monuments, perhaps was the center, or a third, distinguished by a great, tapering tower called an eiffel. She had seen trains for the first time, planes and plane crashes, Ted Heath and Rosie O'Donnell and Louis Pasteur, George Costanza, Oprah Winfrey and Queen Noor, Wolf Blitzer and Adolf Hitler, all for the first time. She had understood Adolf Hitler immediately, wondered if he wasn't in some way a creation of Keepers, placed in a position of power to cause mayhem and slow the growth of human population. Stalin the same, and communism, which had obviously been contrived by Keepers to reduce human economic vitality.

She could see that they had worked hard, all through the last century, to stop the march of man. As they had failed, they had been forced to hide in the tunnels that were their traditional means of movement through cities, and there they had been trapped. She'd seen enough in the dungeons below this city to know what had happened. The humans had invaded their places, somehow getting past the ancient blinds that concealed Keeper passages from man's eyes.

Then she clicked past a picture that startled her. She went back to it. A huge room, a woman on a stage singing. The music was of no importance, but the leather-clad creature had a glow about her that Lilith recognized instantly. She watched. There came a close-up of the woman's face. Lilith watched with the greatest care. Because this . . . no, the woman wasn't a Keeper. Then the picture flashed to another view of the woman singing in another context. Words began to move up the screen: "Silver Dreams," and the woman on the screen sang, *"Silver dreams fly me away, silver dreams save my soul . . ."* Her voice was hard-edged and yet resonant, much richer than a normal human voice. It was interrupted by a hollering male: "Call 1-800-999-0020 right now, and you get not only Leo's greatest hits, we'll add Leo Patterson Intimate Moments, both for $19.98. Remember, these special Leo editions are not sold in stores."

Behind the screaming words, the voice of Leo Patterson continued. Slowly, Lilith came to her feet. She knew what she was looking at, she knew precisely. This lovely creature was a blooded human being. Then, abruptly, the scene changed to an idiot kissing a crocodile.

Lilith sat stunned. *Blooded!* Oh, joy, there was life yet in this benighted world, and look how they loved her! There had been a huge audience, the man screaming his words from excitement! And blooded, blooded, so feeding. Yes, she would be an ally, she must be.

Lilith paced, thinking how to get into the SONY. How to go in the pictures? Was there a tunnel inside? Oh, she had to go!

She rushed to the SONY, but it was attached by mere rope to the wall. Nobody could be inside, it was too small. So, by what enchantment, then . . .

Oh, the humans were so great, and she was so small, but there was this blooded woman somewhere, somebody to help her, to love her.

She rushed up and down the floor, up and down, trying to think, to understand. But she understood nothing, she knew that.

There had been a number. "Call," he had said. That was it, the thing that contained voices that stood on a small table—it also had a pad arranged with numbers. She went to it, pressed the correct sequence.

Nothing happened. She did it again. Still nothing. A hard knot evolved in her throat. She might survive if she found this bloodling. Survive! She had not thought of this possibility. She'd been trying to understand how to be rendered to ash and not dismembered, that was all she had hoped to achieve.

But now—she pressed the numbers again, then again.

Or perhaps this thing had nothing to do with it. She went to the SONY, held the wand to her face, and shouted the numbers. Then she shouted them at the images on the screen. Then she pressed them into the pad on the wand.

Nothing, nothing, nothing!

What might it be, then? She went back to the thing on the table. She had picked the part of it up that appeared designed to fit against the head and heard buzzings and beeps. She did this again. The buzzing lingered for a moment, then became a series of beeps.

Pressing buttons, she eventually got a voice saying, "The number you have dialed, 3336699, is not in service. Please check the number and try again."

She pressed the number the man had shouted. "The number you have dialed requires that a one be dialed first."

She did it again.

"Heartstrings Music, your order, please."

"Hey, sister, put Leo on the line."

"Excuse me."

"Gimme Leo, sister."

"You want the Patterson album?"

"Say again, sweetheart? I'm not getting your drift."

"Do you want the Patterson special?"

It was gibberish. Lilith put the device back in its cradle. Gentle tears rained down on the machine. How she hated this world! Oh, what a hideous, confusing, impossible place! She stood up, went to the window, stared out across the cliffs carved with windows, and screamed.

Outside, birds were flushed by the sound. On a roof across the way, men stopped their work and held their ears, then looked with wide eyes in the direction of this place. She stepped back out of view. She threw herself back onto the sleeping couch.

Suddenly there was a noise. It was a bell ringing very rapidly, repeating itself in intervals. It seemed to invite her to pick up the speaking instrument. She did so.

"Good afternoon, Mrs. Perdu, we have you checking out today."

What did this mean? She had no idea. "Perdu" could be the name of the creature she'd stunned and later eaten, which had been in here when she arrived. Its remains were dust on the floor of the clothing cupboard. "Okay, mister."

"Okay! Well, actually it's three-thirty, and we do need the room."

"Sure thing, kid."

"So when will you be out?"

"I will be out when, so okay."

"Excuse me?"

"Okay, kid, we'll do it your way."

"Uh, I'll send up a bellman."

"You do that, sweetheart."

She replaced the speaking and listening piece into its cradle. What to do now? Her one object was to find that exquisite blooded creature, who represented hope and life for her. But the place was a vast maze, and everything was so mysterious. Where might she be if not at the other end of the stated number?

She whipped around, startled by tapping. What was it? At the door, a persistent tapping, then repeated more loudly. She went closer, listened. Breathing through nostrils slightly closed by swelling. Tired, yet young breathing. A male. And yes, she smelled its skin.

She went into the clothing cupboard and drew on some of Perdu's clothes. She chose the ones that seemed most in keeping with her station. The dress glittered with tiny bits of metal sewn to it, and clung to her form very, very tightly.

The tapping came again, louder yet. To the breathing, add muttered words, "Fuckin' bitch . . . c'mon . . ." *Taptaptap! Taptaptap!*

She put on bright red sandals with tall spikes inexplicably fixed to the heels and went lurching across to the door. Who would want to wear such things?

Taptaptap!

She opened the door to a young man in black clothing.

"Miss Perdu, they sent me up to help you with your bags."

The creature had a nice flush. Too bad she was quite full. As he regarded her, she watched the pupils expand. For what reason was she surprising him? She stepped back, allowing him into the room. She did not want to appear unusual. The humans would destroy her in an instant, she was certain of it.

"You going to a party, ma'am?"

"I am going to a party."

"Okay."

She wondered what this "party" might be.

He moved to the cupboard, then turned around.

"Where are they?"

"They?"

"Your bags. Aren't you checking out?"

"I am checking out."

"But your clothes—everything's still hung up."

"You got it, baby."

"You need to pack. Do you understand English?"

"Sure thing."

He muttered, "The hell you do." Then he said, "Where are you from?"

"Egypt."

"Oh, boy. Look, I'm gonna help you." He removed a large, black case from the cupboard, then took some of the clothing and laid it on the couch. "You remember, you packed before you came here?"

"You better believe it."

"Look, my guess is, you have somebody who packs for you at home. I can do this, if you don't mind."

"Okay by me."

He began putting the clothing in the cases that he brought out of the cupboard. His busy hands pushed the dust off the bottoms of the cases, the dust of the real Perdu. He could have massaged Lilith with those strong young hands, but she never wanted to be touched by a human again.

She followed him into the narrow, unadorned corridor. He carried Mrs. Perdu's materials on a gleaming brass platform that rolled along on wheels, a very pretty workman's tool. Then they went into another machine, a small room that had a sliding door. It was like the little moving room aboard *Seven Stars,* and after a moment the doors slid open again. The man pushed his platform with the bags upon it out of the room. Lilith followed, trying to conceal her wonder at the opulence of the hall that spread before them.

Thus did she descend into the glittering, eerie netherworld of man.

You think you have something decent happening at last, and it all goes to hell immediately. What stupid piece of shit had dropped that tab on him?

Some jerk that didn't want him at Stuy, but why not? What was the matter with him that he didn't know? He paced his room. God, but it was small. All these Leo posters, the junk of an infatuated child. But her concert was tonight and everything, and he wanted to be there so damn much. Just to see her. It wasn't much to ask, but when you're dealing with absolute, total grounding, it's a lot. Didn't they realize that she hadn't performed in public since he was a little kid? You never got to see her except on the tube, that was the thing. Shit, though, what would it be—four seconds of watching her run down a red carpet and into a club where he was not allowed?

That Mal had done it. He'd given him the rave flyer, then dropped his tab on him when all of a sudden there were these cops there. Mal Sweeter, that was his name. Sweeter, yeah. Yeah, real sweeter, you prick. Prickface asshole.

He'd been signed up for Classical Lit and Particle Physics and everything, dammit. He'd e-mailed Jack and Sherry and all the kids, they were going to all meet in the city next weekend and do a rave with him and then go back to his place and make this incredible breakfast and crash for the day. He never went outside the law. A CIA kid didn't have latitude, and he respected that. He could rave, but not do drugs or drink, never, no way. It could affect somebody's career, and there was no way he'd ever do anything to hurt his mom and dad.

"Believe it," he shouted into the silence of his room. He'd been in here since they'd returned from the city at four A.M., and he was as hungry as hell. "Mom?" It wasn't that he was mad at them—they'd been very understanding. Dad had said, "I choose to believe my son," and that had meant a lot after two hours in a holding tank with a bunch of scared kids and scum the likes of which he had never even imagined existed before. He'd just been so damn embarrassed, that was it. He'd ridden all the way up here in the backseat, not saying a word. He'd been congealing inside. He wished he could be in the trunk.

When he got up at ten, they were gone, and they'd now been gone all day. Well, that was about par. First, he loses the best thing he ever had in his life because he got royally screwed, then when he can finally face them and try to explain, they're gone.

He went downstairs. The house was quiet. So where were they? Off on some mission, probably. He didn't even know what they did. It involved investigating people, that much he knew. But who and why, he had no idea. Dad had explained to him how "need-to-know" keeps secrets where they belong, but he would at least like to have known if their job was dangerous.

He was in the kitchen when the phone rang.

"Mom!"

"Hi, hon, I'm on my cell. We're just about buried in work, and we've got a concert tonight, so we're going to change down here and then go straight on."

"What're you gonna see?"

"Your heartthrob, Leo herself. It's not your father's kind of music, but we got given the tickets, so he really can't say no."

It was as if his soul had just drained out of his body and buried itself forever six feet under.

"Ian?"

"Mom—"

"Honey?"

"Mom, I . . . I . . . you guys have a good time."

"Well, *I* will. You know how his nibs hates anything post about 1790." She stopped. He listened. The phone in his hand felt like some kind of a lifeline. "Oh, hon, you're disappointed."

He forced himself to be steady and solid. His voice would not break. "Yeah," he said, and listened to the word shatter like glass.

"These tickets were given to us by a very wealthy man, and we can't just not show up. They cost thousands."

"I know what they cost. Ten grand to the Environment Fund for each one."

"The Environment Fund, is that it?"

"Anyway, it doesn't matter if I'm grounded, does it? Even though I didn't do anything except get shafted by some jerk."

"Hon, we would take you if we could. But—"

"You and I could've gone, Mom. He doesn't even want to go. He hates Leo."

"It's a working evening for us." It was Dad's voice, rumbling down the line.

"Hi, Dad."

"Hi, buddy. I just want you to know, it's in the line of work. We're going because we have to."

"Dad, this may sound crazy to you—"

"Try me."

"Could I come down and watch? Be in the crowd outside?"

"Son—"

"We could go out afterward and have a late supper together, then all stay at the apartment."

He should have asked Mom, he definitely should not have done it this way, he'd been a total fool.

"I don't think—"

"Okay, forget it."

"I got you out of night court at four in the morning, and no, I do not think you should break grounding before twenty-four hours are up. Watch it on TV."

"It's not on TV."

"With that publicity hound, I'd have thought it would be."

When he said that, angry sparks shot through Ian. He managed a polite good-bye and hung up the phone. For a moment, he thought that he could not be angrier at his dad. Nobody ever said Paul Ward wasn't arrogant. He'd sit in there staring and not smiling and not even lift a hand in applause. That's exactly what would happen.

Damn Dad and damn the entire world.

Except . . .

No, he shouldn't do this. No, they'd be sure to call here at some point, and . . . he could forward the phone to his cell. Simple.

But no, they'd get back way before he did.

Except . . .

He could just see the entrance, then take the next train home. He'd be here in plenty of time. And at least—well, wasn't this a little crazy, to want this much just to see some girl from a distance who you would never touch, you would never speak to, who would never know you existed.

He hammered numbers into the phone, waited for his cell to ring, then hung them both up. Deed done, he was on his way to the damn *promised land!*

Lilith was made to stand before an altar with other supplicants, and soon found herself confronted by a heavily scented priest with a blue silk ribbon knotted neatly around his neck. She had fallen back on lack of knowledge of English to let the acolytes conduct her through the ritual. She was enmeshed in a whole series of arcane acts involving small inscribed shields that were kept in a packet that, it initially developed, she had left behind in the room.

The young male had retrieved it, and now the priest was completing his rituals with one of the shields. What material was it made of that caused them to value it so? It had not the beauty of gold or lapis lazuli. In fact, she'd never seen anything quite like it before, and there were a dozen of them in the leather packet the young man had handed her with such pride. And this ritual of the priest—what might it mean? Afterward he smiled at her, so she assumed that whatever he had read from her shield had offered good portents.

Man, always calling on his gods, looking to the skies or the entrails of sheep or the blowing of the leaves upon an errant wind for guidance—did he not know, even yet, that time unfolded into the silence of God, and destiny had another name called chance?

"May I call you a cab?" the young man asked.

The intonation suggested a question. Apparently he wished to address her in some new manner, now that the priest had given her the required blessing.

"You may call me a 'cab,'" she said.

Improbably, he rushed into the roadway with a small brass whistle and began blowing it furiously. She was well aware by now that she was at sea among a vast number of customs that were quite beyond her understanding. This would require vigilance and care. Every moment, every new and bizarre request, presented another danger.

Soon, a yellow carriage pulled up at her feet. As a newly invested acolyte or priestess or whatever she was, it seemed that she was expected to go about in this thing. There were many of them on the road; it appeared to be a commonplace enough privilege. She entered the machine.

The young man stared at her. Another man put the cases in a compartment behind. Of a sudden, the smile disappeared from the young man's face. "It takes all kinds," he finally said with a snarl, and slammed the door.

"All kinds," she replied as the vehicle pulled in among the other vehicles of the honored.

"Where to, lady?"

"To where."

"Where you goin'?"

"Allô."

"Shit, lady, you don't speak English. What you do speak? *Parlez-vous français?*"

His incantation was in two languages, she could discern that readily enough. After the conquest and the arrival of the Greek ruler Ptolemaeus, the Egyptians had begun to speak Hellene. Perhaps these had also been conquered, and this "parlez-vous" was a snippet of the language of the conqueror, used as the Egyptians had used Hellene, to display their familiarity with the court of the new pharaoh.

"Parlez-vous français," she responded.

"Ah, bon! Je suis d'Haïti. Si, où est-ce que nous allons?"

"Si, nous allons."

"Pardon? Mais où?"

"Mais? Ah, si!"

"Que?"

The meanings of these words were unclear to her. She struggled to devise a sensible-sounding response. After the ritual, she had been escorted into the vehicle. Now all the questioning made it clear that she had to instruct the driver. Then she recalled the use of the word *change,* by the young man when they were still in the room of the woman Perdu. "I change," she said.

"Okay, back to English. You change. Where do you go?"

"I go where I change."

He hit the steering wheel.

"Leo Patterson," she said. It was a name. It was also where she wanted to go.

"You mean the Music Room? You're going to the concert at the Music Room?"

"The Music Room."

Muttering spells, he accelerated into traffic. The vehicle moved past an array of amazing structures. They were not cliffs carved with rooms as she had first believed, but enormous constructions built by the hand of man. As she had been by the bridge and the great statue in the harbor, she was awed by these human things.

The towers of this place jutted up into a sky of bright, hard blue, smeared with racing white clouds. The air was colder than it had been at home in many a long year, and she enjoyed the feeling of it on her face as it blew in the window.

Suddenly, looking up at the sky, feeling the cool, she realized that she was remembering something from home. It was only a fleeting recollection, but she knew, now, that she had gone beneath a flowering plum tree to sleep, and in her sleep had dreamed, and was dreaming still. . . .

"You okay?"

She used the intonations and accents she had learned from the SONY. "You got that right, buster."

"Hey, Lauren Bacall!"

She had so little idea of what he had just said that she did not even try to reply.

Her heart was leaping in her chest, her skin was prickling, and she felt the most poignant, acute sense that she was missing something important, that another, beloved life—her real life—was passing her by.

"Lady, you can't be taking all that luggage to the Music Room. You're goin' to a hotel. Have to be. So, you tell me, what hotel?"

That was familiar, "hotel." It was the name of the temple in which she had lived and worshiped. "Hotel Royalton."

"No, the Royalton's the one we're leaving. Bye-bye, Royalton, get it? Finished. No more."

Ah, yes. "Leo Patterson," she repeated, hoping that this might elicit further results.

This was apparently the correct response, because the driver's face illuminated with a broad smile of a kind she had not seen in a very long time. The humans were monsters, but a smile is a smile, and she could not help but respond in kind.

"Leo lives at the Sherry," he said.

"Yes."

They went up and down some streets, crossed a wide plaza, and pulled up before one of the great towers. "I can drive the wagon," Lilith said. "I have done it before."

She could see in a small mirror the expression on the driver's face, which revealed that this comment was not expected. So her thought that he had stopped from fatigue was wrong.

The door was suddenly flung open by a male in resplendent clothing, obviously a human of great importance. She was guided out as others placed her bags on a rolling platform. So the ritual was to be repeated here. Man had always enjoyed ritual, but this business of being unable to so much as walk three steps without yet more of it was absurd.

She was conducted to another altar in the opulent new temple, and again did the ritual with the card. "I am already a 'cab,' " she explained to the priest when he began to swipe the thing through the various magical sigils that were employed here.

He glanced at her in such an odd way that she decided that she was growing overconfident, and stopped speaking.

"I don't see your reservation, Mrs. Perdu."

"Ah, good."

"No, I don't have a reservation for you. Let me—" He signaled another priest, who came majestically forward, his eyebrows raised, his chin high. If she understood anything at all about religion, her response had caused a higher priest to be engaged in the ceremony, which was all to the good.

"Yes, Mr. Friedman?"

The first priest replied in an incancatory undertone. "We don't have a reservation here."

The other murmured. "She looks like she's dressed for a party."

Now they whispered. Lilith heard every sound, of course. "The cabbie told the door that she's going to the Patterson do."

"Oh, Jesus. Put her in a suite."

Now they both turned to her with great smiles on their faces. "Welcome to the Sherry-Netherland, Mrs. Perdu. You'll be in the Rose Suite, very nice." He rang a little bell. More of the creatures swarmed over her trolley of bags.

"Leo is here?"

"Oh, I believe that she's rehearsing over at the club."

"Ah. I will go there."

"Would you care for the hotel to provide you with a car and driver for your stay?"

"Yes."

"Very good. And when will you be leaving this evening? I think that the club's only—oh, ten minutes at most. Fifteen. Perhaps seven-thirty?"

"Seven-thirty."

They went into another of the rising and falling compartments, this one far more opulent than the Royalton, as was the entire place. She was beginning to see that the entry and exit rituals were the only religious aspect of the place. These were really apartments of rooms where people stopped to rest. She wondered if they all carried their possessions about like this all the time. What sort of arcane lives must they live if they did this, darting about like flies, never stopping in any one place for long?

The chambers they gave her had sun pouring in the tall windows, illuminating the rose pink decorations, the tables and chairs, and the stuffed couches and such very nicely. Instead of one room, there were a number of rooms. In this one was placed sitting furniture, in another a broad table. At the far end of the wide, tapestry-thrown floor was another chamber, this one containing a large couch made of gleaming brass. She had not seen so much space, or such nice space, since she was at home.

The inevitable young man who had come with her laid the bags upon the couch in the other room. "How long will you be with us?" he asked.

"For eternity," she replied.

He laughed slightly. "I know what you mean. This is such a great suite."

She saw the water room. It actually had a pool in it. Almost automatically, she stood awaiting service, but he did not comply. She did not know how to order a slave in English, so she said, simply, "Bathe me."

He came in. "Uh—you want to know how to use the bath?" Grinning, his face flushed, he twiddled levers.

Water came out in copious flow, dropping into the pool. She awaited his ministrations, but he backed out of the room. Immediately thereafter, he had withdrawn altogether. "I'll send you a maid," he shouted as he left.

Soon another slave arrived, this one a female, a short, dark Nubian, not one of the tall blacks from Punt. "May I help you?" she asked.

"Give me a hand, sister," Lilith said. She was feeling helpless and frustrated. She had the uneasy feeling that nothing was quite as it seemed.

"That's gonna run over, sweetheart," the Nubian woman said. She made the water stop flowing into the bath. Lilith could have done it, but she was determined to make these slaves act in the way she wanted them to. Surely she could still command a slave.

"Bathe me," she said.

"You want me to give you a bath?"

At last, that response made some sense. She was finally getting through to these idiots. "You got that right, kiddo!"

"Well, lady, I don't think I got hired for givin' nobody no bath. Look, you take your own bath, and I'll put up your clothes. How's that?" She went and busied herself with the bags and the cupboard.

Lilith wasn't going to whip a slave belonging to a temple, but this was getting ridiculous. She removed her clothing and had the bath, soaking until the water grew cool, then cold. The Nubian had left long before, left without a word.

She arose then, and dressed herself, this time in coarse, black leather that reminded her unpleasantly of the beautiful cloak that she had lost.

She went to a window. The light had gone. She knew that she had spent a whole day in the bath, or the better part of it, but she often did this. Or even more time. In Rome, she had once spent a very long time in the baths of Hadrian, at his villa, perhaps a week it had been. He'd had proper slaves that were properly trained.

A box on the wall near to hand commenced ringing. A voice said, when she finally got it properly fitted to her ear: "Your car is waiting."

* * *

Ian hurried through the streets, heading up from Grand Central to the Music Room. There was a big crowd of fans, of course, but that didn't bother him. He'd done this before, at premieres and openings of various kinds. He loved to attend, and he knew the ropes. There were even some familiar faces. The expectant tension in the air told him as he walked up that Leo had not yet arrived.

As soon as he'd began working forward, he noticed an unaccustomed nervousness in the crowd. He saw Ruthie R., a pro autograph collector. "What's the story?"

"Word is she's already inside."

"She'll come out."

"Yeah, sure."

Ian was confident. "She will. I know Leo."

He watched some shadow arrivals, so called because the TV crews killed their lights as soon as they saw it was a nobody. It was kind of fun to watch the nobodies think they were getting the big *entrada,* then having their lights cut. Mean fun.

Then, electricity. A second later, excitement. The *E!* crew hurried out onto the mat. This one was for real. Huge excitement. Autographs jostled to the rope. The limo door was drawn open by a flunkie, and out came Penelope Cruz. She was splendid in a white silk dress as slight as a breeze. After a few seconds with *E!* she made a fabulous entrance, glowing under the lights like the goddess that she was. She actually stopped on the other side for a couple of seconds. She was signing, God love her grace, Penny.

Ruthie R. made her move, Ian giving her the help she needed. And then the actress was right there, looking absolutely amazing up close, so perfect, so rich, so . . . human that Ian felt for a moment levitated by her mere presence. This was star quality, this was what it was all about.

They began to come in thick then, one after another, the most stunning array of genuine bigs that anybody even in this jaded NYC crowd had ever seen. Bowie, Clooney, Gibson, Paltrow, Roberts, Zellweger: it looked like the academies. But no Leo. So they waited, making a recognition game around the passage of moguls. Ian saw his parents go in, watched them with hungry eyes. How he would love to be with them, to be going in there, to—oh, shit, it was an awful moment for him, no other way to describe it. He kept well back. Dad was terrifyingly observant, like some kind of juiced-up eagle or something. He could count the hairs on a speeding rat, Dad could.

Then he noticed—as they all were noticing—that a car had pulled up at the front, a particularly magnificent car, and that it was quiet and dark, nothing moving. *E!* started its setup. More cameras arrived. "Michael Jackson," the whisper ran.

"Here we go," Ruthie murmured.

The driver came around and opened the door. A woman began to emerge, blond, tall. The crowd seemed to utter a sigh. This was not Leo.

But this woman—Ian had never seen anybody like her. She was oddly but fabulously dressed, in a black leather business suit with no shirt and apparently no damn bra. Her hair was blond and soft, lingering like smoke around her head. She looked about twenty, twenty-three, no more than that. Her eyes were powder blue.

"Who *is* that?"

"It's the most beautiful woman in the world," somebody said.

As she came forward, Ian had the strange feeling that she was connecting with him. Then an actual, physical shock went through him, as if she'd reached out across the thirty feet of space and people and brazenly put her hand on his crotch. The sensation was so real and so pleasurable that an erection shot up like the mushroom cloud over Hiroshima.

She stopped. She was directly opposite him, just a few feet away. When their eyes met, he felt a kind of delirium, as if a hundred voices were all shouting at him, demanding something of him, something that he did not understand but wanted to understand.

Who was this woman, and why in the world was she singling him out like this? She said something—uttered what sounded to him like a command—using a language he'd never heard before. She waited for a response. Her face was so incredibly perfect, he almost passed out. She was the most pretty, the sweetest, girl and the sexiest woman he had ever seen all wrapped up into one. Her eyes shone like a perfect blue sky, her lips, complex with laughter, innocent and yet . . . not . . . her lips parted a little. And she was interested in him—*him!* Why was she doing this? What was going on here? He felt himself start to shake. Then the eyes captured his eyes—literally captured them, there was no other word for it. A tide of some kind of fire poured into his brain, like lava flowing out of her and into him.

Then he felt pain—a cuff around his wrist. He looked down. Her hand had darted forward like the head of a snake. She'd grasped his wrist so fast that he couldn't believe it, that her hand could be there, and that her hand could feel so much like steel. She drew him toward her, knocking over the precious ropes beyond which you did not go unless you wanted to get booted. She dragged him right out into the entry aisle. Turning, pushing aside William H. Macy and Meryl Streep, she strode into the lobby of the Music Room, Ian in tow behind her. He stumbled along in his jeans and sweatshirt and fannish sneakers, in a kind of ecstasy of amazed fear.

The lobby was blazing with celebrities, officials from the Environment Fund, bigwigs of every stripe—and him, a kid in street drag being towed along by some kind of a he did not know what.

"Hey, you—"

It was Big Joe Peak, a famous celeb guard. He knew all the groupies by sight.

"She's got my arm!"

"Out. Now. Or you get the cooler."

"Look, I don't want to be here—"

She dragged him off like a puppy on a leash. Big Joe Peak's huge hand closed around his shoulder.

But there, resplendent in green silk, was Leo. Big Joe, Ian—they both froze. Incredibly, Leo did the same. She looked into the woman's eyes just like Ian had, he saw her do it, and he saw an explosion in her, too. But it was different from what had happened to him, it was more. Because Leo seemed to go into some kind of shock. Like, she was trembling. Like, she was going pale. Like, tears were filling her eyes.

Big Joe instantly calculated that this did not add up to what he had been expecting. His hand dropped off Ian's shoulder, but he remained right there, his sour breath washing the back of Ian's neck.

Leo wore emeralds matched to her eyes, and a grand cloud of a dress of the richest, most gorgeous silk Ian had ever seen. Her face was a vision of the purest beauty that there was or ever could be, the chin pointing a little, just enough to make it a heart, to emphasize the innocence that flickered in her eyes and the sensuality that touched her smile like a dangerous shadow.

The eyes widened. The lips dropped open. Then she blinked fast, surveying the woman before her from inside a rain of tears. The silence of the two women spread to the surrounding celebrities. It extended for a beat, then another, and now the whole room fell silent.

"You've come," Leo said. Her voice was faint, trembling.

"I want to see your Keeper."

"My Keeper—my Keeper . . . oh . . . I'm sorry."

The strange woman drew Ian forward, gathered him around the shoulder. Big Joe tried to pull him back.

"Get outa here, fella," she hissed at him. "Take a powder, and fast."

Why in the world was she talking like some film noir black widow or whatever? Whatever, he evaporated like so much sea foam, Big Joe did. She thrust Ian into Leo's face. He could see her chest rising and falling with what must be a thundering heart. Her makeup was running down her cheeks, running in the tears that were spitting from her eyes. "This one," the lady said, "he will be your Keeper."

"H-him?"

"Of course, he is of my blood! Can't you see it?"

Leo looked at him, her eyes now frantic.

"I—don't—get—it," he said through clenched teeth.

But Leo apparently did. She looked him up and down, then said to the woman who held his shoulders, "He's so beautiful."

"Of course he is beautiful. He is of my blood."

Leo reached toward him, her face filling with worship, adoration, even. Her trembling fingertips caressed his cheek. He did not react, could not. He knew that what he was feeling now was shock. He couldn't even begin to imagine what was happening here.

Leo said, "W-will you love me?"

Frantically, he inventoried the past twenty-four hours. Some damn asshole had slipped him LSD at the rave. Because this was not happening. This was not possible. Leo Patterson was not begging him to love her.

The lights flashed. Leo said, "Come with me." She moved off down a side aisle, Ian and the woman following, a very confused Big Joe a few steps behind.

A man rushed up to her. "We're overbooked," he shrieked, "there's been a computer glitch! Jack Nicholson brought six people, and I don't have space!"

"Put these people down in front."

He looked them up and down. "Excuse me, but that's impossible."

"The center table."

"You gave that table to Kitty Carlisle Hart!"

"Put her in the men's room."

"It's full!"

"Then put her in the basement. And Nicholson."

"There's no seating in the basement."

Leo strode off. "Just fix it," she said.

The man looked them up and down. "Who in God's name *are* you? And what are you doing in that—didn't you read the invitation?" The man was looking directly at Ian—glaring, his eyes crazed.

"I—I—don't know. Uh—"

"Oh, God, come on!"

The woman followed him, never varying her regal motion as she progressed through the crowd. Dad and Mom were probably somewhere off in the balconies with the other no-names. He allowed himself a small thrill of pleasure when he considered what they might think when they saw him down here in the glitter and the pomp. Very different from getting caught outside. This was, like, incredibly impressive. Was Dad ever going to wonder what was going on! Thing was, he didn't know either. He had no damn idea, *way* no damn idea! All he knew was, he was with one incredible woman, and he had just met a star who was like a goddess to him, and this star had acted like he was her lord and master.

It was a dream that felt real. He could pinch himself, and it would work, but this was still—well, it just wasn't happening. So okay, let 'er rip.

They got to their table, sat down. There were little caviar thingies on the table, and the waiter brought champagne.

"So," the woman said, "where've you been keeping yourself?"

"Uh, at home."

"I got it. Hey, my handle's Lilith. What's your moniker, buddy?"

"Uh, I'm Ian. Ian Ward."

She lifted her champagne. "Here's lookin' at you, kid."

Chapter Twelve

Stripped

L eo was fighting hard to stop being sick, and George was helping her, holding her as she retched again and again. She'd never had stage fright, and this wasn't stage fright. She had never, ever seen anybody like that woman, never felt anything like she felt right now. Her blood was ringing in her ears, her heart was thundering, and when she shut her eyes during a heave, she saw her again, the most perfect being she had ever beheld.

She shuddered all over. The vampire was a woman, but that was okay. She was completely fabulous, more so even than Miriam. Leo could see now why she had been so careless as to leave a remnant on the dock: she was imperious, an empress of vampires, if they had that. God only knew where she had come from, but Leo absolutely adored her and wanted to serve her and give her happiness and be for her what she had so briefly been for Miriam, that and more. And the boy—of her blood, she had said. He looked it, too, shining, a young Apollo with wisdom and hardness in his eyes. Leo thought: I am going to feel him inside me, and she screamed a little and staggered, then forced herself to soldier on.

"The blood is a magnet," Sarah had said. "Other vampires will drive you wild."

She had wanted so badly to be loved, and she was going to be loved. She was, her. She imagined him. He'd be huge, a wild, savage post sweeping upward, and his muscles would glow in the candlelight, and he would just plain break her in two, he would be so powerful and take so so so long.

"We're on ten minutes ago," George said.

"Oh, Christ. Makeup. Hair."

George clapped. "Kids!"

She went into the dressing room, and Nilda immediately began getting her costume on her. She would wear black leather boots up to the knee, a complex, thonged dress covered with silks and held together by breakaways, and a black collar around her neck dotted with diamonds and emeralds. That was it, nothing under, nothing else. She had a plan for this show; it wouldn't just be music. Until that woman had showed up, she hadn't been sure if she would dare to execute this outrageous plan. But now she would. For sure.

She was going to do it for them, for the angels in the front row, the god and the goddess, and unless hell damn well swallowed her, she was going to fuck their brains out tonight, both of them, until she was spent to ash.

Francie and Lester did makeup and hair. The black lipstick was the good kind that doesn't dry out your lips. Her hair was sprayed, teased, transformed from Maurice's elegant creation into something out of a wilder, harder reality.

"How can I do this?" she whispered.

"You can," George said. "You're so wonderful."

But he didn't know what she was going to do, nobody did but Nilda, who had to have guessed. So his words meant nothing. She felt like a nervous schoolgirl now, like she had the time she'd done a striptease for Bobby Carney and Dan Belton when they were all eleven years old, the way it had felt when she sat naked in Bobby's lap, with her leg over Dan's bare leg, and felt them both as hard as little twigs in their shorts. She had been thrilled and incredibly embarrassed to be the only one naked, and when they had parted her legs, she had felt like she felt right now, deliciously helpless and deliciously, wonderfully exposed. It had never been like that again, except once with Miri and Sarah, in the back of Miri's car, racing downtown in the deep of a wild and druggy night.

I am going to do this, she told herself. I am going to. She took a deep breath, wished with all her soul for a beautiful cigarette. But there could be no cigarette now, not when her voice had to be huge and perfect and as delicate as a chime.

"Okay," she said, as hair and makeup pulled away and she stepped toward the crack in the curtains. "Let's go to the office."

Lilith almost could not release the boy's hand. His beauty had appalled her, had made her instantly desperate. He sat beside her in his rags, glowing with the purest glow she had ever seen from a body. He was not just a Keeper, he was more than a Keeper. From all the Keepers, there was something missing. She had never understood what it was. But something was missing from their eyes that was not missing from this boy's eyes.

She wanted only to embrace him, to press her lips against his, to taste his delicious mouth and breathe his intoxicating breath. Never in this life had she wanted to be under a male, but she wanted so badly to be under this glorious creature that she could hardly bear to sit. If she wasn't in a room full of humans, she would have cast herself on the floor at his feet.

He was not only Apollo, he was Gilgamesh, he was Osiris, he was every imagined lover, he was the boys who had laid her in the golden bowers of child's play and pressed on her until she wept from pleasure.

The boys of childhood? She recalled with gasping force that she dreamed about a boy such as this, a boy who was waiting for her. Yes, he was her husband. Her husband! Oh, yes, and he was waiting.

But where?

She saw a town of stone houses with spreading roofs of wheat-thatch, and in the middle of the square was a beautiful fountain, the Fountain of the Hours. Sitting there was a boy with long legs and tan, muscled arms, dangling his hand in among the fish. He looked up, and his eyes filled with smiles. "Lilith," he said, his voice ringing like the bells of memory.

For a moment, she was actually frantic. He was her husband, they'd just gotten married, she had to get back to him!

Then the lights went out. She sucked breath, tensed, immediately ready for an attack. Silence fell. After a short delay, the beautiful creature

Leo appeared, prancing out onto a little dais. She wore black clothing, tight, and black boots. Her long limbs swayed in the air as she moved around on the stage, keeping time with the rough beat being emitted by men with various musical instruments. Lights played about, flattering her with their brilliance.

I used to be a woman!

What is that?

The fuck is that?

She pointed a leather-clad stick at a male human who sat nearby.

You made me a woman, told me I was a woman.

What is that?

The fuck is that?

She threw off a piece of the clothing. There came from the darkness a stir of movement. The others were reacting strongly to this ritual. Lilith sensed that they disliked it.

I chose what you made me,

I love what I am,

A wo-man, a woo-o-o-man.

I belong to the moonlight.

I am your mother.

You rest in my arms . . .

The music was low now, repetitive, dangerous and yet soft. She was moving more and more directly in front of this table. Lilith began to get the impression that she was singing *to* her.

I will give you every part of me,

Just let me love you, please let me.

Let me let me, please let me,

O let me let me, please let me . . .

She came down off the stage and reached out for Lilith's hand. Her touch was cool and soft, and as the fingers closed, Lilith could feel a firmness that sent a little thrill through her.

Let me let me, please let me, let me let me, please let me . . .

Then Lilith was rising, she was going up on the stage with her, and Leo was guiding her hands, taking her fingers to the snaps and the hooks. She was scented like a maiden and had curved breasts that she now exposed, to the gasps of the faces upraised out there in the shadows.

Let me let me, please let me, let me let me, please let me . . .

The voice was rough but soft, trembling on the stillness. Lilith almost moaned when the singing stopped, it was so gorgeous—like listening to some seductive whisper of the earth itself. She looked out across the room. It was difficult to see out from under the lights, but she knew that she stood before the audience now.

This ritual, then, was about her. The music pounded and sounded gentle at the same time. Leo undulated, and Lilith longed to touch that smooth skin of hers. But also, she wanted the boy. His uplifted face was bright with desire, she could see that.

Leo seemed to know, to be called, perhaps, by the blood, for she leaned down to him, still moving to the music, her breasts like cream in the light, and stretched out her hand as far as she could. "Come on," she said to him, "come on, baby."

"Uh—I—me?"

Let me please let me, let me please let me . . .

She drew the cringing boy closer, smiling at him, urging him until finally he came onto the stage, and in the lights his face was so dear and somehow familiar that Lilith had to fight bursting into tears of joy.

Somewhere, sometime, there had been for her such a boy. "Only an hour," he had said, had promised . . .

Back in the depths of time . . .

So far back that the moment had dipped below the horizon of the real.

Now the dream was here.

"We're entertaining people, here," Leo muttered.

"I—how do I—"

Leo dropped to her knees before him, took his hands to her cheeks. *"Let me please let me,"* she sang.

Watching this, Lilith saw his cheeks flush, saw his pupils dilate, felt the increased heat that flowed from his body.

Leo began unzipping his trousers, and he, a fixed, tense smile on his fresh young face, resisted her, clumsily shuffling, trying to turn away.

Let me let me, please let me. Let me let me, please let me . . .

* * *

His mind had gone numb, he knew that. Looking down at Leo's face was like looking through water. He could feel her hands fooling with his zipper, but he couldn't believe—no—that she would do this on a stage. They were on a stage, yes, that was real. And standing over there in a flaring rush of light was the goddess of the world. She was tall, she had eyes like searchlights, lips that welcomed, and she was looking at him with liquid desire. She was jealous, he could see that.

His pants slipped down to his knees, instantly followed by his underpants.

He looked down, but she was already standing. She came to him, her face fierce now, and with a gesture of greater power than he would have thought possible, ripped his shirt open.

Let me please let me, let me please let me . . .

It was a nightmare, the naked-in-a-crowd nightmare. But it was real, it was happening. The audience was totally silent. He turned away from them, but she put her arms around him and danced with him, her body rubbing him, and he heard, out there, soft clapping as they danced and the drums muttered. He felt the warm, stage-bright air against his skin, and her fingers tight on his buttocks, her long nails just worrying the sensitive rim of his anus.

The stage seemed to get tiny as Becky struggled with a shock so great it had almost knocked her cold. She shook her head, but the stage was still there, two balconies below them, and on it was Ian with his clothes off, and Leo Patterson naked but for a G-string, dancing dirty with him. The most beautiful damn woman in the world stood a couple of feet away, getting out of her ill-fitting clothes.

She joined them, and the three began dancing together.

A few members of the audience were clapping softly to the jungle rumble of the drums, but most were dead silent, as shocked and amazed, Becky knew, as she was.

Paul's hand in hers was cold, hard iron.

She felt the sudden scalding of woe that comes to those who have unexpectedly lost. Even what Ian was doing here was a mystery. He looked bewildered, and his hands kept hopping about like nervous little birds as he pitifully tried to conceal himself. Becky thought that it was the blood: the blood had drawn both Leo and Ian to the vampire. What other explanation could there be? Somehow, they knew or felt by instinct, or the vampire knew—in any case, they had come together, and now they were together, and now Paul would take their lives.

"Let me let me, let me let me," Leo sang. The three of them, more beautiful than the most perfect of statues, danced slowly naked before the stunned-silent audience. They stood face to face, their pale backs and buttocks exposed.

Becky was almost afraid to look at her husband, because of what she feared she would see. But she did look, she had to look—and she saw the worst thing, the most terrible thing that she could possibly see: his eyes were totally blank. He could have been a doll, for all the life that flickered there.

The man was devastated.

"What's happening?" he asked, "what's happening . . ."

Leo broke away from Ian and the vampire. She turned and stepped to the proscenium. Then she bent far forward and slowly came up, until she was leaning far back, her legs spread so wide that her vagina was open to the gaze of the audience.

Somebody yelled something. A flower was thrown, then something heavier.

Ian went to her. Becky had not seen him naked in years, and the perfection of his body—the gleaming muscles, the graceful proportions, shocked her and then embarrassed her, for she found herself looking upon his member with a woman's evaluative interest, not a mother's clinical concern. Then the vampire joined them.

Becky was absolutely fascinated, she could not help but be. In all these years, she had never seen an intact female vampire naked in light. And it was a sight, easily three shades whiter than Leo, who was already pale. Its skin was so completely without the slightest blemish or wrinkle, it looked more like a white latex suit than a body. The mound of Venus was graced by—of all things—blond ringlets. She had her hands over her breasts.

The spectacle of the three naked people on the stage was unforgettable, especially with Leo now doing a limbo beneath an invisible pole, flashing her dark-infested cunt.

They were the most naked, most exposed people Becky had ever seen.

Cameras clicked and clicked, videotape rolled. There was going to be a fantastic sensation because of this. The tabloids were going to go wild. Every TV show in the country would be clamoring for Ian Ward.

How pitiful, and how unimaginably terrible.

Paul stood. He began to slide toward the aisle. Becky followed him. She was glad, because something obviously had to be done, and she didn't know what that would be. She just wanted to save her boy, because one thing was very, very clear: he was in awful trouble.

Paul's heart had been ripped to pieces inside his chest. His soul was plunging down a black shaft of despair. He had known that one day his son might turn, but there had been no sign, no damn sign.

He had to fix what was happening here. No matter what, he had to fix it, and that meant getting Ian off that stage and away from those creatures right now.

The decision made, he began pushing his way toward the aisle. When he reached it, he leaped down the steps from one balcony to the next. Behind him, Becky called in a loud whisper, "Paul, Paul." He couldn't wait, though, because if they got his son, then whatever last chance he might have was over. If Ian had never tasted blood—and Paul suspected from his body language on the stage that he was still totally clueless—then they were going to feed it to him, and if that happened, it was going to be over for Ian. He'd be more than addicted, in Paul's opinion. His body would change, would turn against him, would become unable to live without the food of the vampire.

"What's the plan, dammit!"

He turned on her, almost flared at her. But when he saw that terrified, brave face, the lips tight, the eyes hollow with a mother's fear, he could not help but love her, and the hand that had wanted to push her away instead drew her to him.

"The plan is, we're going down there and getting our kid off that stage, and we are going to do that right now." He started toward one of the doors into the main floor—doors that were each guarded by two armed security personnel. But he stopped, and not because of the guards.

Misinterpreting his hesitation, Becky said, "We can take them."

On the way down the stairs, Paul had experienced something that was totally unexpected, that had never touched him before, not like this. As he had turned away from the nightmare on the stage, he had felt what had to be among the deepest, sweetest emotions he had ever known. He wanted the woman on the stage, and badly, so badly that he felt as if a sort of electrical arc had blasted through him, shorting out his good sense, his morality, everything—except, of course, the duty that kept him hunting down the thieves of human life.

He charged straight toward the guards who stood before the nearest door into the lobby, ignoring their guns. He was a big man and an efficient, well-trained fighter, and he doubled one of them over with a piston-hard blow to his stomach as the other one fumbled for his weapon. The man dropped his head enough for Paul to shove it downward as he slammed a knee into his jaw. The guard, a heavy man with a jiggling pot, dropped like a bag of sand.

Throwing the doors wide, Paul burst through into the auditorium. The music was screaming, Leo was prancing, the vampire standing behind her as still and careful as a snake. Ian had crept to the edge of the stage, was struggling with his pants.

There were no aisles here, just this sea of little tables with arrogant pricks sitting at them in tuxedos, eyeing each other's trophy girls or salivating over the burlesque parody unfolding on the stage.

The music sounded like something from another planet—a bad planet. He couldn't understand the words, but the whole effect was vaguely familiar. He'd heard it a thousand times, in fact, blasting out of the coffin-sized speakers that covered one wall of Ian's room.

Pushing tables over, tossing people aside like so many rag dolls, Paul made his way toward the stage. He was a hundred feet away when somebody tackled him from behind. Hunching his shoulders, whipping his torso forward, he flipped him up and over his head. It was another guard, who went crashing into five or six of the little tables, then disappeared into a heap of dresses, diamonds, and lurching tuxedos.

Leo was staring out into the lights, obviously aware that there was a disturbance out there. But she kept up her performance, still naked, still prancing around, moving like she was on speed. Another body slammed into him from behind, tackling him NFL style. Crunching down on somebody with his left foot, he yanked himself away from the clawing hands. He was within fifty feet of the stage now, and panic was spreading like a tidal wave out from the point where he was crashing through the audience.

Women screamed, men cursed, and Leo finally stopped dancing when she saw guards vaulting up onto the stage. Paul roared his son's name, roared it with all his might, but he could see no reaction from Ian, who was standing about two feet from the band's speakers, which were still blasting away. A guy appeared in front of Paul. He grabbed the tux's lapels, lifted, and dropped the flouncing, squirming man into the heap behind him.

"Ian! Ian!"

Two, then three, guards slammed into him, each shock staggering him. A pistol came out, crashed into the side of his head, making sparks in his eyes and causing the room to take wing and go racing crazily off to the left. He knew what this meant: it meant that he was falling. If he did, he felt that he would not see his son again.

His arms clawed air, as, despite being festooned with at least six strong men, he kept moving toward that stage. "Ian! Ian!"

He reached the edge of the proscenium, grabbed onto its lip—and watched a door close back in the shadows behind the band, and knew that Ian had been ushered through that door with the others. "Ian!"

He went down, then, a huge, roaring grizzly overwhelmed by wolves. Fists smashed into his face again and again, shoes crunched into his ribs, and he ended up compressed under a good thousand pounds of male bone and muscle, his mouth forced open, his tongue pressed against the filthy floor.

Next, his arms were pulled back, cuffs were jammed on his wrists, and the weight on him lessened. When they turned him over, he found himself looking up into twenty angry, scared faces.

Twenty, he thought, isn't bad. He said, "That's my son up there."

One or two of the guards glanced at the empty stage, but nobody reacted. He repeated it, screaming at the top of his lungs, yelling until his voice was the only sound in the room.

The problem was, there was nobody up there—nobody except Becky, whom he saw going into the backstage area.

They dragged him to his feet and started manhandling him out of the theater. Behind him, the audience settled down. The audience began to clap. They wanted their baby back.

"What the fuck was that?" Leo demanded as George dropped a sable around her.

"A nut," George said. "It happens."

"Ian!" A female voice echoed from behind them.

"Mom?"

As Leo looked toward the sound, a frown crossing her face, Lilith heard and knew instantly what was happening. She took the boy by his arm and drew him to her. He grabbed a feather boa that Leo had used in her act and held it in front of Lilith, seeking to shield her breasts from view. Being unaware of the notion of privacy herself, she did not respond. For her, clothing had to do with ritual, not concealment. But she understood the boy's desire to cover her. She knew the mind of man, after all, in great detail.

Drawing the feathers around herself, she took him in her arms and kissed him. He sprang up between his legs so quickly that she broke away and laughed.

"Ian!" The mother called again.

"Mom?"

"We gotta take a powder," Lilith told Leo.

"I—who's the kid, anyway?"

"His moniker is Ian. Look, get a move on."

"My mother—" the boy pleaded.

"She cannot be your mother!" Lilith said. "Your mother is a Keeper."

"Oh, my God," Leo said.

He tried to break away. "Mom!"

"Ian, where are you?"

Lilith kissed him again, this time with all the depth of passion that she possessed. In the kiss, her loneliness washed away, disappearing as easily as dew on the fronds of morning. She held him to her nakedness, covering them both with the feathered shawl, drawing him into the softness and warmth of her. For a long moment he resisted her, but then his muscles seemed to tremble as if from some deep upheaval, and his arms grew tight around her.

"This way," Leo whispered, and Lilith went, drawing Ian with a gentle but insistent hand. As he had come onto the stage, he came with them now.

"Don't look back," she said when the woman called Ian again, her voice sharp in the gloom and silence of the backstage. Far away, as if on another world, the audience was clamoring for their darling Leo.

"Where are we going?" Ian asked.

"Someplace close by, to get to know each other," Leo said.

Ian regarded Lilith. "Who are you? What's your name?"

That was better. That was very much better. "Lilith," she said.

Leo stopped, stumbled, then recovered herself. "That's the name of the mother of them all."

Lilith smiled, watching cheerfully as a pallor spread over the sweet creature's face. So she knew the meaning of the name. Lilith gave her as warm a smile as it was in her power to give. Leo rushed to her and threw her arms around her, weeping.

"There's no time for this now."

But she couldn't stop, she was clearly beside herself. It was the wrong place: they had not escaped. The human woman would soon appear again.

"Ian!"

"I have to go to my mom!"

"Ian, this chance will not come again. Spend an hour with us."

"An hour?"

She drew him on.

"Ian!"

"Mom, it's only an hour."

"*Ian!*"

A metal door opened. Beyond it was a magnificent black equipage like the one that had brought her here.

They threw themselves into the back of the thing, and Lilith found herself in a very plush little chamber. Immediately, it began to move. In the front sat a driver, never looking back. He was isolated by a glass window.

"Hey, this is all right," Lilith said.

Leo shuffled a white stick out of a small package, put it to her lips, and lit one end. She shook as she did it. When she exhaled, a ghastly odor filled the small room. Lilith had noticed other humans doing this—Ibrahim, for example, among the men—but she had not seen it up close, not until this moment.

"What is that?"

"You don't know what a cigarette is?" Ian asked.

"You better believe I do, buddy."

"Okay. Because you'd have to be some kind of a—look, Miss Patterson, uh, where are we going?"

Leo smiled. "Ask her."

"So where are we going?"

"A little hideaway somewhere. We gotta talk."

"You sound like Joan Crawford imitating James Cagney. Who are you?"

"English isn't my lingo, bud. I learned it from . . . perhaps from bums."

Leo laughed. "Let me ask you this. Would you like to go home to Momma, or to one of the most beautiful places in the world with us?"

"Leo, my name is Ian Ward, and I don't know what I'm doing here."

Leo Patterson smoked hard. So, the name had told her something, something that she did not wish to hear. It had left, judging from the steadiness and inlooking of her eyes, a residue of suspicion, and more than a little fear.

"We'll go to my place on St. Barts," Leo said.

"St. Barts! I can't go to St. Barts!"

"You can go," Lilith said. "Think of it. Us. Together. For just a little while."

"Five hours there, we'll be on the ground by two."

"My parents—"

"You'll be back tomorrow before midnight. I guarantee it."

Lilith saw that Leo was cold toward the boy, cold and suspicious. In fact, she seemed a little unbalanced, so suspicious was she. Lilith would not pass judgment, though. It was obvious that much about this situation remained hidden from her. Whatever this St. Bart's was, it must be a pleasant place. Perhaps there would be pools in which to swim, and maids to anoint her with oil, and some fresh-blooded humans to satisfy what hunger she might feel.

"I can't do this," Ian moaned.

"But Ian," Lilith said, "you want to."

"How do you know that?"

"Because you lean against my shoulder when you say you can't. Shall I order you? I have the right, you know."

"She does."

"Nobody can order me except my mom and dad."

"I can, but I won't. Come for fun."

"Look, Ian," Leo said, "there are probably a hundred million guys just like you who would give their blood to do this. So don't blow it."

"Leo, I owe it to my folks. I can't just disappear on them."

"I have a palace in Egypt," Lilith said. "Take a look at my palace."

"Now, *that's* far away! And no, I'm definitely not going."

"Grace, will you call ahead and tell them to get the plane ready? I could be going anywhere, so they should plan accordingly."

"Yes, ma'am," a female voice said out of a box.

"We'll go to St. Barts."

That seemed to calm him. His eyes kept devouring Leo. He was dying to be with her, Lilith could feel it. Why was the male such a blind and fickle creature?

"Anybody want a drink?" Leo asked.

"Sure."

"What'll it be, kid?" Lilith asked Ian.

"Uh, Cutty and soda?"

"*Cutty?* The only Scotch in here is—what is this?" Leo reached into a compartment made of wood and polished to a gloss. "Johnnie Walker Blue Label."

She poured the liquid into tumblers and filled them with what Lilith had discovered at the Royalton Hotel was called "ice," a substance that, if left on a couch, for example, slowly sank into it and disappeared. To what it might touch, it communicated coldness. This was a form of hard snow. In the early times, she had lived in places where snow came with the winter season, but of late that had not been true.

"Is it illegal?" Ian asked.

Leo shrugged. "Everything's illegal somewhere."

He took his drink, lifted the glass in the way humans had from time immemorial. Leo lifted her glass. Lilith watched them, smiling softly.

"Madonna," Leo said, gazing dog-eyed back at her.

Lilith did not know the meaning of the word, and did not ask. She let the creature adore her with her eyes, though.

Becky had lost Paul, and she was going to lose Ian if this cab didn't step on it. Paul had been taken in, of all the damn things, on a disorderly conduct rap. She couldn't follow him, so she called their lawyer from the cab, told him to go down and get him out. Morris didn't ask any questions, but his voice said that he certainly wanted to. The Wards had given him a busy few days.

"Where do you think they're headed?"

"Upstate. Goin' out on the West Side Highway."

"Keep with them."

"You got it."

She watched the limo's tail lights as it headed up the ramp onto the highway.

"They're crossing the GW Bridge. You still want me to stay with 'em?"

"Sure thing." She hardly glanced at the magnificence of New York spreading out along the Hudson as they proceeded across the bridge.

She wished she could predict their destination. She had been derelict in not researching Leo Patterson more carefully. Had she been unwilling within herself to help Paul, for fear of what the consequences could be for Ian? Or had it been more subtle than that, a gradual loss of faith that had come from all the years of endless, futile investigation?

Either way, she didn't have a clue about Leo's life, and therefore no idea where this journey might take them. She had an inspiration: she tried Ian's cell phone, jabbing in the numbers and telling herself she was damn well senile not to have done this before.

And then she heard his voice. "Hi, Mom."

"Ian, for God's sake!"

"Mom, I'm fine, I'm with Leo and some girlfriend of hers. Mom, please let me do this."

"I want you to listen to me. You are in danger, Ian. You have to get out of that car, and you have to do it now."

"It's going sixty miles an hour. Can you see me?"

"Of course I can see you! Look, there's going to be a light. There has to be a light. The second it stops, you get out of there and you run, Ian. You run!"

She watched the limo leave the bridge, then head down Route 17, going south. There were no lights around here, but there were lights on Route 17. "Close it up," she said.

"You ain't gonna get me shot at?"

She managed a laugh. "Heavens, no. That's Leo Patterson's car. I'm her hairdresser."

"Where's she goin' this time? Paris? London?"

For a moment, she didn't get what he was driving at. Then she did. Teterboro Airport was a few miles south of here. Her urgency intensified. She leaned forward, staring at the limo.

A light came up . . . green. "Goddammit!" Then another—yellow. The limo sped up, got closer, closer yet. Red.

The limo slipped through, but the cab had to stop.

"Please!"

"They goin' t'Teterboro. You'll catch up."

And sure enough, they turned into the airport. She called Ian again, but this time got his message.

Could she charter a plane here, on the spot? She had no idea. But she did know this: no matter who had given birth to him, that was her son in that car, and she was not going to let them get her son, not now and not ever. If they did, there would be only one reason that they had: she was dead.

* * *

Leo watched the two of them, the nervous kid with his red cheeks and semipermanent boner, and the fabulous blond woman wrapped in a cheap feather stage prop. She wriggled in her seat, wishing she was sitting where Ian got to sit.

Ian Ward, Christ. She knew Paul Ward had a kid, and in Ian's strong face, his steel-blue eyes, she could see a shadow of him. What the hell was happening? And why did she want him so desperately? It wasn't just his looks, it was something else that had made her drop to her knees before him on the stage, and thrill—just absolutely *thrill*—to be bending there in homage to his beauty.

But fucking *Paul Ward?*

And then it smacked her in the face like a tap from a blackjack: this was Miri's baby. This was who she'd been carrying all those years ago.

Oh, God, oh

She reached his hand, took it. And there, yes, in the line of the jaw, in the laughter hidden in the lips, in the careful sculpture of the nose—it was her, beloved Miri was there too—Miri and Paul, their baby.

This was a full-fledged vampire boy, this was. "What's your mother's name?" she asked.

"Rebecca Ward."

"Your real mother?"

"She is my real mother, and listen—"

They hadn't told him. They damn well had not told the poor kid! He didn't feed, either, she would bet on that.

Lilith, on the other hand, did, and Lilith was just beginning to get a little hungry, she could see by the way she rubbed herself here and there, like an addict with the itchies. Leo knew the state well.

Lilith . . . she whispered the legendary name in her throat.

"Yes?"

"I was . . . thinking."

"You kids don't know each other, do ya?" Lilith said in her odd English.

To Leo's ear, she spoke as if she'd learned from a talking computer programmed by Sydney Greenstreet.

"No," Ian said. "I don't know her. I'm a fan."

"A fan? Like, flit, flit, flit?" She moved a languid hand in the smoky air.

"No, it means a person who really goes for a certain star."

"Which star?"

"Her."

Lilith gave her the most wonderful, most thrilling look. It was more than a stripping look, it was a render-you-naked-and-fill-your-holes-and-soul look. Leo squirmed with delight when Lilith reached across and touched her breast. "You're one sensitive kid," she said.

They pulled up in front of the main building. Grace got out quickly and threw the door open. "We've had a cab on our tail the whole way," she said to Leo in an undertone.

"Better tell security if they try to come in."

"Uh, I have to go," Ian said.

"Sure," Leo agreed, "go." Excellent.

"Okay?"

"I said yes. So go! You're being followed anyway. By whoever called you a few minutes ago, would be my guess. Mommy Becky." She looked back down the long drive that led out to Route 17. "Here she comes."

Ian walked a few steps away, waving. The lights of the cab approached.

"What's the situation?" Lilith asked.

"We're going to the Caribbean. I guess he isn't."

"Ian—"

Lilith turned her back on Ian, for a moment concealing Leo from him. As easily as a human being might pick up a small dog, Lilith lifted her. She locked onto her lips. For a moment, Leo resisted, then just went limp in the steel arms. Lilith's tongue rampaged into her mouth and snaked its way deep down her throat. She stiffened, raising her head to try to accommodate its bulk. It was just like this with Miri, they kissed you almost senseless.

She got wet, soaked, raining between her legs. The desire was so great that it made her hurt, made her scream around the blasting kiss.

Then Lilith released her. "Get on the program, sister," she whispered. "I want the kid with us."

The cab arrived—and George came out. Leo saw Ian's face freeze, then fall as if some youthful confidence had just been shattered. "I have clothes," George said to Leo. He held out two shopping bags. Ian still wore his jeans, but he went for the Leo sweatshirt and the black pullover he'd been wearing before he arrived on the stage.

Lilith was indifferent to the clothes, seemingly impervious to the cold October air. The feathery wrap Ian had given her blew about her.

Leo said to Ian, "She wants you to come." She paused. "I want you to come."

"Look, I don't belong here. I don't know what I'm supposed to be doing, I—"

"Please," Lilith said. "Was that your frail in the talking machine?"

"My mother . . . she was supposed to be here." He gazed off down the road.

Leo thought fast. She had to make this work. She had to have Lilith and Ian both.

She took his hand. "At least take a look at my plane."

"What kind of plane?"

"Come look."

Glancing back, he allowed her to lead him to the apron where they parked the planes. Her sky blue Gulfstream IV stood under the lights. It was, quite frankly, magnificent. It had better be, for $18 million.

She squeezed Ian's hand. "Come on, take a look."

He didn't move.

She drew him toward the steps. "It's a really amazing plane." She started up the steps. Lilith was right behind him, staying close. Leo saw that she was discreetly cutting off his escape. So they were kidnapping him. Paul Ward's kid? Oh, well.

"Hey, Lauren, hey, Jack," she called to her pilots as they entered. "Ready to roll?"

"We're cleared," Lauren said. "Not a lot of traffic at this hour."

"Lauren's my pilot. Timmy?"

The attendant was in the galley. He came forward and drew the door closed. "Have a seat," Leo said.

Ian said, "Look, I better not do this."

Lilith laid an arm around his shoulders. "Don't let it get to you, kid. It's gonna be one hell of a ride."

For part of the taxi, Lilith stood like a sentinel, close to Ian, who had sunk down in one of the armchairs. Leo had her plane decorated like a comfortable den from a lovely home circa about 1920. Forward was her bedroom, all chintz and girlish frills. The couches and chairs in this compartment made into beds. It didn't look like it, but she could sleep twelve in here, slumber-party style. With the plane's six-thousand-mile range, that capability came in handy.

She could see the smile hovering on Ian's face as they gathered speed. What kid wouldn't smile, considering where he was and who he was with?

They took off, soaring into the sky on the two powerful engines.

"Well, I'm in huge trouble," Ian said.

"How do they punish you?" Leo asked.

"Grounding. This is, like, grounded for life. Until age twenty-one."

The deck canted steeply, and the plane shuddered as it rose. Lilith's eyes moved quickly about, and Leo had the impression that she'd never flown before.

Leo asked her, "How old are you?"

The eyes stopped their nervous hunting, connected with hers. Lilith said, "As old as you."

Leo smiled to herself. A typical Keeper answer, exactly the sort of thing Miri would have said.

Leo went over to the boy, who was peering out a window, looking back at the rapidly disappearing lights of New York. She got down beside him in the big seat. Lilith watched them with the molten eyes of a cobra. Leo stroked his hair. "Don't be scared, little boy," she said, "don't be scared."

CHAPTER THIRTEEN

Night Journeys

W hat. In. Hell. Are. You. Saying!"
Paul had roared, his voice resounding with the rage of somebody who's just lost big.

She had cried, choking her sobs past a throat almost closed by fear.

Agony. No other word for it. You try his cell and try it and try it. You get onto the FAA, you scream for the plane's flight plan—which terminates in the dead middle of the Atlantic. Best guess—a Caribbean destination. Or hey, Europe. Or the Middle East. And what about Latin America—yeah, there's that, too. In a long-range Gulfer like that, they could be in goddamn Ulan Bator by now.

Agony. You wake up sick with fear and dragging from the worst dreams a human being can know, that your beautiful son is being force-fed red blood and gagging and gobbling and, oh, God, *loving it!*

You start drinking early, and you smoke like Satan at a sermon. You pull in every damn marker you've got, you who are an outcast, the wife of an outcast, and you get just exactly friggin' nowhere, baby.

Tick tock, the hours are passing, and your dear beloved innocent heart is being damn well corrupted and polluted beyond all belief and knowledge.

And you know that the silent man at your side is being tortured by a more horrible torture than even you know, which is the knowledge that if his own son, child of the body and the heart, is corrupted, then he will have to put him to death as if his brilliant angel of a boy was a rabid cur.

They had plotted, planned, worked, performed miracles on their communications equipment. Now, three days after they had started tracking, they were at a sleek Upper East Side highrise, on their way up to the thirty-fifth-floor apartment of one George D'Alessio, Leo Patterson's very well concealed chief of staff.

The names of Leo's staff were a skillfully kept secret, and George had proved infuriatingly—and surprisingly—hard to find. But Becky had used her search skills well, and her access to various intelligence databases, and she had identified him.

They came out into a long, ill-lit hallway with a gray carpet and walls. A faint smell of something frying lingered in the air. This building was essential Upper East Side—a lobby that glittered with chandeliers and mirrors, but upstairs the place was as pretty as a prison. Apartment 3541 was a two-bedroom unit. He rented it for $3,700 a month, and lived in it alone.

But when you are breaking in on somebody, you never assume that they are unarmed, asleep, or alone. You assume that they have a nervous dog, a number of supporters, and are wide awake and know you are coming. And they are very, very well armed.

They stopped at the door. It was three-fifteen in the morning, the favorite time for an action of this kind. They carried small pistols and full official fake identification. Also lock picks. They already knew precisely what kind of locks they were up against, and had wax patterns of the keys. Becky had come yesterday to do that prep. She'd also determined that there was no alarm system on the unit. George relied on anonymity to shield him from intruders, foolish boy. It wouldn't have mattered, anyway. Commercial alarms relied on magnets. Piece of cake.

He was gay, George was, but very private about it. *Salon* had even speculated that he was Leo's secret lover. A secret lover was involved, but it wasn't her. His secret lover was a twenty-two-year-old kid called Bobby Parr. Somebody had spent a lot of money on Bobby to make him look about fourteen. It was legal, though, all of it. Becky had looked hard for a way to haul George in, maybe before the same bored (but now slightly confused) judge who had kindly dropped charges both on Ian and Paul.

"Don't tear him apart," Paul said.

He watched her slip a plastic key into the first lock. It was a little stiff—these plastic babies made from wax impressions almost always were—but it turned over the lock with a loud click.

"*Goddammit!*" she hissed, feeling like a damn fool.

"Congratulations," he whispered, his voice dripping sarcasm. Pros did not click.

She went for the second lock, which was much more complex, and had to file the skeleton a few times before she got a positive result. She opened the door a bare inch, then stuck a wire through. A moment later, the safety chain was hanging free, and the door was wide.

Paul stepped in. Becky came behind him, closed the door. Both standing absolutely still, they methodically surveyed their surroundings. Nothing moving very well. Next step: Paul put on his night-vision lenses and made the same survey, this time looking carefully for things like tripwires, or somebody sleeping on the living room couch, anything unexpected.

The living space was an L, with a dinette and small kitchen off to the right. To the left was a corridor that led to the two bedrooms.

You would have thought that somebody like this—a professional organizer—would have a spotless apartment, or at least a clean one, but this place was filthy, every surface piled high with dishes, ashtrays, old newspapers, you name it. The only movement was the scuttling of roaches. At night here in *chez* George, they ruled. Paul took a step toward the corridor, looked into the first bedroom.

For a moment, he wasn't sure what he was dealing with, but then he understood. This was a dungeon, something used in S&M sex play. He saw a wooden frame, obviously homemade, with wrist and ankle straps nailed to it. There was an open massage table with more straps. On an old desk were two or three dildos, an enema bag in a puddle, and various implements—pliers, razors, a box of salt, and a paddle.

"Jesus wept," Becky said, her voice barely a whisper.

"An active fantasy life."

"Maybe we can use it on him."

"You aren't gonna get anything out of this scum with torture."

"I believe it."

They went toward the second bedroom, hanging back in the hall until they had completely surveyed the space. On the rickety bed lay George and his boy toy, both sound asleep. The difference between them was that George was chained to the bed, and boy toy was as free as the wind and as naked as a plump little piglet.

"Looks like Georgie is the bottom," Paul breathed.

"You think the chains are real?"

"They're fastened to the bedframe."

"Ready to rock and roll?"

"Let's do it, sweet."

She took her syringe out of her bag and lifted it to the faint light that drifted in from between the slats of the closed blinds. She stepped silently to the boy's bedside, found some free space on his upper arm, and swabbed it. The boy sighed a little, as if he thought he had been kissed. Well, he had been, but by a powerful anesthetic. She inserted the needle into the deadened skin, then withdrew it. She stood gazing down at him, listening for his breathing to change. He would wake up tomorrow afternoon with no awareness of any of this, none at all.

She made a hand signal to Paul, who came into the room. Georgie wouldn't have it so easy. Georgie was about to wake up eating a gun.

Paul stood over him. He looked down at the stark, handsome features of the professional assistant. Beside him, his friend's pudgy face was now as slack as a dead hog's. His breath, which had been rattling, seemed all but gone.

"Coma's a ten," he murmured to Becky. Then he pulled out his police special, went down beside Georgie, and shoved it in between his half-parted lips hard enough to chip a few pearlies. The eyes came open, the head tried to turn away. Paul shoved harder, and Georgie went, *"Gwulllggg!"*

Becky came in with a complicated collection of straps from the dungeon and proceeded to start trussing up boy toy, who resisted her the same way a dead fish resists being lifted out of a creel.

"Okay," Paul said to Georgie, his voice booming, "we're feds, but we don't play by the rules. We're looking for your lady fair. We know she left the country in her plane. Where did she go, Georgie?" He withdrew the gun a few inches, just far enough to enable him to talk.

"What the fuck—"

The gun went back, taking chunks of tooth with it, causing groaning and much gobbling against the barrel. "I told you we don't play by the rules. So I'm gonna pull out the gun again, and this time you're gonna tell me what I want to know." Again, he withdrew the barrel.

"Please! Jesus! I'm hurt!" He spat, and Paul slapped him.

"Swallow it. Where is she?"

"What is this about?"

Translation: he knew. Paul pistol-whipped him hard enough to cause a cry, but not hard enough to grant him the brief respite of unconsciousness.

"Jesus, Paul," Becky said.

"Take it easy," Georgie gasped. "Gimme a chance."

Paul swung the pistol back.

"Gimme a chance to talk! Jesus fucking Christ, you hurt me!"

"So talk."

"They went somewhere in Europe or the Middle East. They refueled in the Azores. I know because I wire transferred more funds to one of her credit cards. Oh, Christ, what is this about?"

"You're gonna go to your grave never knowing the answer to that question. Now, I am gonna ask you again. We know she refueled in the Azores. We know she took off headed for the Middle East, which is where we lost her. Where did she go, Georgie, boy?"

"I haven't heard from her."

Paul had hit him the first time with cool method and not a whole lot of power. If he did it again, though, it was really going to hurt the guy, and Paul didn't like that. He'd hurt too damn many people in his long career. He said, "Your buddy's not in too good shape."

George's eyes started darting around frantically when he realized that his friend was comatose. Becky raised the now-empty syringe into his view. Paul said, "One more dose, and he's off to meet his maker."

"Oh, no, don't. Don't, please!"

She turned the syringe, moved it toward the boy's neck.

"He's a wonderful, special person!"

"Mr. Wonderful's gotta die so El Bitch can keep on keeping on. That's a damn shame."

Becky sank the needle into Mr. Wonderful's neck.

"Talk."

"No! Please!"

"She go to Libya? Iraq?"

Becky prepared to push the plunger that would send exactly nothing into boy toy's bloodstream. "Okay," Paul said. "Kill him."

"No! No, wait! Oh, for God's sake. Listen, I think she went to Egypt."

"We checked Egypt. No cigar."

"The plane didn't land in Egypt."

"It did."

"Hold up," Paul said to Becky.

From his years of experience, Paul was reasonably sure that George wasn't lying. If they lied, they relaxed. They always believed the lie would work. It was the truth that they distrusted, that made them prepare for another blow.

The problem was, they had checked every airport in Europe and the Middle East, and had not found Leo's Gulfstream registered as either landed or having passed through. It had not been tracked by either European or Israeli ground control, nor by the Israeli military, which watched every plane that crossed north of a line from Algiers to Bahrain—assuming that the information CIA had gotten from them was genuine and complete. Given the tormented and complex relationship between American and Israeli intelligence, one could never be sure.

Could the plane have gone down? Anything was possible.

Unless— "Did Leo have her passport?"

He nodded.

"What about her friend?"

"I don't even know her name."

Paul pulled back. "We're done," he said to Becky.

"Done?"

"We're done!" He began to leave.

"We don't—"

"Yes, we do."

She followed him out. From the bedroom behind them came a rattle of chains and a loud cry, as Georgie realized that they were both tied up.

"You forgot something," she said.

"Sorry," Paul said as he hurried back into the bedroom.

"Jesus! I thought you were gonna leave us like this!"

"Why, Georgie, I'd never do that." He taped up the creep's mouth. Only when his boyfriend woke up, which would be a good ten hours from now, would they be able to raise anything approaching an alarm. They'd have to attract the attention of somebody going down this sound-deadened corridor. Fine.

"What's the story?" Becky asked as they entered the service elevator they'd come up in.

"Egypt."

"Egypt says no."

"Somebody was bribed."

"So, we go to Egypt."

They returned to Ian's apartment and booked a flight to Cairo on Air France, with a stop in Paris to meet Jean Bocage. They would fly together from there to Cairo, where they would be met by the head of the Egyptian Special Environmental Police, General Adel Karas, universally known as Kari. Paul had never worked with him. They didn't take their guns, only what electronics they'd managed to pry out of Briggsie. He couldn't absolutely flat turn down a mission to recover their own son, not even Briggsie. Bocage and Kari had to provide the weapons, though.

Paul and Becky sat side by side in business class, silently waiting out the long midatlantic hours between JFK and Paris.

"Why did you do it, Paul?"

"What?"

"Set Ian up the way you did."

"I didn't."

"Bullshit. If you'd left well enough alone—"

He turned toward her, his face stricken. "Jesus Christ, look what happened! He was just goddamn fucking *magnetized* to them!"

"If he hadn't felt so humiliated and ashamed, maybe he wouldn't have gone."

"The boy was kidnapped!" He threw himself back against his seat. "Fucking kidnapped."

She fell silent, regretting the fight. Paul had not caused this to happen. The blood had caused it, that mystical, fearful blood of theirs.

As the plane droned on, Paul would fall asleep—which was something he had done very little of since Ian's departure—and when he did, she would hear him moan.

It was a bedroom sound, full of heat, not the moan of a man tormented by loss. Finally, it got loud enough to begin to embarrass the other passengers.

She shook him awake.

He opened his eyes. "Uh, yes? Oh—what . . ."

She leaned close to him, kissed his cold, slack lips. "You were dreaming about the vampire," she said, knowing that it was true and unable to conceal the sadness in her voice.

"I love you," he said.

Yes, she thought, the same way you'd love a good hunting dog. She wanted him right here and now, in this airplane, in front of everybody. She wanted to proclaim it to the world, to the vampires, and above all to that damn blood: this man is mine.

"It's the most beautiful one I've ever seen," he said. "Makes goddamn Blaylock look like a nun."

She squeezed his hand, but did not reply. She couldn't, not without revealing her sadness to him, in the tears that would fill her voice.

He wanted to be loyal to her, but it was hard not to at least in his imagination contemplate what it would be like with that gorgeous creature. His desire, though, was like something that had been grafted into his brain by some mad scientist. It felt alien and unreal, even though it stirred him like no other feeling he'd ever known, not even his feeling for Miri.

He slept again, and was disturbed again by images of the vampire, her breasts like smooth snow peaks, her eyes as merry as a child's and as slow as a tiger's. The danger was what did it, made her irresistible. The dark side of the feminine was there, he thought, to teach you who you really were.

"Maybe she's just a dream," he said when he woke up.

"A nightmare."

Outside the window, he could see the City of Light, gray and vast in predawn rain. They landed, then, and as he faced the reality of Ian's loss in this new place, Paul thought that she was exactly right about that. No matter how much it sweated him, the dream of the vampire was indeed a nightmare.

Jean came forward out of the crowd as soon as they cleared customs. His embrace, in the French manner of greeting, marked much more than a simple reunion between friends. The three of them had faced death together. That made you more than friends.

"Paul," Jean said. "Please accept—" Then he saw Becky and fell silent. He embraced her, the continued silence speaking his admiration for her, and his respect for the sanctity of their marriage. Paul suspected that Jean had loved her, once. Maybe he still did. "We're ready to go," Jean said. "Unless you wish to freshen up—a shower, perhaps, in the VIP suite?"

"Let's keep moving," Paul said. It turned out that the Egyptian air force was providing transportation from here to Cairo. The plane, a small official jet, was waiting for them in the private international area. On the way, Bocage said, "You will meet Kari. He is on the plane. He is—well, you will meet him."

"I've heard a lot about him."

"I have worked with him for years, Paul, my friend. He is—he is like you."

Paul looked sharply at Bocage. "So?"

"In the blood a little, I think."

Paul thought that he should have been amazed, but he wasn't. There was really so much they didn't know about the vampire, and therefore about the world we live in. How long had the vampire been here, and was it something that had come from some other place, or was it an earthly evolution? Why were there people like him, and now apparently also like this Egyptian, who also bore elements of the strange, complex blood of the vampire in their own veins, but without any corresponding need to feed on their fellow man?

Paul's blood contained an array of six anomalous cells, the most important of which was the T-4 lymphocyte which gave his immune system extraordinary reactivity and power. The Sarah Roberts papers revealed numerous experiments involving attempts to transfer this cell into the human body. She could achieve a temporary antiaging effect, but it didn't last more than a few hours.

Paul's platelets also had a life span of years rather than days and were extraordinarily proactive in healing. A wound requiring stitches in a normal person would heal on its own in hours.

Unfortunately, as strong as all this made him, his heart had simply endured too much stress over the years, and his ravenous lust for red meat, nearly raw, had taken its toll in blood vessel damage.

He was even more interested to meet General Karas now. Maybe he knew something about the origins of people like himself and Paul.

"Paul," Bocage asked as they went toward the waiting plane, "have I upset you?"

"I'm thinking."

"I had no idea there were others," Becky said.

"I was surprised when he told me."

"I didn't think anything could surprise you," Paul said, laughing a little. Bocage was an impressive man, highly skilled. When Paul followed Miriam Blaylock from Bangkok to Paris with his old team, ignoring the French operation, Bocage had trapped them all very neatly. He had insisted on something that in those days had been complete anathema to Paul—that they work together. Paul was obsessed with how easy it was for some vampires to blend in with human society, and he had lived in constant fear of moles and plants.

Jean's professionalism had defeated his fears. They had sterilized Paris together, shoulder to shoulder, working their way through the vast complex of catacombs and ancient mines that twisted beneath the city, in the process rooting out over a hundred of the creatures. Subsequently, missing persons cases had become as rare here as they now were in New York, down from thousands a year to just a couple hundred, with few of those remaining open for long.

Paul saw that they would be on a Citation III, which was standing outside the glass wall at the far end of the lobby they had just entered. The plane was white, in Egyptian military livery. He knew planes, and this jet would get them to Cairo in about six hours. Good.

There were no longer any customs to worry about. They had gone from the world of commercial air travel to another level altogether, where the hindrances of borders more or less evaporated. Their luggage, for example, would have caused no end of official questions, given that it consisted, among other things, of military-grade satellite navigation equipment, night-vision goggles, special microphones and listening devices, climbing equipment, forger's tools, and a subminiaturized drone aircraft protected by diplomatic seals. The drone folded into a case the size and shape of a golf bag, and could remain aloft for six hours without recharging its fuel cell. The thing about the craft that was so valuable was that the vampire's body temperature dropped steadily between feedings, and the drone carried a temperature-sensitive camera that could easily identify one from thousands of feet away, even in a crowd.

The legendary general met them at the door of the plane. "Colonel Ward," he said, "Mrs. Ward. It's really a privilege." As they continued into the plane, he added, "I only wish that the circumstances could be more pleasant."

The moment they sat down, he spoke into the intercom. As the plane started off, the steward secured the door.

General Karas was a trim man, his eyes set in a perpetual expression of surprise. His uniform was exquisitely tailored, but rumpled from constant movement. He had a cocked, restless quality, an uneasiness that seemed to dominate his personality.

"I thought we'd gotten them all," he said, "until this wretched situation arose."

"We've been watching missing persons reports for fifteen years," Paul said. "We never saw a trace of the old pattern reemerging in the United States."

"How many lives have you saved? In America?"

"Over the fifteen years," Becky said, "about fifty thousand."

"My God, that's what I keep telling my government. But nobody wants this. Nobody is interested. Nothing like that in Egypt, they say. That's why they give the assignment to a Copt." He rolled his eyes and swept a nervous hand along the leather arm of his chair, and the imposing general suddenly looked like an agitated little boy. "We took our last one just months ago. It had been living in the Corniche, can you imagine, in Cairo! We found things in there—coin from the reign of Cleopatra, for the love of all that is holy. All manner of treasure in that filthy hole. It will go to the Department of Antiquities." He leaned forward, his eyes suddenly glaring, his hands now gripping the chair arms as if he was considering launching himself toward them. "We nailed it to the door of its damned hole, to draw others. And we watched. This new one showed up about six months later. It had already killed a child and possibly a Bedouin in the desert, my God. The thing about it is that it is magnificently beautiful—tall and slim and blond. Very powerful and athletic— you should see it run, leap—my God. You would think that it was an American damned movie star. It took the child"—he made a sipping motion, his pinkie extended— "as easily as milady at her tea."

Jean said, "You're sure it came out of the desert?"

Karas gave him a careful, appraising look. "You know, in Egypt—you would be surprised, I am sure—we keep better records than your media would have you believe. We are not damned third-world idiots, chewing rice and scuttling about in a perpetual state of confusion." He raised an eyebrow, giving his face an almost comical cast, as if he wanted to lessen the criticism implied in his remark. Then he laughed, the easy, sophisticated chuckle of a man used to power. "So I can say with certainty," he continued, "that we have not had any sort of pattern of missing persons that would fit the existence of another vampire. How this one got to Egypt and where it came from are questions that I would very much like to answer. Except that it was here to eat, of course."

"It fits the description of the one that appeared in New York a few days ago," Becky said.

Karas stared at her. Paul had not often seen such careful appraisal in a human face. This man was highly intelligent, that was clear. "Ah, it's in your country."

"Perhaps," Paul said.

Karas raised his eyebrows.

"It's possible that it's returned, in the company of a blooded woman . . . and our son."

Karas gazed down at the front of his tunic, nervously dusting his medals with his fingers. "I have a daughter, Hamida," he said in a soft, caressing tone. "Like me—like you, Paul, but worse, because my wife Violet, also—" He smiled, as tormented an expression as Paul had ever seen. So his wife was a carrier, too. That meant that the daughter would have even more of the blood factors than either parent. She wouldn't be as extreme a case as Ian, but it would be in that direction. "I have also wondered what the effect would be, if she came into—how do you say—proximity, yes—proximity to a vampire."

"It was like some kind of black magic," Becky said. "You have no idea."

They flew on, heading east beneath a hard gray sky, the stately waves of the Mediterranean sweeping beneath them. At length the steward served a meal of tangy *mulukhiya* soup with rice, followed by a variety of *shawarma* meats and vegetables. Afterwards, there was coffee, served with a variety of *um-ali,* small, intensely flavored sweets.

Paul ate, and watched Becky eating, and thought that it was the first real meal they'd had since Ian's abduction. He hadn't been able to eat on the plane over, let alone before that. Now, though, knowing that they were going into action, that they were getting closer to Ian—they were both hungry, and that was good.

The sun was glaring into the windscreen of the cockpit when the intercom warbled. Karas listened for a moment, then said, "We're landing in twenty minutes. And there is good news."

Paul felt Becky stiffen. Ian had been found wandering the streets of Cairo, or asleep in a hotel room, or safe somewhere else, but safe, please God, safe.

Ian had not been found. None of them had been found. But Leo's plane had been located. It was at the airport at Beni Suef, a hundred klicks south of Cairo. The pilots, now under house arrest, were more than willing to talk to the authorities. They were being held at the Mena House in Cairo. Karas concluded, "Her plane is now impounded, of course."

"I wonder if we should do that?"

Karas smiled. "It's on Egyptian soil illegally."

"Impounding the plane brings in customs. What if they give the case to the police?"

Karas sank into thought. "The relationship between my unit and the police is complicated. We are old Egypt—by which I mean, men from before the coming of the Muslims. No Muslims in my unit. The consequence is, we have not unlimited power. We must let the military and the police deal with the plane according to established protocols."

"You can't risk explanations, is what you're saying. Your system's just like ours—a tarbaby."

"A tarbaby is what?"

"Something that sticks to you when you touch it."

He laughed heartily then, and quickly finished his coffee as the steward cleaned up. "Us Copts, we are a tarbaby for Egypt! That's quite good. You know, I'm not actually even a Copt. My family is unbroken in its line, from the time before. Kawaat is our forbear, the eldest son of Khu'fu." He laughed softly. "My great-great-grandfather two hundred times removed was a bastard of this prince."

Paul watched the man, saw the sadness in his eyes, the complex little smile that played there. Normally, he would have found it impossible to believe such a statement. But with this man, no.

"That's four thousand years ago," Becky said. "You're saying your family goes back that far?"

Karas gave her a careful look. "In Egypt, such things are not strange. Julius Caesar was a guest in our house." He lifted a glass. "We gave him wine kept cool by being immersed in a spring." The smile returned, blossomed. "This, I believe, is refrigerated, forgive me."

"Being immersed in a spring is better?"

"The coolness is softer, you know."

The plane shuddered, the engine noise dropped, and they began descending toward Cairo, the great city that lay almost hidden in the clouds far below.

CHAPTER FOURTEEN

The Underworld

Ian lay naked, deliciously exposed, in a state of fairy tale wonder . . . aside from being as hungry as a horse. Beside him and keeping him warm in the cool of this strange cave of Lilith's, Leo was cuddled close. He lay thinking, full of questions about this place and these people. The cave was full of things that looked ancient Egyptian to him, wonderful chairs and divans, exotic linen hangings, all of it, if not exactly crisp and new, then certainly serviceable. But why nothing modern? And, strangest of all, where was the kitchen, and where oh where was the damned food?

They had some stuff from the plane, but let's face it, they'd been in here for days, and he was beginning to wonder if linen was edible. There was water, at least. You got it in these fabulously carved diorite bowls she had around, out of pools with beautiful mosaics of fish and lobsters and crabs and octopi in them. Getting a drink made him hungry.

The thing about it that was good—that was actually amazing—was that both of these women were totally sold on him, to the point that they sort of competed for him in a laughing kind of a way. He turned on his side and buried his face in Leo's neck, just to be sure he still could.

She sighed and stretched. A week ago, she had been this distant, iconic figure, a picture to gaze at during lonely sessions with Sally Five. Now here she was in the warm, sweet-scented flesh. She was a kid who had been made hard by everybody always wanting stuff from her. She told him she was thirty-one, but twenty-five was a more believable number when you saw her up close. She was really cuddly. This was a girl who wanted to be held. If he whispered "I love you," to her, she would look at him with damp, sex-besotted eyes.

Lilith had a more sort of servile approach. She acted like he was some kind of a god or a king or something. Him, a kid from East Mill, N.Y., the son of a couple of civil service types—let's face it, not exactly somebody you knelt in front of and hugged around the waist, for the love of Mike. She would look up with stars in her eyes. He'd smile down at her and quietly wonder what the hell?

If he listened carefully, he could hear her breathing right now, hear the faint swish of her flowing robes as she moved about the room. Somehow, in a darkness so deep that he could not see a finger an inch from his eye, she was pacing like a restless animal in a zoo. Back and forth she went, back and forth.

She was not so easy to understand. Sometimes she was just as vulnerable and needful as Leo. Other times she was harsh, cold. She had long, dark moods that didn't make any sense. At times—like now—she was downright creepy. And what was she doing living out here like this in this crazy place, anyway? He'd asked her why she was in a damn cave and not in a house, and where in ding-dong was the food? Her answer was to hold him and gaze at him and cry.

They'd had fun in the plane, teaching Lilith to speak better English. This "Here's looking at you, kid" approach of hers was not working. She claimed to have learned it from watching Humphrey Bogart movies, an obvious lie. No doubt she'd had a bad teacher, and some sort of Egyptian rule of etiquette prevented her from saying so. Or pride. She had enormous pride. At the least sign that she'd made some sort of mistake, her chin would rise, her alabaster cheeks would flush the color of faded roses, and her voice would go all clipped and sullen. Lilith had never made love to him, but there was hardly time, was there, given that he and Leo did it probably five times a day.

He buried his face in Leo's neck, inhaling the sweetness of her skin. Her lips moved, she muttered garbled dream talk. As many times as he'd done it with her, the hollow-gut thrill of it still made him squirm as his body became ready again. He lay an arm across her spongy breasts and sought her lips with his. She uttered a complicated little sound, a happy sound, and drew him close, wrapping her arms around him.

"I love you," she whispered.

"I love you," he whispered. It felt warm right down into the middle of his heart. He laid his lips against her cheek, felt her smile come up under them. Then she turned and they were kissing. His spirit slipped on light and secret steps into the world of her spirit.

This was love, and this was amazing. It was his Leo dream, and he was living it. One thing he knew about this kid: she might be a great lay, but she was no more experienced than him. That made it even more fun, to discover great stuff together.

Lily would watch, sitting in a chair with her chin in her hand, and tap her foot if it took longer than she liked. So he said nothing to the swooping form out there in the dark, as he slid closer to Leo. He let her know with a gentle thrust of his hips that he was ready. There came in response a low murmur, then a sigh—comfortable, silky, prolonged—that was one of the sexiest things she did, the way it made him feel so wanted and so welcome. He went on top of her, felt her fingers caressing him down below, then entered her under their gentle guidance.

He went slowly, proceeding into their private territory of pleasure by careful degrees. After his first bursting tries, he'd learned to prolong it by breathing deep and stroking slow, and if he started to come too quick, he stopped and lay absolutely still and pictured in his mind the pasty, pimple-spotted face of the Child in his sound cubicle way back down the tunnel to nowhere that ended at East Mill High.

Despite the white heat of the situation, that was one thought that could be counted on to cool him down every time. So he did it now, while she squirmed and moaned and whispered, "Hit me, hit me hard as you can, baby, oh please. . . ."

And then he felt, along the short hairs of his neck, moving air. It was as if a bat had fluttered past. When it came again, he gasped and jerked back—and bumped against Lilith, who was looming over them. But then her lips replaced her breath, and he felt her tongue against the skin of his neck. She was more beautiful than Leo, much more, and he had wondered what she would be like and why she wouldn't do it. But nothing had been said.

Sometimes Leo and Lilith went off alone into the depths of the cave, and when they came back, Leo was always flushed and sweating and didn't want to make love. So he figured they were getting off somehow together, but he was batteries not included.

Now Lilith's hands came firmly along the sides of his buttocks and lifted him out of Leo, who made a little sound in her throat—"oh." And then Lilith, who might as well have the eyes of a cat, was under him instead of Leo, and trembling like a girl.

It hit Ian that she was a newbie, and he said, "Oh, hey," trying to put a reassuring smile in his voice. "Ready to try me on for size, babe?"

Lilith had paced and sweated, trying to stay away, smelling their rising heat and juices, feeling her own vaginal muscles undulate helplessly as she touched herself and listened. She dared not let him find out how different she was, not until he was introduced to blood and eating comfortably and so hers.

He was not hers now. There was danger. He had never fed, but he could feed, and when he did, his blood would open like a flowing, liquid flower and fill him with the exquisite sensations of his sleeping Keeper being. He would never return to the eating of foliage and animal flesh, not after he had tasted the liquid flesh of man.

But before—oh, it was very dangerous before. If he knew, if he understood what was happening to him, then this sweet child of a ruthless vampire hunter would recoil and run, and she would have to kill the most beautiful and important creature on earth.

Leo had told her how the father, Paul Ward, killed Keepers, and how this boy was the son of a lovely Keeper woman and this monster, part Keeper and part man.

Ian was almost pure Keeper. He was to be worshiped, to be adored, to be served, and she had not served a man in so long that she literally could not remember. She loved being at his service, longed to be filled with his child, hoped to flood his life with every happiness she could bestow.

Her love of this brilliant and muscled boy had displaced even her dream-husband, who waited for her in the mists of time and memory. She had left him beside the Fountain of the Hours in his land far away, which maybe existed only in her mind.

Ian, however, was here now. He was making love to Leo—and that was another thing, he was so sexual, so very capable, that the merest thought of him would make her want to go off deep into her cave, down the tunnels and across the black rivers, to a place where she could howl and claw the walls and mourn. The thick scent of Leo's steaming *yuni,* the faintly hydraulic sound of their coupling, the faint glow of their rocking bodies—it was too much.

She just had to, *had* to. "Oh, Leo," she whispered, "please forgive me."

"Are you sure?" Leo said, warning in her voice.

She would take Leo with her into the deep cave, and Leo would use her tongue to produce orgasms in her, and she would bellow his name, *Ian, Ian,* where the boy could not hear. But it wasn't enough, not the clinical suction of another woman. "We have to get him to feed," she would say. But Leo never seemed to entirely agree. But obviously they had to! How could he come truly alive without it? As he was now, he was only a ghost. Of course, she wouldn't know that. She had never seen a male Keeper in his glory, and thus could not know what a real man was actually like. She was satisfied with these narrow human wraiths, because they were all she knew.

Now came a moment that she had been longing for ever since she looked into his blazing, glorious eyes in the lobby of the Music Room. She was going to touch what she had gazed at with such longing when it danced to Leo's tune. She lifted her hands, poised them above the length of the shaft. She could feel its heat.

And yet, she hesitated. She was lost in time, and the memories that came to her now were flickers only, of a husband she once had treasured, but to whom she had never yet given herself. There had been a wedding, but not yet a wedding night, in the romance of her lost past, or her mind.

Should she remain loyal to a dream?

She drew her hands closer, closer. "Come *on,*" he said, laughing.

Then he took them and pressed them against him.

Oh, the heat of it, the pulsing of it, the ancient dignity of it, and how lonely she was! She sobbed aloud, and he comforted her, laying a sacred hand on her cheek and saying in his soft, strong male voice, "It's okay, baby, it's okay." Then, "Are you a virgin, Lily?"

She answered casually, not realizing how strange it must sound: "I don't know." Then she crouched between his legs and held it until the end was tight and gleaming in the tiny light, and kissed it, being careful to keep her tongue far back in her mouth. If she could drink him, perhaps the pleasure of giving him pleasure would be enough. But no, the thought made her frantic. She had to feel him in her, no matter the consequences, and she had to do it now.

Then Leo was there, on her from behind, working her soaked lips with that quick and efficient tongue. It felt good enough—abstractly so—and she let it go on while she kissed Ian's miraculously erect penis and cried and cried.

Frantically, Leo tried to satisfy her. She could not, must not, take him. The second he was in her, he was going to know that something was radically different. Leo had explored Miri's vagina, and Lilith's was much stranger, lined with muscles that were almost as hard as cartilage. If Ian didn't know what he was doing—and that was not in question—then he was going to get hurt in there, or at the very least become aware that it was very odd.

What would happen then was anybody's guess. Incredibly, the Wards had raised him without giving him any information about vampires, let alone that he was himself a time bomb, wanting only a sip of living human blood to awaken the shadow that slept within him.

Lilith knew exactly what he was, and she was possessed to get him to eat some poor soul's blood. He could be her lover, make her pregnant, even.

When he'd gotten on her plane, all Leo had been able to think about was Ian's body. She'd been wild for him. She knew it was the magic of the blood—that he was, in the end, just another slack-jawed seventeen-year-old fan—but God, the blood was good at making her see past what was commonplace about him. This prosaic little bridge-and-tunnel person revealed inner qualities to her that quickly elevated him beyond the status of sex toy to another status entirely, that of lover.

She had never had a real lover. She had never known what it was to be unashamedly wanted by a man. He wanted her, though, wanted her so bad that he'd woo and sweat until he got her. He was sweet and gentle and generous, open-minded and kind and wonderfully, excitingly strong. And he was so in love that he would just fold himself around her and hold on for dear life, and it was so wonderful.

She had to fight to suppress her jealousy when Lilith showed interest. But Lilith was a great vampire, and she was going to get her way. Leo was just an episode. If she interfered, she'd be brushed aside.

Leo did not want to see him living the vampire life. What was it—a chance to outlive everybody you loved? Great. You'd get tired of life and fed up with life and still have to go on. Worse, you had to kill other human beings in order to live, and that was just plain awful, you never got over it. Even the serial killer—the night she'd done him, she was exultant: a guilt-free kill at last.

No damn way. He haunted her now, the same as the others. If he deserved to die for his crimes, that was up to a jury, not some girl who had no idea what he really was or had really done.

Oh, Jesus, she wouldn't wish the vampire life on a dog.

Lilith was getting restless, trying to come away from her mouth. Leo worked harder. This could all be so beautiful, if Lilith could control herself. This could all work, somehow. Love would do it, it would make them whole, all three of them. But this was not the way.

Now Ian felt Lilith's body squirming. Leo was—what was she doing? There was a strange sort of struggle going on in the dark down there. Lilith finally wanted to make love, which was great. But was Leo jealous or pissed or something? She kept trying to get down between their legs and sort of put herself between them. It was damned embarrassing. One thing to be watched—that was fun, it made you feel like a star, it was thrilling. But this—with her fooling around down there, her face pushing, her mouth smacking—this was way creepy.

"Take it easy," he rasped. Then there was a shuffle, and for a moment he felt a very strange sensation, as if he'd been put into some kind of pipe, cold and hard. "Hey, what is that?" They had him in some kind of a tube, and it felt really strange. "What is that, man?"

Suddenly he was afraid. This was a very weird situation out here in the middle of nowhere in a damn cave, for chrissakes, in the middle of a trackless desert they'd had to cross for two days in a Land Rover. And now this strange thing was happening.

His heart started hammering: they were castrating him, they were crazies. He'd known it, felt it, they were crazies and they were castrating him and he was never gonna get out of this hole alive.

When kids disappeared, this must be one of the things that happened to them.

He reared back, struggling to get himself out of whatever it was, grabbing for himself and feeling—whoa. *Whoa!* He tried to stay cool. "Jesus Christ, what the fuck's goin' on with you, Lily?" Man, you sure can squeak, still, little boy.

There was another shuffle, a muffled cry from Lilith . . . and suddenly Leo was there in her place. The pain lessened as he was directed into her comfortable hole. Oh, jeez, this was right, this was just exactly right.

She went up and down, up and down, faster and faster, pinching his nipples as she rode him. Three strokes and he was boiling hot, he was contracting into a bright intense light of pure pleasure, and then he was over once, over twice, over and over and *over.*

"Wow," he said.

"Wow," she said. She giggled back in her throat, pumped him a couple more times, and dismounted. "Okay?"

A face came in the darkness, lips kissing lips. He whispered into the kiss, "I love you, I love you so. . . ." Then he realized that the face was Lilith's, which startled him for a second, but was actually okay. He let it stand. "I love you, Lilith," he said.

And he decided to prove something to her. What the hell, he could, so he should. He got out of the bed. "Lily?"

Silence.

"Lily?"

A hoarse sound, hardly even a reply.

"I can't see a friggin' thing, so you gotta come here." She drew near him, then; he could smell her soft, waxy odor. "Let me ask you girls a question. 'Cause, you know, I mean, it's no big deal, but it'd help me figure out what I'm supposed to do around here. No offense, Lily, but are you a lesbian?"

There came a choked, inarticulate sound from the dark.

"Because I know—it's okay—you two go off." He coughed. "You don't need to. I mean, I'm totally okay with it, you know? If you have, uh, some kind of a problem down below—like what I felt—was that you?"

He was almost knocked off his feet, Lilith slammed against him so hard. Her arms were like steel cables around his waist—it was odd, the way it felt—and her face was jammed into his crotch, and she was gobbling at him like some kind of—well, he didn't know. But it was all strange again, and he didn't like it.

Anyway, he had nothing left. So he had to stand there beside the bed with this poor woman chewing at his bag and crying. He put his hand on her head and stroked her hair, sort of gently pushing at her, trying to give her a message that this was not going to go down.

She didn't stop. If anything, she got more wild, like a dog that's getting pushed away from its food bowl. Finally, he lifted her head away from him. "Okay, listen, later I'm gonna go down on you. 'Cause I think you need it in the worst possible way." She tried to go back, but he pushed her away more firmly. "Nope. You wait an hour, then I'm gonna lie you down and spread your legs and I'm gonna run one more pair of panties up the mast." If he could—but he didn't add anything about that. They'd cross that bridge.

"I adore you," she whispered.

The husky shudder in her voice touched him, because of the tension of need that it revealed. He kissed the top of her head. She was so strange, a blond woman who lived in a cave in Egypt. She'd explained that it had been created by her father, who was kind of eccentric. Which was okay, except it was too bad that he hadn't thought to include a kitchen. Which got him to a very important issue that had to be brought up.

"Look," he said into the dark, "if we're gonna not do anything here for a while, could we order a pizza or something? I ate the last of the wilted crudities from the plane this afternoon, and I'm seventeen, and anorexia isn't my shtick."

"Order a pizza," Lilith said slowly. "A . . . piazza?"

"We can't order a pizza," Leo said.

"And light a damn candle. I'm sick of not being able to see anything."

There was movement. Then a click of flints, which Lilith used with amazing ease.

When her face appeared in the candlelight, Leo gasped, and Ian saw why. He couldn't stop staring, there was just no way. Lilith's eyes were sunken; her cheeks were raw and soaked with tears. Her nose was dribbling, and her mouth described a sorrowing line. But it didn't only make you think of sadness, this face, it made you think of something else. Because in those eyes there was a real mean gleam, and in the line of those lips a knife's lethal edge.

"Look," Ian said, "uh, why are you crying?"

She met his eyes with the glowing pits of her own. A sob racked her. Leo went to her, and she sank into her arms. Ian went, too—hey, why not? He held them both. They rode the dark together, the three of them.

Lilith broke away. This was not going well. Leo was making her absolutely furious. If the girl didn't follow along, she was going to have to be controlled.

"Hey," Ian said, "you know, if it's some kink you're into, Lily, and you, like—you know, you think I'm just a kid—kids are educated these days. I'm cool with it. I just want us all to be—you know, what we can be."

"We go to Cairo," she said.

"Hey, that's cool. To a very good restaurant, I hope."

"Cairo—it's a long drive," Leo said quickly. "Why don't I go out to—there must be some little town—I can get us Arab food."

"Sounds not good."

"No, it's lamb and rice and stuff. Really good."

"Pizza would be really good. You're talking about edible."

"Maybe there's a pizza place. There's pizza places in Egypt."

"We go to Cairo."

"No!"

Lilith felt anger flare. There could be only one reason that Leo didn't want to go to Cairo. She had to be famished herself. Lilith wanted food, that was certain. So Leo did not want Ian to feed. She was trying to "save"

him from the great life that awaited him. There was a foolish and sentimental side to this human girl.

"Leo," she said, "come with me." She took her hand, very firmly.

"Hey, what about Cairo? Two for and one against, Leo. If you don't
want to go, that's cool, you can stay here. Lilith and I are going, am I right,
Lily?"

"In a short time," Lilith said. "We must have a private moment."

"You never stop," Ian said.

Lilith would change Leo Patterson's attitude. She would change it
completely. But she needed privacy to do it, a place so far from here that
not even the loudest, most awful of screams would echo back.

Leo whimpered as she was taken down first one flight of steps and
then another, down into the depths of this horrible place. They came into
a small room with thick, stinking air. Lilith shut the ancient wooden door.
Leo was alone with her now, in the bowels of the earth. No scream, no
matter how loud, would penetrate to the dreaming boy upstairs—as if he,
in his pitiful state, would even hear it for what it was.

Lilith shoved her against the wall. "How dare you, you stupid creature! I ought to kill you."

"I'm ready."

"I thought you were so beautiful. And look at you, blooded by a
Keeper! You should be grateful."

"Grateful? You must be insane!"

"A grand life, power, wealth—it all comes from the blood, my blood.
And you should be grateful."

"What are you people, anyway? Where are you from?"

"The shores of the Red Sea."

"Whatever the truth is, that's not it."

Lilith slapped Leo across the face so hard that she was momentarily in
another world of flashing lights and sounds like cannons.

"Do it! Do it! My life's not worth anything anyway! It's hell! It's been
hell ever since—" She remembered Miri and gentle Sarah, and the love
and trust she had found in their arms. She tried to go on, but she could
not, she broke down and wept bitterly.

Lilith grabbed her and thrust her to the floor so hard it felt as if her knees had exploded. "Kneel when you speak to your betters," she said mildly. "You should not seek to prevent him from discovering his true nature. It is his right to be an overlord to man."

"Yeah, look what happened to all the other overlords."

"He will be greater than either man or Keeper. He's a new kind of being."

"He'll have to slink around in the night killing people just like the rest of us. It's no life, Lilith."

"He is the work of God!"

"God has nothing to do with you or your unholy species or anything about you."

"Be quiet and don't display your ignorance. We do the work of God."

"Then why are you getting killed off? God must not think a whole hell of a lot of you. In fact, God must think you're real crappy workers."

Lilith's eyes became stone.

"Paul Ward is going to kill you. I give you a week."

"Why is this, that he kills us, the father of a man who is mostly of my kind? Paul Ward bears my blood also."

"He'll kill you, and my guess is, he'll do it so that you don't quite die. That's the way they do it—they leave you bloodless and dismembered."

"I know what they do! Do you think I didn't see? I have seen it, all of it—the horror of it, by all that's holy!" She sprang at Leo. "Listen to me! You will cooperate. You will stop trying to turn him against me. Or you will suffer. I know how to torture like you would not believe. I can place you in unspeakable agony and leave you like that for a thousand years. Oh, don't smirk at me, you wretched creature."

"I'm not smirking at you, I'm scared of you! Please, let's try to make an accommodation. We can live our way, and he can live his way, and we can all be lovers. Please, it'll be wonderful."

Leo felt herself lifted up, then penetrated from below by a steel fist. Something inside her was grabbed and squeezed, and the pain was so total and so amazing that her legs thrust out and her head flew back and her arms flailed wildly and she screamed and screamed and screamed.

When it finally ended, she was lying in a heap, gasping.

"I can leave you like that for a hundred ages, suffering just like that."

"Oh, Jesus, Jesus . . ."

"You obey me in everything, and I will leave you alone. Otherwise—well, I have worse than what you felt, and I have no mercy. Remember that, *I have no mercy!*"

As Lilith spoke, her voice changed, and suddenly Leo was hearing what was behind that façade of driven-snow beauty—a scared little voice, the voice of an actress playing a role she thought was way out of her league.

"I am indeed going to show him how to drink blood," Lilith said. "And you're going to help me."

"No."

"No? You say that now?"

"Kill me. Do it. Set me on fire inside. Anything would be better than helping you do that to him."

"Come," Lilith said, but Leo could not come, she could not rise from the floor, not with the punishment she'd taken. Lilith muttered something in her own language. Once, Leo had wanted to learn Prime. Now she loathed the very sound of it, the gutturals and the leaping, bell-like overtones. No human throat could utter such sounds, anyway.

Lilith took her under the shoulders and dragged her. She scuffed along, moaning. They went down a narrow, dark tunnel and then into a wider area, equally dark.

Lilith threw her off into the blackness. She landed in a heap of what felt like lumber. It was hard and it hurt, and she cried out. There came a small laugh, not quite a chuckle—more intimate than that. Then she felt tickling, as if some sort of tick or mite was rushing over her skin. She slapped at it and encountered something that filled her hand like a cluster of wet pencils.

There came a long sigh. Leo listened, but it was not repeated. "Lilith?"

Nothing.

Leo backed into the dark. But she did not come up against a wall, not at all. Instead, she ended up in a confusing tangle of long objects, heavy and covered with dust—dust that ran on her, seething at her lips and the edges of her eyes, making the undersides of her fingernails itch and her vagina and anus burn. She opened her mouth, instinct crying out, and the itching, burning sensation invaded her throat.

The taste was fuzzy and stinging and oddly crisp, like the fried pork rinds they sell in bodegas, if you got some that were moldy. An involuntary cough sent a gust of it out into the air. She gagged, her throat going taut as the extreme dryness of the material absorbed every trace of moisture in her mouth. And then she felt a tightening against her breast, then pain, and looked down and saw there a skull, one wrinkled eye staring up at her out of its gaping socket, and a long, pointed thing like a cuttlebone thrusting out of its round, toothless orifice into her skin.

The drop of blood that appeared there seemed to send an electricity through the whole chamber, and all the bones began to rustle, and the dust to sift and flow. "Never let them touch you," Sarah Roberts had warned her. Now she knew why. She had been thrown into a dungeon of dead vampires, creatures who had wronged their pale mistress.

Leo gagged and struggled, feeling her own urine hurry down her legs, as she dragged her fingers through the living muck that was filling her mouth, burning her sinuses and eating her eyes.

Then Lilith stepped back. As the door closed, the light began to dim. Leo cried out, a jagged gargle, and writhed and twisted, then came to her feet and pranced in the surging bones and skulls, feeling herself being devoured away by inches. She begged God for help, she begged Jesus, she begged and tore at her cracking skin, at her bleeding privates, as she fought her way to that door.

When she got there, she banged and clawed and pleaded and lost hope in the secret way of those who know that they are without an avenue of escape, and her cries became the hopeless tears of the frightened little girl she really was, the lost little girl who had only in these past few days, now, for the first time in her life, felt the comfort of love.

The door clicked. She hammered, she pleaded, she felt runnels of blood speeding down her thighs. The door opened a little. A whisper: "You will obey me."

Before she could answer, the door slammed again. Bones, bits of flesh, corpse dust—it was all sliding toward her, the famished remains of the undead clinging to her, eating into her, devouring her alive. She hammered at the door, she clawed, she howled, driven in just these few seconds to a state beyond the known world of fear, to a place where even in darkest dark, human beings do not go.

Where she bled, where her skin was torn and pulled away, a particle of awareness followed. She was *not* being killed, she was being transformed into a mass of bones and blood and particles that would still have awareness and life, that would be consumed and then lie here with these others, melded with them forever, in perpetual agony and longing.

Hands—cold, like steel—clasped her waist and drew her out of the morass. With a hermetic *thunk*, the door was shut behind her.

She was thrown—then she was in water, deep, black water. She was tumbling in it, unable to tell which way was up, tumbling and spitting, her hands pushing at the filth that caked her body.

She struggled, she flailed—and suddenly her hand rose into air and came back down to the surface of the water with a bright snap of sound and a stinging thrill to the palm. Her face broke clear, then, and she sucked in the air of darkness, sucked it with more gratitude than she had ever felt in her life.

There came then the thought: If I do not live endless life, I have to live endless death. The horror of it was beyond her capacity even to consider. No matter how evil, she had to do whatever was necessary to avoid this. She pulled herself up onto the bank of the freezing underground pool. Breath swept her grateful lungs, clean breath, as pure as the dead, ancient air of this hell pit could offer. Shivering, her naked body still tormented here and there by clumps of sodden undead material, she lay on the bank. She said, "I'll help you," and her soul wept.

"You will be bright, cheerful and enthusiastic."

"Yes."

"You will encourage him and support me."

"Yes."

Lilith lifted her, brought her off her feet, face to face. "Let's be clear. I let you out because I need you. But remember, I'm on a mission, and *I have no mercy*. Remember what it means."

"Yes."

"Smile."

How could she? How could she ever? "I—"

Lilith grabbed her hair and began yanking her toward the door.

"No!"

"Smile!"

She forced a grin—and Lilith slapped it away.

"One more chance. Right now."

From somewhere inside she hadn't known was there, Leo found a fraction of joy—the invincible center of her humanity—and somehow lifted it into her face, and she made from it with a craftsman's patient care, a little smile.

"Let's get you cleaned up. He'll be wondering where we are."

She hurried her along yet another corridor, this one winding steeply upward.

"Lilith?"

"Yes, child?"

"Who were they?"

"That is an execution chamber. They are put in and left."

"Why were they executed?"

She stopped, turned on her. Her dark eyes bore into Leo's. "They violated my will," she said. Not so much in the words but in their tone, Leo heard the most power she had ever heard conveyed in a voice.

She went off then, and Leo followed. Never had she hated herself so much, hated her blood, hated Miri for giving it to her.

She had millions. She was famous and powerful. Maybe somewhere on this earth, there would be a cure.

Twice, Lilith opened doors that were like black submarine hatches. Each one they passed offered a wider corridor, more light, and sweeter air.

"Lilith! Please, Lilith, wait."

"What is it?"

"Is there any way—if you would reconsider. If you need him to get you pregnant, then he can do it the way he is, surely."

Lilith gave her a kindly look. "My dear child, he belongs to a higher race than man. He can't continue living as they do! You cannot imagine what he'll be like in his glory. For both of us, child!"

They came into an area of stone pools. The air was sharp with sulfur, and the water was wreathed by steam. This was not far from the living quarters, which could be seen as a pool of dim light at the end of a near tunnel.

"This is my bath," Lilith said. She helped Leo into the embracing water, then sat back on some cushions that Leo noticed were clouded by mildew. She began to sing. Her voice was soft but penetrating as she uttered the sighing words of love or death among her kind—who knew what they meant?

Drawn by the haunting beauty of the melody and Lilith's miraculous voice, Ian appeared in the doorway. He was wearing a white linen tunic over his gleaming, well-muscled young body. Leo loved him with her eyes. She wanted the best for him, the best of all the world!

"Come in," Lilith said, "we're going to give each other baths."

Lilith went behind Ian and drew off his tunic. She slapped his backside, which made him jump and laugh. "In with you," she said.

"You be careful, you'll get it worse."

"Oh, I'm *so* scared." She popped him again on the backside, and he scampered down beside Leo.

"Oh, my," he said, stretching himself out, "oh, this feels—damn, Lily, what *is* this?"

"Just water. My water. It's what keeps me young."

She came in, also, swam lithely out into the deep orange center of it, then treaded water, smiling at them. "Smile, Leo," she said, "you're not smiling."

Ian grabbed Leo and made her yell in surprise. Then she felt his knuckles digging into her ribs. She squirmed and heard as if on some vast distance—across a black ocean, down a yawning cave—the tinkle of her own laughter.

"She's smiling now," Ian yelled happily. "She's laughing!"

He dunked her, and in the haze of the sulfurous water, she could see Lilith's long, white legs, and then, right before her face, Ian's penis, half-awake.

It broke her heart to see it, for it brought back to her, all at once and in an instant, all the happiness of the past few days, that had been so great and seemed so eternal, and had just ended so completely.

Her hand went out, touched it. She looked at her own fingers on it, knew by his sudden stillness that he was ready to go again, God love this boy. She stroked it, and that familiar, velvety penis skin felt so nice beneath her touch. It came up, and her eyes began to sting and she lifted herself above the water and shook them out, relieved that she would also shake away any sign of the tears that were there.

Lilith was right in her face, treading water, smiling. She also smiled, grinned from ear to ear, and belted out a laugh.

Leo laughed back, a crackling sound like a crow. Didn't he hear the coldness of it? Was he deaf?

The three of them embraced on the wet, sulfur-smelling floor, in the steam and the heat and the silence of inner earth. Then Lilith said, "Tonight, Cairo."

"Cairo," Ian said.

"Cairo," Leo agreed. Her voice lilted because she made it lilt, but her heart was weeping, and her soul screamed silently in its secret hell, The horror, the horror.

CHAPTER FIFTEEN

Innocence Lost

P aul counted the seconds as the satellite image was slowly produced by the printer. The four of them were clustered around it, eager for this crucial picture to appear.

"Perhaps there," Karas said, "just south of Al-Wasta." He went to the telephone, spoke quickly in Arabic, listened, hung up. "It's got three parties in it, according to the police." He paused. "Maybe four."

Becky turned to him. Jean Bocage looked up from the satellite image. Paul said, "What does that mean?"

"Perhaps it's the wrong vehicle."

Paul looked at the Range Rover, hardly distinguishable from above. But the computer had circled it. It was the same vehicle that they had tracked from near the Monastery of St. Anthony in the Arabian Desert. Now it had turned south, though. Why would they go south?

"Beni Suef," Becky whispered. "Oh, God, they're leaving."

"Trying to," Jean Bocage responded. "Remember, their pilots are in Cairo."

"Unless they called them. What if they're on their way?"

"They are in their hotel at this moment," Karas said. "They have not been called, and they have not left."

Becky's brow shone with sweat. Paul touched her hand, was not reassured by the quick jerk of movement with which she drew away. How profoundly did she blame him?

"Let's put the drone up," he said. He stepped down out of the reconnaissance van and pulled the plane's long case out of the rear stowage. Jean helped him carry it onto the desert as Becky and Karas descended from the truck to watch.

Jean said, "That's an impressive unit."

"Let's hope."

They were out beyond Sahara City in the ancient desert, positioned to pounce on the Range Rover when it appeared. It was the only one the satellite had found that the Egyptian police had—supposedly—confirmed as containing just three passengers. They knew that Leo had rented a Ranger Rover in Beni Suef, where they had landed. It had been carefully and intelligently done, the rental, from a small local firm rather than an international company, and for lots of delicious U.S. dollars. But the owner remembered very definitely the three Americans who had rented it, and how odd he found it that they didn't want a driver. He had been persuaded not to check their documentation, no doubt by more of that sweet money of Leo's.

Since the rental had been discovered, the Egyptian police had been under instructions to report the vehicle if they saw it. They had not been given arrest orders, any more than they would have been asked to pick up a cobra and bring it in. Ordinary police did not have the expertise to deal with a vampire.

The printer came to life again, its whining just loud enough to be heard over the communications van's roaring air-conditioning. Becky went back in as Paul struggled with the wings of the drone.

"Help me with this thing," he said to Jean. Working together, they got it screwed and snapped together. Its wings were eight feet long, enabling it almost to hover. The stall speed was just thirty-two miles an hour. They carried the drone out onto the desert. Paul turned on the cameras, made sure the telemetry was working, then used the remote control to turn on the engine, which made a high-pitched hissing sound, like compressed air.

The plane, sky blue, rolled quickly across the desert and bounded into flight. Gaining a feel for the remote control, Paul dipped first one wing and then the other, almost stalled it, then got into controlled flight. He set the autopilot for fifteen hundred feet. The device began going up in slow spirals, but before it had risen five hundred feet, its camouflage had made it completely invisible against the desert sky.

"Give me the coordinates," Paul yelled into the half-open side door of the truck.

Becky came out. "This is hot off the printer," she said.

He took the sheet of coordinates from the satellite and input the location, direction, and speed of the Range Rover into the system. Far above, the silent and invisible craft stopped spiraling and took off in pursuit. The screen on the navigator displayed a detailed image of the terrain the drone was covering superimposed on a map.

"My God," Karas said.

"You're not supposed to see this damn thing," Paul replied.

"Do the Israelis have this?"

"Come on, General, give me a break."

"Just kidding, Paul. Of course the Israelis have it. They get all your toys, whether you offer them or not."

"Not my department."

He laughed suddenly. "We have it," he said.

"Why doesn't that surprise me?" Paul said.

"Egypt has this?" Jean asked. "We don't have it."

"Why doesn't that surprise me?" Karas said.

They watched the screen as the land unfolded below the drone. Soon the outskirts of Beni Suef appeared, looking from above as if they were bombed out. The highway was easy to find but hard to observe, because it was close to the Nile and lined by palm trees.

"At El Maharaqa it becomes a motorway. It's wider, much easier to deal with."

"That's in the direction of Cairo?"

"Unfortunately."

Paul took the drone down to an altitude of three hundred feet, then out over the Nile. He dropped it farther, until the side-looking camera's view was almost parallel to the roadway. With magnification, they ended up with a useful image of the traffic. Slowly, he increased the speed of the drone until it was moving faster than the traffic.

"There," Becky said.

It was a Range Rover—but it was going north. Paul turned the dial that increased the magnification, but the vehicle shot past the south-bound drone. "Goddammit, now I've gotta make a turn."

As he struggled with the controls, the image on the screen gyrated wildly. Something on the control panel buzzed. Using his pilot's knowledge, he straightened out the stick, got his bearings, concentrated on his instruments. "Okay," he said, "piece of cake. Sort of."

They were going north now, catching up with the traffic headed toward Cairo. And there was the Range Rover again.

"The Egyptian and his battle with the sun," Karas said. "Which explains the police uncertainty."

His point was that the windows were tinted deeply. Another Range Rover passed the first, also with tinted windows.

"Great," Becky said.

Paul's heart sank. He couldn't see the license plates, and so had no way to tell anything useful about either vehicle.

"We're in trouble," Jean said needlessly. He was there for the extraordinary weapons that he brought. Alone in the world, the French had developed a purpose-designed gun for vampire hunting. It fired a bullet that split into five separate explosive heads in a tight pattern. A direct hit by even one of those heads meant instant and total control over even the quickest and most powerful vampire.

But to use a weapon, they needed to find a vampire. Above all, they needed to find Ian. He's an intelligent boy, Paul kept telling himself, he's careful and he's smart. But he was also seventeen and horny, and Paul had seen the damn thing in that theater, the awesome beauty of it.

"We need to get a tail on both cars," Becky said.

"That's out." They had never used outsiders in their work, never.

"It's not out, Paul, goddammit, it's Ian's life!"

"Becky—"

"Paul, shut up. General—"

He had gone back in the van and was already on the phone. Paul keyed in the code that caused the drone to return to base, then followed Becky toward the van.

"You don't need to control it anymore?" Jean asked.

"They say not. We'll see if it lands or crashes."

After the white sun of the desert, the van's interior seemed almost black. Karas offered Paul a Coke, which he took and knocked back almost in a single swallow.

"We're following all the Range Rovers in the area," Karas said, "the old-fashioned way." He smiled. "We don't really have one of your planes."

"Why doesn't that surprise me?"

"We need to move," Becky said. "Why don't we just get a car and tail these people ourselves?"

"Becky—"

"Paul, he's your son!"

"Goddamn it, I'm suffering just as much as you are, Becky."

She glared at him.

"Hey, this is me."

"Paul, excuse me, but you're playing with model airplanes, and he's out there all alone with that damn thing."

"The plane is coming in."

"You gave him no knowledge, and therefore he has no defenses. Paul, he's not an experiment, and you have no right to play God!"

The edge of hysteria in her voice scared him, because whenever he opened his mouth, he could hear it in his own. Their judgment was impaired by panic, both of them.

He said, "I want him back as bad as you do."

"Then act like it!"

"Becky," Karas said gently, "if we commit ourselves to following a car before we have a definite confirmation and it's the wrong one, then where are we?"

"Look, we know the license of the car they rented. So we get an ID on it and go after that vehicle. It could not be more simple."

"Until the creature observes that it is being followed," Jean said gently. "As it will."

Nobody spoke. They all knew just how hard this was going to be. You could not trail a vampire without being noticed.

"Her plane has to be dealt with," Becky said firmly, "in case she has access to other pilots."

"I'll have it drained of fuel," Karas said. "If anybody attempts to use it, they'll have to buy more. We'll be alerted." His cell phone warbled, and he extracted it from a side pocket. He spoke on it in Arabic for a full minute, then closed it. "The vehicle we were observing stopped for petrol, and the police got a good look at the occupants. Only one now, a driver of Al-Ireya. They gave up the Range Rover in Beni Suef. They are no longer using it."

Becky's face turned pink. Her hands were clutched into fists. Paul wanted to be sick.

"And their movements?" Jean asked.

"Only this is confirmed: there are three of them, believed to be Americans. Two young women and a young man."

"You're on them? Following them?" Her voice sang like wind slicing wire. She was on the far edge, about to break, Paul could hear it.

Karas looked toward him. "We could try it."

"No," Paul said.

"You do it, General."

"I—"

"Do it!"

"Becky, it won't work!" Bocage's voice caused her to whirl round. But it also caused her to pause, to think.

The vampire's great intelligence meant that you surprised them in their lairs or not at all, and you relied on their two weaknesses: the predator's instinct to live in isolation, and the vampire's arrogant certainty that he could always outwit the human being.

"Then what's next?" she asked. Paul tried to take her hand. She pulled away from him.

It was late in the afternoon, and the lengthening of the shadows meant a quiet increase in the terror of the two parents. Becky was smoking again, and the lower the sun went, the more she puffed and strode back and forth. Paul knew how fearsome she could be in battle. The woman would not stop, not for anything, but she had to have something to fight.

"I say we go to Cairo," she announced.

"And leave our access to satellite information, the drone, all the electronics?" Jean loved electronics.

"If they're going to Cairo, they're going to eat," she said. "We will find evidence—murders."

"Perhaps, and perhaps not," Karas said.

"You don't investigate murders in Egypt?"

"Of course we do, Becky, come on. But it's an immense city. Extremely complex. A remnant—you know how well they hide them, or destroy them."

"I hate this damn third-world crap! If somebody disappears, surely there'll be a police record."

"We all have the same problems," Jean said. "Even in France, missing persons investigations are less intense."

"Even in France," Becky said bitterly. The fact that Jean Bocage's unit had remained intact all these years was a source of bitter jealousy.

"You know," Karas said thoughtfully, "it took a child last time. Maybe it prefers them. If so, then we will certainly have an investigation. It's not like some old fellow who sells cigarette papers evaporating from his accustomed street corner, the disappearance of a child."

"Yeah, in NYC it took a damn fisherman, of all things. Do you investigate the disappearance of fishermen?"

"Sir, there's a call from police communications."

Karas grabbed the telephone. This time, the conversation was more terse. He hung up. "An officer reports three Americans, two women and a man, came down off a bus from the south just a short time ago. A blond woman, a dark-haired woman he recognized as Leo Patterson, and a young man."

Becky's hand clutched Paul's.

"They're in a taxi. We have its number. We're watching its movements."

Paul said, "They're not being careful." An ordinary tail was working—for the moment. But how long would it last?

"How much underground in Cairo, General?"

He shook his head. "Vast amounts, stretching even under the Nile. A fantastic labyrinth."

"Let's move," Becky said.

This time, nobody argued.

* * *

Lilith's course was clear: she would teach the boy to feed, then kill the father, who would be nearby attempting to reach his son. Already, some of his lieutenants were following them, thick creatures in a small car. She said nothing of them to Ian and Leo. Why should she? She could shake off human followers whenever she needed to.

She reflected on how much she had changed since she was last in this city, the confused mistress of a world she did not realize had ceased to exist. In the past weeks, she had absorbed knowledge as well as languages. Human life was far more complex than it had been when she used to walk the streets of man. There was much more ritual. In addition to religious ritual, there was economic ritual. She understood that she had not been involved in religious activity in the New York hotels, but in the economic process of buying hotel space and transportation with credit cards, which withdrew funds from the accounts of the creature she had consumed at the Royalton Hotel, Genevive Perdu. She also knew that Genevive Perdu's cards would eventually cease to function, when her absence from the life of the community was finally noticed.

Leo had explained about passports and visas, but so far she had solved all their problems with money. She sat now beside the driver, a small book opened on her lap. "Old Cairo," she said.

The driver increased the speed of the vehicle. Lilith observed by the lack of tension of his body that he was unaware of the police tail.

"Have you never seen Cairo?" Lilith asked Ian.

He was silent, staring out the window, sheathed in the cloak she had given him. She touched his shoulders. How she enjoyed being tentative with him, lowering her eyes at his approach, drawing command from his unsure young voice.

"We've got to get some more ordinary clothes," Ian said at last. "We look like circus freaks."

"Freaks?"

"You know what it means," Leo murmured.

Lilith did not reply. When she first laid eyes on Leo, she had loved her immediately, for the blood that flowed in her veins. But Leo wasn't working out; she was not the loyal servant that Keepers expected when they infused their blood into human veins. She did not want to kill Leo. In fact, without Leo, she wasn't at all sure how to get out of Egypt, if that should be needed. There would be no more boat trips, not after the experience of the airplane. She'd seen much larger ones, too. Huge ones. They must be palaces within, palaces indeed. Egyptair—the very word was magic.

"That's a mosque," Ian said. "It's magnificent."

"That's the Al-Muayyad Mosque," Leo said, "I think." She was consulting the illustrated guide she'd bought from among the hundreds frantically offered in the bus station. "He's taking us to the bazaar section. Are you taking us to the bazaar section?"

"Bazaar, yes, as you say."

Ian leaned forward, touched Leo's shoulder. "Are you okay?"

"Quit asking me that!"

"You sound funny, and it's bothering me, Leo."

She turned, and Lilith saw in her eyes hard jewels of hate. Then the eyes fixed on Ian and became instantly soft. "I have a little cold."

"Good, because I don't think you should be crying."

"She isn't crying. She's happy. We're all happy, it's exciting!"

"I'm happy, Ian. I'm so happy that we're here, and Cairo is so wonderful, and Lilith and you are so wonderful, and everything is just wonderful."

The dullness of her tone communicated the truth: she had become unreliable. But would she betray her mistress, knowing where she would be put? Or did she cherish some absurd hope of escape?

The taxi stopped. They were disembarking in a region packed with selling booths and humanity. It was a labyrinth, like Rome—although Leo had said that Rome, as Lilith recalled it, with its endless colonnades and soldiery and roaring, fragrant amphitheater, was now in ruins.

They went out of the vehicle and found themselves surrounded by a great chaos of tiny shops brimming with every imaginable object. If ever anyone doubted that humankind was a trinket-loving species, they had only to come to a paradise of trinkets like this absurd place.

"We're getting you out of that awful thing," Leo said to Ian.

"Awful" meant that she did not care for the treasure that hung so gracefully on Ian's broad shoulders. "We will not get him out of it," Lilith said. "He looks wonderful." It was the skin of a philosopher called Moses Maimonides, whom she had won in a game of Tarochi with Al-Malik Al-Afdal Saladin, vizier of Egypt. She had particularly wanted Maimonides, because he had been so dogged about spreading the annoying rumor that she was a divorcée.

"Come on, Lilith, he looks like Dracula's grandson."

"Dracul? What do you know of Dracul?" He was a Keeper of the northern mountains, not somebody whose name this girl should know.

Leo rolled her eyes, an expression suggesting to Lilith that she thought her a fool. Lilith came another regretful step closer to ending the threat of Leo.

"Look, Ian, look at this." Leo held up a white blouse. "This is great, you'll look wonderful in it. And very Egyptian."

When they paused, the three lieutenants of the father who were following also stopped. As Leo and Ian fingered garments, Lilith looked their pursuers over, glancing out of the sides of her eyes. This situation could change very quickly.

"The thing is wonderful," she told Ian. "Buy it."

Leo did it for him, and he strolled away wearing it, the cloak slung over his shoulder. They moved deeper into the tangle of little shops, the stalkers never far behind. Lilith said nothing about them. She didn't trust Leo enough.

Here, there were hanging masses of colorful sweets, there a tiny tea bar, and across the way a coffee room. There were shops with silver and gold, with all manner of smoked eyeglass and walking stick and sash, and shoes of all sorts, black leather, velvet, and the endless, overly elaborate "sneakers." Lilith wore a sandal, and it served her well. There were also many devices that emitted artificialized music. They piped it from the instruments and singers into mechanisms that transfigured it into spark, the atmospheric vibrations of which were detected by other devices, which were sold in gaudy tin shells, no doubt to disguise the fact that the sound that they emitted was obviously no longer music, but the mere jittering of the spark.

The stalkers were closer now, pretending interest in the bins of trinkets and baubles to cover their steady progress. Her heart began humming; she had no further illusions about the danger posed by man.

She gazed up. The sun could not be seen between the rollicking stacks of rooms that wound along the alleyway, but she could tell by the pearl color of the sky that night was already well arisen in the east.

Sometimes, at a moment such as this, she would sense other vistas, as if she had seen them in some far place, a better place than this. Useless dreams, bitter dreams. But how had she come here? And what of the Keepers? Moses Maimonides had been telling a foolish story, that she'd been the first wife of the first man, but so difficult that he divorced her in favor of Eve—an equally unfortunate liaison, if the Bible story was to be believed. But something had indeed happened in the place where she was supposed to have birthed her legion of demons, her old dwelling on the shores of the Blood Sea. I'm a scientist, she thought suddenly . . . and suddenly wanted to cry.

Leo said, "Look at that place. No women allowed." She laughed. "You want to get a coffee, and we'll sit on the bench with the other gals?"

That was not needed now, that could not be done, they were in a hurry.

Ian looked toward the coffee bar.

"Let's find him something to eat, Leo. He doesn't need coffee, he needs food." She caressed his cheek. She wanted him so badly, was desperate for him, and found herself glorying in that fact. Yes, glorying, that was the right word. It was glorious to want a man, and to have the man she wanted beside her, awaiting only a little change in diet to make him truly hers.

"Uh, I'll get a coffee," Ian said. When they'd been out in the desert living in a cave, he hadn't thought about calling his mom and dad. There was no phone, and his cell didn't even come close to working. But here—they were on his mind now, in a very major way. He'd done wrong coming here like this. But the women, God, they were like some kind of wonderful dream. He'd given the dream too much time, though, and he needed to go in there and try the phone. The fact that the women couldn't come in made it a good place. He wasn't sure how they'd react to his calling his folks. Probably not real well.

He entered the smoky coffee bar, where he didn't want to be at all. A kid in a kaftan or whatever brought him a tiny cup of coffee and a big water pipe. He'd give it a shot, but he'd once smoked part of one of Dad's cigars, and that was an experience he would never have again until hell froze over. That thing had been—wow. You never forgot something that made you that sick.

So, okay, he thought, as he took a deep puff on the water pipe, okay, Mom and Dad, how do I do this? I get taken to damn Egypt in this incredible plane by Leo herself and her really cute friend, and we go out and live in a cave and I had no cell coverage. Does that sound believable? Nah, because it's true. But, Mom and Dad, it was so totally incredible and wonderful, you just have no idea. No idea. It was the adventure of a lifetime, see, and—shit. Shit, the truth of the matter was, when he went home, he was going to be grounded until death us do part.

So if he pulled out his cell and called, what happened? He looked out the window. Leo and Lily were on the bench, facing out into the street. He took out his phone. The coffee came. He thought about the phone. Maybe it wouldn't work. "Thing was, Dad, I didn't know my cell wouldn't work."

The coffee was real sweet, but actually kind of good. He was sort of fascinated by this situation. The farthest thing in the world from what Leo, or Mom for that matter, would approve of. A man-only place like this was so completely antifeminist that it was almost funny, in his opinion, but this was the Arab world, where women were not considered equal. He'd never say this, but it was actually kind of nice to go in a place and all of a sudden a whole set of tensions and issues that you didn't even know you had were left at the door. The fuckathons were great, no other way to say it, but having a little piece of time and space to himself, this was also good. So he allowed the kid to pour him another coffee. It deadened his appetite a little, too.

He looked again at the pay phone. How did you make a call from Egypt? He really had no idea. But he could try. He had to be able to say that he had tried. He got up and went over to it, contemplated how it might work.

And then Lilith was standing in the door. Her face was as blank as a piece of statuary. For a second, she didn't even look alive, and it was a little odd—more than a little. Her eyes were just—they were like pieces of stone. For all the world, she looked like she was damn well going to go for his throat.

Slowly, he put down the phone. His mind hurried along in the situation. Were they prepared to stop him from calling home? Had he actually *been* kidnapped?

He left some Egyptian pounds and walked out.

"Let's go," Lilith said. They moved on, but they did not stroll.

"What's the big hurry?"

"You're hungry."

"Look, I was just gonna call my folks. I mean, Jesus, they have no damn idea where I am."

"We'll eat, then call."

Now they were getting into a dark area, still full of people, though. They conferred together in low voices, the two of them. They were up to something. Ian had no intention of doing drugs, if that was what this was about. No way, especially not in a foreign country. In East Mill, if kids got caught with grass by one of the deps, they had to, like, share. That was as far as it went. But you might get put in prison here, à la *Midnight Express* or something. His mom and dad had rented that movie and forced him to watch it, and it had definitely made an impression. You did not want to rot in any third-world jails.

"What's up?"

"We're exploring," Lilith said.

"Are we looking for anything in particular? Because this looks like a dead end."

"It's not a dead end."

"Okay. Look, if they have opium dens here or something, count me out."

Leo laughed, a low sound in the gloom. "This isn't about drugs."

"Okay, fine. If it isn't about drugs, what is it about? Because there aren't exactly any tourist attractions in the slums."

Lilith came close to him, squeezed his hand. "It's a wonderful surprise," she said.

He took his hand back. "I need to call my mom and dad."

"Are you ready?" Lilith said softly to Leo. Why was she talking like that? They were looking for something. What in hell was it?

Leo was standing near the wall of one of the old tenements. There was a sort of opening there—just a crack, really. Nobody could get in there.

"Ready," Leo said. Whereupon she stepped into the crack and was gone.

Lilith pushed him, and he felt a scrape and a pretty hard bump to the side of his head, and he was in this absolutely dark space. Then she came in behind him, her breath hissing.

"What is this place?"

"A passageway into another street."

"A secret passageway."

Lilith dragged him on, and all of a sudden they were outside again, and this street was so different that he was almost ready to believe that he'd gone into a parallel universe or something. The crowds were well dressed, there were regular stores with lighted windows, places like Fendi and Louis Vuitton.

He looked back toward where they had come out, but it wasn't there anymore. "How did we do that?"

"Cairo's full of those passages."

She should know, considering that it was her town.

"Over there," Leo said.

"I see it."

All Ian saw was a kid of about twelve spearing butts from the sidewalk and field-stripping them into a little bag, tobacco that probably ended up in the damn water pipes.

"I'll take it," Lilith said. She strode across the street, threading the Cairo traffic with an agility that would have startled anybody who hadn't been in bed with her.

He noticed that Leo's arm had come around him. "Run," she said, barely breathing, not moving her mouth. He turned to her. Had he heard that right? "Run," she whispered again. She was shaking so much she had to use him for support.

"What?"

"You have no time. Run."

"Where?" But he was getting scared now, for sure. Something was wrong, no doubt at all, not now. Then he saw something happen that looked very strange. It had to do with Lilith and the kid. She bent down to him, and he looked up at her. Then she sort of covered him with the folds of her clothing, and he seemed to disappear inside his own clothes. When she stood up, she had something in her hands that looked like a pile of the kid's clothes, but there was no kid.

"Hey!"

She did not hear Ian, or did not acknowledge his cry. The traffic kept roaring past. The thronged sidewalks were just the same. Except one thing was not the same. Lilith slipped into one of those cunning alleys and came out again, and not even the kid's clothes were there anymore.

She trotted back across the street. "Well," she said, "who's next?"

"What happened to that kid?"

"He went down the alley. I thought he could lead us to a good tobacconist, but I was wrong."

Leo, whose arm was still around him, seemed as stiff and cold as a corpse. By contrast, Lilith was flushed so red that she looked like she was having some kind of high-blood-pressure attack or something. She looked not so good, actually, and Ian kind of did not like her like this. Her eyes were—now the word was *sharp*. They were glittering and sharp and made him think of some kind of—well, actually, not even an animal. There was something really creepy in there. The word *monster* came to mind.

"Want to do another?" she breathed. She was kind of . . . seething.

"Another what?"

She threw her head back and laughed silently, but the look on her face—eyes closed tight, teeth bared, nostrils flaring—was pure agony.

People flowed around them like an excited river. There was a faintly spicy smell on the air, the scent of the East. At the end of the street the moon had appeared over the horizon, fat and almost red, looking as if you could lay a ladder to it.

Leo had removed an object from her purse, a wicked-looking thing with what looked like a hooked blade on the end of it.

"What's that?"

Lilith's head turned toward him with the startling suddenness of an insect's. "She uses it to eat."

Leo gave him what he thought was the saddest smile he had ever seen in his life, an unforgettably sad smile. "We have a small problem. You'll see."

"A problem?"

"Lilith, I can't handle a crowded street like this. I've got to find a quieter area."

Lilith stalked off. Ian didn't follow. He watched her. Not even the way she moved was the same.

"Come on," she said. Her voice was so completely empty of emotion that it sounded kind of like a machine.

They moved quickly, passing through one crowded street after another, going by what seemed like some kind of instinct, or maybe it was just random, Ian wasn't sure.

This time it was Leo who went up to somebody. He noticed that she had tears on her face.

"What's the matter?"

"Nothing, love. We're merely doing what we came to do."

"We came to eat and buy clothes and stuff. I want to see the pyramids."

Leo was talking to an old man, who kept smiling and making gestures. Then Ian understood: these people they were going up to were dealers. The two women were making buys.

"I'm not into drugs," he said firmly, "especially not in foreign countries." He'd been as close to a bust as he ever intended to get.

Leo dropped some change, which tinkled on the ground. The money around here was like tin or something, it didn't sound very valuable. But the old man wanted it, because he went down and started scrabbling around on the sidewalk.

They were in a sort of colonnade. A little farther on, there was a flower seller, and you could smell the odor of her strong Egyptian cigarettes and the softer scent of her flowers in the dim space.

Leo and the guy were both trying to get the money when Ian saw that thing in her hand, the hooked thing. A second later, the old man made a squawking sound and lurched away from Leo. But she held him and put her mouth against his neck. Ian saw his face, which grimaced as he tried to twist away from her. Then there was a sound—*ssssuuuuoooo*—and the skin suddenly went so tight that the guy's lips stretched back and his teeth appeared. Another of the sounds, and his eyes collapsed. His head started looking like a skull.

"Go, take some," Lilith said.

Ian was too shocked to move. He didn't know what he was seeing, except that Leo Patterson was obviously killing an old Egyptian guy somehow by sucking on him.

Oh, Christ, a vampire sucks your neck. But people weren't vampires. Vampires were comic-book shit . . . weren't they?

Suddenly he was grabbed from behind—it was Lilith, and she pressed him toward the man, toward his oozing neck. He reared back, tried to get away, but she was damn strong. She thrust his face straight into the man's wound. He tried to turn his head, but she mashed his mouth right onto it, made his lips skid in the blood. It did what his own blood did to him, which was to sting and feel like something crawling in his mouth, and taste all horrible and good at the same time.

Loathsome. It was loathsome. When she finally let him turn his head aside, she growled. Actually growled. He heard the frustration in it, the rage. She let him go.

The man was dead, which any damn fool could see. Ian scrambled to his feet. "What—what did you do?"

Leo smiled a bedroom smile. She was flushed now, too, and stank of raw blood.

"You're killing people! You're going around killing people! This is crazy!"

Lilith leaped at him, but he jumped back. The taste of the blood was hideous, it was like a living thing crawling around in his mouth. They were loonies, they drank people's blood. They were a couple of total freaks, they were horrible, and he was all alone with them way the hell out here with not even his passport, thanks to bribe-happy Leo.

Lilith came after him. "It's lovely, it's going to be lovely," she said.

"There's a hidden world," Leo said, but he hardly heard her. He was thinking of only one thing now, and that was getting the hell away from these sick and crazy people as fast as he could go. He turned around, and he ran. He ran wildly and blindly, and behind him he heard the roar of a lion, he swore to it, and he understood that Leo's strange warning had been for real, damn sure it had.

They were both monsters. Leo wanted to help him, though, but she was scared to death of Lilith. God, what was the world really like, if stuff like this was real?

He dashed around a corner, stopping just long enough to yank his cell phone out of his pocket. This had to work, for sure. He ran farther down the street, punching 911 as he went. He got a three-toned beep unlike any he'd ever heard before.

He ducked into a store and ignored the man with the CDs who came rushing up, all excited to see an American. He jabbed 01, which he thought was the U.S. country code, into the dial pad, and then their number. This time, a different set of crazy tones came out.

Then Lilith was there, striding into the doorway. Her skin was rose-red, and her eyes were flashing with pure rage. She seemed taller and more imposing than ever. There was not one trace of the young girl he had known.

The shopkeeper said in English, "Do you see that?"

"Get it away from me!"

He ran to the back of the shop, pushed aside some curtains. Here was a tiny room with some stools in it and a whole lot of boxes of CDs. Behind him, he heard a snarl and then the high-pitched screaming of the shop owner. He didn't know what was happening, he just kept running, this time out into a narrow, dark alley that seemed to lead exactly nowhere.

There were a couple of doors, though, and he could hear music. He went in one.

He was in an apartment building with a totally dark hall. The smell of cooking was strong, and there was music playing from inside apartments, Arab music, wailing, sorrowful, women moaning—he supposed—about men they'd lost or wanted. Groping his way, he found stairs that were lit just a tiny bit from light leaking under doors. He vaulted the stairs, one flight, two flights, then hammered at random on a door that had light under it.

A little girl of maybe twelve answered. She was wearing black clothes and she had big, black eyes. She was a very, very pretty child, with a grave expression on her little face. Inside, Ian could see people eating their evening meal around a low table—three men, with women standing behind them near the kitchen door. Everybody was smoking and had been laughing, but now they had all turned toward the door. It was as if a moment in time had been captured—he was standing there catching his breath, the girl was looking up at him, the men's hands were frozen in the act of moving food to their mouths or to the plates, the women were turned toward him, their faces dark with suspicion.

He said, "Excuse me, may I borrow your phone?"

There was a silence. He took out his cell phone, pointed to it. "I can't make it work." He tried to smile, but that only made the girl back away and the men start coming to their feet. The women slipped into the kitchen.

One of the men came forward and made a speech, smiling and gesturing toward the food.

"No, no, thank you. I need to use the phone." He held his closed fist beside his head and said, "Hello, hello, telephone."

The man seemed to understand, but he continued shaking his head. Then one of the younger ones said, "No. No here."

They didn't have a damn phone. Smiling, he backed out of the apartment. Maybe nobody in the building had a phone. Probably didn't. But there was an alternative. By now, the two women must have lost him. Cairo was a big place. So the thing to do was to find a cop. He'd been abducted after all, kidnapped, by crazy people. Who in the world would think that actually drinking blood was going to do anything but make you sick? Those girls were way, way crazy, and they were going to get hepatitis or AIDS or something, not to mention ending up spending their worthless lives in a damn Egyptian jail, which was definitely for the best. Beautiful girls, too bad.

He went downstairs, then out into the alley. It twisted and turned; it must be really ancient. He went along it until it opened into a little square.

There was a dry fountain, there were a few closed shops, that was it. Cats ran away as he entered the open space. But he saw another entrance and went that way. No matter what, he was eventually going to come out on a big street. It had to happen, the city wasn't all alleys.

He came to another turning. It had gotten quiet. No open apartment windows around here. This was like a secret Cairo back in here, where everybody had already died or something. His heart was hammering. Could a kid get a heart attack?

Something closed around his arm—a steel cuff. He twisted away, his cries echoing up and down the alley, making cats leap into the shadows and pigeons mumble nervously in their perches.

They'd been right on top of him the whole time. He'd thought he'd lost them, but he hadn't even been close. She took his other arm and forced him to face her. There was nothing he could do; she was way stronger than he'd realized.

She shook her head, and the scarf that had been concealing it fell away. He saw dark pits where her eyes had been, and her mouth was a hazy black circle. Her skin was as white as the petals of the lilies that choked the entrance to her cave.

A shock of true fear went through him, something he had never known before, something few people ever know. It made him instantly as cold as if he had been rolled naked in snow for an hour. It dulled his senses, causing the world to seem to recede, to become shadowy and unreal . . . dangerously unreal. Only the face before him was real, and it was a truly terrible face—neither man nor woman, but something else, something that suggested the human but very clearly was not that.

And then the mouth came to his mouth, and he tasted a raw, wet, sharp taste, vileness absolute. He tried to closed his jaws, but her tongue was like a steel bar. It came crushing into his mouth and down his gullet, making him gag and retch.

Something hot was coming into him, being pumped down into his stomach, knotting and burning there, and he thought in the little part of his mind that was still functioning, she's vomiting in me, and his whole body lurched, and he knew he was getting a seizure.

She thrust him away from her so hard that he flew through the air and hit the base of the fountain. Quivering nausea overcame him and he doubled at the waist, his jaw opening wide, his tongue protruding until it felt like it was going to come off.

And then the fire came, the fire from inside him. A child was screaming in the fire, a child was dying. What had been a terrible agony almost immediately became a terrible, terrible pleasure. Where there had been retching and seizing, twisting muscles and nausea, now came a hot, shivering blast of sensation so delicious that it made the world start racing around him like a crazy, high-speed merry-go-round, and made him scream now in ecstasy.

The thing that he'd called Lilith and thought a girl rose up and stepped back, keeping away from him. It covered itself with its veil and turned away. He saw it only vaguely, disappearing into the night. He lay there, uncaring, only aware of the fire in him. It was like the moment of climax, a somehow stretched, wound-up intensity of delight that never went away.

He sat up. Still, it continued. He stood. Still. He took a few steps.

Despite the pleasure, he thrust his fingers into his throat and tried to make himself vomit, but all that came up was the sound of his own dry gagging. He sank down, sitting on the edge of the fountain. He'd never felt anything like how he felt now. And how he felt now was real weird. He wanted something. But what? His body—he *wanted* something! He twisted, turned . . . and a scent came to him, a scent so good that it drew him to suck air hard, seeking for more.

Salt, sweet, something burned by the sun, something raw . . .

He jumped to his feet. He had to have this. He had to have it now. They hadn't fed him in days, damn them. He patted his pockets. Wallet was there. He had to get to this food. Oh, God—oh, smell that, *smell that!* He trotted to the edge of the square. Where was it coming from? Down an alley—yeah, over there. He strode along the alley, passing a restaurant kitchen lit by shuddering fluorescent lamps, reeking of hot fat. Not from there. But then the odor came again, clear now, clear and strong.

He burst out into a crowded street. There was light, bustle, cars, and throngs on the sidewalks, people sitting at coffee shops, in open-front restaurants, shopping, strolling.

He screamed. Men turned, raising eyebrows, stopping their talk. He staggered, he couldn't believe it—it was *them,* they smelled like that, the people, the men and women, the darting children. They smelled so wonderful he couldn't stand it, he twisted and turned, he clutched his head in an agony of lust—but what lust? Not sex, no, something else—he needed something else. He doubled over, gagging, his stomach suddenly fighting the blood that lay there. Horrible banging in his chest, a gut-twisting sensation deep, as if the blood he'd been fed was coming alive, a dragon swimming in the well of his gut.

A dragon that needed more. Needed more to get bigger. He took another staggering step—and before him was a woman. She was lightly veiled, otherwise dressed in Western clothes. Her hair was dark, gleaming, her eyes were dark also.

The odor was overwhelming. It split him in half, it maddened him. He went toward her. She saw, stared curiously with those huge eyes. He saw shimmering there a puff of eternity—soul, yes. We do go on, he thought. But the *smell*—oh, oh—he took another step, his hands came up—people were making way. Afraid. Good, yes, let them fear him.

He had the apple, he had to cut the skin, had to get at the flesh within, to make it bleed, so he could lick, could suck, could swallow. His hands were tight on her shoulder, her arms. She was babbling now, her voice going high. It was as if he'd caught a chicken in a barnyard, a starving man.

His body howled blood, blood, blood—

No, crazy! Crazy! Bum trip, help. Help me, God—

Then the taste of her skin, *the taste of her skin!* Salt sweeping into him, salt and sunburn and wicked sweat . . . and under it the flower of the blood. His jaw began to tighten, his throat to suck. Distantly, he heard her babble turn to screams, was aware that she was kicking and twisting. He'd gotten strong, though. Iron, like Lilith. She could not prevail.

A voice cried out. Above. Far above. Arabic, high, a cry that filled the air, that swept into his heart and beat with his heart. He didn't understand the words that shot down into him, deep into him where his humanity was whispering its last.

The old voice, rich with years of prayer, spread its message through all the cells of his body, washing, cleansing, dousing the fires of him as if with purest water.

He raised his head. High in the dark above the street, he saw a towering minaret. There was no muezzin there, no old man, but rather just the empty tower and a couple of loudspeakers. But the meaning of the call could not be mistaken, not by the deep goodness that abided within Ian Ward, in which his father did not have the courage to believe, but which was there nevertheless, what of common humanity that belonged to him.

He screamed, leaping back. The woman had become a pillar of fire, glorious golden flames rising off her skin that made him cry out from the pain of the heat, the beauty. He was seeing a common, ordinary soul in all its reality, and seeing the preciousness of the life to which it was attached. Beyond words, beyond ideas, in the airy meat of mind itself, he saw what she was and why she was here, and the grandeur of it caused him to turn away in agony, that he had even considered taking this life or any life.

He burned, though, burned to eat blood. Also, he saw that the blood was only an incident in a larger process. It was not about feeding on the liquid itself, but the life it bore and ultimately the meaning of that life.

He could not steal that, no. *He could not!*

But he wanted to, oh, with every screaming cell he wanted to. He went for her, stopped himself, stood shuddering, his teeth bared, while the glorious being cringed away. He fell, staggered, got up again, then loped off through the crowd, wanting to get to the mosque, to drink and eat of the sacredness there—prayers now seemed like healing fumes to him, for what he had become had nothing to do with something so simple as a new way of eating. Predator versus prey, the elegance of nature's way. No, what he had become was an etheric beast, and he needed the goodness of man to fortress him against the cruel dark sacred that now swarmed about inside him, famished and seeking the ruin of the world.

As he loped and staggered, fell and came to his feet again, a boy came up to him—soft, concerned eyes—and took him by the hand. He saw in the eyes the truth, that the boy was being guided not only by his own childish compassion but by the whole vast wisdom of a species.

The boy took him closer to the mosque—closed doors—crying out as they went—and the doors opened, and they went in. Ian fell on the wide floor, in the scent of the room, dry and faintly sweet, and beside him the boy and two old men prayed their incomprehensible prayers, and water from heaven poured down, cooling Ian's fire, leaching the dragon within him of its heat, settling it like a lizard on a cold morning.

Ian began to feel quieter, quieter and lighter . . . and better. At length, he stood. The boy smiled up at him. One of the old men, still crouched in prayer, snored softly. The other smiled his wrecked old smile.

"Help me," Ian said.

Chapter Sixteen

The Poisoned Boy

One moment she was standing beside Leo, the next she was gone. Leo could not run after her, she was too fast—so fast, indeed, that she seemed like a shadow darting off down the alleyway.

Leo didn't move. She hardly dared breathe. But Lilith had gone running after Ian. The thing cared only about Ian, had completely put her out of its mind.

Still, she stood there. Dared she attempt escape? The creature had all kinds of powers. It was quick as lightning, it was hideously strong. Also smart, so maybe this was a trick.

Cars passed at the end of the alley. In the distance, somebody called out, a sonorous old voice on a minaret. Behind a lit basement window, a telephone rang.

She took a deep breath. And then she decided: I'll try to run. She went in the opposite direction that Lilith had gone. The possibility of surviving presented itself, and she wanted to survive, she wanted badly to survive.

She could get in her plane and be back in New York in a few hours. She could stop in Paris and get a huge suite at the Crillion and live like an empress for a month. She could go down to Mustique and take a house and hole up across the entire winter, flying to some huge, trackless city like Rio or Mexico City when she was hungry, and eat there without fear of being caught.

But she didn't want to eat again, not ever.

So what would she do? She had to eat if she was going to live. She ran hard, up and down alleys, along streets, through buildings, ignoring the occasional voice that called out as she passed an open door or dashed through a shop, in the front and out the back. She had to put as much of Cairo between her and Lilith as possible. But she was also running from another monster, one that ran right with her, for it was in her, and was her.

Then she came out into a street—she saw lights, cars. Breathing hard, she hurried along the sidewalk. She was looking for a taxi. In seconds, three of them were looking for her. She jumped in the closest one. "Mena Hotel," she said.

Her one chance was to get on her plane and get out of Egypt. She had bought her way past officials for Lilith and Ian, who were passportless, and had to pay a little more for Egyptian visas for herself and her crew. Without having to worry about the two with no passports, leaving would be easy enough.

She would get the finest doctors in the world. If there was a way, they would find it. But what of all the people she'd killed—what would bring them back? There were children without mothers or fathers, parents with lost kids—how did she help them? Did she go to prison for them, maybe end up getting the death penalty? She was one of history's worst serial killers. She, Leo Patterson, who had never been loved.

With Miriam it had all been so miraculous and amazing and wonderful, but Miriam had been almost human, and Lilith was not even close. Still, you had to grant one thing to Lilith: she made you see the truth.

She watched the lights passing, the streets thronged with people, even as late as it was. Cairo did not have the reputation it deserved. From what she could see, it was an intimate, sophisticated city with a flavor similar to Paris, but at once more exotic and at the same time friendly, almost familial. It was one of those cities that felt instantly like home, and she wondered if in some past life she had perhaps spent time here.

There was none of that faintly sinister cast that came over certain cities at night, the wary, haunted atmosphere of a dangerous place. Cairenes were used to being out and about, and they did not expect trouble. When this all ended, she decided, she was going to come back and explore Egypt.

"Mena," the driver said. He turned around and smiled as she thrust money into his hands. She was not careful with money. She spent until it was gone, then called her man at Coutt's Bank and told him to refill whatever needed refilling, or George did it just by monitoring her accounts. No matter how much she spent, every year at her financial meeting, it turned out she was richer than she had been the year before, usually by millions.

She didn't want to die, she didn't want to go to prison, she wanted to be free. Maybe a complete blood transfusion. Maybe something else, some kind of cancer drug, who the hell knew?

Sarah Roberts had tried everything to save herself, even complete blood replacement. "It gets into your cells, it becomes part of you."

Okay, shut up! Take it one day at a time. The important thing is that Lilith and her cave are behind you.

At the desk she said to the clerk, "Please call Captain Williams for me. Tell him Miss Patterson is ready to roll." If Williams was out, he wouldn't be far away. That was the rule: when she called, they had to be ready to start within an hour.

"Patterson is at the front desk of the Mena," General Karas said, his voice tight with suppressed excitement.

"Ian?" Paul asked.

Karas gave his head a curt shake no. "She came in a cab. The driver is being questioned now."

His cell phone rang again.

"Bill, please," Jean said to the waiter. Then, in French, which was much spoken here, "It's not this magnificent food, for which we could not be more grateful. We have an unfortunate emergency and must go at once."

Karas hung up. As they left Shepheard's, he said, "He picked her up in Old Cairo. She was alone. He did not see anyone with her when she came toward the taxi. At the hotel, they say that she asked for her pilot to make ready. He's been told to respond just as if all was completely normal." They got into Karas's limousine and headed for the Mena.

"This isn't a vampire," Becky said. "It's—" She looked at Karas.

"You've read the Roberts papers on blood mixing?" Dr. Sarah Roberts had left behind a number of papers about the blood of the vampire, including its curious relationship to human blood. She had left pitiful reports on her attempts to remove it from her system.

"I've read them," Karas said. "We've never encountered one of those—what do you call them? Do you give them a name?"

"Things," Jean said. "We had two in Paris."

"What happened?" Karas asked. "Were they as difficult to deal with?"

Jean shrugged.

"You blew them apart, right, Jean?"

"They were like the others. Very quick. As smart, I don't know. We killed them."

A vampire was a tough creature, and Paul could scarcely imagine what one of those phosphorus-tipped high-explosive bullets would do to an ordinary human body. "You shot them?"

"If you shoot a human being with one of my guns, he is not there anymore," Jean said. "It's just—you know—a spray of blood."

"Are they fast, or—what are we to expect?" Karas asked.

"They're very fast," Becky said. "Sarah was fast. She was canny. And when she went down—her eyes. I think that the consciousness lingers, just like in the full-blooded creature."

Nobody spoke for a time.

"Vampires are damn clever," Paul said at last.

"I am thinking also of a trap," Jean said.

"To trap us? Kill us?"

"Your boy is the bait, obviously. If it is a trap. Think if the four of us were killed. They would gain so much. Their freedom."

Suddenly they were at the Mena. Paul realized that he was scared. Terrified. "Patterson knows what I look like," he said.

"I'll do the collar," Karas responded.

"If there's a problem?" Becky's cheeks were drawn tight, her eyes were swimming.

Without answering, Karas entered the hotel. His Egyptian team was so smooth and practiced that even another professional couldn't see the stakeout.

"He's got an impressive operation," Paul said.

Jean nodded.

Karas stood in the doorway chatting with one of his operatives, who had materialized out of a passing crowd of businessmen. They spoke in Arabic, gesturing and smiling as if they were friends enjoying a chance meeting. Then the general disappeared into the hotel.

They waited. The only sound in the car was that of Jean stroking his pistol, which gleamed cold blue in his lap.

Leo at first simply turned away from the Egyptian who came toward her from the front of the lobby. But that didn't stop him, hardly. He came closer, a stocky man smiling from behind a brush mustache. She noted that he was wearing a Savile Row suit, but he was still obviously a fan, and the very last thing she wanted to deal with right now was a fan.

Where in hell was Williams? She pulled out her cell phone and called him again. "Let's go," she said when he answered. "I'm getting bothered down here."

"Then we'll go up," the businessman said.

"Come *on*," she said into the phone, then to the businessman: "Get the fuck outa here."

"I'm sorry," he said and opened his jacket. There was a gun there. She looked at the gleaming steel of it, the worn, well-used butt. Everything got slow and quiet. Her eyes returned to the smiling face, then went back down to the huge sidearm. The man's hand came onto her shoulder, and they began moving toward the elevators. She was aware of people behind her, many people. Then the elevator opened, and she was pushed inside.

"Don't turn around," the man said. Something, presumably the gun, was thrust hard into her back. "If you move a single muscle, I will fire."

The elevator rose, its motor whirring. There were also other sounds—breathing, the busy ticking of half a dozen wristwatches, her own jagged heartbeat. She thought, Is everybody always surprised to die?

But she would not die. They weren't going to bother to burn her to ash and scatter it to the winds. On the contrary, she was going to end up like the poor creatures in Lilith's trap, or like Miriam and Sarah, languishing somewhere in tortured silence.

"You are faster, you are stronger," Miriam had said. "Trust your blood. Your blood will defend itself."

The elevator stopped. She heard the doors open. "Back out," the gunman said.

"Who are you? Is this about my visa? Because if it is—"

A voice spoke from behind her: "It's not about your visa, Leo."

Paul Ward! Unmistakable! Automatically, she started to turn toward that familiar tone.

The gun thrust into her back so hard she staggered forward, back into the elevator. "I said, don't turn around." This time, they held her arms from behind.

She was marched down the hallway to a suite, which was opened immediately by a policeman. Inside, Williams and the rest of the crew were seated together on a couch, being watched by an armed man. A dozen more armed men stood around. The room was thick with cigarette smoke.

"Now turn."

Her eyes went from one cold face to the next. A man she did not know, either European or American. Paul Ward. Becky Ward. Two more unknowns, both Egyptian. All were pointing guns at her. Behind her, she could feel another one thrusting into her back. Only when a phone rang in the pocket of someone elsewhere in the room was there a stirring. She could hear a voice speaking low in the background, in Arabic.

"Where is our son?" Ward asked her. His manner was mild.

Becky Ward had an odd sort of a smile on her face. "Tell us," she said, "and we'll let you go."

They would tear her to pieces to get this information, she had no doubt of it. As she thought how hopeless her situation was, tears began.

"Tell us."

Miserably, certain of what it would bring, she whispered the truth, a truth they would never believe. "I don't know," she said.

She closed her eyes, waited. But there was a silence. Then a crisp, accented voice said, "He's at a police station in Old Cairo, on the Sharia Ahmad Omar."

"Let's go," Ward said.

"What about this one?"

"Bring it. Don't let it out of your sight."

"I'm a human being!"

"Were."

A tall, narrow man with those same ice-cold eyes opened his jacket and withdrew yet another monstrous pistol. He ejected a shell into his hand. "It has bullets like this," he said in French-accented English. "That's a phosphorus tip, that light part. The bullet explodes inside you. What it doesn't vaporize, catches fire."

She stared at the huge bullets with their angry white tips, dull silver shells, and long black casings.

The next thing she knew, they were going back downstairs. "I want you to run," the Frenchman said. "Please do it, I would be so happy."

His voice shook with hate. But she wasn't hated. She was Leo, one of the great stars. She was beloved.

The Egyptian, who was apparently some sort of commander, stood face to face with her in the elevator. He was smiling the most hate-filled smile she had ever seen. "How many people have you killed?" he asked.

They had called her "it," had referred to her being human in the past tense. "I want to see somebody from the embassy," she said. "I want a lawyer."

Nobody spoke. Then she could hear Paul Ward, and she thought he was laughing. Becky laid her arm halfway across his broad back, and she knew that the sound was not laughter.

"I didn't understand. I didn't know about the killing," she said. Even as she uttered the words, she felt the lie. Sarah had told her everything, had urged her not to be blooded. But she had wanted it and had loved it . . . for a while.

"Blaylock blooded you without telling you?" Ward asked without turning around. "I don't think so."

"No, she did. She did exactly that."

He whirled, so fast that the elevator shuddered as it glided into the lobby. "You were begging for it! I was there, remember? You begged for it, and you got it, and you've loved it. Loved it! So don't lie to me, you vicious piece of filth."

"I was gonna switch to people who beat criminal raps," she said miserably. "I have to eat."

The street in front of the hotel was jammed with police vehicles. There were two truckloads of officers with machine guns, three police cars with their lights flashing, an ambulance, a limousine, and a black SUV.

"We want it in the car with us," Ward said to the Egyptian.

"I agree."

Then she was shoved into the limousine. The four of them surrounded her, two on the back seat, two on jumpseats, so that she was on the floor.

A moment later the entourage started off, the vehicles screaming through the streets at high speed.

"Did it feed him blood?"

"Lilith?"

"Did the damn thing feed my son blood?"

She hated to say it. "I hope not, but I don't know."

The Frenchman fingered his pistol. On the Egyptian's face was a subtle smile, an expression worthy of a Zen master. Paul Ward glared at her out of eyes glittering with hate so pure it seemed curiously innocent, like Lilith's hate, like her smile. She thought, They're part vampire, both men.

They drove on through Cairo night, and Leo was vaguely aware of great monuments outside the windows, of lighted buildings and long rows of shopfronts, as she waited for the time that could not be far off, when they would destroy her. How strange it was that she was so calm. It was a funny thing, a small but crucial thing, that had swept away her fear and all desire to survive. She had seen the way Becky and Paul Ward held hands. Something about that wordless, continuous contact suggested that they were giving each other strength. It came—had to come—from the fierceness of their love for their son.

Tears stung her eyes. She was to be a sacrifice, in a sense, to the silent god of this love. It had been a desire to be loved—so natural and so human—that had tempted her to her blooding. "I love him," she said.

Paul Ward turned red. Becky's hand clutched his.

God, they were going to blast her to bits somewhere in some alley and leave her forever, wash her down the sewer or something.

They pulled up to a police station. Paul and Becky burst out of the car and ran inside. Two less guarding her. Leo grew watchful.

Becky ran up the short flight of steps calling out, "Ian, Ian," and she heard—she *heard*—that young, unfinished voice reply, "Mom!"

She ran faster—then she saw him. She saw him in a cruelly bright room sitting on a green plastic chair. There were four uniformed policemen there, two old men, and a boy of perhaps twelve. When she appeared in the doorway, Paul right behind her, the boy came to his feet and, smiling, presented himself.

"He helped me," Ian said.

Becky threw her arms around the thin frame. Paul stuffed money in his hands.

A policeman came forward. "Mr. and Mrs. Ward," he said, "he's only a little weaver's apprentice, he's not worth all those dollars!"

"He's worth every penny," Paul said.

"Well, then, God has smiled on the maker of rugs. But your son— we've lost our passport and, I think, gotten sick from smoking a water pipe. But all is well, God is good."

She looked Ian up and down, frantic lest she see the flush of the blood-fed vampire. It wasn't there—or was it? Never mind, she flew into his arms. He rocked back, then she felt his arms come up as he embraced her—and knew in an instant that he was too strong.

Paul came beside her and fumbled toward him. "Son," he said. But then he, too, fell silent. Everyone in the room watched them. Everyone in the room sensed the power of the emotions involved.

General Karas said to the police captain, "We'll be taking him. There's nothing to be concerned about the papers. There will be new papers tomorrow."

The captain saluted, and with Becky on one side of him and Paul on the other, Ian was conducted out of the station.

Becky's heart was breaking; she knew that this wiry creature was no longer a human being in the sense that he had been before, and she did not want to face that and did not want Paul to know it, but she could see by the stricken look on her husband's face that he did know, and he knew also what he had to do, and he was desolate.

"Mom, Dad, I'm so sorry. I'm so damn sorry."

"You know what we do?"

"What do we do?"

"I'll tell you in a minute," Paul said.

They were moving down the corridor. Karas was behind them, Jean before them. Two of Karas's operatives were ahead of him. These men had deployed for a simple reason: Ian was a vampire in custody, and that was a very dangerous situation.

How could they see it? From that faint blush, for one thing. He'd fed—not a lot, or not recently, but he had definitely fed. The second tell-tale was the way he moved, like a big cat trying to conceal its power.

They got into the back of the SUV. Ian gasped when he saw the iron cage inside, saw that it was open.

"Get in," Paul said.

"Dad?"

Paul drew his pistol. Becky looked at it. Ian looked at it. And Ian burst into tears. "Was that blood," he asked, "did she put blood in me?"

The pistol did not waver. "Get in," Paul repeated, gesturing toward the cage.

"Dad, why?"

"You know." He stopped, his voice catching. Becky thought, Don't cry, Paul, don't start.

"Dad, I'm not an animal. I haven't done anything except come here without a passport. And what kind of gun is that? Why do you even have a gun?"

Becky took his arm. "Come on."

"Becky!"

"Paul, we owe him an explanation."

"We owe him nothing!"

"Baby, have you ever killed anybody?"

"Mom, no. But she—it—it has. And so did Leo. They sucked people's blood, you guys. It was horrible and gross, it was unbelievable. What are they? And why am I even involved, here?"

"How did you meet them?" Paul asked.

He sounded calmer now, but the gun was still right there, three inches from Ian's belly. Becky forced herself not to do what her heart screamed at her to do, and just throw herself between child and weapon. At least maybe there was a chance to get him away from the cage.

"Come on," she said, taking Ian's hand. She moved toward an empty police car. "We need time," she told Karas.

He looked toward Paul. "Okay?"

"Okay."

They got in the back of the car, Ian between them. Becky didn't want to take her gun out, but she had to treat the situation professionally. She put it in her lap.

Ian looked down at it. Then he looked at the one his dad was holding on him. "Oh, my God," he whispered. "What have I done?"

"We're part of a unit that hunts vampires," Paul said. "That's the secret this family's lived with all these years."

His eyes went slowly from one of them to the other. "*Your* secret!" He fixed on his father. "Why didn't you tell me?"

"There was no need for you to know."

"*What?* Are you crazy?"

"You know what you are?"

"I—something is very strange and wrong. It's real wrong."

"You're the child of a vampire," Paul said quietly.

The words hung there.

"Mom?"

What should she say? "I love you."

"But—is this true? You guys?"

Paul's gun wavered. For the first time since Becky had known him, his professionalism faltered. He uttered a great, ragged sound that was somewhere between a father's sobbing anguish and the rage of a predator, and grabbed his son and held him close. "We'll find a way to help you. We will find a way."

"What's happening, Dad, Mom? I'm not okay, am I?" Voice rising: "I'm *way* not okay!"

"I made a huge mistake. I should have told you, should have warned you. I've been a damn, damn—goddammit!"

"Ian, a vampire was made pregnant by your dad. She was . . . you know—she was killed . . . and we saved you."

"Okay, and you killed this vampire, who was my mother." He laughed, silent agony. "My mother the vampire."

"We raised you as our own. And hoped—"

"I'd never find out. So that's why I've lived like this, in this trap of a life, stuck at that Podunk schools—so you could keep an eye on me. And what would've happened if I turned out to be one of them? You would've just blown my brains out one day? Without warning? Mom and Dad?" He looked from one of them to the other. "Are you going to now?"

"Ian, the vampire tricked me. When I made love to her, I didn't know what she was."

"That I know to be a lie."

Becky was confused. "It's not a lie." It had been part of the bedrock of their life together. Paul had been seduced. It was all an accident.

"Because you can feel it. You know instantly."

"How?" Becky asked.

Her son reddened. "Because you can."

There was a silence as Paul's face collapsed, revealing his inner agony. "It's the blood," he rasped, "the blood controls you."

"You knew what Blaylock was? And yet you . . . stayed with her? My God, Paul."

"I loved her. I loved her so." His haunted eyes fixed on Ian. "Tell me, son, tell me now. Did you feed?" His finger, Becky saw, strayed to the trigger of his pistol. His eyes were half closed, like a man contemplating a chess move.

"Lilith forced blood down my throat."

"And you—you . . . after that, you fed. You fed on your own."

For a moment, Becky thought that Ian was never going to react. It was like teetering on the edge of a cliff. Then he did—he reared back, his hands became fists, and he screamed, a totally unrestrained, raw bellow of savage terror.

The next instant, he lunged for the car door, trying to cross over her. She knew why, that he wanted to run, was desperate to get out of there, to just run and run—but from what? From the knowledge he had fed, or from the fact that he was longing to, or out of fear of the very idea?

At that moment, the boy who had been in the police station appeared at the door. He was hand in hand with one of the policemen. The child's solemn presence brought silence. The policeman spoke. "He wishes me to say that God has saved your son from—" He lowered his eyes. "We do not speak of it."

Ian seemed calmed by the presence of the child, just another Cairo street kid, less than nobody. "He stopped me from what—what I was about to do."

Paul looked at the boy. "My son didn't hurt anybody?"

The child replied to Paul in Arabic.

"He wishes me to say that God has saved your son, because of what is in his heart."

Ian turned toward his father, his back now to Becky. But Becky's heart was soaring; she knew that he was still with them, that he had not killed.

"Dad—"

Paul's finger slid off his trigger, hesitated in the air for a second. Then he put his gun away, tucking it deep beneath his shoulder. He opened his arms, and Ian flew into them. Becky put her hands on their shoulders, pressed herself to them.

Such is the way forgiveness happens, because it seeks like this to explode from the soul and declare itself in the world. It seeks the light, this living, brilliant presence that inhabits us. Such was the way Ian forgave his parents, with an embrace and instantly.

"I'm so damn sorry," Paul said.

"I never hurt anybody, Dad. I never would, not ever."

The policeman said, "Thank you, sirs and lady."

The boy was gone. "Where is he?"

The policeman shrugged, smiled. "In Cairo—"

After another silence, Ian said, "Lilith is still out there."

"Maybe we should let her go this time, son."

Becky snatched a surprised breath. Paul was tricking him, seeking for him to reveal himself. She wanted to say something, but she kept her jaw clenched. Paul was right. Vampires were very, very clever. Consummate actors. They had to be sure.

"Dad, you can't let her go. That's totally the wrong thing to do."

A smile flickered in his eyes. Becky's heart leaped again. Another test passed.

Paul made a call. "Let Patterson go," he said into the phone. "In five minutes. Let her escape. Make it look damned good." He closed the phone. "Okay, son," he said, "listen to me."

"Okay."

"We might be able to bait a trap for Lilith."

"Paul?" What was he saying? Should they trust Ian this far, to share their plans with him?

"She'll come for him."

"Paul, no."

"He's our best chance, Becky."

"Paul, *no!*"

"In a couple of minutes, Leo is going to get out. There's going to be a lot of confusion. And you're going to use that confusion. You're going to use it to stage your own escape. You'll run for dear life. Cross the street and go along the far side. You see that building with the shadow—the narrow shadow just beside the spice shop?"

Becky saw nothing. The wall beside the spice shop appeared to be blank.

"Yeah," Ian said, "I see it."

"I've been watching your girlfriend. She's right there."

"She's not my girlfriend!"

"During the ruckus, you get out of the car and you go in that direction. Not straight there. Make it look good. She'll call you. When she does, go to her."

"Dad, no way!"

"He's right, Paul. No way."

"You'll be relieved to see her. Throw yourself in her arms."

He was still testing, and it was a monstrously clever test.

"Okay," Ian said. "What does this get us?"

"It gets us Lilith." Paul drew a leader from his pocket.

Becky looked at the small silver object the size of a credit card. "Don't ask him to do this!"

"Son, your mother is right. This is dangerous. But that creature out there is also dangerous. It's the most dangerous vampire I've ever encountered, and I've been doing this for twenty years. You take this leader, you put it in your pocket."

Ian took the instrument.

"It'll enable us to follow you. At some point, we'll get a shot."

"You'll shoot her?"

"Just like that."

He put the transmission device in his pocket. "What if she finds it?"

"Lie. Tell her it's an amulet. They're not technological. It's one of their vulnerabilities."

At that moment, there was a shout from ahead. Through the windshield, Paul saw Leo rise up beside the limo, then jump fully ten feet into traffic. Moving like a gazelle, she avoided two trucks, a bus, and about four taxicabs.

Chased by a dozen officers, she raced off down the street.

Lilith had considered returning home, but she couldn't risk that now, not with Leo and Ian both captured. She realized that they would inevitably give her cave away. A place hidden from human eyes for centuries would soon be invaded.

As she watched the movements in front of the police station, she considered her alternatives. Leo was in the first car, guarded by two police. Ian was two cars back with his parents. Probably he was feeling very loyal to them right now. Probably, he was still in ecstasy from his feeding. But that would wear off, to be replaced by the hunger. She'd lived with the hunger all of her life. Bearing it, feeding it, facing it again—this was nothing to her. But to him, caught up in it for the first time, it was going to be an agony beyond hell, a relentless, unstoppable craving that nothing but more blood could relieve.

He was also a devotee of the senses. His desires were fiery, his lusts fierce. No matter how angry he might be at her, or how afraid, there was still a chance that she could seduce him.

She stood in a darkened corner, visible from the street only by her own kind. She doubted that these people would be able to see her. Certainly they showed no sign. Nobody so much as glanced in this direction.

Behind her, a stair led steeply down, a very worn stair. Below was the ancient labyrinth of the Keepers, known as the Prime Keep, where all the records were kept and the truths were known.

Now, very suddenly, there came an eruption from the first car. Leo leaped out of it and began racing off. Lilith did not move. Let Leo try. Let Leo get shot. It would save trouble.

She watched the car with the boy, her body tense, her breath shallow. She was trembling, counting the seconds.

And then it happened, and she almost laughed, she almost clapped. He came dashing out—oh, what a grand spectacle of a boy! And look, he was speeding through traffic with wonderful grace. What a specimen he was, what a perfect, amazing creature: a blend of two species, more powerful, she suspected, than either by itself.

He was what they had tried and failed to create in the deep past, a new being. Time and nature, though, had worked their silent wisdom, and here he was—and she reached out as quick as a darting hornet, grabbed his wrist, and drew him in.

They would all see him disappear, of course they would. So speed was of the essence.

He struggled against her like a lively little fish on a line. She hardly felt his resistance, dragging him along, hearing him bump and bounce against the stairs.

Then, suddenly, she did feel it. With a roar of anger, he broke away from her. She stopped, looked back and up at him.

"My, my, blood makes my boy strong."

"Just cool it. Nobody drags me anywhere."

"I'll have to remember that phrase, 'Cool it.' Cool my intensity?"

"That's right. You fed me blood."

"Come on, we'll talk later."

"I feel incredible."

Happiness tingled at the edges of her heart. He'd sounded angry a moment ago. Now he sounded different, less so.

Was this an act, then? She reached up, took his hand. "I'll be gentle."

His palm was dry, hot from the blood he'd consumed. That was normal. But also, there was no tension, and under these circumstances, that was not. She laughed a little. "Come on," she trilled, "I have miracles to show you."

Leo was running hard when she heard Ian's shout, and turned to see something that surprised her and disturbed her enough even to slow her down. He was disappearing into a vampire hole. She had not understood that he would still want to be with Lilith, not after how he'd reacted before.

Then she thought, No. She just thought, Absolutely not, no. She turned up an alley, easily leaving the cops behind. Being that she'd just fed, she was at her physical and mental best. What Miri had said was so true; the blood did indeed take care of itself. That was why she'd made this escape, and why she now thought she'd be able to follow vampire sign, at least for the next few hours. She could follow them into the tunnels, and her superacute senses would enable her to find them.

She found a crack, pushed at it, then noticed something. There were no cops behind her. They hadn't even turned up the alley. Had she been so fast that they'd already lost her? She slid her fingers along the crack, feeling for the right spot. Lilith could have done this in an instant, so fast she would seem to literally disappear before your eyes, but Leo was not nearly as skilled, not even at her peak.

Finally, though, she found the single loose place in the masonry and shook it. The crack widened, and she stepped through.

Behind her, the masonry silently slid closed. For hundreds of years, vampires had been carrying their victims down the steep stairway that she now descended, into the dark depths.

This must not be a repeat of her blundering failure in New York. She had to save this boy. It felt like the most important thing she'd ever done—maybe the only important thing she'd ever done.

She listened—off in one direction, dripping. She scraped at the wall, was rewarded with a single strip of faint green light. It was enough, though. She took a few steps deeper into the tunnel. She could not get lost here, because if she did, she would sure as hell not end up blundering out into any men's departments.

Paul and Kari could both, as it turned out, enter the vampire's hidden world. Paul wondered how much vampire blood ran in Kari's veins, and what his history was. But there was no time to discuss that now, not as they dropped down the steep, curving steps of a vampire hole.

He and Becky, Kari and Jean—at least this was true: this was probably the best damn team that had ever been assembled.

Becky was following the signal from Ian's transmitter on one of the modified PalmPilots provided by Jean. "Over there," she whispered. "Twenty yards."

They pulled on night-vision equipment, got out their guns. They moved fast, Kari at the lead. In these tunnels, it would be all too easy for the telltale to go out of range, which would be an unthinkable disaster.

From now on, nothing would be said. The least sound could spell disaster. A vampire that was aware it was being chased was a dangerous creature indeed, and Paul would never assume that this one would be so stupid as to imagine they wouldn't be trying.

The telltale's signal indicated that Ian had suddenly slowed.

The tunnel, which had been dropping steeply, began to become wet. Soon, they were treading six inches of water. Paul knew that they were passing under the Nile, heading toward the Giza Plateau, where the pyramids stood.

Then the green dot on the telltale began going faster, then much faster. Ian had gotten through the water and was running. The group sped up as much as they could. It seemed like ages before they were finally out of the water.

As they were going up the far side, a sound came back to them, a long, echoing cry. Becky gasped. She was behind Paul, and he could feel her pressing against him. Another cry, and this time there was a responsive sound in her throat. Paul knew what he himself was going through. A mother's pain had to be worse.

They were running now, and Paul became aware of his heart, which was laboring noticeably. The tunnel was too narrow for him to drop to the back, so he had to keep up Kari's pace. "You need a heart cath," his doctor had said. "Within a year, for sure." Pain started, a band around his chest. It rose into his jaw. He did not slacken his pace.

Suddenly Leo came into a gleaming, shimmering wonderland. She did not at first know what she was seeing . . . and when she did realize that they were pictures, then she didn't understand. They were shining like mirrors that reflected the day. Each one was huge, forty or fifty feet long, twenty feet high. In them, figures drifted slowly along, flags waved as if underwater, the sun flared down on temples and palaces and long walled cities.

She saw the Pyramid of Cheops flaring white and new, on its pinnacle a huge golden stone with what looked like an eye carved in it. On the Nile stood graceful ships, their sails painted with the images of gods.

It was the past, captured in some sort of frozen mirrors.

Then she heard a cry, just a short distance away.

"Ian!"

"Leo?"

"Over here!"

He came out from behind one of them. "It's incredible, Leo. Look at it all. Look at it!"

The whole of man's past was here, preserved in wonderful detail by a mind that collected things and obsessively kept them, even things as ephemeral as the light of other days.

"Ian, I'm here to—"

One of the mirrors exploded, crashing to a million pieces as Lilith came flying through it, leaping like a maddened panther straight at Leo's throat.

Leo took the blow against her upper chest and head and went down like a rock, smashing into another of the mirrors as she fell. Then Lilith was astride her.

"Ian, run, get away from her!"

"My folks are coming! It's okay!"

When she heard that, Lilith began shaking Leo by the shoulders, slamming her head again and again into the stone floor. Shards of mirror, still blazing with the light of the past, flew up around her like a multicolored halo and then were stained with pink, then with thick red.

Leo felt her skull being shattered, her brains growing loose in her head, then splashing out in chunks. She tried to stop Lilith, but she couldn't even begin.

"You did it, you ruined it all," Lilith wailed as she smashed Leo again and again into the floor.

Then Leo saw Ian behind her with a large piece of mirror. As a stately procession moved across it, he lifted it high and smashed it downward, crushing it into Lilith's back.

Lilith grunted but didn't even slow down. The vampire could take far more punishment than that. But not the human being, and the agony of the blows began to seem to Leo to be farther and farther away. Then she felt sphincters give way, felt warm liquid flowing out of her down below, heard Ian's cries as he strove to pull Lilith off her.

Lilith stood up. Leo felt a curious, electrical tingling all over her body. She lifted herself, confused that Lilith had let her live—and then realized that she had not risen, had not moved at all. Lilith had let her live, all right, but like this, in the undead state, lying here amid the stars of the mirrors, in this great hall of the human past.

"Why did you kill her? Why did you have to do that?"

"She's dangerous, Ian. She's dangerous to us."

In her helpless mind, she called out to Ian—*get away, run, do it now!* There was no sound.

"Come with me, Ian, come here."

Run, Ian!

He turned away. But Lilith had him, snap, her hand around his right arm. He tugged, but it was no use. In a moment, Ian's face was thrust down into Leo's. She was looking straight into his terrified eyes. Then his face was being pressed past hers into her neck. For a long moment, he did not breathe. Longer. Longer still. He squirmed, he tried to twist his head away.

No, Ian, don't, no, Ian!

He took a long breath gurgling with her blood, and as he did, she heard him groan and felt him begin to tremble.

Lilith backed away.

Ian, no! Don't taste it, Ian!

She felt his tongue darting out, touching it, felt his arms coming around her, getting purchase. Then his teeth, he was tearing into her, and it hurt but she could not move, he was biting right through to the artery. Then he was shaking, he was struggling, she could feel it, she could hear soft, desperately urgent sounds as she knew his mind screamed no to his ravenous gut, *no, no Ian—*

There was a roar, a vast shattering of glass, a whole cosmos erupting around her and over her. Lilith passed overhead in a graceful arc, a comet trailing blood and smoke.

It is always complicated until the defeat, and then it is always simple. So it had been for the others, and so it was for her. Lilith knew that she was tremendously damaged. She knew that one entire side of her body was not working. She saw the guns, the humans behind them visible only as dark hulks, so covered with equipment that they weren't even recognizable.

How odd that her dream would come back to her now, of something so simple as a dusty yellow road that crossed a field of wheat, then wound off toward a village. But it was all in fog, unfocused, hard to see.

Riding on another great roar which she knew came from the barrel of a gun, the dream got clearer. She saw now the shady bower where she had been sleeping, saw the sun peeking in around the plum blossoms. Far from feeling the pain of the bullets that were disintegrating her, she felt the pleasing stiffness that follows good sleep.

In the roaring and the smoke, she stretched deliciously. At the same time, she was aware of blood spraying everywhere and voices and shattering glass and a terrible and yet beautiful death scene, with her broken body blowing like a leaf amid myriad tiny reflections, a rainbow of color and red death.

Her eyes fluttered open. Bees hummed in the flowers of the tree that concealed her. Far away, she heard a bell tolling. She had to go, she'd overslept.

She stood, went to the edge of the shade, and pushed aside some of the long, loose branches that hung like a concealing curtain around the base of the tree. She stepped forth into the sleepy thrall of a summer afternoon.

The moment Becky saw Ian crouching there, the dying vampires dropped into the past for her. Paul and the others would finish them off. Her mission was to help her son. She yanked off the night-vision goggles, unneeded in this miraculous place, and rushed to him.

He knelt beside Leo, his face covered with blood.

Paul came, as she knew he would.

"Dad?"

The pistol moved, the barrel pointed.

"Dad?"

She heard the click of the action being cocked, soft, efficient.

"Dad?"

Silence.

She looked at Paul. His face was hard—sad but so very hard. "Kari," he said hoarsely. "Jean. We have this one to do."

Becky was stunned, totally. "He didn't feed!"

Paul closed his eyes, shook his head slightly.

She put her hand around the barrel of his gun, forcing herself to bear its heat. But she didn't turn it aside.

"Dad?"

It was like a dance, slow dance in a sea of blood, as they came forward, came toward Ian. Ian began to get to his feet. It looked like he'd been at Leo, looked exactly like that. She heard the snicker of rounds being chambered. They would all fire at once. He'd be gone in an instant. They would leave nothing to linger, they would not be cruel.

Becky knew what had to be done. Trembling, the sorrow pouring through her like a Niagara Falls of pain, she removed her hand.

"Mom?"

The guns came up.

She couldn't look. She averted her eyes—and saw that Leo's body wasn't desiccated. For an instant, this seemed simply a little wrong. Then it seemed a lot wrong.

"He didn't feed!" She grabbed him and went for the floor.

The guns roared, sending more of the precious mirrors shattering into ignorant rainbow shards. Heat seared her back, then she lay in a galaxy of sparkling instants, red flowers shuddering in ancient breeze, a dog's hip, a golden broken eye. And beneath her, the gasping, gagging, crying body of her son.

They sat up. She hugged him. Like soldiers who have been near an exploding shell, they touched each other in the miracle of survival. She looked up at the three men, Kari, Jean, and Paul. "Look at the body," she said with the thick care of somebody so shocked that they can barely form words, "he did not feed on that woman."

Paul sank down, had to be held up by Kari and Jean. She thought he was crying, but it wasn't that. His skin was gray, his breathing sounded shallow, he dropped his gun with a great crash to the floor.

"Chest," he gasped, "gotta catch my breath, here."

Then Ian was on him, holding his father in his bloody hands, drawing him down, taking his big head in his lap.

The room still glowed brightly. A few of the strange glass paintings had been shattered, but there were hundreds more in great frames, rows and rows of them.

"It's all of civilization," Jean breathed. "This is the treasure house of the ages."

They gathered, then, around their fallen comrade. They'd done it before, all of them, many times. They were efficient, and in a surprisingly short time Paul was outside, having been taken to the surface through the Queen's Chamber beneath the Pyramid of Cheops, which held the hidden door to this extraordinary place of record.

As they moved up the narrow, spiraling tunnel to the surface, Kari and Ian carrying Paul, Jean's gun sounded again and again behind them. He was destroying the two vampires utterly, pulverizing them, making certain that no trace of life remained in them. If they had souls to release, they were released. The blood sank into the earth and deeper, even more secret chambers.

Then Jean, also, went to the surface. In the dark and silence he left behind rats came, and cats came, and long albino crocodiles.

CHAPTER SEVENTEEN

The Veils of Night

Lilith crossed the dell where the plum-blossom tree grew, and made her way along the ridge that swept downward to the fields of Eden, and beyond them their village nestled among its trees. On the shimmering distance stood the red pyramid, glowing in the late sun. None knew who had built it, or any of the pyramids that were scattered across the countries of the sky, but they were said to be the knots that held the carpet of the universe together.

Two columns of smoke rose, one from the inn and one from the baker's. Skyward, white clouds dreamed along the blue, and great, dark birds circled lazily.

The bell kept ringing and ringing. Then she saw snatches of color appearing along the road near the village gate. What was this? People were coming out. She looked around, but there was nobody else here. They were coming out to meet her, and ringing the bell for her.

And then she remembered something that it seemed very strange to have forgotten, it having happened only an hour ago. She had come here with her husband—been brought here, in fact, weeping and afraid.

She touched her cheek. Oh, yes, she had been weeping, and so recently that her eyes were still damp. As she kept making her way down the hillside, the ringing of the bell got louder, and the voices of the towns-people rose to an excited chatter.

What was this? There was nothing in the wedding rite about this. So why were they . . . why? She stopped, attempting to understand what was happening. And then, in that moment, maybe because she noticed and maybe because it was just time, she experienced the true vastness of her own memories of the past hour, and immediately sank down in the road.

There was a world inside her, a huge world in all its gaudy and terrible ages. Still on her knees, she turned, looking back toward the plum-blossom tree, thinking that something in the fruit had made her swoon. But no, this was no ordinary fever. Under the tree, she had dreamed a magnificent and terrible dream, the whole life of a world.

Then everyone was there, the children sweating from their play, the adults dusty from scything the fields. A man came to her, whom she knew was her father. "Have you forgotten Adam?"

Adam!

The group parted, opening her way to the square around which the village was built. There was the fountain, playing merrily in the late light, and sitting beside it was a tall young man with the powerful shoulders of a hardworking farmer.

As she went forward, he came to his feet. He gazed down at her. "It's been more than an hour," he said.

"I slept so hard! I feel like I've been up there forever."

He took her in his arms. It was—oh—like magic to feel the strength of him draw her up so easily so close. When he laid his lips upon hers, she felt as if she had truly come home. But when they stopped, she felt a fearsome thirst, as if she was dry to her marrow. She leaned to the fountain and drank of the clear, cold water. Down at the bottom, she could see the bright fish speeding, the ones that generations of children had tamed until they could hold them cupped in their hands.

The water seemed to flow directly into her veins, cleansing her.

"What happens?" he asked.

"Happens?"

"You remember . . . you went on the wisdom journey."

How long ago that seemed—as if yesterday was somewhere off in history, before their world had been shattered by its wars, and the survivors had rejoined God.

"You have a dream. It's a very long and terrible dream." She stopped, then. She could not tell him the truth of what she remembered—that she had been asleep not for an hour, but for eons . . . and what had transpired in those terrible times, in that place that was beyond the beyond. "In your dream," she said hastily, "you wave a magic wand, and a world full of simple creatures becomes a world full of searchers like we were, before God embraced us."

"What is the secret? Why is it so dangerous?"

"It's God's business," she said nervously. How could he understand that his young wife had woven good out of threads of evil? How could she ever say what she really remembered? "Ur-th," she said.

"What's that?"

"The name I gave it, the place I dreamed about."

"One Place All? That's a good name for a world."

For the breadth of an instant, she seemed to hear the great roar of an ocean, but she knew that it was another sea, the sea of humanity that had been spawned in her dream.

She looked up, wondering where in the sky they might be, for in her heart, she felt that her dream had been enacted somewhere, that the towering anguish of soul that oppressed her now was a wound from a secret life in the eons.

"You have never looked more beautiful," he said.

She slipped her hand into his and lowered her eyes. She was still a maiden, and this was to be their consummation evening.

"I want to walk," she said.

Watched by all the village, they went up toward the Wheat Road that led into their fields, where they harvested the grain that was the staple of their lives. The dream—the awful, monstrous dream—was awash in blood. She felt it trickling down her arms, glutting her mouth, roiling in her belly. She pushed away that madness.

But it did not leave her. No, her hour beneath the plum-blossom tree had changed her, just as the boy master had told her it would. "God has chosen you for reasons that are God's. But a world depends upon it, Lilith. Say yes."

Was that really just yesterday that the sacred child had come knocking, so terrifying her parents and causing her fiancée to beg her to stay?

"I'm so glad," she said.

He took her hand, and when he did, she felt how profoundly she was changing. The terrible dream was lifting as a veil lifts, releasing her from a burden that seemed ages long and horrible.

As they passed the briar-rose tower her great-great-grandfather had made, every rose entered her heart. She became roses. As they passed the bakery where the twisted loaves had been put out for taking, she became the fragrance of twisted bread. So also, passing the toy shop with its painted dolls, she became a bright-eyed toy lying in the lap of the lonely child who had made the universe.

When they returned to the fountain, the purple of evening had risen in the east, and the fields were shuddering off the heat of the day.

"In my dream," she said, "I was a monster."

He laughed and splashed her with water from the fountain. "You'd never be a monster. You're remembering somebody else's dream."

"I am a monster."

With all the town come quietly around, the women in their aprons and the men in their harvesting smocks, the children, some naked, some in play clothes or work clothes—with everybody drawing near—they kissed. Softly, softly came the wordless humming of the marriage song, as they drew closer and closer yet. She who had become the rose and the bread became now the pleasure of their love.

Later, when they were eating bread with their candle on the table between them, he asked her, "What was your dream, then? What's the secret of the plum-blossom tree?"

"It was only a dream."

"Do you miss it?"

"It's over and done now. Time for me to forget."

And so he kissed her again, and she surrendered to his kisses, and they went before the fire and cuddled together in the fleece rug that had come in her dowry. Gently, they came together naked, the innocent girl shown by the innocent boy what he knew of the way of naked pleasure.

Late and very late, while he lay softly sleeping, a shadow stole into the firelight. She sucked a startled breath when she realized that the boy master was there, gazing down at her with grave eyes.

"I come to tell you of the girl-child you are carrying, that she will follow in your path, and sleep beneath the plum-blossom tree."

"I am not carrying a child."

The eyes now laughed a little, and she understood, suddenly, that she was. She had been for a few hours already, since the moment her marriage had been consummated.

"It worked the first time?"

He nodded.

Just for an instant, she looked directly and deeply into those impossible eyes of his, and her heart almost cracked to pieces, for she had seen there the name and past of her child. She sobbed aloud, but he took her in his arms and quieted her against his narrow breast.

"I'll never be able to love her!"

"You will love her. You will serve and protect her."

"I don't want her! Not that—creature."

"Leo has fought hard and suffered much in my behalf. She spent a whole life without love. Lilith, she has so much to offer."

"Please, give her to somebody else."

"All the bells of heaven are ringing," he whispered. "Can you hear them?"

It was true, there were bells greater than the one in their signal tower, ringing somewhere very high.

"Oh, master, master, I did evil. I did horrible, dark things to them. Please, how can I ever forgive myself? And how can I ever love that child?"

"I'm not a master," he said. "I'm only a weaver's apprentice. Don't you remember me, coming with my rugs to your village?"

"You're a great master, and you can help me. You have to, because I'm in agony, I can't bear what I remember, I can't bear what I was!"

"If I told you that you had left behind a couple who will give to earth a whole new evolution of man?"

"I don't understand."

"Then know this, the secret of the enemy: it's the pressure of battle that makes us strong, and victory that gives life its sweetness, which is why I always tell my clients to love their enemies. You were their enemy, child. You gave them their strength, you and those creatures you made."

"I made?"

"In our dream, we made them, you and I. We made them and flooded man's world with them, and when he found them, he found himself."

She shook her head. "I just want to forget."

He kissed her forehead. "Then only remember that you did my work well."

A great light came splashing like a wave across the raw and jagged wound of her memory, leaving it cleansed as if with sweet sea foam. His kiss also put her to sleep like a rocked baby. He covered her with the fleece blanket, close beside her husband. None saw him go down the Wheat Road, then out beyond the red pyramid to the edge of the world. While they all slept, he crossed the bridge of the rising moons, then went along the star path that carries the eternal children between the worlds, on their dark mission of awakening.

Lilith slept at last, a sleep that had seemed an eternity in coming, the warm and blessed sleep of a girl in her marriage bed. Her dream slipped backward in memory, its voices of Egypt and Rome and America fading, of Ian and Becky and Paul, of the kings and pharaohs and vampires, of the crackle of torches and the hissing of the ocean, of the laughter of the jackal—all those strange, improbable voices—called ever more distantly, echoing and then not, slipping away. They were lifted from her spirit at last, as the veils of night passed swiftly and softly over the land, blessing all who rested therein with healing sleep.

EPILOGUE

The Kiss

It stood in an ancient part of Cairo, had stood there for perhaps a thousand years. To the street, it offered little promise, but behind its old walls were wonders. In the ancient manner, it was built around courtyards. Perhaps it had started life as a Roman *praetoria*, an elaborate roadside inn fit for an emperor, when this spot was in the countryside, on the road to Heliopolis. After that, the number of rooms along the west wall suggested that part of it, at least, had become a *khan*, a caravanserai.

The place had belonged to the family Karas since the days of the Mamelukes, and many a soldier had girded himself in armor here and marched to meet the battles of history. But it was not the history of the family Karas that interested Ian Ward, it was a girl, the third daughter of Adel Karas, Hamida. He had first seen Hamida behind a latticed window, watching as his father was brought back from the hospital, his heart newly catheterized by Dr. Radwan Faraj, a small man with a neat beard and a catalog of ancient jokes delivered in improbable English.

Dad had almost died, but he was getting better fast. If they weren't careful, he'd soon be back in the vampire ruin beneath the Giza Plateau, before the scientists were let in and it fulfilled its destiny as the archaeological wonder of the world, the hall where the record of man was stored.

Now he waited for Hamida beside a fountain in the Karases' first and largest courtyard. He sat on its edge, watching slow carp moving in the clear, cool water that bubbled up from a copper flower in its center. The fountain itself was tiled in an intricate design of lilies.

More flowers festooned a plum tree that stood a short distance away. He was really more interested in the tree than the fountain, and most especially in the cool patch of grass concealed beneath its shade.

He dragged his fingers in the water, letting the carp come up and nibble at them. Far away in the house, his mother was singing. In all of his life, she had never done this, not before now. A great burden had been lifted from her shoulders, he knew, when it had become clear that he was not going to feed. It wasn't that he didn't want to, but that he absolutely would not, not ever. The way it had felt within him—as if he had briefly been a god—would haunt him forever, but his reverence for life went deep, arising as it did out of the love that was the truest definition of his soul.

Then the bells jangled that indicated that the outside door was being opened. He raised his eyes. Hamida came down the long colonnade and into the courtyard. He had loved beautiful women, but never one like Hamida. He had not known what innocence was before he met her, or just how pure the eyes of a girl could be. He had been drawn to her by an overwhelming power, greater even than the power that had drawn him to Leo, even than Lilith's hypnotizing beauty.

Hamida laughed when she saw him. She drew off her dark glasses and came down beside him. She'd been at the hairdresser. As a Copt, she did not seek the mystery of sunna. She would never wear the Muslim veil, nor did this house seek to find itself in the path of the Prophet's own family. The olive skin of her face and her great, dark eyes were framed by beautiful black hair, now freshly and fetchingly curled.

"Do you know what's so funny?" she said.

He shook his head.

"I thought you'd end up here. This fountain has a legend attached to it."

"So does everything in the house."

"But this one is special." When she looked up at him out of those wonderful eyes, he saw nothing else, heard nobody else—which was as well, because he probably didn't need to see the parents assembled along the second-story colonnade, tasting of young love from afar.

"There was a boy living here some time ago—"

"A boy you knew?" She had no brothers.

Again, she laughed. "Ian, this is Egypt. I'm talking about at least a couple of thousand years. Anyway, he was waiting for his lover to return. She had promised him it would only be an hour. One hour went by, and no lover. Two hours, no lover. But he had promised her that he would wait. So he stayed there. He stayed there all night and all day, and then more nights and more days—right where you're sitting now—and nobody could budge him. The story is, he stayed there not just for weeks or months or years, but for a thousand thousand years, listening to the water and watching the carp, just like you've been doing."

"Except I've only been here thirty minutes. Not even an hour."

"In Egypt, you don't know. Time is different here, Ian. There are eternities around every corner."

He gazed at her. How he loved the sound of her voice. He knew that it was the blood, the blood of the Karases and the Wards . . . Lilith living on within them. But he would never feed, and she was as innocent as he once had been, without the least idea even of what a vampire was. He only knew this: like him, she could speak many languages, like him she knew math and physics and the poets (unlike him, the Egyptian and Arab and Persian poets, also) and hungered and thirsted to understand the wonders of the world.

"So what happened to him?"

"One day, late in the afternoon, there came a tinkle of that bell over there. He looked up—he had no hope by now, he wasn't crazy—and there, in the doorway, was his lover. She came to him in beauty greater than he had ever remembered, and sat down where I am sitting, and he said, 'Where have you been so long?' And she said, 'Just down to the river to wash my hair.' He got angry at her and would not believe her. But he loved her so much, he forgave her, and when he would ask her what it was that had taken so long, sometimes she would laugh and sometimes she would cry, but she would never tell him."

"That's it? That's the whole story?"

"Is it too Egyptian? I'm so sorry." She tossed her head, and in that moment he knew that he must marry her, that he belonged to Hamida already. "Forever after that," she continued, "people would whisper that these two lovers had been a thousand years apart, and hadn't died, and maybe they were djin or something. He would laugh when he heard that in the coffeehouse or the market, and say, 'No, you're mistaken, it was only an hour that I waited.' So that's why we call it the Fountain of the Hours."

He had long since lost interest in the story. She herself was the story that interested him. He gazed toward the plum tree and the concealing shadows beneath it. "What's it called? Since everything here has a name."

"Oh, it keeps its name a secret."

"How can a tree keep a secret?"

"It's an Egyptian tree. Want to see if it'll tell us?"

His arm around her waist, he drew her toward the plum tree . . . or so it appeared to him. In the colonnade above, of course, her parents both thought, She's taking him to kiss him. Violet knew that her actions would be seemly. Adel rumbled uneasily in his throat. "Be quiet," Violet whispered. Becky's hand touched hers, an intimate gesture of motherly complicity. Both women already knew that Hamida and Ian would marry, as certainly as the two Niles become one.

"What's going on?" Paul asked.

"There is coffee for us on the veranda," Violet said.

"You didn't call for coffee," Adel said in Egyptian.

"We will go to the veranda, husband."

The parents went quietly away and watched feluccas and tourist boats going along the Nile, and the pyramids shimmering in the late sun.

"Look at that," Violet said.

Again it came, a light flickering at the top of the Great Pyramid— nothing much, just a flash in the setting sun.

"It's a reflection," Paul said. "A tourist's sunglasses."

Violet smiled across her coffee cup. Adel said, "In this country, nothing is quite as certain as that."

Beneath the old plum tree, Ian and Hamida listened for secrets, but heard only a little breeze whispering in its flowers.

"What's it saying, Ian?"

"I love you, Hamida."

They came closer, twining their fingers.

"My father used to get mad if a boy wanted to kiss me. But I'm older now."

He would have done it into the night and eternity, but she turned her head away after only a moment. "We must go to them now. They'll be expecting us on the veranda."

"That wasn't much of a kiss."

"Oh, no? It was eternal."

"Three seconds?"

"All kisses are eternal."